HARMONY'S DESIRE

ALEXANDRA RISLEY

HARMONY'S DESIRE

©Alexandra Risley

English Translation by Olga Núñez Miret, 2019

Interior Design: Alexandra Risley
Cover: H. Kramer
Photographs:
Dmytro Sandratskyi/Adobestock.com
kharchenkoirina/Adobestock.com
moofushi/Adobestock.com
mipan/Adobestock.com

Twitter: @AlexRisley
Instagram: @AlexandraRisley
Facebook: http://www.facebook.com/alexandrarisley
Goodreads: http://www.goodreads/alexrisley

Translator's note

When I was contacted by the author, Alexandra Risley, about a possible translation of her popular novel *El deseo de Harmony*, I was thrilled. As a reader, I love historical fiction, and a Victorian romance fit the bill perfectly. The author, who lives in the United States, is an anglophile and had visited the UK and done a lot of research on the topic and the era, as will become clear when you read the book.

We discussed what kind of translation she was interested in. Her main aim was to reach as many readers as possible, and to focus on the romance and love story, the story of Harmony, a girl with big dreams but whose circumstances conspire against her. She is a true character, and I'm sure you'll become as fond of her as I have. We chose to go with British English spelling for the sake of consistency, but I tried to keep the language as neutral and straightforward as possible, rather than pursue complex turns of phrase or complicated expressions that might have been used at the time, but would not add anything to the plot or the feel of the story.

One of the things you might wonder about in the story is the author's choice of point of view. Rather than offering her readers only her main character's perspective, the author has chosen an omniscient point of view, and that means we can read the story from different characters' perspective as it progresses, although Harmony's point of view is the dominant one. I know some readers worry about "head-hopping" and this is a topic I discussed with the author. I found her reasoning behind the use of this point of view illuminating, and I thought I had to share it with you, in case you have concerns. What she told me is that she wanted to tell the story from the point of view that fell more natural during each scene and the one that gave the reader the vantage insight into the action and thoughts of those present. I know not everybody appreciates the use of that narrative style, and therefore I recommend that you check a sample of the book first to see how you get on. As a reader, I must admit it can be odd to begin with but after a short while you realize you are in a privileged position, as if you were a voyeur not only privy to the action from as many perspectives as you like, but also to the minds of those involved. Omniscient indeed!

I hope you'll enjoy the story, and if you do, don't forget to tell others. We might manage to convince the author to translate more of her works into English.

It's bitterly cold out, and I'm depressed.
Hamlet, Act 1, Scene 1

Prologue

Ascot Racecourse, Berkshire.
Fall 1880

'Are you reading that ghastly book again, Miss George?'

The aforementioned and her small retinue jumped up on noticing the presence of Mrs. Penelope Andersen looming over them, all high-and-mighty. The governess had creeped like a lizard under the tree where Harmony was reading to the Jensen twins and to her good friend, Fanny Thornton, passages from A Woman's Journey around the World, the thrilling tome by Mrs. Ida Pfeiffer, unfairly banned from their lessons.

The sermon from the previous week, during the geography lesson, burned fresh in the memory of the students. Then, Harmony, the oldest and brightest of Penelope's pupils, had cited the controversial traveller to settle an argument about the location of the Isle of Java. Her eyes had almost popped out of their sockets on observing the daring, and even the petulance with which the snotty-nosed girl mentioned the reckless wanderings of Ida Pfeiffer, that infamous emancipated housewife and inveterate vagabond, included in her not less gruesome book. But what almost sent her into a catalepsy attack was the discovery of the said volume, which the girl carried with her with devotion almost reverential, as one would have expected her to carry the study guides or the etiquette manuals for ladies.

'Not at all surprising for the niece of the inveterate John Talbot,' growled Penelope under-her-breath. 'I thought I had asked you to leave it at home.'

'Mrs. Andersen, I brought it to keep us amused while we wait for the races to start.' Harmony hid the book behind her back, in a protective gesture, in case Mrs. Andersen decided to tear it to pieces as an exemplary punishment. She doubted she could locate another one available on the bargain shelf at Hatchards. 'It is a lovely day for reading, don't you think?' She contemplated the manicured lawns and well-tended natural areas of the equestrian complex of Ascot. That time of the year, at least ten different golden tones had painted the leaves of poplars and birches. 'It's a shame to think that people come to watch those horrible jockeys whipping the horses instead of enjoying these sublime landscapes.'

Aware of the kind-hearted and sweet character of her student, Penelope folded her arms and frowned. 'And did it not occur to you to bring a novel, or a poetry book, or a more appropriate reading material, Miss George?'

'I did not think it was not appropriate, Miss Andersen. We are not in class.'

'Harmony, I am fully responsible for your education, inside of the classroom as well as outside of it. You know that I will not confiscate that thing,' she said, twisting her mouth in a gesture of disgust, as if it had been a bag full of filth, 'only because Mr. Talbot is not opposed to you having those kinds of... experiences.'

Harmony would have liked to be able to tell her governess that Uncle John did not see favourably her interest in those kinds of "experiences". The truth was he did not show the slightest concern for the manner in which she chose to occupy her time. But, would it have been worth her effort? She was convinced that Miss Andersen would have already noticed the scarce interest Mr. Talbot showed towards any matters pertaining to his niece.

'But I must caution you,' the governess insisted, shaking her index finger in a threatening manner, 'that I do not wish to see you holding that poor excuse for a book in public again or I will be left with no other option but to remove it from you and hurl it into the closest bonfire. Have I made myself sufficiently clear?'

Harmony let out a defeated sigh. 'Absolutely clear, Miss Andersen.'

'Good,' Miss Andersen stood up, straight like a broom handle. 'The races are about to begin. We shall go and take our places. Stand up and start walking!'

As Miss Andersen began to walk ahead, Fanny gazed kindly at her friend. They had both been sharing the keen and edifying services of Miss Andersen for several years. The Jensen twins, only thirteen years old, whom they had just met, had run away from the famous and terrifying Miss Andersen, leaving a dust trail behind. 'It would be wiser for you to leave Mrs. Pfeiffer at home from now on,' she whispered, to ensure her words were for Harmony's ears only.

'Goodness! I hadn't realised that we were also forbidden to think for ourselves,' replied Harmony, oozing sarcasm. 'Ah! One of these days,

Andersen will find a way to infiltrate our thoughts. Mine will cause her an attack of apoplexy.'

Fanny laughed, discreetly. Harmony put the book away in her purse, shook off the bits of straw from her skirt and strode towards the racecourse stands with her friend and the governess. 'Miss Andersen, why don't you like Mrs. Pfeiffer's book?' Harmony inquired while she and the others ascended the stairs that led to the boxes reserved for the most exclusive spectators.

'I cannot believe you feel you should ask me such a question,' the woman grumbled without slowing her pace. 'You should already know it, otherwise, all those years I have dedicated to your instruction will have been an utter waste of time.' Andersen paused in her reprimand to observe the desolate expression of the young woman. After a few seconds she started talking again, her tone softer and kinder. 'Listen, Harmony, it is noble that you feel attracted to travelling and to foreign cultures, but there are more serious and professional books —'

'Those written by old and boring diplomats?'

'I don't mean that! What would your opinion be of a madwoman who sets off alone on a journey around the world, with only a few pounds in her pocket, confronting the dangers of those uncivilized lands, setting camp at the mercy of the elements, and only the good Lord knows what else?'

It only took the girl a few seconds to come up with a reply. 'That she is a lucky madwoman!'

'Lord in Heaven, grant me patience,' whispered Penelope under-her-breath.

Penelope rubbed her temple. She could feel a headache brewing. Harmony George was not like any of the students she had been in charge of educating in the twenty-seven years of her unblemished career. For that same reason, she had never treated her as she had the rest. She had always needed to employ a cajoling discourse, a controlled hand and a tonne of patience. She had seen dozens of girls sharing a similar nature to that of Harmony, restless and misunderstood, being led astray like a straw hat caught up in a gale. In general, those same girls who were trying to attract the attention of their parents with their quarrelsome behaviours ended up doing something stupid that ruined their chances, and in some cases, ended up condemned to social ostracism.

Penelope had seen dozens of girls forced into marriage with the first idiot who had seduced them, a few ruined and forgotten, one who had been sent to a convent abroad due to an inconvenient pregnancy, and another who had ended up in a lunatic asylum due to an aberrant and dishonourable explosion of femininity. Luckily, she had not been entrusted with the care of any of those harlots… until John Talbot and his wife, Minnie, had put her in charge of their niece with a curious sense of urgency, perhaps because Harmony was showing all the signs of going down dangerous paths, and they were only trying to avoid her becoming an inconvenience and an embarrassment in the future. After all, she was an orphan with a loose tongue, careless, and had no other family in the whole world except an aunt and an uncle, both apathetic and only interested in attending balls and social functions. To sum up: the girl embodied all the qualities of an incipient libertine.

Luckily, it could hardly be said that she was beautiful, at least in a conventional way, because, otherwise, some ruffian would already have set his eyes on her and, without a doubt, would have caused her ruin. With that damned hair, thick and curly, more difficult to tame than a pack of wild dogs, she could hardly understand how she managed to keep her head straight. The maid had to spend hours and hours on her, using all kinds of curling irons and pomades to try to give it a moderately civilized appearance, always ending up with a terrible backache. Harmony's features were soft, but not very feminine. Her eyes, black like bottomless pitches, had a sullen and frightening look. If that wasn't bad enough, those square incisors of hers, huge like sugar cubes, were definitely unbecoming.

Regardless of all that, Penelope had grown fond of the girl. She had solemnly promised herself that she would not allow Harmony to suffer the same fate as so many other wretched girls, nor would she allow her bad behaviour to reflect badly on her and discredit her, her governess, too. After all, Penelope hoped to carry on pursuing her profession until the end of her life. She had taken her under her wing as an act of faith and, at the same time, of Christian charity. And if she hadn't, she would have already resigned from her risky mentoring assignment, especially considering that miserly Mr Talbot already owed her several months of pay.

'My darling girl, those are not the kinds of things a respectable woman would do,' she concluded. 'And, it goes without saying; she is a terrible role model for Fanny and you. What eligible gentleman would wish to marry a girl interested in travelling alone? Not a single one. End of discussion.'

They walked across an exquisitely decorated salon, overlooking the racecourse. A handful of aristocrats were elegantly sipping their drinks and conversing while they waited for the equestrian spectacle to start. Others directed their shining opera glasses towards the horse boxes, in an attempt to catch a glimpse of the action. The women showed off elaborate dresses and hats created using a multitude of materials: furs, the feathers of exotic birds and flowers. The men wore elegant three-piece suits in light colours, ties decorated with precious pins and the tallest of top hats.

There, surrounded by such a parade of hens and peacocks, Harmony George felt out of place. In the past, she had accompanied her aunt and uncle to a couple of races, but never one so sumptuous, and she had never dreamed of ascending to the box occupied by the best of the aristocracy, to the watchtower of the big gamblers, full of Lords prepared to lose a fortune in exchange for a bit of fun.

Iolanthe, the horse trained at Uncle John's stables, would run in a highly anticipated race later that morning. Mr Talbot could not stop talking about that blessed animal, about the training sessions in which it had outshone all others, and about his incipient friendship with the buyer, the Duke of Waldegrave, who had paid an incommensurate sum for it. He also went on and on about the improvement in his reputation as an equestrian tradesman such a transaction would bring. Nobody would ever dare to refer to him as a horse dealer again.

Harmony could not fully comprehend the fascination all men felt for racehorses, and even less that of men such as Waldegrave and the rest of the noblemen seated around her, who clearly did not need to pin their hopes on making a fortune on an animal's legs. Their situation was the complete opposite to that of her Uncle John, whose financial situation had been in dire straits before crossing his path with the eccentric duke and managing to sell him the dumb horse.

The half-brother of Harmony's father had once been a rich and well-respected man, but all the splendour he had surrounded himself with had disappeared due to his ruinous investments. For a long while, John Talbot's animals had been the laughing stock of his rivals; therefore, his credibility had vanished. The result of that race could signal his return to the business, or at least that was what he had kept saying the whole week.

Harmony stretched her neck in an attempt at catching sight of her uncle, who was chattering with a group of gentlemen that seemed aloof. John was still talking about Iolanthe, about his winner's legs and the smoothness of his gallop, while Aunt Minnie stuffed her mouth full of canapés. Miss Andersen, with a disapproving look on her face, was waiting her turn to talk to John, perhaps to remind him of the payment of her overdue fees.

As they were about to occupy the only seats available, far away from the action, Harmony and Fanny met a pair of lovely girls who invited them to sit next to them in a choice location. Sally Whitfield had come with her older brother and his wife, and Esther Collins with her father and her step-mother. It did not require a second look to realise that they belonged to well-off families, and that troubled Harmony to begin with. Fanny, who was by no means poor, convinced her that they should accept the invitation of the two kind girls and that persuaded her to acquiesce. At least the four of them were in agreement about their discomfort at having to attend such a tedious race.

And that was when the distinguished owner of the horse everybody was talking about made his appearance. Those present suddenly fell silent, their curious gazes, full of reverence, following his every step, as Devlin Sawyer, the Duke of Waldegrave, walked stately towards his exclusive box, right behind the balusters of the royal box.

Without intending to, Harmony also ended up falling prey to snooping. She had never seen him at such a short distance, and she had to admit that he grew more handsome the closest he came. He was dressed in the latest fashion, with trousers, waistcoat and a frockcoat in pearl grey, his button hole sporting a small bunch of freesias. A silver necktie tied in a graceful bow perfectly adorned his immaculate white linen shirt. His long and lank black hair, fastened by a delicate silk ribbon, was crowned by a magnificent top hat, which emphasised his long and masculine visage.

Harmony delighted in the spectacle before her eyes. She took her time gazing at that snow-white skin, and those small, emerald green eyes of his that squinted when exposed directly to the sun to become two narrow slits. She noticed his dark eyelashes and bushy brows. She lingered on his nose, straight and masculine, on his small mouth, and those rosy, luscious lips... and wondered what one would feel after being kissed by such a mouth.

He wasn't alone, she realised after a few slow seconds of guilty scrutiny. There was a lady on his arm, the most beautiful woman Harmony had ever seen. She was a lovely brunette, with blue eyes, wearing a figure-hugging pink dress. She had a simple and lovely hat on, pretty discreet, in no way similar to the horrors the rest of the women wore. She noticed that the looks those present addressed at the couple varied between admiration and envy.

Well, it was to be expected, she told herself without sharing the same feeling. Such beauty, distinction, and prosperity could not fail but raise bitterness in some. If there was such a thing as perfection in this world, those two were its embodiment, without a doubt.

'Who is with him, Sally?' Ester asked, without removing her gaze from the couple.

'I don't know!'

'You don't know? And you are always boasting that you know everybody who is anybody in London!'

'Well, I've never seen that woman before,' protested the other girl, her pride pricked. 'Have you forgotten that he prefers foreign women? She might be another cousin of Princess Alexandra.'

'Do you know her?' Esther asked, addressing Harmony and Fanny.

'No, of course not,' replied the latter.

Harmony hardly managed to shake her head. She didn't need to scrutinize the lady in question; judging by her delicate demeanour and her expensive dress it was evident that she was a member of the aristocracy, and she had never been even close to such an exclusive world.

'I hope he has not gone fishing in the same contaminated waters again,' reflected Sally in a sad tone of voice. 'We had more than enough with the high and mighty Danish girl and the scissors' lunatic, and I hope he did too.'

'Have those been his fiancées?' Fanny inquired, perplexed.

'The least notorious, as far as we know.'

'Yes, pretty, but depraved to the core,' added Esther, wincing. 'I wouldn't be surprised if this one ended up being the same.' The four pair of eyes stared into the girl Waldegrave paraded on his arm with evident pride. 'Lady Colvile, Laurel, is the worst of the lot. She made a terrible scene at the Parliament's New Year Ball. They say that Waldegrave arrived with another woman and that drove her crazy. Afterwards, they had a shouting match in her house, so loud that it could be heard from the pavement. The woman grabbed a pair of scissors and tried to slash her own jugular right in front of him.'

'How terrible!' murmured Harmony while she kept looking at the duke, who had taken a seat next to his beautiful companion.

How could anybody lose her head like that for a man, no matter how handsome and charming he was?

'What happened afterwards?' Fanny asked eagerly. 'Did she manage it?'

'Well, she was so pathetic that she couldn't even find the vein and ended up with a gash in the middle of her throat,' concluded Esther, exasperated. 'And what did she achieve? She is now unable to wear any open-neck dresses and has the worst possible kind of reputation, that of being crazy and pusillanimous. Although I've heard she's had a reputation for being mad since she was a child.'

'Waldegrave didn't go back to her, of course,' explained the other girl. 'And I hope he never does. She does not deserve him.'

'Honestly. I would prefer...' Fanny lowered her voice, as if she were about to reveal a secret. 'What I mean is, I'd prefer people to call me the worst nicknames and insults to being called 'pusillanimous'.'

In unison, the other girls mumbled words of agreement that dissolved into general laughter. It was true, Harmony thought to herself. Having a reputation for being pusillanimous was the worst fate possible.

The race started shortly afterwards. Fanny, Esther, and Sally seemed to have managed to find something in the show to keep them entertained, even if it was only in order to criticise the ridiculous attires worn by some of the ladies and their hats, which brought to mind birds' nests and deer antlers. Harmony, by contrast, pretended to follow with interest the struggle between the jockeys and, from time to time, would turn her eyes back towards Waldegrave. He was cheering his horse, Iolanthe, as was doing his beautiful friend, who was hopping excitedly, with her opera glasses firmly held in front of her eyes.

She could not fathom why, all of a sudden, she had become so fascinated by that man, beyond his apparent beauty, and his protective attitude towards the beautiful stranger, which clearly evidenced an affable and kind character. It was amazing the way he looked at her, as if he would be prepared to step in the path of a bullet for her, as if she was the only living being for miles around. The smile, at once ecstatic and tender, which he beamed at her conjured up pleasure, like the feeling of warm water against a frozen skin; and the shining in his eyes hinted at... love?

Ignoring the direction her own daydreams were following, Harmony quietly wondered how it would feel to be the cause of such a smile, the object of the feeling betrayed by those eyes.

Suddenly, she felt very silly. Clearly, Waldegrave was much taken with that young girl, whom everybody looked at curiously and with delight, for whatever reason, and whom she had unwittingly started to feel envious of. Harmony would never be the object of the attentions of a man like the duke. She had never managed to raise the interest of anybody, even of those in her close proximity! The woman's beauty reminded her of her own dullness, of her insignificance. The Talbots had hardly glanced at her since they landed from their carriage to check if she was still there.

She was a nobody, only a sad orphan girl. She had no charms or spark. She arose neither admiration nor love.

The ecstatic screams of the multitude brought her back from her pitiful ruminations. The spectators congratulated each other and cheered the triumph of Iolanthe, Waldegrave's horse. The duke, filled to the brim with pleasure, was now lifting his brunette companion and making her spin in the air. Harmony looked away from the scene, trying hard to pay attention to the chatter of Fanny and her new friends, whose relatives had also bet on Iolanthe. She glanced again at Uncle John who, excited like a hen that had just laid an egg, scrambled to penetrate the circle of aristocrats closing in around Waldegrave. The torrent of flattery he had so carefully prepared would have to wait a little longer.

After a few minutes, the crowd quieted down and even Uncle John had a chance to pay tribute to the horse's owner. Harmony could not help but turn to look at him. This time he was alone, saying goodbye to the gamblers who had approached to greet him. Harmony looked around him trying to catch a glimpse of the beautiful brunette he had seemed inseparable of before; she was shocked when she saw her in a secluded corner, talking discreetly to an attractive blond man. She was intrigued because the same man had been part, only a few minutes earlier, of the group surrounding Waldegrave and congratulating him, but even more so, she was intrigued by the fact that he and the brunette seemed to be talking in private. The desolate expression on the girl's face and her sad eyes made her look away. He, on the other hand, seemed annoyed, but no less hurt.

What was taking place there? It looked like a lovers' quarrel. She guessed there must be some history between them. And Waldegrave, immersed in his equine chatter, had failed to notice it.

Harmony did not feel she should mention what she had witnessed to Fanny, Esther, and Sally. It was not proper to turn the drama of two people into gossip material, because what she had seen strongly suggested a tragic love story. She looked again at the duke, anxious to see if he had noticed the scene. And in a fleeting and unexpected stroke of luck, the green eyes that had mesmerised her so an instant ago, met hers again.

Harmony froze. She held her breath unwittingly, and her throat closed whilst Waldegrave's gaze, fascinating and thrilling without even trying, held her as if in a trance. Those eyes bore so deeply into her that she felt her core tighten; but although she could feel her cheeks burning, she did not look away, absorbing it for as long as it lasted without daring to move a single muscle. She took in his beauty, scrutinised his visage, enjoyed the crumbs she was given, and that felt sufficient to her.

However, what in her own imaginary world had felt like a full minute had not lasted more than a couple of seconds. Right when Harmony was about to offer him a smile, clothed in the feminine shyness overwhelming her, Waldebrake broke off the exchange. And he did it with an impatient and haughty gesture, almost rudely. Without wasting more time, he strode towards his beautiful friend, who was waiting, sitting in a corner, her shoulders slumped and she had the saddest look on her face Harmoney had ever seen. A look that echoed her own sadness.

It took the girl a few anxious seconds to realise that her pitiful person had not arisen the slightest interest on Waldegrave. There was no gentle nod, and a smile would have been totally out of the question. She doubted he had as much as seen her. She felt a quick and sharp pain, like a bee's sting.

Ashamed and annoyed at herself for weaving such stupid fantasies, and even more for harbouring such ridiculous feelings, she dropped on the nearest chair.

Chapter 1

An early dusting of snow covered the gardens of the ducal property of Waldegrave Terrace. In a few hours, the unexpected midnight thunderstorm had swallowed up the manicured fields and enveloped in a white cloak the hills of Hampstead Heath as far as the eye could see. The incredibly tall pines, their branches covered in icicles, sprouted in the growing morning light. The wind rocked them with a gentle sway, shaking their branches, spreading the sleet in an unrelenting shower. But not even the iciness of the land could compare with their owner's gloomy mood.

With an almost insane absent-mindedness, Devlin Sawyer, standing in front of his study's Spartan chimney, observed the red-hot logs in the hearth until they burned to ashes. In the scorching darkness of the room, the reflection of the flames danced on his eyes, drawing diabolical shapes in his irises and distorting his face that grew tense and fierce as he clenched his mandible. Anybody who saw him would have sworn he was in the presence of a creature of the night.

His left hand was closed in a tight fist, and his right was holding a glass of liquor that since the previous night had been filling up and emptying at a worrying speed; his body and the mind, however, resisted the solace of drunkenness. His rage kept him sober. The jealousy and a heart whose breakage he'd never openly admit were mushrooming inside his chest in a spiral of pain.

A few hours ago, his mansion had been the stage of a sumptuous charity ball; hundreds of wealthy and influential people had paraded through his halls, had drunk the most select bottles of his cellars until they had felt sated, and the servants had filled them up with exquisite dishes. Waldegrave Terrace had not seen such a celebration in a long time, since the times of the old duke, perhaps. The broadsheets had not spared compliments when extolling the party. Right then, many of the attendees were sleeping in the guest rooms and others were seated around the breakfast table to discuss the ins and outs of the gala or where wandering around the mansion looking for some alcohol leftovers. He, however, had done nothing but languish in that remote refuge; his mind going over and over the words of the woman who had left him once the night was over, the same woman in front of whom he had laid out his whole world recently… the woman whose hand he had planned to ask in marriage at the end of the night.

Devlin wished he could hate her for having struck him such a direct blow but, as things were, that was unlikely. Victory Brandon, the widow of Lovelance, had got a hold inside of his veins like a merciless drug; her charms had turned him into the ruin of a man he now knew he was.

She had made him think that she had fallen in love with him, and that had made him reconsider the possibility of getting chained to a woman when he had avoided it his whole life. And all for what? To have his affections thrown back at him with a cruel lash of the whip, straight to his soul. To end up like a poor jilted devil, like so many people he knew who always annoyed him with their dismal love stories. All that to finally come to the realisation that he meant nothing for the only woman deserving of his attention. The only one who had managed to make him kneel down at her feet.

Yes, "a damned duke," he thought bitterly before taking the last sip of brandy, the proud owner of one of the oldest and most revered titles in England, meant nothing to her; she preferred the favours of an ordinary small-town count, who until recently had but been little better than a beggar.

The rage that consumed him made him hurl the crystal glass at the roaring fireplace. The whole set-up had been a massive waste of time: the arrangements to make his acquaintances attend the ball, to convince them to leave huge sums of money on the betting tables, and to agree to become benefactors of the Mary Alice Bird Foundation for the Widows in Need of Great Britain, founded by Lady Lovelance, which he had supported without giving it a second thought.

Earlier he'd thought she'd taken advantage of him but later he dismissed that idea to realise that anybody who was disinterested enough to set-up a house for poor widows could not be accused of being greedy. That left his hand tied, without anything he could use to reproach her, which increased his frustration. He had hardly had a chance to express his amazement at the fireworks that had put an end to the evening when Victory asked him to stop trying to win her over because her heart already belonged to somebody. Devlin had interrogated her about it, and she had ended up confessing that she was talking about Casper Pleydell-Bouverie, Count of Radnor.

Just thinking about him intensified his need to hit somebody.

A noise at the door distracted his attention from the charred firewood and his irate thoughts. Limsey, the mansion's elderly butler, solemnly entered the study. The servant's furrowed brow and his glum countenance reflected the worry that had consumed him since he had learned, from one of the maids, that his master had spent the last six hours locked there.

'Good morning, Your Grace,' he said, after clearing his throat.

Devlin did not reply. He only glanced, frowning, in his direction, silently warning him that he was not welcome. Behind Limsey, a maid carrying a silver tray sneaked in. The girl, quieter and faster than a mouse, deposited the item over the small table where Devlin's late father used to take his breakfast.

'What is that?' he inquired, annoyed.

'Your breakfast,' the butler answered immediately.

'I have not asked for it, Limsey.'

'Of course, Your Grace, I took the liberty of asking for it myself. I imagined that...'

'I don't pay you to take liberties!' The roaring voice of the duke set the glass panes on the doors of the bookshelves and the stained glass windows shaking. 'Or to imagine!'

Limsey nodded. 'I beg for your forgiveness, Your Grace.' He addressed a meaningful glance to the young maid, who hurried out of the study, tray in hand, back to the kitchen. He cleared his throat and afterwards spoke, carefully enunciating each word. His eyes wandered, paying special attention to the liquor table and the two empty bottles resting next to the writing desk. 'If I could be allowed to make an observation, Your Grace has an easy sleep, and I had never before seen you stay up, awake, until morning in the study.'

Devlin laughed bitterly. He picked up the glass decanter and poured another glass of brandy before dropping on the leather chair in front of the fireplace.

'My poor old and sentimental Limsey,' he mumbled, made aware of the man's intentions by his solemn choice of words. 'Years and years looking after my father and his pathetic drinking sessions and now you get upset because I "stay up", as you put it, one night with a bottle of brandy.'

'That is the reason, precisely, Your Grace,' the servant replied with unexpected determination. 'It would be a disaster if you were to acquire your late father's habits.'

The silence that flooded the chamber propitiated some memories of the old duke. However, neither of them expressed their thoughts.

'Some guests wish to say goodbye to you before they leave,' Limsey carried on, giving his voice a monotonous and obsequious tone. 'What shall I tell them, Your Grace?'

'Tell them that I am in my chamber, mounted astride a woman and I have expressly asked not to be disturbed,' he mumbled.

Limsey's gaze betrayed surprise and desolation.

'Pardon... Your Grace?'

'Relay that to them, word by word!'

Limsey watched as his master looked away and stood there for a while, his brow etched. His master had never been foul-mouthed or a despot who treated his servants cruelly, and even less a sombre and sullen drunkard. To be fair, the duke, who before used to be such a restrained and proper man, had begun to behave in an alarming manner due to the romantic setback that had already become the talk of the mansion's servants' quarters. Limsey was starting to worry about the sanity of his young master, whom he had known from the first moment he opened his eyes to this world.

Poor boy, he thought, praying that the alcohol would not become the comfort he would come to depend on to calm his private dramas.

'Well,' he said in the end, but Waldegrave had already forgotten his presence. His eyes had gone back to the burning logs and to his gloomy thoughts.

A groom gestured at the butler from the door. Limsey walked towards him and collected the message.

'Your Grace, Lord Fenton has just arrived.'

Waldegrave snorted as he rubbed his long, black and untidy hair reluctantly.

'I am not in the mood for an unannounced visit.'

'But, Your Grace, you have a meeting with the viscount arranged for today.'

'I don't remember it,' he lied.

'I am sorry to hear that, because I do remember it.' With a determined stride and self-confidence born of a long friendship, the Viscount of Felton entered Waldegrave's study. 'Good morning, Limsey.'

'Good morning, My Lord.' The butler greeted him with a respectful bow. 'Shall I bring you a drink? Have you already had breakfast?'

'Don't worry about me, Limsey.'

'Well, if you don't need anything else, I will leave you.'

Devlin stood up as soon as Limsey closed the double door. Unexpectedly, his upset about that inconvenient visit lessened. A slight wobble betrayed his incipient drunkenness, making him curse under his breath. He could feel his friend's judgmental gaze on him.

'My good friend... Always such an early riser,' he mumbled sarcastically. He walked to the decanter and poured two glasses of the amber liquid. 'Care for a drink?'

'Devlin, it's only eight in the morning.'

'Bah! It's freezing cold outside!' He snorted, looking out the window, where a heavy curtain allowed only a peek at the outside world. How passionately he hated the snow! 'Don't dare tell me that you have never breakfasted with a good glass of Armagnac to warm yourself up.'

'I can see you have been "breakfasting" since yesterday evening.' Felton dragged the words slowly as he gazed over the empty bottles by the desk. 'I didn't know you had grown so fond of cognac.' Waldegrave shrugged. 'Look, we can leave work for another time.' He added with an obsequious gesture, 'You should be aware that I know what happened yesterday.'

'You do? What might you be referring to?' He offered the glass to Felton, who rejected it with a brusque shake of his head and a serious gaze.

'Devlin, I beg you. Lady Lovelance told Clarissa, of course.'

'Felton, somebody should tell you,' he joked after taking another sip of his glass, 'that gossiping is a woman's hobby. Don't let your wife and her friends get you involved in that kind of nonsense.'

The viscount, who was as patient as a saint, did not appear offended. He simply looked at him with a trace of compassion. 'It would be better for you if you admitted that you are angry at her.'

'Angry?' he snorted. 'Do you think I am one of those men who lose their sleep over a skirt? How little you know me, Felton.'

The viscount sighed, frustrated. He did not have the slightest idea of how to deal with such an embarrassing situation. He'd only agreed to intervene at the insistence of his wife. Until that moment, he had only known Waldegrave to behave like a cold and rational man. Yet, the man had never before been scorned by a woman he had grown to care about more than he would ever admit.

Oh well, he thought dryly, there had to come a time when he would be denied the sweetness of love, just as it happened to the rest of us mortals. 'Then, there is no ill feeling towards our dear Lady Lovelance?' he piped up finally.

'But of course not. I was surprised by her decision. That was all.'

'Well…' He pretended to believe the poor excuse so as not to torture him anymore. 'In that case, what is happening? Have you already decided what to do with that horse you bought last autumn? I told you it wasn't a good investment.'

Devlin growled on remembering another one of his troubles. The horse he had bought from the dealer whose name he no longer remembered, had obtained an average of two victories and eighteen loses in the last few months. Smoke-and-mirrors; that was what Iolanthe—the specimen he had fallen in love with at first sight—was. He had not requested an expert valuation and he had paid no attention to the genealogy or to the morphological details that only a skilful breeder could assess before reaching a firm agreement with the seller.

He had acknowledged, in the quiet of his own thoughts, what seemed to be his main problem. He always allowed himself to be dazzled by the misleading appearance of things, and when he'd finally see the substance that confirmed his mistake, it'd already be too late.

He had hardly paid any attention to Iolanthe's constant loses at the races, bewitched as he was by Lady Lovelance and her charity project, but now that he was finally alert, awake from his pathetic dream of true love, he was able to examine what was happening around him with wise eyes. He was not a man used to lose, but it seemed that victory had abandoned him, in more ways than one.

And, although he did not know why, he had the feeling that his debacle had started the day of Iolanthe's first race.

'Damn…' he growled, trying to retrieve the name of the damned swindler from somewhere in his brain.

'Talbot,' offered Felton. 'Why don't you bring a lawsuit against his pigpen? He will carry on selling animals of doubtful quality…'

'A duke lowering himself to the level of a stable hand?' He snorted before taking another sip from his glass. 'My ancestors will curse me.'

'But that horse is a fraud. Gresham confirmed it.'

'Everybody is aware of my impulsive decision to buy it, Felton.'

The other man raised an eyebrow.

'And what will you do then?'

'Nothing. That bastard's reputation will collapse of its own accord. I do not have the slightest doubt about it. For now, I'll settle for not bumping into him anywhere.'

The viscount huffed, then ran an urgent hand through his hair. It was rare to find somebody like Waldegrave these days; a man for whom the word "pride" had such an unusual meaning.

'I am afraid you will have to meet him at least one more time. Clarissa has invited his family to the Christmas ball. You understand how it is; it was before all this happened, but I doubt that vile man will dare to attend.'

'That would be a relief.' Devlin grunted, and then gave a twisted grin.

Felton smiled in sympathy.

'You should have something to eat, and perhaps bathe...' He slapped the duke's back. 'Yesterday's party has left you exhausted.'

Due to Felton's insistence, and despite his developing migraine, Devlin agreed to talk about the draft bills being debated in Parliament. All of them related to the ambitious project to electrify London, the endeavour he had felt so passionate about before stupidly falling in love. These were changing times, and History remembered the names of capable and resolute men, not of the wimps who went around feeling sorry for themselves because of some skirt.

When his bench colleague retired, an impulsive idea crossed his mind. He called one of the grooms to his presence, scrawled a note and gave it to him. The boy left to fulfil his mission, and Devlin returned to the chair in front of the fire after pouring himself another drink.

Perhaps that would not solve his problems, but at least it would offer him some brief and pleasant solace. And that would suffice, for the time being.

Harmony descended from the Thorton's carriage with extreme caution. That time of the evening, the cobblestones of Chamber Street were a treacherous trap made of thin ice. Dear Lord! The recent snowstorm had wreaked havoc in the city. During the journey there and back, she had seen Londoners struggle to remove the snow accumulated in front of the doors, on the roofs and the gutters of the houses. Even the authorities had intervened and sent employees to clear up the way for the carriages. Thoroughfares were blocked due to the innumerable minor accidents: horses slipping and falling in the middle of the road, the heavy wheels of carriages getting stuck on the ice and mud, and there were also some pedestrians who had stumbled and ended up on the floor after trying to cross the street without paying due attention.

The buildings along Whitechapel were covered in a white sheet that hid their defiled facades, stained due to ash and slovenliness. Only half of the shops remained open, while the shopkeepers kept trying to maintain their doors clean. The city chimneys worked in unison, sending onto the skies a cloud of soot that dissolved into the grey and thick clouds. Under the bridges, the pauper families crowded around a fire, seeking refuge and warmth.

London had taken on a chaotic atmosphere that only children seemed immune to. Harmony had seen a group of noisy kids seizing the opportunity provided by the storm to play in Russell Square, hurling snowballs at each other or making snowmen with the few items they had at hand. The memories of very far-off Christmases, with her parents, flashed in her mind and a sad smile darkened her visage. Ages ago, that time of the year had been her most yearned for, the one she most enjoyed. Now, she had to make an effort to appreciate the beauty of the snow, and the approach of the seasonal festivities brought her no joy.

She held on tightly to the house fence. With great difficulty, she managed to reach the door without stepping onto the layers of ice mixed with mud and stones. Trudy, one of only two servants in her relatives' employment, greeted her with a smile as she let her in.

'How was tea, Miss?' she asked her while she took her woollen coat, her hat, and her gloves.

'Better than the dirty water Woodrow regales us with,' she replied as she shook the snow off her boots at the door. Trudy let out a giggle, hoping the cook would not hear her. 'Ah, Trudy, I wish you could see Sally's house. It's a palace! They have electric lights and a heating system that actually works.'

After the first meeting with Sally and Esther at the Ascot racecourse, the previous autumn, Fanny and Harmony had become good friends with them. They were often invited to their meetings and afternoon tea; they spent entire days playing board games, going for walks, and chatting to those two young women who had gained an important place in their hearts.

'I am very happy that you have made good friends, Miss.'

Harmony was about to carry on praising the magnificent property of the Whitfield family, their fabulous dogs, their enormous garden with the semi-frozen lake, but some overheard grunts coming from the hall distracted her attention.

'Your uncle arrived not long since,' Trudy explained. 'He is not in a good mood.'

'What a surprise!'

She walked along the corridor to the parlour where she glimpsed at Aunt Minnie having tea in her favourite chair. Uncle John, standing by the window, could be hardly said to exhibit a similarly calm demeanour. He was shaking a newspaper up in the air as if he was trying to take his bad mood on it for some reason. Perhaps his horses had lost a race once again.

It did not surprise her in the slightest.

'After all I've done for that insufferably conceited man,' he said, irate, 'and look how he repays me. What unbearable rudeness! I've told you a thousand times, Minnie. Those people are no better than us; no matter how many titles they have and what posh schools they've attended.'

'Or their money,' the woman mumbled after swallowing a sandwich.

'Yes! Or their money!'

'But, darling, don't take it so much to heart,' his wife said, her mouth still stuffed with food. 'Even the most important people can make a mistake.'

'Not to take it to heart? A mistake?' he croaked, indignant. 'Do you think that pompous Croesus does not have at his disposal an army of servants to breathe on his behalf, if required?'

'John, darling, I think you are overstating things.'

'Minnie, this is an insult to our family, and to my honour,' John growled, stiffening up and shaking his index finger at eye level, overtaken by what appeared to be a rightful rage.

'Is something the matter, Uncle?' Harmony intervened.

The Talbots hadn't even heard her arrive. The man glanced at her, annoyed, and shook a dismissive hand in her direction. 'I don't think a snotty-nosed little girl like you would understand such things.'

He dropped the newspaper on the sofa while he carried on ranting and raving. Harmony sat down and rescued the crumpled piece of paper, hoping to discover the reason for such racket. Her heart jumped in her chest as soon as she saw the portrait of the face she had been trying to avoid thinking about in recent times. Her mind made a Herculean effort to try to keep at bay recent memories involving a horse race and a pair of eyes looking without seeing, which had caused a small wound in her chest, right where her heart was.

She read the whole item, although she was already aware of what was written there thanks to her conversation that afternoon with Sally Whitfield, and she could not find the reason for such turmoil. 'Is this what has upset you so much, Uncle? A charity ball?'

The man looked at her incredulous and irate at the same time.

'We haven't received an invitation! Don't you realise what that means? I've become aware that he hosted a colossal party at his mansion thanks to a vulgar feature in the newspaper, and we were not there.'

'But those kinds of balls are for charitable people... people with a big fortune.'

'How would you know about it?' he grumbled.

'Sally told me. Her father sent a banker's cheque. He could not attend because he is visiting the continent.'

That very same afternoon, at Sally's house, the talking point had been the charity ball at Waldegrave Terrace, where they had collected funds for an institution for destitute widows. Her friend, who had attended accompanied by her brother Caleb and his wife, had expanded describing the smallest details of the event. She was the one who revealed the identity of the young woman in whose company Waldegrave had been seen in Ascot: none other than the founder of the institution, a widow herself, Baroness Lovelance, who had danced with the duke, and whom, it was rumoured, she'd be marrying shortly.

'So, now that you have rich friends, you think yourself important,' Aunt Minnie splattered.

Harmony looked at her, frowning. How she despised her, and her puffed up, beetroot-red face! She'd never smiled at her, unless it was a sneer. Minnie Talbot was a treacherous woman who had made her life miserable since she was a child. She did not make much of an effort to hide her animosity towards her husband's niece that, if anything, seemed to be increasing with the passing of time.

'Did you know about the ball and you didn't think to say anything?' asked her uncle.

'I had no idea you enjoyed going to such balls, Uncle John.'

'And who would dislike the idea of rubbing shoulders with the aristocracy? I would have managed to get myself invited by the duke if I had been apprised of that information in time.' He straightened the lapels of his fur-lined jacket, feigning an elegant demeanour. 'I can be generous too, once in a while.'

The young woman held back a mischievous guffaw. John was no less abhorrent than his wife. She had difficulty believing that such a trickster, a fast-talking and mean man like him was related to his father, who had always been an example of virtue and generosity. 'It costs five hundred pounds to reserve a place,' she informed them, guessing at the reaction that would follow her words.

Aunt Minnie almost choked on the sandwiches. John, on the other hand, blinked repeatedly, rendered speechless by the surprise. He swallowed hard and rubbed his shiny head, which only sported a few tufts of hair on the sides. Harmony smiled, discreetly, on having exposed him.

'Do you believe, perhaps, that your uncle is a miser,' John complained a few seconds later, 'unwilling to give five hundred pounds to a destitute widow?'

'Are you insane?' retorted Minnie, her eyes bulging. 'I would never have allowed you to pay a thousand pounds for two dinners, even if it were in the magnificent mansion of the Duke of Waldegrave, and they served the most exquisite delicacies ever tasted,' she said, slobbering, her eyes glazed over, lost in some imaginary banquet. She gobbled down more biscuits to placate her appetite, the same that had turned her into a woman as rotund as a Yorkshire pregnant sow.

'Uncle John you have just saved one thousand pounds.'

'In any case, Waldegrave should not have excluded me, don't you think, Minnie? He should have invited me in recognition of our businesses in common and our incipient friendship!'

'Incipient friendship?' The girl repeated with a rueful grimace of disbelief. 'He simply bought one of your horses, and it has not won a single race since October.'

'Shut up! You understand nothing about horseracing.'

'That might be so, Uncle John, but it is the truth. You've swindled him!'

John's eyes seemed to have burst out of their orbits.

'How do you dare call me a swindler?'

She stared at him, managing to swallow—she hardly knew how—the words that she'd always wished to shout at him.

'You are becoming unbearable!' Mrs Talbot reprimanded her, again. 'Your governess is useless.

Miss Andersen is a saint because she looks after my education despite your lack of payment, the young woman thought, gritting her teeth

'Although, thinking about it, I can't see how anybody could possibly turn this insolent girl into a Lady,' said Aunt Minnie with a huff.

'Oh, of course, dear Aunt,' the sarcasm in Harmony's voice became almost audible. 'You are the expert in how to be a Lady.'

'I will not tolerate further insults!' John stormed towards her, and she cowered in her chair. 'You are so ungrateful! Have you forgotten that Minnie and I took you in when your parents took leave of this world?'

Harmony remembered that day with amazing clarity and had never stopped hating it. Her parents had become consumptive, and they had dragged her out of her home to prevent her from coming to the same end. When the Georges died, away from her, the authorities could not have taken her to a worse place than the house of John Talbot—her only living relative—and his despicable wife. She would have preferred a children's home.

'Bringing you up caused a terrible upset to us that we agreed to bear because we are compassionate, unlike you,' Aunt Minnie finished with a self-satisfied look that put her teeth on edge. 'My John and I have given up everything for you, and is this how you pay us back? With your affronts and your misbehaviour?'

'You are no longer a child,' John added, arms akimbo, 'you're about to be one-and-twenty...'

'Yes, Sir! One-and-twenty!'

She could not wait for the arrival of the twelfth of January, because that day she would get rid forever of the yoke John and Minnie Talbot's custody had imposed on her. According to her father's will, when she reached that age she'd take control of her inheritance that until then had been kept under the control of her legal guardian, in accordance with the law. She was convinced that the total amount would be, at the very least, a small fortune that would allow her to live free from worry for a few years.

She had dreamt of that twelfth of January. She had prepared for that moment. She had made plans that she expected to put into practice when she became the mistress of her own life. And those same plans were the ones keeping her alive and her hope fluttering inside, like a butterfly caught up in a net, waiting to be freed.

That was the reason why she bore it all with admirable strength. Harmony was not a silly girl and knew she had to show restraint. It was not convenient for her to fight with those two because they could throw her out in the street at a moment's notice. She forced herself to calm down and pretended to feel remorseful. Think about the twelfth of January, her inner voice repeated, as it did every time she was about to lose her head. 'I apologise if my words have given you offence in any way. It was not my intention,' she could feel the words burning her voice box inside.

'That is much better.'

'I hope you are telling the truth.'

'I am, Aunt Minnie.' Or should I say, Aunt Piggy? she thought.

'Now, retire to your room,' ordered John.

She did not wait to be told again. She nodded energetically and marched directly to her room, muttering curse words only audible inside the intimacy of her own mind. She hated living with the Talbots. She was eagerly awaiting the twelfth of January and the chance she had been anticipating half of her life.

She climbed the stairs, two at a time, up to the third floor, where the attic where she had slept in since she was ten was located. She hurried into the narrow bedroom. The creepy screech of the door on opening and closing comforted her. It signalled that she was safe, in her private sanctuary inside that nest of predators.

She was fond of her bedroom, although it was not different to Trudy's or

Mrs Woodrow's; it was only a cold living space, its walls covered in green wallpaper hollowed out by the damp and the weather. The roof was slanted, made up of decayed wooden beams. The only window overlooked a brick wall, and the old pipes reverberated during the night like the howls of a wounded animal. There were other bedrooms in better condition in the house, but Minnie had refused to offer her any of them, arguing that she could not spare any of the decent rooms reserved for visitors.

'What proper lady does not have at her disposal a comfortable room to offer her guests?' she had said at the time.

She bolted the door and afterwards dropped on the small bed. The cold made her teeth chatter, and she curled up and wrapped herself in the starched bed cover. She glared at the stove, that useless piece of junk. She felt like kicking it, but that would have required her to get up and disrupt her rest. Instead, she decided to control that feeling and she curled up tight on the sheets, like a little girl.

In a few moments, she started poking under the mattress until she found Mrs Ida Pfeiffer's book. There it was, in the same place as usual. She caressed the cover, without lifting her head from the pillow, and she rejoiced in the beauty of its title, the perfect choice of words: A Woman's Journey around the World. It sounded like poetry to her. She got goose bumps every time she read it. She savoured it repeatedly, because, to her, it tasted like fate. Because that was her fate.

She, like Mrs Pfeiffer, would take every penny she had and would escape that awful hovel, leaving behind those horrible people, and she would embark on a journey of adventure. And nobody would ever again dare tell her what to do.

Chapter 2

December was moving at a snail's pace for Harmony. The more she wanted the time to rush, the more it seemed to get stuck, like the wheels of the carriages in the thick snow. The days slowed down to a trickle; the gap between her and her wish for the twelfth of January turned into an exasperating chasm.

As luck would have it, she'd recently had some good times with her friends. After class, they'd meet to have tea, to go for a drive around the city, or, if it was too cold, they'd stay in, working on Christmas crafts by the chimney while enjoying a hot chocolate. Miss Andersen was in favour of the friendship of her pupils with the young gentry, whom she considered a good example to follow and, therefore, she did not object to these meetings when their studies were over.

During one of her most recent visits to the Whitfield's, Harmony had helped to decorate the Christmas tree. They placed the glass baubles, the little porcelain angels, and hundreds of candles all over the huge pine tree, making it shine like fireflies on its branches. Once they had placed the star at the top, the girls stepped back to look at it in awe, marvelling at the effect their hands had achieved. Harmony had never seen a tree as big and as beautiful; the Talbots usually had little taste in decorating theirs, only doing it to be seen to comply with a bothersome convention of the season. And they hardly participated in its creation, leaving it all in the hands of Trudy, whom Harmony usually ended up helping with the humble decorations.

On another occasion, the girls had embroidered doilies and tablecloths under the guidance of Mrs Bonifonte, Sally's governess, who was an artist with a needle, while they rehearsed Christmas carols. Esther had sat at the piano to accompany the voices with the energetic tunes from the keyboard.

Such moments gave comfort to Harmony, prevented her from thinking about the Talbots, and helped her cope with the time she had left until she reached her longed-for independence. Since that argument about Waldegrave and his stupid horse, Minnie and John had been treating her worse than ever. They had forbidden Trudy to clean her bedroom, to wash her clothes or to render her any service, as a punishment for having called John a swindler and for suggesting that Minnie was not a lady.

Her friends would never know what those afternoons of laughter and the relaxed atmosphere meant to her. She delighted in the company of those young women who, despite their high status, their families' fortunes and their contacts, had much in common with her. She felt often sad when she thought that she would not see them for a long time. Once she set off on her journey, she'd spend months in the high seas and in other places she was eager to visit. She did not have any idea of when she'd return to London. She promised herself she would write to them regularly to avoid losing contact.

It was not difficult to love Esther, the youngest of the group. She was lively, a dreamer, and a born optimist. Her child-like lips always had a smile to offer, or a comforting word when Harmony was feeling sad. A while back and without asking her anything, the girls had realised her relationship with her guardians was terrible. It didn't take long for the girls to learn the story of how she had ended up under the care of John Talbot and his wife in full detail. From that moment on, they had done nothing but support her, to such point that, sometimes, it made her feel uncomfortable because she had never had a chance to become used to solidarity and kindness for its own sake without feeling a little suspicious. Esther showed her the most empathy because she had lost her mother four years earlier and from then on she had had to put up with an apathetic and unfeeling step-mother. Sometimes Harmony wondered how Esther managed to smile all the time, even after having recently lost the most important person in her life.

As if all that was not enough, Esther was also pretty. Petite, delicate, and a brunette, she was the one who attracted all the boys' looks wherever they went.

'Esther, what is this?'

'It's an angel.'

'An angel?' Sally displayed with a horrified expression the amorphous bit of mass just out of the oven that was meant to be a biscuit. 'Do you truly think this abomination is an angel?'

'It's a fallen angel,' the other one replied with a shrug. She never appeared upset, even when she had reasons to feel that way, and when something seemed to bother her; she limited herself to complain in a joking tone, unwilling to let anything ruin her good mood. Her spirit and inextinguishable energy were the glue that kept the group together.

'Oh, I suppose the fall has left him unrecognisable,' Fanny cut in as she beat the eggs, unable to contain her laughter.

'It looks more like a squashed bird,' said Harmony as she kneaded beside her.

'Sally, don't bother me!' Esther defended herself by throwing a prune at her. 'You should have told Mrs Jenkins to bring some moulds from the shop. It's difficult to model the shapes without having one.'

'The moulds are around, somewhere, but I don't know where,' said Sally.

'Enough, girls. What is truly important is how it tastes,' stated Fanny. 'We will cover them up in whipped cream if necessary.'

Fanny was refined, a born diplomat, and clever like no other girl Harmony had ever met. She was the one she knew best, due to the years they had been studying together under the supervision of Miss Andersen. They had become friends overnight, and Fanny was kind, a good study partner. She had not felt threatened when the governess had offered Harmony a place in the classes, which were supposed to be exclusive. She was not as well-off as the other two young women. Her father was a clerk at the Bank of England, and her mother a photographer's assistant, but her grace and elegance came naturally to her. What most girls had to learn, sometimes with a great deal of effort, was pure instinct for her.

Perhaps Fanny wasn't as beautiful as Esther, but her kindness and her good manners made her shine brighter than the prettier girls did. 'There is no lady more beautiful than the one who stands out for her moderation', the governess used to say when talking about Fanny, who would roll her eyes at the comment when Miss Andersen was not looking. According to Fanny, who never stopped joking about her big nose and her brow that was "as endless as the Sahara Desert", it was all a lie.

'All right. Harmony, try one!' said Sally.

The aforementioned, awaken from her own thoughts, blinked on hearing Sally's subtle command. She was worried about making a faux-pas her new friends would not forgive; if she praised excessively the taste of a biscuit that did not deserve it, they might decide she was a hypocrite, but if she did not like it and she was honest about it, she risked hurting them with her opinion.

She dismissed her doubts with a shake of her head. She took a biscuit; it was still warm from the tray that Esther offered her and she bit into it under the expectant look of the other three. It smelled good, but it had the texture of a piece of cardboard as she chewed on it. And it tasted the same way, unfortunately.

'Well?' Sally wanted to know.

She forced herself to swallow, with difficulty. 'I am sorry. It's... disgusting.'

Her hostess opened her eyes wide, ready to complain.

Sally Whitfield could be taken for a rich girl, spoilt and arrogant, but whoever thought that did not know the truth. The daughter of Thomas Whitfield, one of the most powerful industrialists of England, was not at all as Harmony had imagined at first. As time passed, she had discovered that she was compassionate, and she participated in charity work, not to keep up appearances but because she and her family had learned that those who give the most are always the ones who have the most. Sally knew how to listen, she was gentle and, although sometimes she could be stubborn and show evidence of the aggressive character that had turned her father, the son of a fisherman, into a winner, she was a truly lovely and charming human being. Harmony had come to understand that the reason why she had sought her friendship and that of Fanny that day at Ascot was because she felt more comfortable among humble youths—as she had been once herself—than surrounded by stupid and frivolous ton girls.

A second later, the theatre Sally had built up using the horrible biscuits collapsed, and she burst out laughing. The rest of the girls did the same, to Harmony's relief.

After trying for themselves the unfortunate culinary creation, the other girls proceeded to tidy up the mess.

'Why don't we donate them to charity?' Fanny suggested.

'Forget about that,' Sally retorted. 'Paupers have already enough problems and don't need to add stomach upset to their list. I am tired of baking inedible biscuits and of embroidering shapeless booties,' she moaned as she untied her apron. 'We should go skating in Hampstead Heath.'

The Whitfields were not there to oppose such a notion, and elderly Mrs Bonifonte was napping in her room at that precise instant. The road was clear.

After being subjected to the girls' persuasive chatter, the Whitfield's coachman drove them to the North of London, where a festive atmosphere was beginning to take hold of each square and corner. The houses were already seasonally decorated with garlands made of holly and ivy, and with bells and candles on the windows to keep the bad spirits at bay. The street markets, packed with buyers, exhibited the season's produce. The snow, which had upset the pedestrians earlier on, was now joyfully welcome. The shop windows were decorated with simple snowmen and signs highlighting Christmas offers to tempt passers-by.

After three-quarters-of-an-hour journey, they ended up surrounded by people who, like them, sought the most daring of winter pastimes. The white promontories of Parliament Hill congregated, like every year, a myriad of daring people who, mounted on wooden planks that had become improvised sleds, hurled themselves downhill, sliding on the snow.

Further away, a small crowd stumbled across Lake Highgate, its surface now a vast sheet of solid ice. People wore tick overcoats, gloves, and woollen or fur hats or mufflers, to keep the bitter cold away. Wearing boots with steel blades on, dozens of impetuous people slid over the ice; some with more energy than elegance. The crowd's screams flitted between joy and the fear of falling down.

Without wasting any more time, Esther and Sally put their skates on, then helped Fanny and Harmony afterwards. Unfortunately, Harmony shared the shoe-size of the instigator of that minor misdemeanour; therefore, she had a pair of skates ready to borrow. She was far from being a skilled skater and realised this was not the moment to try to prove anything. She simply glided cautiously holding onto Fanny's hand, who seemed as apprehensive as she was, and put all her effort into not falling down. They were soon overcome by laughter on seeing their friends falling on their bottoms. Once, twice, three times.

And because public humiliation was part-and-parcel of the risks of ice-skating, it was not long before they followed their example, landing on the ground rather ungracefully.

Harmony knew that those moments of total joy were fleeting as winter time was mean with the hours of daylight, therefore she was not surprised when she raised her head and noticed the sky was of a lead grey colour. She was not worried about getting to the Talbots after dark—she never knew where they were, or what time they would be back—but the other girls had families who would not allow them to arrive home late.

When they were feeling frozen stiff and their eagerness for entertainment sated, they decided to go to town to have a hot chocolate. Hampstead was a charming and ancient parochial hamlet where people lived removed from the hustle-and-bustle so typical of the big cities. Humble shops and houses made of stone and plaster stood crammed along the narrow cobbled streets that were covered in snow. In the vicinity, they glimpsed at an ale-house, an inn, and a travels bookshop. Harmony glued her eyes and the palms of the hands to the shop window.

'Damn,' she whispered as she wiped away the thin layer of ice to look inside the shop. It was closed.

'The day is over,' Sally said, smiling. 'We'll come back some other day.'

'I didn't know you liked travel books,' Esther said.

'Like them?' Fanny interrupted, amused. 'Miss Andersen almost threw her out of class once because of one of those books. She said it had been written by a female adventurer without a proper sense of morality.'

'Is that true, Harmony?' Esther asked.

'Yes,' she laughed, cupping her hands on the window to try to peep inside the shop. 'Mrs Ida Pfeiffer, but she is not immoral, she's a woman with an amazing good luck.'

But what Harmony was passionate about was not travel books but travel itself, or, perhaps, the experiences women travellers narrated, the adventures in faraway lands, in mystical and inspiring locations. Right behind the door, there seemed to be a mountain of books she could not wait to explore.

They entered an unassuming bakery where the shopkeeper offered them hot chocolate and freshly baked carrot cake. Harmony took the first sip of the sweet and thick drink, her cheeks blooming bright pink. While they devoured the cake, the conversation moved onto the magical book by Mrs Pfeiffer, and Harmony promised to bring it to their next meeting to read them some paragraphs about the cannibal tribe of the Batak.

Fifteen minutes later, they left the bakery. They walked to the carriage, where the coachman was waiting for them, an anguished look on his face while he checked his pocket watch, presumably for the umpteenth time. Nearby, they heard the light trot of a horse on the cobblestones; a few seconds later the narrow street revealed the shape of a nimble and brazen rider. Harmony stopped dead on recognising a familiar face. The smile she was wearing at the time suddenly abandoned her.

Waldegrave.

He looked impressive in his overcoat, its lapels, and cuffs trimmed with mink, an attire she would find extravagant and ridiculous if a mere mortal wore it; a man other than him. A smart Homburg hat crowned his head, hardly keeping contained the silky strands of dark and long hair. His expression, like that day in Ascot, was wild and handsome, but his colour was rosy. Waldegrave moved, confident and elegant, atop a strong bay horse snorting white puffs of steam.

'Your Grace,' Sally called out to him, always so daring. Harmony admired that quality of hers, never feeling intimidated by anybody. 'Good afternoon. What a pleasure to meet you. We had forgotten we were in close proximity to your property.'

'Miss Whitfield.'

The determined and velvety voice of the duke startled Harmony; a wave of pleasant sensations settled inside her stomach.

Waldegrave offered a sharp nod to the young woman he'd met a few days earlier at the charity ball. He glanced quickly over her three companions; as he had not been formally introduced to any of them he only muttered a curt 'good afternoon.'

'I hope you are enjoying your visit to Hampstead,' he carried on in his usual severe tone.

'Oh, yes. Charming!' Sally replied, smiling. 'Isn't it lovely that the snow has decided to turn up early this season? It looks like we'll have a white Christmas, like in Dickens' stories...' Sally carried on talking as if she was a wind-up toy, and that gave Harmony a chance to study Waldegrave in detail. He appeared restless, perhaps upset. She wondered, absent-mindedly, if he might have fought with his fiancée, Lady Lovelance.

'Oh, what an unforgivable oversight!' Sally said suddenly. 'I am in the company of Miss Collins, Miss Thorton, and Miss George.' Suffering from a sudden attack of nerves, Harmony swiped the corners of her mouth with the back of her hand, worried that some trace of cake might be clinging onto them. 'Miss George is Mr Talbot's niece. You have met him, Your Grace; he sold you the magnificent horse that won Ascot in September... What was it called? Ah, yes, Iolanthe!'

Harmony desperately wished for a landslide to come crashing down the nearest hill and bury her. Sally could have kept that bit of information to herself.

For the first time in the conversation, Waldegrave looked at her, and as was to be expected, with a frown. His features showed a trace of distaste and resentment on learning she was related to the dealer who had sold him that fraud called Iolanthe. It wasn't a favourable calling card, she was well aware of it, and that made her look away and avoid the condemning gaze she did not deserve.

'I see.'

No polite comment accompanied that curt mumble, only a perplexed silence from her friends. Harmony hoped her blushing would be mistaken for a reaction to the intense cold.

'Your Grace, we were planning a ride on a sleigh around Hampstead Heath this weekend,' Sally said, looking somewhat confused. 'Perhaps we could have the pleasure of your company.'

Please, make him say no, Harmony begged in her thoughts. She was not capable of enduring more discourtesies from him.

'I am afraid it won't be possible, young ladies. Perhaps another time.'

'Very well,' Sally replied, her confidence intact.

'Ladies, I must leave you now. Please, send my regards to your family on my behalf,' he told the only person he knew. 'And to your uncle,' he added, sharply, looking, or, better said, piercing Harmony with his stare. 'Tell him that if he knows what is good for him he should never come near me again. Good evening.'

Harmony felt as if they had punched her in the stomach. She kept looking at him, sceptical and hurt, as he galloped away.

'Oh, my God! What was that?' Esther whispered when Waldegrave had disappeared around the corner.

'Harmony George,' Sally, astounded, stared fixedly at her, 'What have you done to Waldegrave?'

Back in the city, and with her pride still shaken, she felt obliged to tell her friends the reason why the duke had treated her with such lack of courtesy. Despite their deep admiration for Waldegrave, they did not hesitate in taking Harmony's side.

Devlin spurred the bay gelding on the last stretch of the way to the mansion. He had left at midday to avoid having to see Anita Marinov after the maid had been to wake her up and tell her she had to leave. Four days was more than he could bear the company of a woman who only offered him her bed and conversation so dull that at times it felt like torture.

On his ride around Hampstead, he had been assessing possible locations for the new London electric power plant, in a desperate attempt at keeping his mind busy with work matters. Devlin was the English owner of the Continental Edison Company, having acquired the patents of the North American inventor to install—in partnership with the government—the first street lighting system in the United Kingdom.

Luckily, he had managed to achieve his objective that day; he'd visited the hamlet and returned with several ideas churning in his head. He even had time to do something he had never done before; to visit the alehouse and drink a few pints with the local drunkards who, stupefied by alcohol, did not recognise him.

His recent bad luck, however, had come back to haunt him with that final encounter, a reminder that he, Devlin Sawyer, the bloody Duke of Waldegrave, had been swindled by a lowly farmer. It was hard enough to avoid the jokes of his acquaintances, who laughed at him due to Iolanthe's repeated defeats, but to now have four snobbish brats poking fun at his bad luck as well was too much to bear.

'Good evening, Your Grace.'

'Good evening, Limsey.'

'Did you enjoy your ride, Your Grace?'

'Something like that.' He gave the butler his overcoat, gloves and hat. 'Any objections from Miss Marinov?'

'Some, but everything is back in order now,' Limsey affirmed with his usual aplomb. 'The lady left Waldegrave Terrace a few hours ago.'

'Did she say anything before leaving?' Devlin was convinced the woman would not have left without causing a ruckus.

Limsey cleared his throat. 'She threatened to eviscerate your delicate parts, Your Grace, in a very vulgar language. If I may offer some advice, I would be careful if I were you.'

Devlin chuckled to himself. He had always thought that Anita had the body of an odalisque and the mouth of a sailor.

'This letter arrived for you.' The butler offered him a silver tray where a cream-coloured envelope lay.

Devlin identified the busy and feminine writing of his mother and the crest stamped on the envelope with emerald-coloured lacquer. It had to be another apology for not having attended the charity ball.

It was lucky she didn't, he thought bitterly. He thanked his butler, picked up the letter, and retired to read it in the privacy of his study.

Devlin could not say that he had an excellent relationship with his mother. For years, a comfortable coldness had nested between him and the majestic Duchess of Waldegrave, but that did not mean they did not exchange correspondence quite often. While he tried, once more, to forget the reasons for such distance, he broke the seal and started to read.

Dear Devlin,

I read in the newspaper that your charity ball was a big success. I'm so happy! I feel so proud of you and of your friend, good Lady Lovelance. I see that you did not miss me at all. Even so, please, apologise to her on my behalf for not having been in your company.

With thanks to the Lord and to the medication Dr Shapiro prescribed me, the infection situation has improved. My eye looks better and it hardly hurts any longer. I hope the eye drops will help me get completely over this inconvenience soon.

On the other hand, I have news from Lady Colvile, Laurel. Her sister, Lady Burghill, who came to visit me a few days ago, told me that her health has improved exponentially. She told me that she appears calmer, more mature, and she has not had a temper tantrum in a long time. She said that she has even started painting again. Isn't that marvellous?

I am thinking of visiting her one of these days. She has been on my mind often, and I am sure it will do her good to have a bit of company.

Devil, I think you should write to Laurel. I am sure that you know that any act of kindness on your part might make a difference to her recovery.

I leave it to your conscience, darling.

With all my love,

Your Mother.

Devlin was pleased that his mother, Corine, was getting over her ailment, but he did not understand what she was trying to achieve by acquainting him with Lady Colvile's state of health, and even less, asking him to write to her.

Laurel had only left a trail of bad memories in his life; memories he was not prepared to resurrect by exchanging correspondence with her, and not even his mother's subtle manipulation would make him change his mind.

He placed the letter in one of his desk drawers. He would have time enough to reply, although the subject of Lady Colvile would not come into his consideration.

Once back at her guardians' house, Harmony greeted Trudy and prepared to go back to her room. When she had hardly climbed three steps up, she was forced to stop.

'Have you noticed how dark it is outside?' echoed her uncle's voice. She was afraid and surprised in the same measure when she turned to find him standing at the door of the dining room.

'Yes, yes, Uncle John. I'm very sorry. The Whitfield's coachman had problems with the traffic,' she lied. 'You know the city is in a mess with the snow and all that...'

'Yes, yes. It's fine, but I don't want it to happen again. Go wash your hands. Gertrude is about to serve dinner.'

After freshening up and changing her clothes, Harmony entered the dining-room where the Talbots awaited. She sat down, feeling a slight heaviness in her stomach. Something wasn't right there, and she knew it from the moment her uncle had caught her arriving home in the dark.

She carried on eating her soup and ignored the futile conversation of the couple. It was curious to notice that they didn't seem to pay any attention to each other, as if they lived in parallel worlds without any link between them. At one point, Harmony had concluded that the Talbots had not had any children because they were too selfish. And because nobody listened to her in that house, she was not going to pay any attention either, until the Talbots mentioned her.

'But, darling, how will we take her?' Mrs Talbot moaned, piercing Harmony with her eyes. 'A dress for a soirée like that one will cost us a small fortune.'

'We will manage, Minnie. The viscountess has specified that she wants to see the three of us. If we turn up without Harmony she will take offence.'

'Offence?' The woman insisted. 'She'll be offended because we will deprive her of the company of this little savage who is completely ignorant of how to behave with propriety at an aristocratic event? She will shame us, I warn you.'

Harmony took a moment to realise they were talking about the Christmas ball organised by Lord and Lady Fenton, the charming couple she had met at one of Iolanthe's races, before the debacle. Clarissa, the wife of the viscount, had behaved charmingly, despite her uncle's bothersome flattery, and had gladly invited them to attend the event. 'You don't have to take me,' she whispered, downplaying the issue.

'I insist that you must go!'

'John, this is not acceptable. This girl will embarrass us. You know how she is. She is not ready to be seen in society.'

'Harmony is polite when she wants to be, isn't it so, dear?' Harmony didn't speak, so he carried on, 'You have a good governess, although a bit costly and well-to-do friends. You will manage, won't you? You will help your uncle make a good impression on the Feltons.'

Aunt Minnie stamped her feet. 'But you're not to talk to anybody,' she mumbled, looking both angry and resigned. 'And sit in a corner somewhere. Oh, I think I've lost my appetite!'

Minnie Talbot wasn't hungry, and Harmony George would go to a ball at a viscount's mansion. The world's turned upside down, Harmony thought.

'All right,' she finally said after swallowing a bite. She had to admit that tormenting her uncle's wife caused her great pleasure. 'I will hold back from talking with a full mouth and from filling up my bag with the leftovers, if that makes you happy, Uncle John.'

Her uncle seemed pleased. 'Tell me, Harmony. Did you have a good day at the Whitfield's?'

That question baffled her even more than their insistence that she attend the Christmas ball. Her Uncle John ignoring her taunts was something she would never have believed possible, even less that he would express an interest in her activities. Now she had no doubt. Something odd was happening. 'Yes,' she mumbled. 'On the way home I met somebody.'

'Who, if we are allowed to know?'

'The Duke of Waldegrave.'

Uncle John frowned.

'Oh, it can't be!' Aunt Minnie screamed again, now heartbroken. 'And you had to look as slovenly as you usually do. His Grace will think that we cannot afford to dress you properly.'

What else could he think, when you only buy me rags, Aunt Piggy? she thought.

'He sent you a message,' she told her uncle. '"Tell your uncle not to come near me again in his life, if he knows what's good for him".'

Silence filled the room for a few seconds. Talbot cursed under his breath and Aunt Minnie shouted for Trudy, asking her to bring the migraine powders.

'Perhaps it would be better if we didn't show our faces there. I bet the duke has also been invited to attend. If he crosses paths with you, you might get into trouble.'

'I have nothing to hide. Waldegrave insisted on buying the horse without listening to anybody else's opinion. If it didn't work out as he expected, it is not my problem,' he replied, coldly, a moment later.

'It is obvious that he is upset, Uncle. We shouldn't go.'

'We will go anyway. I'll talk to him, and I'll explain that the horse has not brought him any winnings because its trainers are mediocre and soft.' He looked at her in a strange way that gave her goosebumps. 'Sometimes, Harmony, the beasts do not respond as expected because we don't use with them the required strictness. But after a bit of harsh discipline, they end up becoming creatures that toe the line.'

Harmony stared at him gloomily. 'Are you still talking about horses, Uncle John?'

Talbot's evil laughter scared her even more. 'No, dear,' he said, then sipped his glass of wine. 'This conversation has reminded me of what I've wanted to talk to you about the whole day. I think it's time to find you a husband.'

Harmony felt her heart give a painful jolt in her chest, startling her. She looked at him, unable to believe her ears. 'A husband?' The words burned her lips.

'Of course.'

She opened her mouth but did not manage to make a sound. The plans she'd been weaving for years bore no relation at all with finding a husband. There was no room for anybody else in her future.

'I don't want a husband!'

'Don't be silly,' Uncle Minnie, whom Trudy was looking after, moaned. 'Why wouldn't you want a husband? You are a woman. Not a very exemplary one, granted, but a woman, after all.'

Harmony glared at her. 'Not all women marry, Aunt Minnie.'

'I know that. The unfortunate ones who have no assets, education or beauty are condemned to spinsterhood. You are not exactly in that position, but it would not go amiss to show a little bit of interest. I have seen worse cases than yours and they have managed somehow,' she said scornfully.

'But... I don't want to get married.

'And what do you expect to become if it is not the wife of a respectable man?' John concluded.

'I don't know...'

'Look, we have thought about it very carefully, and we are sure it will be the best for you.'

The best for me? she screamed inside her head. How the hell would Minnie Talbot know what the best for her was?

'I thought of Andrew Curson,' Uncle John said.

'What?' The girl howled. Her self-control was dissolving more and more as the seconds passed. 'No, Uncle! No, please!'

She would never allow them to marry her to that infamous midget who used his small stature to stare at Harmony's and other ladies' busts as if that physical characteristic gave him the right to do it. She would rather drink a bottle full of arsenic and then set herself on fire than marry a depraved man like Andrew Curson.

'He is one of the best jockeys in England,' John countered.

'And what of that? He is also a lazy pigmy!'

'Don't you mock small people,' diminutive Aunt Minnie growled, obviously taking it personally. 'If he was tall, he would have to do something else. And, you are not precisely a beauty. I don't think you can aspire to much more, to tell you the truth.'

'But it is not about that. It is that... he is a bad person and I don't like him.' Harmony's words tumbled out of her mouth at full speed. She could not believe what was happening to her. She wished it was a nightmare.

'Nobody says you have to like it. It is enough that I give my approval as your legal guardian.'

'Don't do that to me, Uncle,' she begged, overwhelmed by desperation.

'Please, don't make me marry Curson.'

Uncle John laughed. 'Don't worry. Perhaps it won't be Curson. There might be another man better than him.'

The world is full of better men than Andrew Curson, Harmony thought, irate.

'But you can be sure of one thing: you will get married and pretty soon.'

She couldn't believe it. That had to be what Uncle John was referring to earlier when he talked about 'discipline'. A husband would handle her as he pleased, would make her walk the straight and narrow path, would rob her of her identity and turn her into a docile creature.

She could hardly believe that the beautiful day she had spent in the company of her friends could end up so badly. She noticed Trudy's compassionate glance from the other side of the table as she ministered to Uncle John now. Unable to endure the situation any longer and overwhelmed by nausea and pain, she stepped away from the table and rushed to her bedroom, luckily, without being stopped.

Minnie patted her hair and gave an exasperated sigh. 'When will you tell her?' she grumbled, as soon as the young woman had disappeared through the door.

'Soon,' her husband replied, sombrely.

Chapter 3

If the Whitfield Mansion had dazzled her, the home of Lord and Lady Fenton, the hosts of the Christmas Ball, had a similar effect. Harmony wandered around the entry hall, her eyes glued to the ceiling with its marble freezes and golden decorations. The majestic crystal chandeliers showered harmoniously the whole space with electric light. Impressive sculptures adorned every corner, surely real antiques from the Hellenic Period.

By her side, the governess smiled like a debutante and flinched every few minutes, whispering praises about the viscount and his wife, for their refined taste and their undeniable wealth. The Talbots, who walked closely behind, on the other hand, expressed their thoughts at full volume. Without holding back the inappropriate comments, they made assumptions about the cost of each ornament and criticised their artistic value despite their colossal ignorance. It was lucky for Harmony that they had allowed Miss Andersen to accompany them. Thanks to her finesse and her characteristic authority, the woman kept things under control and ingeniously managed to slow down her guardians' mischief. If that had not been the case, Harmony would have ended up embarrassed by the end of the night, without a doubt.

She was determined to make an effort and to behave well at the ball to avoid disappointing her governess, even with the threat of a forced marriage hanging over her head, like the sword of Damocles. Harmony had spent the last few days racking her brains to find a way out, any shortcut to prevent her uncle from forcing her to get married to Andrew Curson or any other among his horrendous acquaintances. She had sought Miss Andersen's help, but as she had feared, her governess supported John's decision of finding her a prospective husband. She had turned her back on her.

'You are of the right age to become the lady of a house,' she had explained to her one day after their lessons. Her severe expression had showed the same conviction as her uncle's. 'There is no other possible fate for an orphan lady who is well-educated and of a good family.'

'And do you think I am all that, Miss Andersen?' she'd asked.

'No,' the woman had replied with shattering honesty, as she had come to expect. 'But you will have to learn it all as you go along, dear. There's no other option.'

There's no other option, kept going around and around in her head even now. Miss Andersen was a woman full of virtues, but her narrow-mindedness impinged on everything else. For her, a woman without a husband was only a minuscule human being, without any voice or worth.

'But what I'm definitely against,' the governess had added, after pondering about it for a while, 'is your uncle's decision to do it so soon. You could wait another year, at most, while the appropriate gentleman comes along; somebody you could become fond of in the end. And I think his choice, that pedestrian jockey, is foolish.' Then, she had concluded, with a patronising smile, 'God willing, you will soon meet somebody more respectable.'

Only her friends had shown her sympathy, but there was little they could do to help her avoid the dark fate that probably awaited her. She remembered with nostalgia the previous weekend: the four had met at the Collins' house to exchange presents. After that, Esther, Fanny, and Sally had to leave with their families to spend Christmas Eve in the countryside. She had received delightful presents that had made her cry: a beautiful shawl made of silk and feathers, a pair of pearl earrings, and the most prized of all, the memoirs of Maria Graham, another famous traveller, which the girls had found in the Hampstead bookshop. Harmony felt sorry because she had only given them worthless trinkets. She was missing them terribly during their absence.

In the middle of the ballroom stood a brilliant Christmas tree, at least twenty feet tall, decorated with lit candles and delicate ornaments. Harmony guessed that there were thousands of lights, mixing with the coloured baubles, the crystal figurines and the gold satin bows covering it from top to bottom. The central staircase had also been decorated with ribbons, holly wreaths, and beautiful greenhouse flower arrangements. On a platform near the tree, an elegant orchestra was playing waltzes.

The place was full to the brim with ladies covered in jewels; all were dressed up in the latest fashion. The gentlemen, all in dark formal attire, and many in tailcoats, also excelled. Although Harmony was not as interested in fashion as other girls of her age, she had heard about Charles Frederick Worth, whose designs were the favourites of the wealthiest women. Princess

Alexandra and Empress Eugenia, the wife of Napoleon III, were his best-known clients. Monsieur Worth had revolutionised the world of female fashion with his exquisite embroidered bodices, choice luxury fabrics and the shape of the skirts, flat on the front and voluminous on the back. The dresses, coveted by women all over Europe, came with the couturier's signature—like true artworks—and were created following his own ideas rather than the demands of his clients, laying the foundations of what would become known as haute couture.

Harmony's frock wasn't a Worth, but at least it came from the shop of a decent dressmaker. Earlier that day, a mean-looking woman, who seemed tired, had handed her a box containing the only dress that had merited Aunt Minnie's approval. The outfit was made of chenille with lace—very flimsy at first sight—on the sleeves and the bodice. Harmony made do with it and completed her attire with the pearl earrings she had received as a present. The maid had worked hard to try to tame her hair; the result was passable. She could not complain.

They moved forward until they reached the hosts who, as demanded by the rules of protocol and good manners, were being complimented by the guests on their arrival. Harmony's heavy heart turned into true despair when she glimpsed at the person standing next to the viscount and his wife. The Duke of Waldegrave.

Heaven's above! He looked so beautiful; it hurt to look at him. His hair was combed back, emphasising his masculine beauty and revealing the symmetrical shape of his face. The tall forehead, the long mandible, and the slender neck. It was evident that he did not need to use any pomade to keep his hair under control, only a silk ribbon to hold it back at the nape. Confronted with such a vision of perfection, Harmony feared she looked a sorry sight.

'Talbot family, welcome to Felton House!' Viscount Felton, a young, dark, and handsome man said with a gentle smile, although he seemed slightly tense at that particular moment.

'My Lord, Madam,' greeted Uncle John with excessive pomp and a bow that his companions imitated. 'What a grand ball! And how generous of you to invite our humble family!' He glanced at Waldegrave, who was looking at him as if he were a fly landed on the dining-room table. 'The splendour of a gentleman speaks louder about him than his wealth. As you well know, My Lord. It is not common currency these days.' He looked at the duke again. 'Good evening, Your Grace.'

Harmony swallowed hard. The tone of resentment John had used was evident to anybody who had heard him speak, but most of them ignored the reason for it, thanks be given to the Lord. The main recipient of said resentment was Waldegrave himself, who replied with a 'good evening' hardly audible through his gritted teeth.

Felton seemed befuddled by Talbot's long-winded speech. He looked at his wife, in an obvious attempt to seek assistance.

'Mrs Talbot, I hope you find the banquet to your liking,' said casually the viscountess, a beautiful and voluptuous blonde, attired in an extravagant shiny garnet-coloured satin dress. 'Tonight we have a fabulous chef in our kitchen. He has cooked for no other than the King of Belgium.'

Aunt Minnie burst out laughing so loudly that it made all the aristocrats there jump. Good grief! Mrs Andersen must be dying of embarrassment faced with such a neigh, thought Harmony.

'I am sure I will, Madam,' John Talbot's wife eagerly replied. 'I can't even imagine the delicacies that must be served at the parties of the peers of the realm. I'll taste everything! I promise you!'

The viscountess smiled at her. If she had found Minnie's comment abhorrent, she had concealed it well. Afterwards, she addressed Harmony.

'Miss George, is it?'

'Yes... Yes, Ma-dam,' she stammered. 'Thank you for inviting us. Your house is very pretty and your Christmas tree is... the most gorgeous I've ever seen.'

'Oh, you are very kind.' The brief speech seemed to have made Miss Andersen, who was introduced immediately after, proud. The viscountess addressed the duke afterwards. 'That reminds me of something: Your Grace, you are very quiet this evening, and you have not commented on my tree, which is very rude.' She feigned upset. 'My servants and I worked very hard in its decoration for you to simply ignore it.'

'Lady Felton, you are, by far, the best hostess in the entire London,' he uttered without much enthusiasm. 'You are committing a sin of greed by trying to accumulate even more compliments than you and your tree have already received this evening.' He let out a chortle and added, 'I agree, my dear. God have mercy and don't let Her Majesty hear that our tree is more popular than her own, or she will try to make us pay a heavy price.'

The viscountess laughed, as did the Talbots.

A footman walked by Aunt Minnie, who had obviously lost interest in the conversation, and she grabbed two glasses for her and her husband after asking him where the table with the refreshments was.

'Oh! Do you know Miss George?' the viscountess asked the duke.

A twinge of apprehension exploded inside Harmony's chest. Waldegrave looked at her with his usual furrowed brow, and she wished Lady Felton had kept her mouth shut. His green eyes seemed to reproach her for not having passed his warning onto Talbot. I have, Your Grace, but you don't know my uncle, she wanted to tell him.

'We have not been formally introduced.'

'In that case,' the viscount intervened, 'allow me. Your Grace, Miss Harmony George, niece of Mr Talbot. Miss George, I introduce you to the Duke of Waldegrave, a regular visitor of this house, or at least that was the case until a month or so ago.'

Harmony curtseyed, although she did not miss the mocking and at the same time reproachful tone employed by Lord Fenton.

Waldegrave bowed slightly, like a perfect gentleman. It was an unfortunate moment to remember the vacant gaze he had addressed her with in Ascot, which had made her feel tiny.

Luckily, a long queue of newly arrived guests approached the hosts. The Talbots, Harmony, and Miss Andersen had to keep moving to allow them to greet them as well.

'Please, enjoy the evening!' the viscountess told them all.

'My God, what a rude man!' Aunt Minnie babbled before gulping down a big sip of champagne, once they were sufficiently far away. 'He ignored us as if we were servants!'

'Don't worry,' her husband replied. 'I think I've put him in his place. That conceited man won't dare criticise me or my business.'

Disgusted, Harmony had already lost interest in the gossip of her guardians. Now she was wondering where the duke's fiancée, Lady Lovelance, would be and if she'd attend the ball. It was odd that he was alone when, according to Sally, he had danced with her in a very romantic manner during the charity ball at his mansion. Rumour said that they were very much in love, and they would announce their engagement soon. Perhaps they would do it that very night. Such an idea made her stomach twist into knots.

She turned to look at him once more to find him looking around with a hint of expectation and something very reminiscent of disappointment.

Devlin sighed and shook his head. Why did he harbour the hope that she would turn up? He knew it would not happen and, still, he kept rubbing salt into his poorly healed wounds. Although he had forbidden it to himself, he did nothing but give free rein to a stupid and unconscious desire that seemed to push him into madness at a frantic speed.

Victory had left for Scotland with her lover, the Count of Radnor, and would not return to London until the New Year. But, even if he'd had her before him, what could he tell her to win her back? The pride that ran in the Sawyer family was stout like a thick concrete wall, and on occasion bordered on arrogance. If it would not allow him to directly demand redress from a lowlife horse dealer, it would allow him even less to beg love from a widow. Probably, if he saw her, he would treat her as if she was nobody to him and would pretend that he was not hurt by her rejection.

From a very young age, he had decided to become an ice floe when hurt, to hide his feelings, and he had been very good at it until he met Lady Lovelance. The baroness had found the key that opened all his doors; she had penetrated his soul and had thrown him into an inner turmoil. With her, the generosity, the relaxation, the joy, and the elation had become instinctive reactions he had not experienced with any other woman. He did not mind if they saw him excited in the racecourse boxes next to her, cheering Iolanthe on; or if they spotted him lifting her up upon the horse's victory; or if they found him looking at her with an uncontrollable longing he never managed to sate.

Now, unfortunately, even minor courtesies—like praising the beauty and richness of a Christmas tree, or repaying his own mother's tenderness by writing her a letter—had become very hard, as if an internal padlock had clicked shut and was now sealed, an unconscious reaction to avoid danger, to safeguard his battered heart.

At the ball, he had to face the usual sycophants who would go out of their way to greet him and make sure they covered their quota of flattering, parents who seemed to rub their daughters in his face to make sure he noticed them, comrades-in-arms, and political adversaries who would release their sharp comments. Innumerable young girls appeared very disappointed when he showed no interest in the ball or in conversing.

A footman walked by with a tray full of drinks. Devlin grabbed a glass and in a very ungentlemanly manner knocked it back. The bitter liquid travelled down his throat, burning him and relieving him at the same time. He needed to evoke that feeling of pleasure and oblivion that alcohol granted him. He wished to get drunk so that some fleeting enjoyment, more effective than the four days of sex with Anita Marinov, could remove him from reality.

It was past midnight and Harmony had not yet danced with her first gentleman. Miss Andersen, on the other hand, had taken up the role of the matchmaker. She had spent the whole evening talking to the matrons, to a Scotland Yard officer, to a pair of generals of the Royal Navy, and even to a clergyman, with the only intention of collecting—with admirable

52

discretion—essential details about potential husbands for her young pupil. After a painstaking study, she had added five names to the list. All the prospective candidates came from respectable families, had more than satisfactory incomes, and some of them could even have been considered quite good-looking. The problem was that none of those young men seemed to be aware of Harmony's existence.

Harmony humoured her governess so she would not scold her for not having tried, at the very least. She had talked to some of the gentlemen, pretending to be interested in their stupid topics of conversation, until they left without asking her for a dance. Andersen reproached her for not trying hard enough and insisted that she should do something more than frown on hearing a dull comment. According to her governess, a virtuous lady had to praise the opinions of men and pretend to be dazzled every so often by the nonsense that came out of their mouths. Although afterwards she had tried that, she had ended up empty-handed. And it didn't take a genius to know what was happening. At least Harmony had a theory. If she had been prettier, the gentlemen would have ignored her lack of interaction and would still have asked her for a dance or, at least, would not have left her side after a brief five-minute conversation.

That experience did nothing more than confirm what she already knew: that she was ugly. It wasn't the biggest problem in her life, and she had never been too worried about it but, even so, facing the fact still hurt.

It was not easy to accept the fact that she was rather plain. Her hair looked like a spider's nest, her face was dull, and her teeth… Oh, how she hated her teeth. Fanny had dubbed them 'the Tower of London's gates' because they were huge and stuck out like those of a rabbit. Harmony and her friends used to laugh at each other's flaws, making funny comparisons. Right then, however, she could not see anything funny in her lack of charms.

Tired of bland conversations and of her governess's scolding, the girl began to focus on her feeling of hunger. When had she become so frivolous? She forced herself to ignore the self-pitying thoughts and walked decidedly towards the refreshments and food table. There, a group of ladies and gentlemen had converged, plates in hand, eager to try the Christmas fare. There was a selection of canapés, fruit tartlets, chocolates, Christmas cake, and the traditional Christmas pudding prepared with plums, cream, butter, and brandy. Everything looked delicious. She finally decided to try the pudding. A footman dished it out and offered it to her kindly. She concluded it was delicious after sampling the first bite. The touch of brandy gave it a slightly bitter aftertaste that, mixed with the fruits, resulted in a glorious dessert. The man offered her a glass of homemade wine, which she politely declined.

'Stop immediately! Don't you know that the pudding is fattening?' Harmony jumped on hearing the punitive voice that reached her ears. She turned to find a red-haired young woman standing beside her. She was not reprimanding Harmony, though, but another girl who was eagerly piling up food onto her plate.

'I couldn't care less! I need energy for my next dance!' she replied to her friend, without turning to look at her.

'You'll end up like her,' she insisted, chuckling, as she pointed surreptitiously with her head.

The girls glanced at an obese sickly-looking woman who was resting on a chair, looking like she'd wolfed down an incredible amount of food. Of course, it had to be Aunt Minnie.

Both of them laughed, openly.

'I am famished and this tastes wonderful,' stated the one who was helping herself to pudding. 'Would you like some?'

'No, thanks!' The red-haired girl declined with a wave of the hands. 'I would like to be able to fit into a dress without having to pull at the corset more than necessary. And who comes next on your dance card?'

'Holborn,' replied the other one, looking fed up. She sighed with yearning. 'I hope Waldegrave will ask me to dance with him before the soles of my slippers are done for.'

'I haven't seen him dance with anybody all evening. The only thing he has done is drink. It shows an unforgivable disregard with so many ladies around hoping for more dance partners.'

'Perhaps she has reserved her first dance for his beloved, Lady Lovelance.'

'Marianne, haven't you heard?' whispered the red-haired girl. 'Lady Lovelance and Waldegrave are no longer together. She is now Lord Radnor's lover. Everybody is talking about it.'

'Lord Radnor?' Marianne repeated in the same quiet tone. 'But wasn't he married to Edwina Leyburn?'

'Well, I imagine he left her for the widow,' she grunted with contempt. 'Ah, poor Waldegrave! Luckily for us, he is available once more, don't you think? I hope the silly man gets over his bad mood soon.'

The other one chuckled at her comment.

Harmony lost her appetite. She left her half-eaten plate of food on the table and moved away. That was why Waldegrave looked so serious; that lady had scorned him to run away with another gentleman, probably the same one she had seen her talk to at the racecourse.

Instead of returning to Miss Andersen, Harmony decided to go out onto the back gardens of the mansion that were accessible through a wide glass door. Although it was bitterly cold, she needed to breathe some fresh air, put some distance between herself and the festive music, and that crowd of people who overwhelmed her with a Christmas spirit she did not share.

The garden at Felton House, with its plants naked and covered in snow, was lit by electric lampposts, a luxury for a few privileged families in London. She glimpsed a lovely archway of grapevines, which had probably been fertile in a different era. The place was beautifully decorated with sculptures, plaster urns, and wooden, wrought iron benches.

Uncle John's words echoed in her mind. 'You can be sure of one thing: you will get married and pretty soon.' If her parents were still alive, and they had talked to her about marriage, she would have agreed to it without hesitation, but the fact that it was her uncle who was forcing her into it made her irate. He had no right to decide for her; he had never loved her; he had never shown the slightest affection towards her, and his wife had always treated her with disdain. The only thing the Talbots wanted was to get rid of her in the old-fashioned way, transferring the responsibility to a husband.

She had to do something about it, she thought anxiously, while she rubbed her frozen-stiff arms with her gloved hands. Perhaps she should behave badly towards the gentlemen who approached her, so none of them would show any interest in her, and they would keep running away from her side until there were none left. Until all the men in London thought she was the worst candidate possible to be a wife and rejected her outright. She could scare off each and every future husband Uncle John chose for her.

A slight cough distracted her. She quickly turned and saw a person standing by one of the plaster statues, under the light of one of the lampposts. At first, she thought he was a child, but she dismissed that thought almost immediately; that vicious look could only belong to a satyr. To one in particular: Andrew Curson.

He was wearing a good quality tailcoat and had his hands stuffed inside his trouser pockets in a relaxed pose. His reddish and curly hair shone like fire under the curtain of light.

When she saw him, Harmony opted for leaving the place. She was not afraid of that man, but she preferred to avoid him, as she did in the racecourse and the stables, whenever she had the misfortune of accompanying Uncle John to his events. She'd rather save herself the depraved looks and his conversation that, usually, centred on himself and involved puns and wordplay that she had no difficulty guessing alluded to sex.

'Oh, no, no, don't go please,' he told her, blocking her way. 'Let's stay here. It's a beautiful night.'

Harmony looked at him from head to toe. The head of the young man, who must have been three-and-twenty, only reached up to her jaw. 'Not so much any longer, Mr Curson.'

'Ouch!' He put his right hand on his chest, pretending to be in pain. Afterwards, he offered her one of his sinister smiles. 'I was wondering if we might be able to have a talk in peace, far from that tide of pretentious people.'

'Pretentious people?' Harmony half-smiled and crossed her arms. So, he also shared in Uncle John's jealousy. Perhaps if her aunt and uncle had had a son, he would have been like Andrew Curson. 'How ungrateful, Mr Curson. Aren't they the same people who invited you here tonight? Or have you sneaked in without being invited?'

'I've come with my patron,' he explained, adjusting his cufflinks.

'Good for you.' The young woman made another attempt at leaving, but the little man once more blocked her path.

'Wait,' he insisted. 'Don't leave. I beg you.'

'I don't see why I should stay alone with you.'

'Why do you always run away from me? Why are you always so aggressive? I don't recall having ever done you any harm. Have I, perhaps?'

Harmony opened her mouth to reply, but she could find nothing to say. He was right. Apart from his vulgar attitude, the arrogance that was characteristic of him and the offensive way in which he looked at her, she had nothing to reproach him for.

'That's better,' he said, pleased, and smiled at her again.

Suddenly, she thought she could start to put into practice the simple plan she had been thinking about. If that idiot learned of her worst side, he would get scared and Uncle John would never be able to convince him to marry her. 'And what would you like to talk about, Mr Curson?'

'I don't know,' he said with a shrug. 'I thought that we could get to know each other better in a neutral place. I always see you briefly where I work, where my concentration must remain unbroken. I cannot afford the luxury of watching you or enjoying you as much as I'd like.'

Damn. How did he manage to make every single word that came out of his mouth sound like an insult or innuendo? Harmony was sickened by his effrontery.

'Tell me, what do you like? What impresses a young woman like yourself, Miss George?'

'Size, perhaps,' she replied, pretending that his dirty language did not bother her. She had to do it for the sake of her plan. 'A large size.'

Curson frowned as if he were wondering if he should feel offended, but then he showed her a hint of one of his nasty smiles. 'Naughty girl.'

'I was talking about palaces, carriages, jewels, Mr Curson. What woman would not be impressed by such things?'

The horseman smiled. 'I didn't think you were one of those women.'

'You know nothing about me.'

'It's true, but I didn't take you for the typical social climber. I'll tell you how I see you...' He came perilously close to her, without lifting his gaze off her bodice. 'Like a girl with many unsatisfied desires, fed-up of her life, anxious for new experiences.' Well, at least the nasty rogue was right, although the way he'd said it caused her to feel nauseous. 'I can help you with that, truly I can. In fact, I'd love to do it.'

'It's a very kind offer, but I don't need it,' she replied, stepping back as her instinct demanded.

Curson smiled and let out a detestable, screechy sound. 'What does it matter what you want, Harmony?' he whispered. 'Your uncle has promised me your hand in marriage.'

Her jaw slowly opened, as if unhinged. In that instant, she felt a stabbing pain in her chest, so sharp that she thought it would pierce her insides. Curson took advantage of the surprise that had engulfed her to take the hands out of his pockets and caress with a finger the exposed skin of her collarbone. So it was a done deal already, she thought as her heart sank.

Instinctively, she jumped backwards, slapping off the hand of the shameless individual. 'Don't touch me! Don't you ever dare come near me again!'

'But we will be husband and wife. It is better that you become used to my hands on you, and you should get ready for the things I want to do to you.'

Harmony kept walking backwards until her back hit a hedge.

'Would you like to know something funny? Being a short man has its advantages,' he carried on, saying embarrassing things to her while looking at her in a most lascivious way. 'There are things I can do that a regular size man cannot. Shall I show you?'

In a daring or stupid act, Harmony pushed him to the point of almost making him lose his balance, frustrating his attempt at getting closer. Damn it, she would jump in front of a train rather than marrying that vermin. Oh, yes. If it was necessary, she would slash her wrists with a rusty knife to avoid such a fate.

'I like you like this.' He laughed. 'To be honest, I can't bear the fragile and

57

shy damsels. I want a headstrong, vigorous female like you, Harmony George. A wild mare I can tame and later ride at will!' He moved as if he were atop a moving horse, swirling his hand as if he was holding a riding crop on it. 'It will be funny, my beautiful.'

'You are an evil bastard,' she mumbled while observing with her eyes wide such a demeaning circus show. To tell the truth, she was feeling too sick to faint due to her embarrassment as any other young girl would.

Curson laughed out loud. 'I love your pretty dirty mouth. You and I are alike.'

'No, Curson. We are nothing alike! And it will be best if I tell you now: I'm not going to marry you. You will have to go to the stables to find another wild mare. This one doesn't like ponies.'

Harmony tried to leave again, but Curson, in a desperate gesture, grabbed her bodice to prevent it. The only noises that could be heard were the tear of the poor quality lace and her own moan on realising her dress was ruined. 'Idiot! Look what you've done!'

'Oh, no, you look better than a moment ago!'

This time, Curson had gone further than she was prepared to put up with. Harmony slapped him so hard that the palm of her hand burned. She felt good; she had to admit, having put that rake in his place.

The horseman retreated like a wounded animal, surprised by the girl's daring. With his eyes brimming with anger, he stepped towards her to reply in kind. Harmony felt a fierce burning in her jaw; the little coward's hand had just injured her chin. Damn him! Nobody had ever hit her, not even her aunt and uncle. Overcome by anger, she turned towards him and hit him even harder.

Her attacker, totally defeated, looked at her, panicking. Perhaps he had only just realised what he had done. He had hit a woman in the viscount's garden during the Christmas ball. He started to shake her, showering her with threats that sounded more like entreaties for her not to tell anybody what had happened there.

With hard slaps, Harmony got rid of the desperate grab of the horseman and ran back to the mansion. There, dozens of couples were still dancing the waltz, unaware of the disturbing scene that had taken place only a few yards away. She glimpsed at Uncle John and his wife, who were chatting by a column removed from the crowd. She walked towards them as fast as she could, hiding the torn bodice with a hand and holding her achy cheek with the other.

'Uncle John. You have no idea what just happened to me!'

'What's this scandal? Do you think you are in Covent Garden market, you vulgar girl?'

'Andrew Curson…' She mentioned that name with all the revulsion she could muster, vindicated because now she had something to reproach that awful rake for. She had made an unforgivable mistake underestimating him. 'He has been disrespectful towards me, Uncle! He has behaved like a pig towards me!'

Talbot grew pale. 'What are you talking about?'

'Look what he's done to me!' she removed her hand from her bodice, showing the torn material, and pointed at her jaw that felt red hot. 'He said horrible things to me and slapped me in the garden. That man is a bastard!' she exclaimed, covering up again her battered dress. 'You must tell the viscount so he throws him out, Uncle.'

Talbot was looking at her with his eyes almost popping out of his sockets, but it was not horror what showed on them; it was bewilderment. She knew then that this was the last chance he had to earn her respect as her guardian. He blinked several times, exchanged a confused look with his wife, and inspired deeply before replying. 'Curson is a gentleman, Harmony,' he whispered with astounding coldness. 'He would never behave inappropriately, even less so with his future wife.'

'But… but, Uncle… can't you see?'

'And you say he was disrespectful towards you in the garden?' intruded Aunt Minnie. 'What were you doing there with him, impertinent girl?'

'Nothing, nothing. We were only having a conversation.'

'Having a conversation? Really!,' she blurted out, mockingly. 'Aside from being a harlot, you are also a liar.'

'Uncle John, you can't allow…' She begged him with her eyes.

'Enough. You're calling attention to yourself.'

'I knew something like this would happen,' grumbled Aunt Minnie. 'Where is that useless governess? Why has she left her on her own?'

She turned to look again, imploringly, at her guardian. 'Uncle John, you must seek Curson and make him pay for what he's done to me.'

The man had gone into a state of unshakeable calm. 'Perhaps there has been a misunderstanding.'

'There has been no misunderstanding!'

'This afternoon, I decided to give your hand in marriage to Curson, but I wanted to wait until the end of the evening to let you know. Perhaps the poor man thought that you already knew and wanted to flatter you a little…'

'Flatter me?' she repeated, inflamed. 'Since when one flatters a woman by tearing up her clothes and hitting her?'

'Harmony!' he hissed, looking around cautiously. 'Stop behaving like a lunatic. We are in Viscount Felton's mansion. Show a bit of respect. You are shaming the whole family.'

She looked at him, hurt but not surprised by his behaviour. 'You are not going to do anything, are you?'

'I'll tell Curson that he must behave better...' was all he could promise her. When she made to walk away he added, 'Where on Earth are you going?'

'To talk to the viscountess,' she said with a waving gesture. 'I'll tell her one of her guests assaulted me, and that she must throw him out of her house before he does the same to another young girl. And afterwards, I'll tell her that you, my uncle, did not defend my honour.'

'You wouldn't dare to embarrass me.' He gritted his teeth and clenched his fists. 'Do I need to remind you that you live under my roof and that if I feel so inclined you could end up sleeping on the streets tonight?'

'Under a bridge! One with plenty of vagrants,' interrupted Aunt Minnie who, judging by her huge smile, was enjoying the argument.

Harmony looked at her, horrified. 'All right. I would prefer that to marrying the beast you have chosen for me, John Talbot. I think he could be a more than worthy son of yours.'

'Listen carefully!' he shouted. 'You won't go anywhere, except to the powder room to get that dress mended. You'll come back here and apologise to us and to your future husband for having placed him in such a horrible situation.'

That rogue? She was convinced that he had already run away from Felton House. Harmony let loose a bitter laugh. 'If you think I am going to apologise to Andrew Curson, allow me to make something amply clear. In case you don't remember, I will be of age in less than a month. As soon as that happens, I'll be glad to leave your horrible house.'

'Ungrateful brat,' he growled, frowning so much that his eyes grew almost invisible; the gazes of the guests, little by little, were being drawn towards the discussion of people they clearly thought were poor uncivilised individuals, invited by the viscount and his wife in a clear demonstration of their eccentricity. 'You are arrogant like your father, but you have nothing to boast about.'

'I have the money he left me! I have my inheritance!' shouted Harmony, jutting her chin up, holding onto the only thing she had left, to the ship that would transport her to her dreams, away from that horrible family.

And she could have never believed she would feel as crushed as she did when the man in front of her, with the sound of his words, made the earth crack open and her whole world disappear inside.

'Allow me to make something amply clear, dear niece. You don't have a single penny to your name.'

Chapter 4

The colours of the parlour, the Christmas tree, the lights, and the hothouse flowers, started to melt in her mind in a painful tremor that almost robbed her of her senses. The seconds passed, but she wasn't able to wake up from the sudden nightmare the ball had turned into. Around her, people chatted, laughed, and danced to the rhythm of the music the orchestra kept playing. The clinking of the glasses and the chink of the cutlery on the fine bone china resounded loudly in her ears, like two trains colliding.

'But... my inheritance.'

'It vanished,' her uncle admitted.

'What do you mean "it vanished"?' Her voice had turned into a sickly whine; it mattered not how hard she tried to fill her lungs with oxygen. It was physically impossible, as if they'd been torn to pieces. How could her future have been snatched away in just one second?

'Well, I had to pay my debts somehow, didn't I?'

'Did you use my money?'

'The moneylenders didn't want to listen to me, so I took what your father had left. It wasn't much. It helped me get out of some tight spots. And if it hadn't been for that I'd be in prison now, and you and your aunt would be living in a shelter.'

'God forbid...' mumbled his wife.

'But, everything? All the money?'

'I'm telling you it wasn't much,' he insisted. 'Your father wasn't a rich man.'

'I know that, but I also know there was enough. And the interest...?'

'Ignorant girl... Banks don't pay interest these days. There's nothing left of your inheritance, Harmony. And you don't need it, in any case. Curson is well-off at the moment. In a few years and with a bit of luck, he'll have lots of money. You'll have a good life. You should thank me for what I'm doing for you when you've been so rude.'

'Silly girl,' Aunt Minnie intruded again. 'You've won the lottery and act as if somebody has died.'

Harmony ignored her, as she always did. She only saw Uncle John. 'I don't have anything left and you tell me here? Like... this?'

'We are even. My wife and I took you in and have looked after you for the last ten years; the least you could do is help us cope with some of the load.'

Harmony gathered all her strength, she did not quite know where from, to confront her guardian. If she no longer had her precious inheritance, the one she'd been planning to use to leave England and set off on the journey of her dreams, away from all the misery she had experienced with the Talbots, at least she would not remain silent. 'You had no right!' she burst out. 'This was my inheritance. I had planned on starting a new life with my money, far away from you! You are a—'

'Be careful, Harmony...' He whispered in a threatening manner.

'I can't believe we are related,' she carried on, immune to his warnings, because she had nothing left to fear. 'My father was a gentleman and you are an embarrassment. Thankfully, we don't share the same surname. And you...' she turned to look at Minnie, whose expression, stunned and grotesque, mirrored her husband's. 'I cannot insult you enough, even if I try. Thankfully, you did not have any children you could subject to the torture I've been through.'

And, after saying that, she left their side as soon as she could. On her way, she bumped onto several people, whom she moved out of the way by pushing and elbowing. She no longer needed to maintain the niceties expected of her if her life had been completely ruined, did she? She did not have to pretend to be a refined lady, like Miss Andersen insisted on reminding her. She only wished to escape from that horrible meeting; from those horrendous people she'd never considered part of her family and to run out into the streets. Anywhere was better than next to that pair of monsters.

She glanced at the door she'd entered through before. Her governess—her blond-grey head moving in all directions—was standing there, presumably looking for her. The last thing Harmony wished at that moment was to have to listen to sermons. She would avoid her at all costs and that meant trying to find another exit.

She decided to return to the garden. She knew that all elegant city houses such as this one had a back door that opened into the street, and it could usually be found at the bottom of the garden. Harmony entered the cold yard and wandered through it until she reached the place where the electric lampposts disappeared. There, a deep darkness engulfed her. Without pausing to look around, she crossed a cemetery of trees and bushes covered in snow as she walked along a gravel path. Her mind was assaulted by thousands of new ideas. Perhaps she did not need an inheritance to start a new life. After all, Mrs Ida Pfeiffer had travelled with only a handful of pounds. She could work and save a bit until she could afford a transatlantic ticket and, afterwards, she would work wherever her travels took her.

She only stopped when she managed to make out, at the end of the path, a huge wrought iron door. On the other side, she could see the deserted street, and two mounds of snow that somebody had removed with a shovel. Under the dim light of the moon, the sky stood out, grey and gloomy.

She went to open the door but, to her dismay, saw that it was locked with a padlock bigger than her fist. Of course, nobody would be so silly as to let open the door of their house at midnight. All was lost.

'Damn!' In a pathetic attempt, she started to shake the door, as if she'd manage to open it that way. The frustration, the desperation, and the sudden awareness that she was captive and would never manage to escape the horrific life the Talbots had chosen for her was starting to take a toll on her reason. Her tears flowed, the pain overcoming her until she was almost bent over.

There was only one thing left to do.

Devlin felt like a mean Ebenezer Scrooge in the middle of that party that, he hoped, would finish any minute now.

How long had it been since he had decided to go for that walk? One? Two hours? Once the liquor had slid down his throat without completely easing his anxiety, he had stopped to care. The bottle of whisky was almost empty; soon he'd have to go back to Felton's cellar to get another one. He did not fancy that in the slightest; not when he would have to avoid that crowd of idiots dancing and singing carols while he was dying inside. He didn't want them to see him looking like that: a pathetic drunkard.

He wondered about her whereabouts all of a sudden. Would Lady Lovelance be happy coexisting with the Wiltshire sheep? Would her new lover buy her jewels? Would he support her charity? Would he treat her like a queen, as he had done? In dismay, he rubbed his eyes, which had started to burn. 'Don't cry, damn it. Don't cry,' he growled to himself.

'Damn!'

A nearby scream woke him from his drunken stupor. Devlin stood up, aware that the alcohol had slowed down his reflexes. He moved slowly, his eyesight precarious, and he was not sure he could walk more than a couple of steps without falling flat on his face. Despite that, he walked to the end of the garden from where the scream had emanated, with extreme care. He then had a glimpse of a moaning and vague mass of skirts climbing up the fence. 'Shit, what are you doing?' he shouted, and that made the woman move back down, startled. Their gazes met, but he was unable to focus in the semi-darkness.

'What the hell do you care...?' was the irate reply he got.

The woman started to climb up the iron gate again in a hazardous manner. Devlin felt a familiar shiver running down his spine. He had been in a similar situation recently, but not in a million years would he have imagined this would happen again.

'Oh, no, no... stop doing that.' He ran towards her, fighting the uncomfortable weight he felt in his feet. 'Do you want to slip and break your neck?'

'I will break your neck if you don't leave me alone, pretentious idiot!'

Devlin scratched his head that felt unsteady and untidy like a birds' nest. 'Damn it,' he moaned. No woman had ever spoken to him that way before, at least not without a reason. The alcohol running through his veins didn't help him think logically. He wasn't angry; it would be more accurate to say that he was astonished and rather amused by the girl's reaction. He tried to focus his eyes, frowning and moving closer to her until he finally saw who she was. 'You are Talbot's niece.'

She snorted. 'Oh, I am so happy to see that you have noticed my existence.'

Was it sarcasm what had come out of her mouth? He wasn't certain.

'It is such a great honour that I think I'll start crying this instant.'

'Wait! Stop climbing, you damn fool!' Devil grabbed her ankle hard, stopping her, but she started kicking her leg obstinately.

'Why don't you mind your own business and leave me alone?'

'You've decided to kill yourself on Christmas Day, haven't you?' he insisted, without letting go of the ankle clad in soft stockings. 'Couldn't you wait until the New Year or until tomorrow and make your way to the afterlife in another house, one not belonging to my friends?'

'I am not trying to kill myself!'

'That's what will happen if you don't climb down from there, you silly girl. The metal is slippery due to the sleet. I order you to leave through the front door, like decent people do.'

'I can't...' she whimpered.

66

'Yes, you can. Stop behaving like a spoilt girl and go find an available exit.'

'For the last time, let me go!'

Harmony shook her head fiercely, her mind in a whirl. She thought she'd die of embarrassment when she saw the Duke of Waldegrave contemplating the decadent spectacle she offered trying to climb the metal bars of the door. At first, she did not recognise him. He looked so different. He was clearly drunk; his hair loose and messy cascaded over his shoulders, his frack looking untidy and his bow-tie crooked. She felt a little braver when she realised he had no reason to feel proud of his appearance either.

She shouted at him to let her be, but he insisted in preventing her escape, as if she was in need of a knight in shining armour to come to her rescue. Harmony could kick him on the face and get rid of him in no time—in his state of drunkenness he would immediately collapse—but she did not want to harm him. She did not want to take it out on him who, paradoxically, was the only one who seemed to care about her.

'You are nobody to give me orders, bloody brat,' growled the duke, hugging her thighs—that were encased by the swirl of her skirt—with such intensity that she was thrown out of balance. His face ended up at the height of the swell of her derrière. 'I order you to climb down right this moment or I will drag you down and, in the process, I'll give you a couple of slaps on your backside.'

'You would not dare,' she whined, fighting against his grip and against a rather inappropriate sensation, until she had no option left but to burst out crying. 'You don't know me. You have no idea what I'm going through. You live in your palace, with all the luxuries, imposing your will wherever you go. You don't know the pain, the rage, the impotence. The sensation of having nothing left!' she added as she struggled to look behind her, trying to face him.

Devlin raised an eyebrow ironically. 'Don't be so sure.'

'Release me, Waldegrave,' she begged for the last time. 'I only want to leave, I cannot go back in. Please, let me go…'

'I am not going to do it! Your life is in danger, cry-baby!'

Harmony inhaled deeply before trying her last resort: she let go with one of her hands and elbowed the duke hard on the brow. 'I'm sorry', she whispered when she heard him croak.

Waldegrave let go off her, experiencing the irrepressible need to touch the spot where he had been hit. His state did not help him maintain his balance and he stumbled, falling on his backside on the gravel.

Harmony hurried to climb the short distance to the top, but her worry made her turn around to ensure he had not hurt himself worse than she imagined. Then, her left foot stepped onto a particularly wet iron bar. She slipped spectacularly, clutching the bar only with her hands now, but they weren't strong enough to hold the weight of her body. Her fall was inevitable. The blow was not too hard, because she had not climbed up too high, but that did not prevent her from hurting herself slightly in the coccyx.

She was still lying on the gravel, cursing and moaning, when a threatening shadow fell on her, then an untimely closeness enveloped her so tightly it almost crushed her. She was astonished to see the Duke of Waldegrave sitting astride of her with his knees by her sides, his powerful arms and elbows shackling her forearms, his long hair grazing her cheeks, and his beautiful and irate face inches from hers.

'Damn you, little girl! You have no idea whom you've just hit,' he growled like a beast, a rancid whiff of whisky escaping his lips. Harmony did not mind that; she didn't even fear his threats. She was paralysed, her mind clouded by a fact that should have horrified her but, strangely, caused her a dark pleasure instead. 'I will make you feel sorry for this, I'll show you who is in charge. I'll... I'll...'

The duke's eyes, wide with anger, gazed at her torn dress that was fully visible under the whitish light of the winter moon. The bodice's lace was torn to pieces, revealing the top of her corset and the generous mounds of her breasts that trembled with her ragged breathing. The white steam of his breath, thick due to his exertion, enveloped them like smog, caressing them softly, causing her skin to break with goose bumps. Suddenly, she wondered if his breathing would have the same effect on her nipples too.

Devlin's head spun. He looked at the girl underneath him and froze. Her messy hair spread out on the gravel like a soft blanket. Her cloudy gaze reflected his, as she looked clearly agitated and confused. She was not resisting nor asking to be freed. Then, when he realised that, he found himself enjoying the image he had in front of him—or rather, underneath him—and a delicious sensation flowed down to his groin. Devlin fell prey to an excitement as unwelcome as it was surprising. Without the common sense required to weigh up the consequences, his mouth sought the feminine lips to melt into them in a feverish kiss.

Harmony's world had melted into nothing, and she felt her heart would stop, right at the moment Waldegrave put his lips on hers. She had desired him in secret, and now that he was kissing her she did not know what to do with him; nothing, except keep still and allow the softness of his lips to take possession of her.

She had lost all point of contact with reality, forgetting how absurd it all was, and she ended up believing that the knock on her head had been so hard that she was hallucinating. The Duke of Waldegrave would never kiss her, a simple and plain girl, especially when she'd called him 'idiot' and 'pompous' and had hit him. Then, she decided that if it was a hallucination that could end at any moment, at least she might as well enjoy it while it lasted.

She allowed him to take control without resisting, to caress her in such an intimate manner, and to pour out his warmth over her lips, a warmth that spread to the rest of her body. He made her open her mouth wider and proceeded deeper still, surprising her. His tongue explored the inside of her mouth, looking farther in, moving inside impatiently, as if he'd wanted to examine every nook. Harmony felt the need to use her hands, to touch his hair, which she'd always felt fascinated by, but his hands kept her imprisoned.

After a few seconds, her skin felt more sensitive, and that was because he was atop of her, as if they were having sex. Instinctively, she opened her legs, allowing him to lean on them. Was it really a hallucination? But it felt so real. Her body responded to the sensations in a way she would never have thought possible. Before that night, she did not know what it meant to kiss somebody, but she was sure that nobody else on earth could make her feel what that man did.

Then, things got out of control. With a moan, Waldegrave removed himself from her, letting go of her hands. He started to scramble around the folds of the skirt of her dress. Layer upon layer of material threatened to bury Harmony who, in her state of ashamed excitement, felt a wave of panic flooding her. 'No, wait. Stop!'

Good God. She knew what he was trying to do and would not allow it, no matter what, even though he might have thought he could do whatever he liked to her, due to her submissive attitude. Desperate, she started hitting his shoulders, trying to make him react, but the duke was out of control.

No! She had to prevent this from happening!

Waldegrave had managed to put his hands under her petticoat when a yellow light blinded them. Both of them stopped, their eyes hurt by the unexpected flash that had cooled down any vestige of a fight. Harmony protected her face with the palm of her hand, right at the moment when a surprised gasp followed by an indignant feminine shout echoed through the garden.

She removed her hand and, when her eyes got used to the light, she managed to see the dumbstruck Viscountess of Felton holding a lantern on her hand. Next to her, stood a shocked Miss Andersen, whose face could hardly reflect a bigger disappointment.

Now in Count Felton's study, a male and luxurious chamber that had swallowed Harmony up from the beginning, she couldn't feel more intimidated if the walls were to start closing in on her. The room was panelled in birch, the floor covered in Persian rugs in beautiful geometric patterns, the chairs and sofas circling a low table were upholstered in iridescent gold and burgundy-coloured materials. There was a huge arched mirror above the marble chimney, and a golden clock said a little over two a.m. Farther away there was a mahogany writing desk and, behind it, a huge bookshelf. The room was lit by a sumptuous glass chandelier.

In the time she'd been there, she had looked at the floor most of the time as she yielded to Miss Andersen's tenacious interrogation. With nothing left to lose, she'd told her what had happened with her aunt and uncle, with Andrew Curson, and finally with the Duke of Waldegrave. The governess's face went from surprise to scepticism as fleeting expressions of horror kept pinching her features. One of the viscountess's maids had brought her a blanket to cover her torn bodice with, and a cup of tea that was growing cold on the table without her having had a single sip.

The study's door opened. She saw Uncle John and his wife coming in, their confused expressions bordering on horror. Behind them came the viscount. Harmony could feel her skin go red up to her forehead when she realised her encounter with the duke would now become a topic of discussion for that man she hardly knew. The last one to come in and close the door was Waldegrave. Harmony knew because she noticed his shoes, still wet with sleet and mud.

'I am sorry we had to call this meeting in such...' Lord Fenton took a couple of seconds to find the appropriate word, 'confusing circumstances, but we are under the obligation to solve this situation; no matter how uncomfortable it makes us all feel.' He looked at Harmony and she dropped her eyes to the floor again. 'Especially Miss George,' he added.

Harmony felt the exact moment when all eyes landed on her, and that was when she wished the pattern of the rug would come alive and swallow her whole. This could not be happening, she kept repeating to herself. It had to be a nightmare, or a stage in the delirium she had fallen into after the knock on the head.

'My Lord, My Lady...' Uncle John stood up from the sofa where he'd been sitting with his wife. 'With all due respect, I demand to know why my family has been summoned to this meeting. Whatever my niece has done, it is a family matter of our exclusive concern,' he said looking at the duke, irate.

'I'm afraid it's not that simple.'

Waldegrave respectfully signalled Lord Fenton, asking to speak. For the first time since he had entered the study, Harmony looked at him. Apparently, he had sobered up, because he looked as formal and solemn as usual. In fact, his hair had been wet and combed back meticulously. He looked as if what had taken place before had never happened. Right then, the memories of their passionate kiss overwhelmed her.

'Mr Talbot, tonight I've wronged your family,' he said in a calm voice, his hands behind his back.

'You?' the man inquired, looking at him sideways.

'That's the case. I have…' a fleeting hesitation crossed his eyes, while Harmony prayed all that was only a nightmare, 'harassed your niece. A few minutes ago we met alone in the garden, by pure chance. It was not an arranged encounter, and I have jumped on her to… to kiss her… on the lips.'

After he'd said those words, a loud guffaw shook the room. Aunt Minnie burst out laughing uncontrollably until the gazes of all those present turned towards her, piercing her until she obviously realised Waldegrave was not joking. 'But that's ridiculous!' she said, all traces of humour gone from her expression.

'It isn't, Mrs Talbot,' the duke insisted. 'I'm telling you the truth.'

'But, what the hell?' Uncle John said, looking astonished. 'Harmony, is what this man saying true?'

Harmony opened her mouth to answer, but not a single word came out. Her gaze was fixed on the rug once more. She had never felt so ashamed in her whole life. In part, she had to admit that she was surprised by Waldegrave's attitude, admitting everything with such fortitude.

'Mr Talbot,' the governess said, while caressing her pupil's head in a protective gesture, 'it is not necessary to pester her with questions after what she has endured tonight. I beg you to be gentle.'

'Miss Andersen is right,' Waldegrave agreed. 'There is no need to harass her over something that is my sole responsibility; your niece has not condoned my behaviour at any point. I want to apologise in front of you all for this embarrassing episode, and for putting the young lady in such a compromising situation. It was not my intention to ruin your evening.'

The door opened. Lady Fenton entered the study accompanied by the hurried whisper of her skirts; her expression was considerably less grave than that of the others. She looked almost satisfied. 'I apologise. I was making sure that the rest of the guests were not inventing some gossip.' She sat next to Harmony and smiled at her encouragingly. 'Are you all right, dear? Do you need anything else?' When Harmony shook her head, she added, 'Don't worry, I'll get you a new dress.'

The mention of her torn dress resulted in Harmony blushing even more, if that were physically possible.

'How is everything out there?' asked the viscount.

'It seems that nobody has seen anything. All were far away from the garden at that point but, to make sure, I've left Olga wandering around the hall with her ears pricked. If anybody says something about it, she will tell me straight away.'

'Well, that is a relief,' her husband said with a sigh.

'Don't be so quick, My Lord,' Uncle John mumbled, stepping toward Waldegrave with the fake pompous attitude Harmony hated so much. 'In case you have not noticed, My Lord, the honour of our family has been defiled by this shameful episode. I assure you the trauma we have suffered tonight will remain with us for years to come. In fact, only the Lord knows if we will ever recover. Don't you think we deserve some kind of... compensation for the inconvenience?'

'Compensation?' Lady Felton frowned intensely while her gaze went from Uncle John to the duke.

Harmony thought she would faint with the shame. No! Damn you, Uncle! Don't you dare ask for compensation for this! she thought, holding her head in her hands in desperation. She knew him well and was aware that he would do anything in order to get a good sum of money out of that situation. She hated him even more for that.

'What are you talking about, Talbot?' Waldegrave inquired, looking glum.

'What other thing could I be referring to, Your Grace? It might be the case that none of the guests have found out what you did to my niece in the garden, but each one of us present here knows it. And, believe me: at least I have no intention of forgetting it. I would rather not have to talk to you like this, considering who you are. I admit that I've failed tonight—as the only relative and guardian of Miss George—but as you will understand, I cannot let it rest. The only graceful way out of all this mess would be for you to get married to my niece.'

Devlin heard the words of that vile individual, his blood throbbing in his temples. Had he demanded that he marry that girl, his niece? His luck could not get any worse, for sure. After being discovered by the governess and Lady Felton, the duke realised what he was doing and what he had been about to do. He was lying atop that young girl and kept thinking he was a wretch of the worst kind, a pig, and vermin. His drunkenness had now abandoned him and

72

a stabbing fear had taken its place.

He had no idea how it had all started. How was it possible that a simple walk through the garden—which had taken longer than expected—and a bottle of whisky had caused such a catastrophe? The alcohol was coarsening him and now had got him into a predicament he would not get out of unless a miracle happened.

He knew that marrying the girl was the most honourable solution. Although he did not remember anything, he was aware that he had compromised her, God only knew acting under what bloody spell. He could not imagine a more compromising situation for a young debutant and, of course, that was not something that could be righted with money.

'No, no, no!' John Talbot's niece stood up suddenly, letting out a scream that surprised everybody. When she moved, the blanket covering her slipped down her back and ended up on the sofa, exposing the top of her dress, which was in tatters. Then, Devlin remembered vaguely that he had been staring at the top of those breasts and he had longed to suck them and bite them. Damn it. Had he torn her dress?

He glimpsed Felton's horrified face when he looked away, as a gentleman would do, and then looked back at the girl, who had covered herself again. Of course he had been responsible for tearing up that dress.

'This is madness, Uncle John,' the girl objected. 'It wasn't that bad; I assure you.'

'It wasn't that bad?' Now it was the governess who raised her voice. 'He was lying on top of you, for God's sake! I saw it,' she said to the girl, causing Devlin to lower his head in shame. Would he have raped her if they had not been discovered? He made an effort to reject such horrifying possibility.

'I am sorry,' the governess continued, 'but Mr Talbot is right. The Duke of Waldegrave has been on the verge of disgracing you and such shame can only be repaired when he marries you, my girl.'

'Miss Andersen, don't you think this is a bit rushed?' Lady Felton interrupted, looking fixedly at the governess. 'I know perfectly well that Miss George has been affected by this, but a forced marriage wouldn't help anybody. The duke and your pupil hardly know each other.'

Lady Fenton tapped her foot and frowned slightly. She was a convinced defender of love marriages, even inside the rigid British aristocracy. She, personally, as she had confessed to Felton on occasion, had been married for twenty years, due to her parents' imposition, to a man much older than her. After losing her husband, the woman had become Lord Felton's lover. Then, after months of hesitation, of overcoming conflicts and of tough tests, the viscount had taken her as his wife without paying any attention to the ill-meaning comments of his milieu, who had tried to discredit her by calling her a "merry widow". Lord and Lady Felton loved each other passionately and that was evident to everybody around them. Taking into account the events that had brought them together, one could say that both of them had been the protagonists of a modern fairy-tale.

Devlin let out a soft sigh, grateful for the viscountess's words. But before he could comment, the governess spoke again. 'There will be plenty of time for that, Lady Felton. In my career as a governess I've seen arranged marriages that have been successful. What I have never seen is such gall in order to avoid doing the right thing.'

'I am not avoiding it, Miss Andersen!' protested Waldegrave.

'Please, stop,' the girl begged, and then turned her gaze towards the duke to add, 'Your Grace, I extricate you from any responsibility you might think you have acquired towards me. You are obliged neither to take me as your wife nor to give me any compensation for what has happened. Therefore, let's forget all this. I beg you.'

Devlin blinked and walked slowly towards her. He fixed his gaze on her, on noticing a detail he seemed to be the only one to have observed. He had not been listening to her words, or her noble intention of releasing him from a compulsory marriage; his narrowed eyes stared obstinately at the left side of her jaw, and a shudder of terror shook him from head to toe.

There, a few inches from her delicate chin was beginning to appear a small bruise he was sure he had caused while attacking her to gain control, so he would be allowed to do as he wished. If, until now, his horrendous behaviour in the garden had not been motivation enough to despise his own person, that final piece of evidence had finished up the job.

Devlin knew what to do straight away. 'I don't need to be released from anything, young lady. Your uncle is right. From this moment, I accept my engagement to you, as required by good manners,' he said, stoicism in its purest form oozing out of him. Then, he turned to look at the miserable man he would now inevitably become related to. 'I ask you for the hand of your niece in marriage, Mr Talbot.'

The horse dealer's smile widened so that his yellow teeth were exposed in all their dubious glory, like those of a hyena before a copious banquet.

'I knew you would not shy away from your moral duty, Your Grace.' His arms opened up in an embrace Devlin had no intention to be party to even if his life depended on it. 'You have my blessing and... welcome to the family!'

On her way home, wearing a dark blue outfit belonging to the viscountess that was huge on her, Harmony kept going over recent events in bitter and reticent incredulity. All of a sudden, she was completely ruined, without the backup of her father's inheritance, which her uncle had disposed of. If that weren't enough, she was now engaged to be married to the most arrogant man in London, the Duke of Waldegrave. The same man who had prevented her escape; the same who had immobilised her on the floor with his powerful body and had looked at her irate; the same who had kissed her in a most sensual and sizzling manner; the very same who had frightened her with his sudden rush of passion.

No, her mind could not assimilate all that, not even in a million years. She rubbed her temples, anxiously, to try to alleviate an incipient headache while Aunt Minnie carried on talking about a glorious wedding, with the most appetizing delicacies the British aristocracy had set eyes on in years. No! In centuries. She was talking about a sumptuous reception, about new and powerful contacts, and about the imminent association of the Talbots with royalty. It seemed as if she had hit her head on her way out of Felton House, while Harmony's was about to explode confronted with such a future prospect.

'None of that will happen! There will be no wedding!'

'What do you mean 'no'? The engagement is settled!' Aunt Minnie insisted.

'Uncle John, you cannot be serious!' she said, after sneezing. The chill of the night was becoming too much to bear.

'You are the one who has provoked this, Harmony,' he told her harshly. 'I had no idea that you would go that far to avoid Andrew Curson. Goodness, you must have truly disliked the poor devil to hurl yourself into Waldegrave's arms so blatantly.'

'Uncle John, I didn't…' she protested feebly. She was not going to waste her breath trying to explain what had happened in the garden of Felton House. In any case, it was no concern of his. She remembered, disgusted, the way her uncle had suggested a 'compensation' and, in the end, he had succeeded. He had managed to establish a connection with the Duke of Waldegrave so he could extract a lot of money from him. 'I knew you would take advantage of this. It is what you always do, isn't it?' she accused him.

'No, dear,' he said with a smirk, 'nobody has taken as much advantage of this as you have. You have managed to lure Waldegrave in with your charms, little vixen! I think I have underestimated you all these years. I must say, I'm proud of you. You've managed to come out on top despite being at the bottom of a dark pit. Your father's inheritance wasn't even one thousandth of what

Waldegrave will lay at your feet.'

'My little one,' Aunt Minnie said, taking her hand, and that scared her more than if she had placed a spider under her skirts. She had never called her that; never looked at her with such a cheap imitation of affection. 'You will be a fabulous duchess. You'll see. You will be the most beautiful of all, and I'll be by your side to teach you how to do it.'

Once they'd climbed down the carriage, Harmony ran to her bedroom in the attic, feeling overwhelmed by nausea. She dropped herself on the small bed, after locking the door. She could not believe she was back in this place, when she had been so close to escaping, when she'd been so close to achieving her greatest desire. She could not believe the way her life had completely overturned in a single evening, and she cursed a thousand times her aunt and uncle, Andrew Curson, Miss Andersen and even Waldegrave, for frustrating her escape and later for agreeing to marry her.

How she wished her darling friends could be there to offer her comfort, or at least to listen to her woes. She needed them more than ever, but she would not see them for several weeks.

Then, she did the only thing she could to at that point: she cried until dawn surprised her through the window. She cried remembering her broken dreams, her dashed hopes for the future, and the life she would never know.

Chapter 5

A cold morning dawned over London. The golden hue of the daybreak fought with the leaden grey announcing a heavy snow storm for Christmas Eve. The streets bustled with the festive spirit of the season, but far from that tide of joy, Harmony George's world was collapsing.

She woke up with a soaring fever, a stuffy and runny nose and exhaustion. Curiously, her aunt, now extremely attentive, forbid her from leaving her bed and called the family doctor. After examining her, old and bitter Dr Mortimer concluded she was suffering from a common cold, due to a negligent exposure to the harsh winter weather the previous night. She, on the contrary, was convinced that her ailment was because she had started to slowly die of sadness and, shortly, there would be nothing left of the girl she had been.

Dr Mortimer asked her about the bruise in her jaw and she, evasive, mumbled that she had slipped in the garden; the doctor replied with a rude shrug. Before he left, he gave her some remedies and recommended that they had the room heater repaired, a suggestion that Aunt Minnie followed immediately. Harmony spent the rest of the day lying on her little bed, rereading for the umpteenth time A Woman's Journey around the World and Maria Graham's memoirs, as a way of exorcising her anxiety and forgetting the fact that her life had tumbled down the darkest and deepest well.

Trudy looked after her, since her uncle had lifted the punishment of depriving her of the maid's help. The girl brought her a cup of soup and freshly baked buns Harmony hardly tasted. While she was looking after her, Trudy could not keep her eyes off the purple patch on her chin that, albeit small, clearly evidenced a blow that had little to do with a fall. Neither she nor Dr Mortimer had believed that silly lie.

Mid-afternoon, when she was feeling a little better, the postman brought her a bunch of Christmas cards sent by her friends. Their beautiful cards with drawings of Father Christmas and little bunnies wearing woolly hats and scarfs made her smile. She didn't feel up to sending them any cards back, convinced she would start crying her eyes out if she tried to write a single line.

Later on, she was visited by Miss Andersen who had come to bring her a Christmas present; a beautiful book of poems by John Keats. Harmony wasn't in the mood to talk to her, but agreed to do it because she did not want to seem rude. Of course, she did not miss the opportunity of accusing her of encouraging the marriage to Waldegrave, landing her in the middle of a terrible mess.

'But, my dear girl, don't you think it is a major improvement to have the Duke of Waldegrave as your fiancée rather than that vulgar jockey?' Miss Andersen replied.

'Of course, but,' Harmony said with a sob, 'Miss Andersen, I don't know how to behave like a duchess. I know nothing about that man and, evidently, he does not want to marry me. I'll be a nuisance to him.'

The governess looked at her, raising an eyebrow. 'In that case, he should have thought about all that before laying his hands on you.'

Andersen obviously knew Harmony well and, therefore, did not try to make her feel better by reminding her of the benefits she would be entitled to by becoming a duchess. She promised her she would prepare her for her new life while the engagement lasted and told her that someday she would thank her for it, and that day wasn't as far away as she thought. Then, she left with a big smile, mumbling something about having done her duty.

In the evening, her aunt and uncle left the house to attend a Christmas dinner at Mr Donovan's, a horse dealer of middling success with whom her uncle was trying to go into partnership with. Harmony remained in the house, totally alone, because Trudy had returned to her village to celebrate Christmas with her family. It wasn't easy to convince the girl to leave; the silly girl wanted to stay and look after her, even though her employers would not guarantee her payment for the extra day of work, but finally she managed to send her home.

Harmony spent Christmas Day lying on the sofa of the main parlour, her only company the handkerchief nursing her runny nose, her favourite woolly blanket, a bowl of walnuts and a nutcracker, while outdoors the snow buried the streets of Whitechapel under its pristine whiteness. It was the worst Christmas ever, she pondered, furious, while she contemplated the lit chimney and blew her nose. She wouldn't have cared if the fire from the hearth had spread to the floor, the curtains and the ceiling, and then had burned to ashes the whole house with her inside.

Every so often, somebody knocked at the door which caused her every time to stand up, open the door cursing and shout to the kids who went carolling around the houses for a shilling: 'I have no money! Go away!'

Immediately after, she would bang the door shut and settle down on the sofa like an old hag.

A small group of particularly annoying boys refused to leave after she had sent them away. One of them knocked on the door again with admirable determination. Furious, Harmony threw walnuts at him and, in return, she got pelted with snowballs. 'Damn brats!' At any other time she would have thought it funny, but now she felt miserable, in every respect. The same thing happened a couple of times more until nobody dared to bother her in her convalescence.

After spending the last hour stuck on the sofa, blowing her nose and ranting against that dark Christmas, her mind, subdued by her idleness and her dejection, insisted on going over the facts of the previous night. Waldegrave had immobilised her against the ground and had kissed her there, in the frozen darkness of the garden of Felton House. It had been her first kiss.

Once she had digested that unbelievable fact as the memories kept flooding in, her whole body began to shake. She touched her fingers to her lips, as if she could feel the trace that kiss had left upon them. All that now seemed like a Christmas wish come true, enmeshed with a horror story. She made herself comfortable on the sofa, overwhelmed by a jumble of sensations: the pleasure, of course, the guilt, and the curiosity. Harmony bit her lower lip and closed her eyes to recall the sweet feel of his mouth, the hungry rub of his lips, and the sinful invasion of his tongue. Did everybody kiss like that or was it unique to him?

But then, in the most inexplicable way, he had lost his mind. He had looked at her in a disturbing, reckless and eager way; he had sharply pulled up her skirts, and Harmony had paled in horror. And all the magic had turned into a nightmare. She could not help but wonder what would have happened if Miss Andersen had not appeared to rescue her. Would Waldegrave have raped her? And what if Harmony had not resisted...?

Ugh! She felt ashamed by her obscene speculation. She picked up the nearest pillow and hid her flushed face in it. Perhaps Waldegrave was the most attractive man in London; perhaps she had wanted to be kissed by him; but she was not a hussy, and although she'd had a chance, the thought of seducing him had never crossed her mind.

She wasn't stupid either. She knew beauty wasn't one of her attributes, but it was as if she had provoked him involuntarily. What if Waldegrave was a degenerate? What if he attacked all the women he caught unawares? Esther used to say that some aristocrats are eccentrics, living lives of excess, whims and pleasures, and always did whatever they had a mind to, and even committed crimes against the law that later were ignored. But the duke was not known for behaving in a licentious way.

No, she insisted. After all that chaos, he had behaved as would be expected of him, in an educated and formal manner. He had accepted the responsibility for his actions in front of everybody. He had opted for doing what he thought was the right thing. Why had he done it then? Why had he kissed her?

A knock on the door distracted her from her thoughts. Harmony picked up a handful of walnuts, stood up like a woman possessed, and ran to open the door at a furious pace. But, on realising that it wasn't the singing children or vagrants looking for leftovers, the nuts slipped from her fingers, the rage accompanying her disgust quickly transforming into confusion, and the deep breath she had taken to scream abuse at the intruders ended up becoming a gasp.

'Good evening,' a lonely and cold voice, like the landscape behind him, greeted her. 'I am aware the time is not appropriate for a visit, and I have not announced myself as I should. However, I think it is important that you and I have a conversation right away.'

She held on to the doorknocker so hard that she thought she'd break it, or break her fingers instead. 'My aunt and uncle are not home,' was all she managed to say.

'All the better,' the man said, signalling with his head. 'I'd rather talk to you in private, if you don't mind. I won't take up a lot of your time. Will you let me come in?'

Harmony hesitated but ended up acquiescing, as if she would have dared to slam the door on Duke Waldegrave's face. She moved to one side to allow him to come in, avoiding the trail of walnuts and sleet she had left on the unpolished wooden floor. Waldegrave removed his hat, gloves and overcoat, all covered in minuscule snowflakes, and set them on the same spot where Uncle John usually left his things.

She studied him, hazy with surprise. He was so handsome, so tall, and so elegant that the room around him paled. 'It's Christmas,' she reminded him innocently, in an attempt at breaking the ice. 'Shouldn't you be with your family?'

Waldegrave looked at her with a serious gesture. His facial muscles had tensed up and Harmony worried that she might have unintentionally offended him.

'So should you,' was his sharp reply.

In his short walk to the parlour, she noticed the duke was observing everything, judging it severely. Perhaps it was the first time he had visited a house in the discredited neighbourhood of Whitechapel. Compared to his mansion, built on the edge of Hampstead Heath, that opulent vantage point, he must have thought the Talbots' home was little more than a rat's nest.

Harmony invited him to sit close to the fire. He chose her aunt's favourite place, a chair upholstered in a faded purple material.

'Miss Talbot...'

'George!' she corrected him rudely. She felt offended and hurt that he didn't even know her name. How easy it was for that man to make her feel small and of little importance. She had no other option but to muster all her dignity. 'My name is Harmony, Harmony George.'

'Miss George...' he corrected, although he didn't seem sorry for his mistake. 'I am terribly sorry for my behaviour last night. I don't usually behave that way. I can assure you that what I did was an isolated and unforgivable act that will never happen again.' He paused to shake his head, perhaps in an attempt at clearing his thoughts. 'Frankly, I'm surprised you have agreed to open the door of your house to me since your guardians are not in.'

'I know that you were... that you had drunk too much,' she mumbled. 'You already apologised yesterday.'

'Yes, but as I'm sure you know, something happened between us that was beyond what your governess and the viscountess managed to see.'

He looked ashamedly at Harmony's chin, while she remembered the contact of their mouths and, afterwards, the rushed way in which he had tried to lift her skirts. She had to make a huge effort not to hide her face on the cushion and to maintain her sang-froid.

'And that is even more serious than what your family and the Feltons imagine.'

'And what does it matter?' she replied sadly, without imagining what he was referring to. She shrugged, shivering when she thought that Miss Andersen would tell her off for such an uncouth gesture, so inappropriate for a lady. 'These things happen all the time, don't they? In this world, I mean.'

The duke stared at her with a mixture of astonishment and curiosity, but then his expression changed to a distant one. By the light of the fire, his green eyes glinted with a golden hue. 'My grandfather compromised my grandmother by spending three minutes alone with her in a music parlour. He was telling her that the hostess's grand piano had been played by Salieri in person.'

She blinked, surprised. He, on the other hand, cleared his throat, embarrassed. She realised that situation was miles away from being comparable with what they both had experienced in the garden of Felton House.

'Yes, it happens often, but respectable people face the consequences,' he added.

Utter nonsense! Harmony thought, and she had a much simpler way for him to face the consequences. She could ask him to write her a cheque for ten thousand pounds to forget what happened... she would then disappear... But would that sound too dirty? It would be like stealing a sweet from a baby. Waldegrave was filthy rich; with that arrangement he would not have to put up with her as a wife, and she would be able to leave on her trip quite comfortably. Finally, however, sanity prevailed. 'Your Grace, I insist and intend to free you from your responsibility.'

'I am a gentleman, Miss George. I face my mistakes. As you will surely understand,' he carried on solemnly, 'we can only remedy this error by marrying. Your uncle, as you know, has been more than willing to cooperate in the matter.' He spoke with such grief that it bordered on physical pain, and something inside Harmony cracked. 'It is... the right thing to do. I hope you understand and that you will consent to it in the end.'

'For the love of God,' she said feebly, 'you don't have to do something you not only have no wish for but will also make miserable.'

'The truth is that I have to do it,' he said firmly.

Harmony wasn't convinced. This man was a tyrant and a masochist. He was prepared to do anything to keep his gentlemanly honour intact.

'Tomorrow, I will meet your uncle to discuss the details of our agreement,' he added with extreme coldness after a few moments of awkward silence, as if he were talking about the purchase of another horse. 'I only wanted to apologise to you in private. I didn't think it would be scandalous to come here, as I have already compromised your honour.'

Another brief silence filled the room, until the logs cracked in the fire and a parade of noisy children crossed the street outside the window singing Christmas carols. Harmony silently prayed for them to leave soon. 'Is that it then?' She mumbled when the voices faded away. 'We have to get married.'

He leaned forward in his seat, frowning with confusion. 'Miss George, am I to understand that you feel particularly repelled by the thought of becoming the Duchess of Waldegrave?'

'No. No, Your Grace.' She shook her head intensely, trying to find the right words. 'I just can't understand it. I can't understand how all this happened.'

He nodded, this time showing signs of understanding. 'I don't want to lie to you. You don't... embody the qualities I like in a woman.'

That comment struck her like a lash and made her feel resentful. She dropped her head, ashamed. Nothing would have pleased her more than being able to smile at him mockingly. Perhaps I am not beautiful, Your Grace, or refined, or charming, but at least I'm not pathetic and suicidal, her lips ached to articulate.

'But I don't want to excuse my behaviour either,' the duke carried on. 'I beg you to accept what I can offer you: my respect, my name, and my protection. I'm extremely protective of what's mine.'

With extreme sadness, Harmony had to admit that, a part of her, a tiny little part, wanted to be his, but only if he would be hers as well. But that seemed impossible. Any girl would be joyfully jumping up and down on learning she would be marrying the Duke of Waldegrave. She, on the other hand, felt as if she was cattle being dragged to the slaughterhouse, or a soldier about to enter a bloody battlefield.

He doesn't love me... He'll marry me only because he committed an indiscretion. I will be an inconvenient to him, a pebble in his shoe... He might never kiss me, or take me to his bed, she kept thinking.

Seemingly unaware of her dark thoughts, he continued with great pomp, 'I should remind you that being my wife will come with plenty of advantages. You will have all the clothes you like, a carriage, a coachman, jewels and a monthly allowance for your expenses.'

So, I'll be unhappy, but at least I'll be fashionably dressed, she thought bitterly. Then, a rather promising idea crossed her mind. Even a total fool could predict that such a union would not last. Eventually, the duke would get tired of her and ask for a divorce, and Harmony would be ready to retake her life when that happened. Perhaps, if she saved the money from her allowance, if she put away those 'jewels' that were coming her way to sell them later, and if she gathered the courage necessary to put up with everything that marriage would bring, very soon she could be at the gates of a new beginning.

Because, what other alternative did she have? None! That man was an obstinate mule, and he would never cease trying to restore his bloody honour. As for Uncle John, he was an opportunist who would drag her to the vicarage, if necessary. She could not do anything, not even escape, because she did not have a shilling to support herself. And she was sure that Mrs Pfeiffer would have been disappointed by her absolute inability to improvise.

Of course! she carried on thinking as the duke eyed her with concern, obviously giving her time to think things through. She would get divorced and then she would have licence to do whatever she wanted. She would not care if people looked down on her for being divorced; she would confront her situation with firmness and even finesse. After all, Harmony did not care what people might say. She would not stay there to listen to their gossip.

She only hoped her heart would resist for as long as her marriage lasted. 'All right, Waldegrave. I'll marry you,' she finally burst out.

Devlin nodded his agreement and managed a thin smile. He was aware that there was no going back. He would marry that grim girl, who wore that sullen and mistrustful gaze. May the Lord above help him, because he had no idea what kind of a life awaited him next to her.

He kept asking himself what had pushed him to jump over her. He had gone over and over the few details he managed to remember, because the whisky had submerged him into a sea of blackouts, but that explosion of lust still remained a damn mystery. She wasn't even pretty; she did not look like Victory Brandon or any of the women who had driven him crazy in the past. Talbot's niece was, rather… simple. Yes, a rather plain girl, sickly-looking and sadly pale. Perhaps she had got ill recently, he thought on seeing the purple circles under her eyes and her whitish lips.

And she dared reject him. Harmony George did not offer herself to him like so many daring girls he had met; she did not flatter him or smile at him batting her eyelids. What the hell had made him jump her as if she were the goddess Venus incarnate? His drunkenness or his frustration on not having seen Victory? Would he have done the same if he had met a servant or a matron in the garden?

In any case, Devlin realised he had to pay for his stupidity and there was no other option than to marry her. Felton had tried to dissuade him from it, but he, proud and impulsive, had refused to listen to him.

'I am the Duke of Waldegrave, and my title is one of the oldest and most honourable in the United Kingdom,' he had reminded his friend, puffed up. 'My family has a spotless reputation to preserve, and I'm not going to go down in history as the man who attacked a young girl in the dark and forced her to open her legs!'

The viscount had looked pained as he dabbed at a layer of invisible sweat from his forehead with his handkerchief. 'Devlin, you won't right one mistake by making a worst one. There are other ways of solving these kinds of things! Only a few people know what happened…'

'And one of those is Talbot. You are crazy if you think I'm going to leave such a secret, which could be my ruin, in the hands of the family of a scoundrel, a horse dealer who won't think twice about causing damage.'

He was convinced that the girl's uncle would use his attempted rape to dirty his reputation, even to blackmail him, and he already had enough skeletons in the closet to add one more.

However, that wasn't the whole reason. He had to admit that, on the other hand, he felt miserable for having assaulted a girl to the point of tearing her dress to pieces and bruising her jaw. That was the most anxious blank in his mind. He did not know how and when he had gone from lustful to irate, or had the opposite occurred?

He was scared by that apparent trait of his that he had never thought he had; it made him think of his father, and his mind immediately tried to escape from that memory, horrified, as it usually did.

For that reason, the best option was to get married, he thought now, as the girl fixed him with a determined gaze. Of course, she had not made it easy for him. She truly enjoyed playing hard to get at first. He was on the verge of feeling offended when faced with such stubbornness, as if a girl of her social standing could afford to choose a better suitor. And finally the girl had stopped objecting—attracted, of course, by his talk about money. Devlin sighed and crossed one worry off his long list.

'Well. As I said, I'll discuss the particulars of our agreement with your uncle. He will inform you, in due course, of how the engagement will proceed, and of the wedding date later on.'

He stood up, happy to have completed his task there and ready to retrieve his things and get out of that pigsty that unsettled him so.

'One moment, please,' she detained him with her timid voice, 'I must apologise as well… for having hit you.' Devlin tilted his head, and his eyes darkened. He did not remember having received any blows, although the next morning he had woken up with an unusual headache, which he had attributed to his hangover. 'I am very sorry. You turned up right when…'

Waldegrave raised his hand to stop her discourse. The last thing he wanted was to be reminded that he had behaved like a beast, and she had done what was necessary to defend herself. The damn business turned his stomach. 'Let's leave it, Miss George.'

The girl seemed disappointed; nevertheless, she followed him hurriedly down the corridor.

'I don't really mind that your explanation sounds like an excuse,' she blurted out, and Devlin knew exactly what she was referring to. 'Right now, I do not think it matters. I only ask you to be honest with me. Why did you do it?'

He stopped. Had he heard her correctly? She was giving him permission to pronounce words that would be like sharp knives pointed at her throat. Perfect. If she could bear the truth, he would not deny her an explanation.

'Miss George, you must believe me. Had I been sober, I would never have laid a finger on you.'

The news of the engagement between the Duke of Waldegrave and the—up till then—totally unknown Miss Harmony George, was published on the morning of the twenty-eight of December in the society page of the Telegraph, unleashing a collective commotion and the subsequent storm of miscellaneous opinions.

London wondered where the said girl had turned up from, to which distinguished clan she belonged and, more importantly still: why the most coveted bachelor in the whole kingdom had chosen her among so many perfect candidates to bear the title of Duchess of Waldegrave. Nobody had heard a word about a powerful commercial alliance between families, a love-at-first-sight story, or a scandal that had resulted in a rushed engagement. The people who had bet that his Grace would soon be announcing his nuptials with the widow Lovelance, whom he had seemed totally smitten by, were the most astounded.

When the humble origins of the lucky girl became common knowledge, the matrons, disgusted by such an unfortunate choice, mocked the girl mercilessly. Harmony quickly became the object of envy for a big part of the debutantes, of admiration for others and of curiosity for a large number of gentlemen. The latter were eager to know what qualities she possessed that had captivated the exquisite and righteous Waldegrave.

During all that time, Harmony preferred to stay at home and claimed to be ill, but that didn't keep her out of gossip's reach. Until the end of the year, she received an endless stream of visitors, most of them acquaintances that until then had treated her as if she did not exist. She only met with her dear friend Fanny Thorton, who had returned from her Christmas holiday early, and was the only one to whom she'd confessed the true reason why Waldegrave and she were getting married.

The wedding was set for the third of January. Harmony imagined that the duke intended to take advantage of the absence of most of the people he knew due to the festive season to seal their union and be spared from giving explanations or inviting anybody. She did not mind. The sooner they put an end to that circus, the sooner she could start planning her life as a divorced traveller.

In the meantime, Miss Andersen, as she had promised her, had worked hard to teach her the last few lessons. In them, she had tried to instil on her some notions of how she had to behave amongst the aristocracy and what the responsibilities of a duchess were. Harmony realised that her governess was a little confused by her role, as she had never before had to prepare any pupil for such a haughty position. It was true that some of the Andersen girls had become baronesses, ladies of the upper class, and a few countesses or viscountesses, but she had never before had a future duchess in her bunch of pupils.

Days later she learned that, after the meeting between her uncle and Waldegrave had taken place, the former had received an exorbitant sum of money. Harmony twisted her face on thinking that it was the price paid for her, as if she were a mare. Uncle John must have been rubbing his hands gleefully and planning some illicit business in which to invest that amount, whilst Harmony thought about the poverty he had plunged her into due to his irresponsible behaviour.

New Year's Eve turned up to be a bitter and miserable affair. The table was full of exquisite delicacies: roast beef, turkey, a plum cake and egg nog, which Aunt Minnie had ordered, using, of course, the money the duke had given them. The best liquor also flowed that night, and that attracted a swarm of vagrants and opportunistic sycophants that where somehow related to the Talbots. The men, who had previously looked at Harmony disdainfully, now eyed her with lust, and the women approached her with flattering comments, begging for her friendship and eagerly asking her for advice, so they could 'bag a lord' as well.

It wasn't long before she got fed up with those horrible people and escaped to her attic. It was slightly before midnight when she lay down on her narrow bed to stare at the ceiling. The cheerful buzz from the street and the shouting of the drunkards crowded in the main floor of the house only served to remind her that she was alone in the world. She had been like that for the last ten years.

She missed her parents so; the warmth of a loving home, the family she had before the damn tuberculosis had taken them away. Things would have been so different if they were still alive.

She covered her ears with her fingers when the street-singing got louder

87

and the fireworks—which were released from a boat in the Thames at midnight—exploded over the dark sky of the city. The burst of the blasts mixed in her ears with the howls of the dogs that were terrified by the noise, with the euphoric yells of the drunkards and Harmony's own desperate sighs, heralding an unhappy future.

And that was how the year 1881 started.

Chapter 6

'But, how rude!' screamed Aunt Minnie from her seat inside the landau that had become dwarfed by her rotund body. She was stuffed inside an ostentatious fox coat and looked as if some hairy animal was swallowing her whole but, unfortunately, it was only an impression, and that disappointed Harmony terribly. 'It is not right to perform the wedding at home, as if we were infidels, when the church is only around the corner.'

That third of January, it was snowing heavily. London buzzed under a frozen and vast white blanket; the snowflakes, shaken by the wind, created a hazy mist, as if it were the backdrop of a dream, and the sky had turned into a leaden and infinite vault. The streets were populated by emptiness. The Christmas cheer had given way to the lethargy usual at the beginning of the year. The city chimneys worked at full throttle, proving that people felt cold even in their sanctuaries. While the carriage taking her to her destiny rattled down the street covered in sand, Harmony imagined a family in a pretty house, huddling together in front of the fire, watching the snow falling outside their window from the warmth of their armchairs.

She remembered it was her wedding day, and she was on her way to the mansion of her future husband, where the ceremony would take place. She sighed pitifully and then stared at her hands, immobile on her lap. All the while, the car shook her like the ragdoll she was, silent and inanimate.

Uncle John remained quiet, with the calm of a chess player planning his next move. She exchanged a questioning look with him but broke it off quickly. Before they left the house that morning, he had grabbed her roughly by the arm to give her a 'last piece of advice' that made her stomach churn.

'It is not necessary to be honest in the extreme with your husband. Imagine what a bad impression you will give him if you complain because I was forced to use your miserly inheritance,' he had told her.

'Are you worried that he might demand an explanation from you, Uncle John?' she'd challenged him.

'I'm more worried about Waldegrave getting tired of you too quickly. The duke will soon realise you are an impertinent and ungrateful girl. Your true personality will show through, my dear. I don't know what that governess has taught you, but you will cause embarrassment to the family and will discredit yourself if you bring to light that private episode of our life. And it would be best if you did not speak a single word about Curson. Understood?'

Harmony had looked at him with disdain. Why should she tell Waldegrave anything? The aristocrat did not care for her or for what might happen to her. 'Don't worry. It didn't cross my mind to mention it.'

While the carriage continued its sombre journey, Aunt Minnie did not stop ranting and raving about the weather, about the improvised ceremony, and about the fact that Waldegrave had preferred an intimate and tranquil event with only ten guests at a pompous ceremony at St. Paul's Cathedral. Aunt Minnie complained that she had not had time to inform her sisters in Exeter, her friends, her bridge partners, and that the said wedding was a sad apologia of bad taste, an offence to the Talbot family and to her sweet niece.

Harmony was suspicious of her doubtful solidarity. She only lifted her eyelids when Miss Andersen, sitting by her side, leaned forward and sighed appreciatively on seeing the majestic mansion of Waldegrave Terrace.

She had to admit that it was a beautiful place, surrounded by the woods and lakes of Hampstead Heath, that in springtime were astounding. The place where Keats used to write poems in his youth, the same place where, a few weeks back, Harmony had hurled herself downhill on an improvised sledge, without any inkling that her joy was starting to slip away between her fingers.

'And just imagine that all this is about to become yours,' her aunt droned on, without waiting for a reply, it seemed.

The carriage proceeded up the tree-flanked hill and stopped in front of the imposing grey stone building. As soon as the double doors opened, an impeccably dressed elderly man of weathered features and white hair greeted them. His movements were slow and ceremonious, almost mechanical, as he told them his name was Limsey, and that he was the butler at Waldegrave Terrace.

Harmony shrank when he looked at her harshly.

Uncle John coaxed the man into showing them the mansion, so the Talbots and Miss Andersen stayed with Limsey while Harmony was shown to a room on the third-floor by a maid.

Harmony felt mesmerised when the maid opened the double doors revealing a beautiful bedroom decorated in an overtly feminine fashion. A huge four-posted bed with a canopy, full of plump cushions in all shapes and colours, had pride of place in it. The walls were covered in lilac wallpaper with delicate flower designs.

'Do you like it, Miss?' asked the maid, who had introduced herself as Prudence.

Harmony smiled. At least she was nice, not like that Limsey, who had made it clear that for him Harmony was like a fly in the soup. 'Yes, it is... beautiful.'

'The duke's dressing room is behind there.' She pointed at an oak door. Harmony trembled slightly on learning she would be so close to Waldegrave. So close and yet so far, she thought.

'We will get you ready here. I have everything you need.' The girl started rummaging inside a basket full of bars of soap, little bottles of aromatic oils, and multi-coloured sponges.

'What is that?' Harmony asked, looking quizzically at a corner of the room, although the fact was that she did not need to ask.

'Your dress!' Prudence squeaked excitedly. 'Don't worry if it doesn't fit you perfectly. Mary will make some alterations. She excels with a needle! She'll make it fit like a glove, Miss. I don't honestly think it will require much work. I bet it will look perfect on you.'

Harmony walked slowly towards the dress; it was placed on a mannequin like the ones the dressmakers used to imitate the female silhouette. It was a beautiful creation in oyster-white satin, with embroidered delicate flowers and tiny pearls. The lace veil was next to it, with a pair of shoes and other delicate accessories.

'The duke commissioned it to Monsieur Worth's workshop. They brought it this morning. I couldn't believe it when I saw it. It's a Worth, Miss!'

'But nobody told me... I brought my own dress,' she mumbled.

The dressmaker who had made her dress for the Christmas ball at Felton House had got her a simple and inconspicuous model. With the hurry, she didn't have time to make it to measure. The woman had only rummaged around the back of her workshop and found a dress, commissioned by a girl whose wedding had been cancelled months earlier because her fiancée had shot himself to escape his gambling debts. Harmony had tried it, and not feeling up to being too demanding, had approved it.

'Perhaps this one will fit you better,' Prudence insisted, sweet-talking her.

'I can't wear it.'

Prudence's huge smile slowly disappeared. She looked at her, incredulous.

'But, Miss, it is a very glamorous dress… and I am sure it cost a fortune. Why won't you wear it?'

Harmony didn't reply. She prised her eyes off that beauty which she would under no circumstances use, because that would be admitting to her poverty and to the fact that she did not have anything decent to wear. Using it would be like accepting, ahead of time, the fact that she was now Waldegrave's property, and she would depend on him even for her dress. She realised that she needed to perform that final act of rebellion, to make sure she did not forget who she was and why she was there.

She needed to do that desperately. 'I don't like it,' she lied. 'I'll wear my own dress.'

Prudence hardly managed to nod.

Mary, the maid who was supposed to be making some alterations to the dress, arrived moments later. When Prudence told her that the bride would not use Worth's dress, the girl grew sad, but like the other one, didn't try to dissuade her.

Devlin contemplated himself in the mirror while he waited for his valet to finish polishing his shoes. Then he wondered what on Earth he was doing.

Was he really determined to get married to the niece of that abject man, John Talbot? Did he truly want to tie his life to a dull girl he had only seen a couple of times? Yes, he had some reasons to do that but, what was his strongest motivation? He needed to clarify that, at least for his own sake.

Was it his honour? His worry that the Talbots would discredit him with their rumours for having attacked a girl while he was drunk? His guilt for having tried to force himself on an innocent? Or was it his need to forget Victory?

He snorted. He didn't believe there was anything that would make him forget Lady Lovelance, and even less being tied to a wife with whom he would have nothing to share, not even the bed. He had already decided to renounce his conjugal rights, as that might facilitate an annulment in due course. In any case, she did not attract him. The presence of Harmony George continuously reminded him what an idiot he had been drinking a whole bottle of whisky, and how much he missed the beautiful and ungrateful widow that had broken his heart.

Then, all of a sudden, a thought he hadn't had time to consider popped into his mind. Victory hadn't married Radnor yet. Her decision to stay with him did not have to be final. If Devlin went looking for her, if he tried to persuade her, if he fought a bit for her—something he had never done for a woman—things could still turn out as they should. What was wrong with showing some weakness and crawling a bit if the result was nothing short of his happiness? A duke was, first and foremost, a man.

A painful reflection started to dig at his insides. Perhaps, if he hadn't been such a prideful and arrogant bastard he would have fought for her from the very beginning; he could have avoided that engagement that would tie him to a stranger for life. How many things had he missed on due to these ungodly character traits his social position demanded?

Thank the Lord he still had time to remedy things, he told himself, suddenly full of determination. He had to stop his marriage to Miss George. He would apologise to her and to Mr Talbot and, afterwards, he would send everybody home. He would buy three or four more horses from the horse dealer, if that would appease his indignation. Damn it, he would buy him a new house if that was what was required!

Once all that had finished, he could pursue his true love.

With a purposeful stride, Devlin walked towards the door connecting the two rooms. He was so used to living alone in that fortress and being its lord and master, that the thought of knocking on the door didn't even cross his mind. He turned the handle and opened the door slowly. The hinges, well oiled, didn't make the slightest noise.

Then, he stopped at once when his eyes glimpsed a vast and sinuous patch of skin. With the door ajar, he considered stepping back and returning to his room without making a noise, which was the honourable thing to do, but he felt momentarily unable to move a muscle, not even to blink.

Harmony George was standing inside the copper bathtub, totally naked. Devlin had opened the door right at the moment when the young woman had stood up with a splash and the warm bath water was sliding down her creamy skin.

It was as if he was seeing her for the first time. Beside the bathtub, stood the maid, her back to him luckily.

With her back to him too, unaware of his presence, Harmony was offering him a privileged view of her body, slender and pleasure-evoking: it was a sweet and riotous pleasure. The beauty of her body could not have been guessed under her boring clothes, he quietly observed as he flinched, surprised.

Devlin delighted in the soft bend of her bottom; in the golden shine the electric lights gave her rounded hips; in the graceful journey the water embarked on from the secret place between her legs, down her thighs and calves, until it went to die at the bottom of the bathtub. A treacherous current of pleasure shook him, right in the groin.

His eyes looked for breathing space, focusing on the messy mop of brown hair crowning her body, a cascade of infinite curls which she was now trying to awkwardly settle over her left shoulder. The outline of her elegant back came into full sight, and Devlin imagined taking her from behind.

She started shivering, suddenly. She hugged herself in a candid movement that gave novel insights to Devlin's newly discovered sensations. He smiled unawares, moved by such clear evidence of vulnerability. It put him in mind of one of Bouguereau's delicate angels, whose wings had been mutilated.

It was strange to think that she was the girl about to push him down the cliff, or the gloomy-gazed simpleton that would create an insurmountable distance between him and his only love. In fact, that whole unfortunate story vanished from his head, and his eyes discovered a tempting woman that inspired his desire and his tenderness at the same time. A rare mixture, he— who had always boasted of knowing quite well the female nature—had to admit to. That was the same woman who'd made him lose his head in the garden of Felton House. Here was the answer to his internal controversy.

The succinct memories of that infamous night returned to his mind, right when the magic possessing him began to disappear. His fascination turned into anger when the maid wrapped a towel around the girl's shoulders, depriving him of the vision of her wonderful body.

Frowning, he forced himself to get out of there before being discovered. It wasn't like him crawling around, spying on naked women... and he wasn't one of those men who broke an engagement after having given his word, or those who took rushed decisions, compelled by momentary feelings.

He closed the door with an imperceptible sound, still dazed by the vision he had just relished. After shaking his head to clear his thoughts, he realised that his valet had his clothes ready for him.

There was no turning back.

The ceremony was to take place in the magnificent and intimidating study of the duke. The only bystanders were going to be Mr and Mrs Talbot, Lord and Lady Felton, Miss Andersen, and Miss Fanny Thorton.

When Harmony entered the imposing space on her uncle's arm, the groom betrayed an expression of annoyance. That made her smile. She was sure he was not happy she had rejected his extremely elegant Worth to wear in its place a cheap dress, the only one she could afford. She didn't mind. She concentrated on holding her little bunch of hothouse yellow blossoms and on

94

walking with her chin up, despite the several pair of eyes looking her way: Miss Andersen's and Aunt Minnie's oozed pride, the viscount and vicountess's uncertainty, and Fanny's, oddly, flushed with emotion.

The vicar was a man of middle height and thick grey hair. Judging by the tic in his lower lip, he must have been feeling terribly uncomfortable outside of his vicarage. Or perhaps it was the atmosphere lacking in enthusiasm that seemed to unsettle him.

While the monotonous discourse lasted, Harmony maintained the stillness of a statue, until the moment came to exchange the rings. The duke, immersed in some kind of stupor, picked up the golden ring that his friend, the Viscount of Felton offered him. When he was about to slid it down her finger, something happened that Harmony would never have imagined possible in a man so in control of his emotions as was Waldegrave. The ring slipped off his fingers, hitting the floor with a loud clink. The jewel rolled on the floor, running down the central aisle of the improvised chapel, as if refusing to participate in such an insipid ceremony.

Several pairs of eyes followed the trajectory of the rebellious ring, while the embarrassed groom ran after it. The scene ended when Devlin, with a powerful stomp of his foot, stopped the course of the ring before it slipped down the door of the study. After frustrating the escape of the ring, he returned to the bride's side, with a slight blush in his cheeks.

Nobody in the hall moved a muscle. Nobody showed the tiniest evidence of amusement on witnessing that event that had probably felt miserably pathetic to Devlin, but only because the attendees worked so hard not to show it. Only Harmony, protected by the privacy of her veil and despite her deep sadness, dared to smile. She wasn't poking fun at him. Rather, she had found it charming, in spite of herself.

A few minutes later, the vicar pronounced them husband and wife, and it would have felt the same if he had announced the time of day. They were married now and it was final. Waldegrave uncovered Harmony's visage and discovered her as wife. He deposited a delicate kiss on her cheek, bringing a bit of colour to it, and when Harmony dared to look him in the eyes again, she saw in them something indiscernible.

After surviving the two agonising hours that followed—the time the dinner in honour of the newlyweds lasted—Harmony went upstairs to her bedroom on her own, dragging her feet as if they were made of lead.

She was surprised when the maids curtseyed deeply in her presence, and that reminded her of her new status. The idea almost made her laugh sarcastically. Harmony George, the least bright of Miss Penelope Andersen's pupils, was now the Duchess of Waldegrave.

She allowed Prudence to help her get rid of the bothersome clothes while Mary put hot bricks under the blankets. It had been an exhausting day, and the biggest torture had been to have to tolerate Aunt Minnie's endless chatting during dinner. That woman never stopped talking; now that she thought she had been propelled to the high society, she acted like a windup toy fully charged.

Once she had taken her dress off, she slid a fine lace nightgown on. Mary directed her to sit in front of the dressing table so they could work on her hair. The maid combed it with a silver comb of thick teeth, pulling sometimes quite hard to unknot the mop of hair, but being careful not to cause her any pain. Harmony looked at her in the mirror apologetically, but the girl did not seem bothered by the hard task.

'It is nice to be able to look after you, Your Grace,' Mary noted with an honest smile as she worked. Harmony realised that it would take her time to get used to her new title. 'On the other hand, that horrible Anita, I don't know…'

'Mary! Will you stop talking now?' Prudence scolded her with a chilling look. Mary covered her mouth with her hand, ashamed, and Harmony realised, somewhat concerned, that they were talking about an ex-lover of the Duke.

'I am very sorry, Your Grace,' said Mary.

Harmony looked around the room through the mirror and noticed that her bathtub had been refilled with steamy water. Next to it, there was a wooden stool with a pile of folded towels on it, as well as a flask with rose petals and little bottles of all kinds of essences. It didn't take a genius to realise that the bathtub had not been prepared in readiness for that moment, but for after her wedding night. She blushed deeply, looking away. Then, she noticed that Mary and Prudence were exchanging naughty looks, then turned their eyes towards her.

If you only knew… she thought.

Once they had finished readying her for her wedding night, the maids said goodnight without removing the silly smiles from their faces. Harmony kept looking at the door they had left through and huffed.

Now that she was alone for the first time, she stood up and walked around the room calmly. She examined the space that was full of luxuries she would have never dared dream of having at her disposal. The bed was larger than the attic in the old house at Whitechapel, and covered in sumptuous violet silken bedspreads and blankets. She didn't know how she'd manage to get up the next morning after resting in such a place, she mused, while she tried the fluffy mattress and the big pillows filled with goose feathers.

The exquisite walnut furniture, painted in a creamy colour, shone; so did the spacious chest of drawers, the dressing table with its three oval-shaped mirrors, the chaise-longue upholstered in purple velvet and the breakfast table with its two chairs with elegantly curved legs. The windows were fitted with heavy curtains of spectacular designs that matched the wallpaper. There was a beautiful fireplace in limestone that she could now admire in its entirety, as somebody had been kind enough to light it up. It was a sublime place, she concluded, in the quiet of her own thoughts.

The door opened, all of a sudden, in almost total silence. Harmony looked up, expecting to see Prudence apologising for having forgotten some small detail, but it wasn't the maid who now entered confidently striding in.

It was her husband, the duke.

He wore the white shirt he had on during the ceremony, but without the hard collar. The two first buttons were undone, the sleeves rolled up to the elbows. His hair, loose and lanky, fell carelessly on his wide shoulders. Harmony felt a strange oppression between her chest and her back as she saw him approach with the self-assurance of a man who knows he owns everything he sets his eyes on.

'Hello,' he greeted her in a voice that didn't seem to come from him. His severity had totally abandoned him, and it had been replaced by velvety warmth. She put it down to the tiredness caused by the ceremony. She was also feeling exhausted.

'Hello.'

'Do you like your bedroom?' He looked around slowly, as if it was the first time he was seeing the place. 'You can always change the décor.'

'There is nothing that could make this place more impressive.'

He nodded. 'I am happy to hear that.'

'Has everybody left already?'

'Yes. The last ones to leave were your aunt and uncle.' His voice remained warm and nonchalant. She liked that. 'Your aunt suggested that I should invite them to spend the night here, but it felt highly inappropriate, and I declined.'

Harmony closed her eyes, feeling a renewed wave of shame. 'I'm sorry. I'm very sorry. She is...' She shook her head, unable to find the exact words that best defined her aunt.

'Yes, I know.'

He walked towards her until he was only a couple of steps away from her. Harmony decided to look away demurely. Although his tone of voice was surprisingly kind, she still had reservations about that man. Waldegrave intimidated her still; the fact that she liked him so much despite his dismissive remarks disturbed her.

'My aunt and uncle are very bothersome,' she whispered finally, mortified, rubbing her eyes with the back of her hand. 'I hope you can excuse them. And me too, because it won't be long before I make a blunder as well——'

'What do you mean?'

Waldegrave came even closer, as if she was talking very softly and he wanted to hear her better. Harmony raised her eyes and saw his face a few inches from her own. His fingers went up, catching a thick lock of her hair that then he proceeded to carefully place on her shoulder. That gesture made her tremble; she wasn't sure if it was shame—because her hair had always been the subject of jokes—surprise, or just excitement.

'It is obvious,' she shrugged. 'I don't know how to be a duchess.'

He stared at her in a funny way, obviously weighing up her confession. Harmony thought about retracting her words or saying something else, but she was quite busy trying to work out what she had said wrong. What had disturbed him? She had only intended to be honest.

'Nobody would know exactly how to do it until they became one, don't you think?' he told her, his eyes shining.

'No...' Harmony shook her head slowly, making the heavy curls swing around her head. 'Miss Andersen says that a woman is prepared for such a position from childhood.'

The duke offered her a sarcastic grin.

'Your governess is a know-it-all,' he said in a tone between bored and amused, 'although she has character, I must admit. However, I doubt she has the first idea about how a true duchess must behave.'

'You might be right, but she is good at what she does. I am not her best student, not by a mile, but Fanny is a true lady...'

'How old are you?'

'Twenty.'

He frowned. 'I thought you'd be younger... Why do you still have a governess at twenty years of age?'

'My education started late.' Harmony lowered her eyes, hesitant in case with that revelation she might be airing the shameful facts of her life with the Talbots.

Waldegrave frowned even more deeply, and she began to worry, sweating. Had Uncle John been right when he affirmed that any revelation of such nature would make her husband ashamed of her? She reminded herself to be more careful with what came out of her mouth from then on.

'I don't want you to worry, do you understand?' he replied softly. 'We won't spend much time in London. When the weather improves we'll go to Sudeley, my ancestral castle, in Winchcombe. We'll spend a few days there.'

She nodded quietly, suspecting that was a trick to hide her from his friends and acquaintances. She fought against a feeling of disappointment.

Then, his hand reached for her shoulder, and her self-pity fled her head. The touch was not casual; she felt it close, intimate, full of intention. Stunned by that gesture, she turned to look at him to find him closer than a moment earlier, so close that she thought she had fallen asleep, because it all felt like a dream. His eyes, glassy green, stayed fixed on her. His face wavered between lights and shadows caused by the effect of his long and loose hair framing his face and the light from the fireplace behind him. All at once, the heat in the room no longer came from the fire, but from the body she had in front of her that inched increasingly closer to hers.

'Are you all right, Harmony?' he whispered.

She nodded, the victim of a spell. It was the first time she had heard him say her name, and she liked how it sounded coming from his mouth, and the voluptuous movements his lips made to pronounce it. The echo of his voice got branded on her memory, as did the musky aroma of his fine cologne. She had to bite her lips to stop the smile that was threatening to take hold of her mouth.

'You don't need to worry or be scared,' he carried on, resting his other hand on her waist. Then, he ordered her: 'Turn around.'

She obeyed him without a question. She couldn't speak, and she noticed that the beating of her heart deafened any sound. His hands started to rummage around the line of tiny buttons of her nightgown, and the young woman closed her eyes. With each little snap, a button came undone and the piece of clothing opened a little more. The rite, that he insisted in prolonging, caused her heart to race. When the gown was sufficiently loose, he dropped it on the floor with a slight gasp.

Harmony, still her back to her husband, reacted a bit late. She saw herself totally naked, and a panic attack overwhelmed her, to the point that she wished to pick up the piece of clothing and bury herself under it.

What was happening? She did not want him to see her like that. There was nothing to see. She felt so small she almost burst out crying. She squatted quickly, ready to recover her dignity, and immediately noticed he copied her movement.

'No, no,' he shushed in her ear. His voice sounded delirious, hungry, muffled by her thick hair, where he had buried his face. 'Let me see you. Please.'

Then, she remembered Miss Andersen's words, when Harmony had asked her how she was supposed to behave in her wedding night, assuming— improbable as that was—that she'd have one. The governess had been reluctant to give her the details she was hankering after, perhaps because she did not know much about the subject herself, but she had given her a piece of advice in a grave tone: 'Don't you dare contradict your husband. Whatever he asks you to do, indulge him.'

Determined to follow her governess's advice—even if it meant exposing her insecurities—Harmony stood up. He did the same. She found it extremely hard to turn around allowing him to look at her, as he had asked her, but in the end she did it. Waldegrave stepped back a little, obviously to get a better view and look at her from head to toe. She looked over her shoulder a couple of times while she waited. His measured expression revealed little of what he was thinking. He only pulled at his hair anxiously once he finished observing her.

'I won't hurt you, I promise you,' he said finally, after what felt like a minute. Harmony had the odd feeling that he was trying to convince himself more than her. 'I will never do that again. Turn around and look at me.'

She did as he asked without thinking what his curious words meant. He had not hurt her, not physically.

'What I said that day at your relatives' place is true. I'm going to protect you.' His sincerity was evident in his green eyes, so beautiful that they did not look real. The gentleness of his promise moved her, filling her up with confidence.

'All right,' she nodded, and realised that she was whispering.

Waldegrave's hands moved her hair to one side, placing it on her pale right shoulder. His fingers brushed her skin when they moved, inducing a spasm of pleasure inside her. Harmony saw him lean over her and, without realising it, held her breath. His lips touched a bit of skin between her neck and her earlobe, and Harmony's blood started rushing at a vertiginous speed. She held onto his shirt, clenching her fists and eyes tight, concentrating on the sensations she was experiencing, so sweet and violent at the same time. She had only felt something similar when Waldegrave himself had jumped on top of her on the humid gravel of the garden.

It was going to happen, she thought, her head full of a thick mist of pleasure. She had thought he would abstain, but how mistaken she was! He did not seem disgusted at the thought of touching her; quite the opposite, he seemed to be enjoying it as much as she was. She could guess it by his breath that felt warm on her skin, by his wet lips traveling up and down her neck, and by his hands that moved eagerly around her waist, her back, and her sides.

Then, her doubts reappeared. Harmony remembered his hard words at the Talbots, his statements that had hurt her fragile pride, and everything that was happening stopped making sense.

'What is happening?' he asked, probably aware that Harmony's body was growing cold in his arms.

'You told me that you did not like me and would never lay a finger on me while sober,' she reproached him, and the pain she was feeling inevitably slipped into her words. 'You told me I didn't have the qualities required to be your wife.'

Waldegrave, overwhelmed by his own hurricane of desire, replied in a hoarse voice, without blinking: 'Prove to me that I was wrong.'

Devlin assaulted her with his kisses that were ardent and exacting. He sought her mouth impatiently, found it, and took it with the enthusiasm required to quieten her doubts. She smelt of jasmine and tasted of innocence, he verified on introducing his tongue in her mouth, a delicious cavity that, surely, only he had had the pleasure to taste. The idea injected new passion into his being, as if knowing she was his was enough to heat things up.

He had been debating for hours if he should do what he was doing or not. Once the ceremony finished, he'd hankered for a drink, but his wish to be with Harmony George increased without measure. He could not do both. If he gave into his desire for the girl, he had to give up drink; otherwise, he risked ending up becoming the protagonist of another episode of violence. Finally, the bottle was left behind, forgotten on one of the shelves of his study, and now he was there, ready to claim the rights that until that night had not piqued his interest.

He placed his hands on her head, burying his fingers in her soft hair. Oh, he liked the feeling of the curly hair on the palm of his hand that was rough and exciting. He had found a new fetish, he observed as he grabbed her curls with primitive force. He was careful not to hurt her, but he tangled up her hair firmly enough to let her know how much he liked it.

Still clutching her hair with one hand, he used the other to play with her skin; it was terse in contrast with her frizzy hair. He abandoned himself to both sensations that, although extremely different, excited him in equal manner. Soon, he came across a breast, and he cupped it with the palm of his hand while rubbing the nipple with his thumb.

Harmony panted when Devlin took one of her nipples to his mouth and started suckling it frenziedly. She held tight onto his shirt, obviously caught up in rapture, and that reminded Devlin that he was still fully dressed. He hurried then to lift her into his arms. She looked at him with slight fear. Her eyes revealed that she had not expected that; he thought about telling her that neither had he, but he was unable to speak. He was too eager.

He laid her on the bed with exquisite care, as if she were a fragile object that might break easily. He grunted a bit, irritated at having to remove his hands from her to take off his clothes. He hurried not to have to spend too long away from her skin and that wild hair that put him under some kind of carnal spell.

Once naked, he climbed onto the bed, where she was waiting for him, lying there, with her hands shyly covering her sex. Her creamy skin stood out on the warm violet hue of the blankets. Her hair, spread out over the pillow, looked like a huge fan of curls. The duke swung one of his legs over her slender body to ride astride of her, then leaned forward to admire her closely.

He wondered why he had assumed that she was a simpleton, unsociable and dull. He had even thought at times that she was ugly. Now she did not look like it at all. In fact, right then, he found her charming.

Then, he realised that she was trembling.

He placed a kiss on her forehead to calm her down. He was not sure what words he should use to soothe her. If he promised her that it would not hurt, it would be a lie. As for whispering words of love… they were the greatest of infamies. Why was it so complicated? He was starting to feel the sweat on his brow and back, but his desire, instead of diminishing, increased with the expectation. His hardness threatened to burst.

Deflowering a virgin had always been his most private fantasy but fulfilling it supposed an unthinkable risk; any adventure of such kind was condemned to turn into a scandal and afterwards lead to an inevitable marriage, which was why he had never even considered it. When he had thought he would get married to Victory Brandon, the widow Baroness of Lovelance, he had renounced that pleasure in his mind. Now, however, he was married to Harmony George and nothing prevented him from taking possession of his virginal wife. To hell with his idea of keeping his distance from that girl; to hell with his determination to suffer because of that unwanted marriage.

What was wrong with having a bit of fun together? How would that be the honourable thing to do?

He breathed in deeply with renewed impetus. He slid his fingers up the pale thighs, high, higher up still, until he reached the warm wetness between the female legs that pushed him to the edge of his control. He panted in time with her panting, as if he had pressed a tiny mechanism that flooded both bodies with pleasurable sensations.

Harmony closed her eyes and forgot her modesty. The hands that had been protecting her most intimate place with such obstinacy, now grabbed frenziedly onto the blankets while her back arched as if of its own accord. Devlin's fingers played with her soaking folds in different ways and changing rhythm. She couldn't help but move, enjoying that most intimate and wonderful invasion, as if she'd needed it all her life but had never been aware of it until then.

He stopped suddenly. Harmony saw him lying atop of her, his eyes burning with desire. His mouth covered her in passionate kisses again. She corresponded by caressing his lank hair, so soft that it made her feel as if she was submerging her hand in a warm stream.

Soon, she noticed Devlin's hard and exacting member making its way towards her. She then hugged onto her husband's back, full of confidence, and looked at him with dreamy eyes. For an instant, she wished they could be a couple like any other, one that had reached the vicarage of their own will, or at least in less pitiful conditions. She dreamed that they loved each other; that they had planned for the future and imagined that those sensual acts they were sharing were driven by genuine feelings.

An explosive moan burst from her lips when he penetrated deep inside of her, tearing her virtue. It hadn't been only pain. It was a strange mixture of pain and pleasure, roaring in her body with the same impetus, fighting over which one would impose itself. Harmony accepted them both, knowing instinctively that both emotions were necessary and complementary, like day and night, light and darkness. She absorbed everything with the same attitude, just as her legs locked around Waldegrave's hips, as if motu proprio.

Harmony had hardly come to terms with that novel sensation when she heard her husband cursing under his breath. In his voice there were traces of lassitude and frustration that made him frown, even in his delicious drowsiness. An agonic moan, followed by a violent spasm, took hold of him.

A moment later, he lay in total silence, his body covering hers. The seconds passed, tense and heavy. The only noises in the bedroom came from the fireplace and Waldegrave's lungs. His face was buried in the dense coat that her hair, spread on the pillow, had created.

When Harmony was finally able to open her eyes, still clouded by the sensation of having him inside, she found a totally different man to the one who had just taken possession of her. Worried, she saw him abandon grudgingly the hiding place he had created with her hair. His beautiful face was the image of sorrow. Feeling overwhelmed, she innocently tried to caress his cheek, and he withdrew like a wounded animal, abandoning her.

She missed him straight away; her bed felt horribly icy without that warm body enveloping her, fulfilling her. He didn't even bother to look her in the eye. He got out of bed and, with a tense calm, proceeded to pick up his clothing, piece by piece. Harmony's chest started hurting. She did not understand anything about marital relationships, but knew that something wasn't right. Was he upset with her?

What have I done wrong? she wondered in the silence, holding back a lump in her throat and her eagerness to talk, but she did not have time to verbalise her confusion. Waldegrave walked wearily, to the door that led to his bedroom, his clothes bunched up in a ball under his arm.

Was he leaving?

She sat up to make sure her eyes were not lying to her. She saw him leave the room without saying a word, without looking at her, without saying good night. As soon as the door closed, she released a bewildered sigh.

He was gone.

Chapter 7

Next morning, Mary and Prudence made the bed and picked up diligently the wedding night sheets. They exchanged a complicit look in silence, with a hint of a proud smile, on seeing the dark stain giving away what had happened in that bedroom. It was blindingly obvious that the new duchess was no longer a Miss.

Harmony hardly paid them any attention. She was absorbed contemplating London from her high-up window. Waldegrave Terrace had a privileged location atop the hill that was covered in trees, overlooking Hampstead Heath. The newly discovered views overwhelmed her. The city, far away and phantasmal, hardly poked its outline under the veil of the mist of early January. Contemplating it from a height, Harmony had the weird feeling of being in an unreachable tower, or of being a celestial object prying on the earthly world happenings with certain indifference.

She thought about her husband and how used he would be to looking at the world from his plot of sky. The memory of his mouth and his fingers wandering through her body suddenly gnawed at her. She sighed against the glass pane of the window that steamed up with a blurred grey circle. Her view of London disappeared, falling into oblivion.

She would have loved it if he had stayed to sleep with her. After Waldegrave left her bedroom the previous night, she had cleaned up in silence, aching and suffused by a deep sadness she had no words to describe. She only used a bar of scented soap, a towel, and the hot water from the tap. She had the horrible feeling that the tiny essence bottles, forgotten on the stool, were laughing at her.

At some point in the early hours of the morning, after hardly having slept a wink, she ended up convinced that marital relations were like that. She mocked herself and the anxiety she had felt for hours, for believing she had spotted an expression of sorrow in Waldegrave's face. What did she expect? That he would recite a love poem in the darkness? That he would tell her that he loved her?

She shook her head, trying to dislodge the ideas she did not wish to foster because of how painful they were. She reminded herself that although Waldegrave was very handsome, she did not love him, and he did not love her either. Their relationship was destined for failure and, when the time to separate came, she could start a new life full of travels being totally free. That was what she had planned and that was what would happen.

At once, she felt like going out, like breathing the icy air, like sinking her boots in the snow. The maids helped her put on a pair of long bloomers, a chemise and a corset. Then, they retrieved from the wardrobe appropriate attire for the freezing climate: a white shirt, a stripped woollen grey skirt and a jacket. Finally, a cap, a pink scarf and a pair of gloves. They helped her do her hair and get dressed and, luckily, stopped insisting after a while that she ought to have some breakfast. Harmony's stomach felt as if it had shrunk, and she did not feel able to partake of any food.

A little later, she went down the stairs to the main floor. Her joy didn't last long, because in the hall she met the butler, that evil-looking man who looked at her with poorly-concealed disdain, perhaps because he thought she was not good enough for his master.

'Good morning, Your Grace,' the butler greeted her, with a polite bow.

'Good morning,' she replied, haughtily, trying not to be intimidated as her dear friend Sally would have done in the presence of her aristocratic acquaintances.

'Did you have a good rest?'

'Yes, yes. I'm… about to go out for a bit.'

Limsey made a huge effort to maintain his professional phlegm. That little girl he disliked so much would not bring anything good to Waldegrave Terrace, he was convinced of that, but he could not do anything about it. The duke had insisted on taking her for a wife, and everybody in the house suspected the reasons were very shady and had to do with the acquisition of the horse Iolanthe.

He mentally shook his head, full of worry for the duke. What mess had the poor boy got himself into? He had seen him leave earlier than ever, downcast and desolate, and he had deduced that it had to do with his new marriage, that evidently made him unhappy. At least he had not been drinking, and that comforted him somehow.

106

It was his duty to look after that girl, now the duchess, and he would ensure he complied with it, regardless of his personal opinion. 'In this weather? You will freeze to death.'

The girl glanced at him, with suspicion. 'Thanks for your concern,' she mumbled. 'I'll go out anyway.'

Limsey pressed his lips in an astonished grimace. He promised himself to never take his eyes off that girl who could be the ruin of the family that he— in his own way—had been protecting for years.

'If that's the case, I hope the air of Hampstead does you good, Your Grace.'

'Me too,' she said as she went out.

Harmony stepped onto the cold outside the mansion, wrapping herself tight with her coat and trying to forget Limesy's stuck-up face. She saw that the back entrance of Waldegrave Terrace was as stunning as the façade, with its high windows and its grey stone walls.

The surrounding area was covered in a layer of snow and the ample grounds were not clearly visible. The mist enveloping the city had crept up to that level in only a few minutes, causing even the edge of the forests she knew started where Waldegrave's property ended to disappear.

Harmony felt a bit disappointed. She had to make do with imagining those superb spaces in full springtime, the ground covered in pasture, the trees full of green leaves, the fluffy heather and the flowers in glowing colours, strutting to the sound of the April wind. She imagined a group of kingfishers, kestrels, and woodpeckers gliding through a blue sky to land over some large bushes later. She wondered if she would still be there by the time that landscape bloomed.

She carried on with her walk where she could see more clearly. She noticed, not very far from there, a brick building of rustic construction. Soon, she realised that it was the stable and decided to go and have a look.

Inside, there was a strong smell of hay, leather, and dry manure. Harmony screwed up her face but carried on walking, impelled by a sudden curiosity. The stable was lit by a row of oil-lamps hanging from the walls. The heads of the silent animals stuck out from the top of the doors at the stalls, which extended very far. Waldegrave had many horses, she thought, raising her eyebrows in awe.

She scrutinised the large place with her eyes. There were big bales of hay and piles of sacks of grain in a corner. In another, there was the equipment used for riding and tending to the horses, next to a huge fireplace. Everything was kept in perfect order.

She walked along the vast corridor while she looked at the spectacular animals, all slender and with a shiny coat. They were looking at her curiously as she walked by. One of the horses moved its ears when she reached it. Harmony caressed its mane that was soft and well looked after. It was evident that their owner made sure his animals were kept clean and fit. He remembered that Waldegrave loved racing horses and spent a fortune for their upkeep, according to what Uncle John had told her in more than one occasion.

She carried on walking and then, the horse housed in the next stall powerfully attracted her attention. Sad and downcast, it was languishing inside the confines of that narrow stall. Harmony caressed its head, stricken by its appearance of neglect, although she had never totally sympathised with it. It was Iolanthe.

She remembered the continual defeats that the horse Uncle John had sold Waldegrave had suffered, and she sighed mournfully. It was evident that the poor animal had been dismissed for its bad performance and that was the reason for its desolate look. She had been convinced at the time that selling that beautiful specimen as if it was a champion was an extravagance. It had hardly started to train as a professional, but Uncle John had insisted that it had all the qualities required to become a revelation, or that was what he had told everybody.

She heard footsteps dragging over the earthen floor. Then, an elderly man with greasy hair and long, messy sideburns turned up at the door of the stable. His shoulders jerked to see her there, and he almost tipped his cup of coffee on his dark leader jacket. His eyes, tiny and dark like a deer's, opened wide, obviously on realising that the new duchess was standing there among the beasts, in the rustic stables of Waldegrave Terrace.

'Good morning,' she greeted him in a kind voice, trying to ease his shock.

'Good morning, Your Grace.'

'Sorry, I didn't mean to scare you.'

'Scare me? Not at all!' He laughed and left the cup on a nearby stool. 'I wasn't expecting to find you here, and even less at such an early hour, Your Grace.' He added, with a clumsy bow, 'Congratulations on your nuptials.'

'Thank you.'

'I am Gresham, the veterinary, at your service. If you are thinking about going for a ride, I can ask Timmy to saddle a good mare.'

'No!' she remembered the slight ache between her legs and blushed. 'I haven't come looking for a horse, Mr Gresham. I was simply looking round.'

'I see you have found Iolanthe,' he stated, pointing at the horse. 'But don't grow too fond of him, Your Grace. He is a loser.'

She looked at him, disdainful. 'He's lost a few races, that's all.'

'I hate to contradict you, Ma'am, but the truth is that this horse is a fraud. A crook cheated my master and sold it to him saying that it was a marvel. Unfortunately, that day I was attending the delivery of one of the mares, and I was not able to warn him that it was defective.'

Harmony blinked. Had he said 'defective'? Had Iolanthe, perhaps, some kind of malformation? She examined him from head to hoof. She squatted to look at him through the stable's bars. If he had some malformation, she could not see it. 'What do you mean by 'defective', Mr Gresham?'

The man laughed out loud. 'I am talking about his lineage. It is not completely pure, at least in the eyes of a true specialist,' he mumbled, pointing at his own person.

She stood up slowly. She was starting not to like very much the said Gresham, who had decreed that only a specimen of the purest blood was fit to win a race, as if courage was the exclusive domain of the upper castes.

'It would be more suitable as a carriage horse,' the man added, pedantic. 'Isn't it so, lazy bum?' He shouted at the poor animal. 'Would you like to pull a carriage up to Winchcombe?'

Harmony clenched her jaw. What a horrible man! She had always believed that vets were sensitive people, who loved animals beyond their pedigree, but this man was only interested in the animals that could be exploited for an economic profit.

Gresham jumped when the hooves of a horse approaching echoed nearby. He said goodbye to Harmony and rushed to leave the stable. She ignored him and remained with Iolanthe, who had started to sniff her out intently, as if he had developed a sudden interest in her.

'You should stop listening to that awful man. It's not your fault that my uncle, the crook, has used you,' she told the animal who seemed to reply with a stoic look. 'Who says you cannot be a great champion? Look at you, Iolanthe. People bet money on you, they shout your name every time you run a race.' She caressed his head, getting a satisfied snort in return. 'Yes, you're a winner!'

Waldegrave appeared at the stable's door striding energetically; behind him were Gresham and a boy she imagined was Timmy, the stable boy, who guided the bay horse to remove its harness. The duke was giving his instructions and moving fast and determined down the stable's corridor while the other two men followed him, flustered, trying not to miss a word of his orders.

It looked as if he had performed some physical activity, she deduced, considering the way his chest heaved up and down and his messy black mane that was peppered with tiny snowflakes resembling cotton fluff. When had it started snowing again? She noticed that the duke was wearing the same overcoat trimmed with mink he had worn that day at the village, and black trousers that clung to his long and muscular legs. He was wearing black boots—covered in mud—below his knees.

Waldegrave had yet to notice Harmony's presence, until Gresham said something that caused him to glimpse in her direction. Then, he turned around and their gazes met. To her utter disappointment, the look in his green eyes was one of uncomfortable surprise.

After giving the final instructions to the stable hands and dismissing them, Waldegrave walked towards Harmony stepping slowly, as if he did not wish to reach her before he had decided what to say.

'Good morning.'

'Good morning.'

The silence grew between them for a few seconds.

'I like to ride before breakfast,' he said to justify his early exit, or his appearance. At least that was what Harmony thought. She nodded and smiled slightly. The truth was that he did not look bad at all, but the opposite.

She looked at the door the stable hand had gone through and remembered how flustered they'd looked while he talked to them.

'Is there anything wrong?' she asked.

'No, no. The shed door got stuck with last night's storm.' He shook his hand, downplaying the matter. 'It is nothing important.'

'What an ungrateful blizzard, don't you think?' She laughed anxiously.

Harmony could not ignore his avoiding gaze, his ill-at-ease posture, like that of a child about to be told off for being naughty. She had the painful feeling that it was hard for him to come close to her or talk to her. Perhaps he was repentant for having touched her the previous night. The idea caused her a sharp pain in the deepest recess of her chest.

She made an effort to swallow the lump that had lodged in her throat.

'I came out to have quick look,' she said, trying to sound casual. 'Waldegrave Terrace is impressive. And then I ended up here, at the stable. And I found Iolanthe. When is his next race?'

'There will be no more races for him.'

'What?'

'He's finished. I'm going to sell him.'

She looked at him, confused. 'Finished? He's only three years old!'

Waldegrave sighed tiredly. 'He's no longer profitable, Harmony. I had irrational expectations for this horse, but he has disappointed me, and I didn't even take into account his... anomalies.'

She felt pained by his use of that word, which was as demeaning as the one Gresham had used: 'deformities'. What the hell where he and the vet talking about? Iolanthe looked healthy, despite the harsh treatment he was receiving, and he had also won two difficult races against professional rivals. What did it matter if he wasn't a specimen of the highest purity?

'Why don't we keep him as a riding horse?'

'The decision has been made.'

She regretted hearing that, because it reminded her of her own situation. When the Duke of Waldegrave made a decision, no force of nature could make him change his mind.

'Is that what you do when something is no longer of use to you? Do you get rid of it and that's all?'

Devlin was astonished and had to make an effort to control his expression not to show it. That girl's impudence left him speechless. In any other occasion, he would have come up with one of his cutting retorts, those that made the most resolute of men shut their mouths immediately, but with her, everything was different. He could not join the words together; perhaps because she was right, or because he could not look at her without thinking about the previous night and his deplorable performance.

Damn it. That hadn't happened to him since he was fifteen and he felt terrible. He hated what had happened, being so rushed, as green as an adolescent, and even more with her, who wasn't the most beautiful or the most sensual woman he had ever bedded, by far. Then, why had he spilled his seed in such a shameful way as soon as he had slipped inside of her, even though that was the most glorious place he had ever entered?

He gave thanks to the gods for her being an inexperienced young girl, incapable of understanding the magnitude of what had happened to him.

Harmony, conscious of his hesitation, took advantage of his momentary weakness to carry on challenging him. 'I am sure that you didn't buy him to watch him race. You did it because it is a beautiful animal, didn't you?' She paused and caressed the neck of the animal, which seemed more than happy to count on her, since she were such a competent defender. Devlin decided to prolong his silence to carry on listening to that original little speech.

'Beautiful things have the power of confusing us, of enveloping us, of making us see everything in a better light, and of making us feel better in ourselves,' she carried on.

She was saying all that with a lost and dreamy look, as if she was resorting to her own life experiences. But what experiences could a twenty year old brat have? he wondered, raising an eyebrow smugly.

'And do you think is it such a bad thing to be confused by their beauty?' he finally said, sounding amused despite himself.

She thought about it for an instant, before replying, enigmatically:

'No. It shouldn't be a bad thing if you can accept the thing in question when it shows itself as it truly is.' She blinked, as if trying to capture an elusive idea. 'I mean that you should forgive the fact that Iolanthe's beauty did not also come with all the qualities you imagined in him.'

Devlin could no longer accuse her of being boring or a simpleton. Since the previous night, Harmony George, had shown signs of being an interesting woman, and she had left him speechless on a couple of occasions. First, she had admitted her inexperience in the overvalued art of 'being a duchess'. That, in other words, humility, was such a rare gift in his world that he hardly knew how to react when somebody put it in evidence. And just now, to top it all, she'd blamed him for being frivolous.

'I did a bad business deal, I admit,' he said a moment later, suddenly overcome by a common-sense attack. 'I enjoy keeping race horses, but I don't collect them to admire them or anything like that. Iolanthe...' Why was he telling her all that? Devlin paused for a moment, puzzled, then added, 'Something attracted me to him. I saw something in him, but afterwards...' He was careful not to say that he then got a crush on Victory Brandon and forgot about the stupid animal. 'Afterwards, I think that I opened my eyes and realised that I don't need a beautiful horse but a fast one.'

'I feel sorry for anybody who hasn't come to this world with enough qualities to make you happy,' she said in an audible whisper, seemingly fed up.

'I must remind you that my poor taste does not justify the deception I was a victim of.'

He insinuated about that trickster, her uncle, to her, only to see how she would react. Devlin had no intention of blaming her for anything.

'You should not have closed a business deal without Mr Gresham, the expert, by your side, pointing out all the defects of the poor horse with his condemning finger. I can guarantee you that his concept of beauty would have been more profitable than yours.

To his own surprise, Devlin smiled. For a second he had thought that Harmony would defend her uncle and would try to convince him that the transaction had not been a trick, but even she was aware that he had allowed himself to be swept by an impulse and her guardian had taken advantage of it.

'Don't undervalue beauty, Harmony,' he replied sardonically. 'Plato said that love is the thirst for beauty and goodness.'

The young girl's hand stopped halfway through the caress she was giving the animal. She seemed to be chewing on an idea that left her with quite a bitter aftertaste.

'It might be a good idea to sell Iolanthe,' she said at once, her gaze glued onto the object of their discussion. 'He should be with someone who recognises his value or, perhaps, will even discover his potential. Who knows? He could be a champion; don't be deceived but his 'anomalies'.'

He shook his head. He had faith in the opinion of Waldegrave Terrace's old vet. 'I don't think so. Gresham dismissed him.'

Then, she looked at him with a certain arrogance he thought funny. 'That man would not know the difference between a thrush and a crow.' She looked back at the horse as she walked off. 'Good luck, handsome,' he thought he heard her say.

He followed her outside and, after leaving the stables, they went back to the comfortable refuge offered by the mansion. The blizzard had started again with more intensity after a few hours of truce. The snowflakes now looked like scraps of cotton.

They dropped their coats that were sprinkled with tiny shards of glassy ice in the hands of the servants and sat down to have breakfast by the big fireplace. They enjoyed a splendid meal consisting of sausages, bacon, scrambled eggs, a selection of cheeses, baked beans, toast, coffee, tea and orange juice, then chatted about the palatial property at Winchcombe, where they were due to travel in a few days. Devlin was telling her about Sudeley Castle and the virtues of life in that peaceful region, which was becoming more important thanks to its thriving industrial activity.

Devlin studied the girl intently as they talked, his brow furrowed. She seemed to have a good appetite and tried everything with eagerness. He wondered if John Talbot and his wife had treated her well, and experienced an unexpected bout of worry. He remembered something else she had mentioned the previous night: that her education had started late and that she shared the services of a governess with another pupil. He made a mental note to check Miss George's dossier, which he had commissioned before the wedding and was in his pile of pending documents. That way, her confessions would not catch him unawares.

Luckily, the conversation at the stable had managed to dissolve the tension accumulated since their interaction the previous night. It was good to be able to feel at peace with his wife, at least until he decided what to do with her.

At midday, he took her by the arm for a small tour of the mansion. He showed her the legendary halls of Waldegrave Terrace—where he threw his parties—the music room, the gallery that he felt so proud of—where priceless art pieces were exhibited—the games room, the solarium, the conservatory, and also the terraces that had spectacular views over the city. What impressed her most, though, was the library.

Seeing the tall and wide bookshelves packed with countless volumes seemed to make her a little crazy with enthusiasm. She got carried away striding faster and faster down the corridors, her eyes open wide, so in awe that for a moment Devlin almost had to run after her to keep conversing.

'This is ridiculous!' She stopped before a bookshelf he had hardly ever glanced through. 'You would not be able to read them all even if your life depended on it.'

Devlin cleared his throat. 'To be honest, I hardly ever stray away from the science section.'

'Do you mean Faraday, Morse, and all those?' she said while she ran her index finger over the row of spines, with a concentration reminiscent of that of an archaeologist evaluating a new discovery.

'And others... it's my job,' he hastened to add, in the face of her mocking tone. 'I preside over the Parliament's Commission for Science; I am the youngest member of the Royal Society of London and in my spare time I help develop inventions, thanks to my degree in Physics. It is my tiny contribution so you can read your mystery novels by the reliable light of an electric lamp, for example.'

'Did you say mystery novels? Perhaps I look like a reader of mystery novels,' he heard her whisper while she removed a volume from the bookshelf. He swallowed hard, a little irritated for not having impressed her much with the abridged version of his curriculum. Curious, he squinted to read the cover of the book she had picked up: Travels in Arabia Deserta by Charles Doughty.

There was something wrong with the book, he deduced from the sudden disappointment in her face. Harmony returned the volume to its place and carried on with her scrutiny while she bit her bottom lip in fierce concentration.

He realised he was smiling. Her enthusiasm was refreshing, a big novelty for those old walls that for years had only been visited by cynicism and conceit dressed up as brilliance. The Sawyer's library was one of the best-stocked libraries of the continent, and it grew year on year thanks to the new publications in the market. He liked the fact that somebody showed an appreciation for it.

In spite of that, a small twinge of unease advised him to move away from there. If he dropped his guard, very soon the girl would start to talk, to flatter him, to interfere in his affairs, to look for a way to introduce herself into his life more than he was prepared to allow her, and that was something that Devlin would try to avoid at all costs, if he wished to, at least, survive that marriage. He was determined to be like an iceberg for her and to remove from her head any possibility of a romance...

Although, to be honest, right now she seemed so immersed in her search that she probably had forgotten he was still here.

Devlin cleared his throat and she looked up.

'It may be better to leave you here on your own; that way, you'll be able to choose what to read at your leisure.'

'Devlin...' She smiled at him, bursting with pleasure. He had insisted over breakfast that she should call him by his first name. After all, they were husband and wife and, contrary to what he had thought at some point, he did not find her all that disagreeable. 'Thank you for bringing me here. I'll spend so much time here reading that I won't bother you at all. You won't even notice my presence. I promise you.'

In lieu of a reply, he nodded in silence as he rubbed the nape of his neck with the palm of his hand. Then, he left quietly, but before closing the door behind him, he turned to look at her one last time. She seemed to be possessed by the rows of the damned books.

Curiously, he liked to see her there, in his home.

She didn't know how long had passed since Devlin had left until she started to nod off in one of the Chesterfield chairs in the library, but in that space that seemed so joyfully indefinite, she had enjoyed an interesting narration: The Indian Alps and How We Crossed Them, by a 'Lady Pioneer.'

Harmony discovered in its pages the story of a woman and her husband, an administrator for the East India Company, who went on a journey through the rough and icy region of the Himalayas. Lady Pioneer and her husband had to suffer some deprivations while they reached a height of almost twenty thousand feet above sea level, travelling through one of the most stunning landscapes on earth. Then, they fell ill due to the height and got lost during some stretches of their journey. To top it all, their provisions started to dwindle, adding up to a picture of calamities that contrasted with the spectacular nature of the view. Finally, after travelling for two months, they managed to find their way back home.

She felt that the Lady Pioneer complained too much, particularly considering she had at her service almost a hundred native servants that carried her on a doli. Her exaggerated female sluggishness had turned the journey into torture. Her descriptions of the craggy mountains dusted in snow, of the prairies and the lakes, however, were imposing.

Next to her, on the table, she found a Wedgwood porcelain tea set. On the plate there were only crumbs left of the scones, cream and jam one of the maids had brought her. The half-opened curtain showed a late winter afternoon, the sun not quite peeking out from behind the ashy clouds.

She focused on the book she had on her hands: A Voyage in the Sunbeam, by Annie Brassey, a woman who had managed to drag her whole family in an intrepid voyage on her sailboat. She was about to start reading it when sleep started to besiege her. Shortly after, she fell into a light snooze.

Suddenly, she saw herself in a clearing in the woods. It was covered in snow that reached up to her calves. She wasn't alone; Devlin was by her side. He was holding her hand and guiding her like a seasoned hiker through glacial spots. Harmony squeezed his hand that was stuffed into leather gloves and just followed him. She would have jumped off a cliff if he had asked her to.

Then, without warning, a blizzard caught them in the middle of the wilderness. Devlin ran, hand-in-hand with her, looking for refuge. Harmony followed him through the thick snow, which slowed down their run as if they were walking through quicksand. Finally, they came across a lumberjack's cabin which, although tiny, was clean and had logs piled up to feed the stone fireplace.

Devlin lit a fire inside and Harmony lay atop a thick carpet. For some unknown reason, she was naked. A pressing need raging from her core was taking over, starting in her belly, bubbling up and spreading through her limbs. She had only experienced such intoxicating sensation in a couple of occasions, with a person in particular.

When her husband lay atop her, she knew what he wanted, what he needed. He was also naked, and his body, heavy and warm, fitted in with hers with a celestial precision, as if they were made to slot into one another. Her breathing accelerated, all her insides heating up in response to his intimate invasion as her arms and legs curled around the tense and wide back bearing over her.

Then, a crushing pleasure she'd never imagined lashed at her as if she were a branch in the heart of the blizzard raging outside.

She exhaled a bitter sigh of shock then because she had been pulled out of her shameless dream abruptly, and she didn't quite know how. Devlin was before her, leaning forward, in such a way that their faces were only inches apart. Harmony, her eyes open wide, couldn't say anything, other than what her obvious fearful look—like that of a thief just discovered in flagrante delicto—revealed. The thought that he could learn about that dream, could have seen it, or heard it, horrified her.

His gaze wasn't one of censure, however. It was… she didn't know what his look expressed exactly.

'I am sorry; I didn't mean to scare you,' he whispered, hardly moving a muscle. 'Mary didn't dare to wake you up and came looking for me. It's almost time for dinner.'

She stood up slowly, without establishing visual contact. She still felt very disturbed and ashamed. She realised that at some point she had removed her hairpins and her hair laid spread on the cushions. It wasn't the most proper of appearances, and she rushed to put her hair up to avoid looking like a wild creature.

'I hadn't realised,' she said as an excuse. 'You see? That's what I was talking about.' At least she had the ingenuity of laughing at herself as a way to hide her embarrassment. 'A duchess shouldn't fall asleep in the library, should she?'

'You might find it difficult to believe, but I have seen much more outrageous things,' he whispered. He rescued the book Harmony had been reading, which now lay forgotten on the carpet. A Voyage in the Sunbeam. He raised his eyebrows, somewhat impressed by his discovery. 'Is this your thing, then? Adventures?'

She rubbed her eyes, allowing a smile to grow in her lips. She was on the verge of mentioning Mrs Pfeiffer and her incredible stories in A Woman's Journey around the World which, in comparison, made those other narratives seem like textbooks but, for an instant, Miss Andersen's words echoed in her mind like a fog horn. She had said once that no gentleman would approve of a lady who invested her time in such daring reading materials. Harmony was prepared to defend the cultural worthiness of her books, but more important than that was to prevent his rejection. She could not bear Devlin thinking badly of her and no longer being deferential and subtle.

'It was entertaining,' she only said, shrugging.

'So much so that it put you to sleep.'

He offered her a smile that made her stumble slightly as she stood up. Solicitous, he steadied her and guided her by the arm outside of the room.

'And which are those crimes, more awful than snoring and drooling in full sight of the servants, if I'm allowed to know?' she asked him, more upbeat.

'Ah, well, there is a long list of them,' Devlin said, scratching an eyebrow.

'For me, the worst one is to support one side in parliament when your husband is on the other side... or cheer another horse at the race course.'

Harmony burst out laughing. 'They are both horrible, I imagine!' she agreed. 'But the dukes are also capable of committing the most awful acts.'

'What are you talking about exactly?'

'Staring at a lady at a social event and not greeting her with as much as a nod... or a smile. Turning around and making her feel as if she did not exist, instead.'

There was a brief silence while they climbed up the stairs.

'I don't understand.'

She addressed him with a shy look. 'I am talking about Ascot, in the fall, after Iolanthe's first race. You saw me, and it was as if you were looking into a void.'

Harmony surprised herself by saying that so matter-of-factly, even with a hint of humour. For months, that look had made her feel smaller than an ant, but now she did not feel the same. She felt as if that had happened in another life.

A silence ensued between them.

'Were you there? I don't remember seeing you.' His eyes rolled back as he obviously tried to recall the scene in his memory. After a few seconds, he said, 'Oh. I'm very sorry to have offended you. I have no excuse.'

You didn't offend me; you only broke my heart, she thought. 'I think you were busy. Don't worry!'

Devlin looked at her quizzically, but she decided to drop the issue. She would make sure that no mention of Lady Lovelance became necessary.

'But it's true that it sounds like something I would do.'

'Why should you do something like that?'

'I'm not usually too friendly towards the people I haven't been introduced to.'

Now, they were walking towards Harmony's bedroom in total silence. He had fallen into a reflective mood that was unable to understand, until he finally talked again: 'Well, this is not a formal complaint, but I think I have also been the victim of a generous measure of your rudeness recently.'

'What? What are you talking about?'

'Your wedding dress.'

Now it was Harmony the one left speechless. She had not come up with any justification for her daring decision. She couldn't even remember why she had rejected the magnificent dress designed by Worth that had been left behind, all but forgotten. 'I am sorry.'

He gave a slight nod. 'I should have asked for your opinion before buying it. It was only that I thought you might need it and I pre-empted it. That is all.'

'Thank you.' She smiled. 'I hadn't thought about it that way. Did you choose it?'

'No, it was Lady Felton who did. Her eye for high couture is more trustworthy than mine. She was very disappointed, by the way.'

'I'll apologise to her as well.'

'Are we even, then?'

She thought about it for a little while. 'No.'

'No?'

'I hit you in the head, don't your remember? I am infinitely sorry about that,' she added, her expression truly sorrowful. 'I am sorrier for that than for not wearing the dress. It's the most stupid thing I've ever done. Forgive me.'

She was holding his arm at the time and he patted her hand. 'Although I can't confirm that all my brain functions are in working order after that knock…'

Her anxious screech pierced through his complaint before she realised it was likely to be have said in jest and was amusing, after all.

'The truth is that we are even. I was rude towards you that day in town,' he admitted in a serious tone, leaving her speechless once more. 'I took out on you what had happened with your uncle. I shouldn't have done that, and even less in front of your friends. I didn't even know you then.'

She had never thought she'd hear such a speech, but he seemed determined to keep on surprising her.

'It seems we have gone out of our ways to annoy each other since we met,' he observed with a huge smile. They had stopped in front of Harmony's bedroom. 'How did we end up married?'

He got no other reply than a fleeting and elusive look.

Waldegrave opened the door to her bedroom that was deserted at such time of day. Mary and Prudence must have been busy with the clothes or some other chore. Harmony wished her husband would follow her in, lock the door, kiss her and caress her again like the previous night, but she could not imagine inviting him to come in, even if that was his house, even if she was his wife. That was the reason why she kept quiet.

'We'll see each other at dinner,' Devlin told her on leaving, and she felt too disappointed to reply.

She saw him walking down the long corridor at his stately pace; his steps echoing farther and farther away on the marble floor. She had the weird sensation that he was moving away from her in more ways than one.

Dinner was short and there were not many words exchanged between the spouses. Once the polite conversational subjects were exhausted, Harmony wondered if he was planning on visiting her later. She hoped he would. The idea started to go around and around in her head, like a bird of prey circling in the air.

And if he did, how should she behave? Was it appropriate if she asked him if there was anything wrong, or were those kinds of subjects completely off-limits?

They said goodnight a little later, and although Harmony waited for him all night long, Waldegrave never crossed her bedroom door.

Chapter 8

The weather did not improve in Hampstead Heath in the next few days, except for inside the old mansion of Waldegrave Terrace, where an atmosphere of peace that none of its inhabitants could have predicted settled in.

Harmony adapted quickly to the house routine. Most of the servants held onto the belief that the young girl was a trained gold-digger, a witch that would prove despotic and bossy. Yet, they soon realised she had the malice of a day-old chick so they began to treat her with the same respect and obsequiousness they showed the duke. All except for Limsey, who had reservations and preferred to remain reserved and keep his glacial façade.

In the morning, the spouses breakfasted together, once Waldegrave had returned from his usual morning ride. Afterwards, to pass the time, Harmony entered the library, alternating between narrations written by women travellers and the novels she found here and there. It didn't take her long to realise that she was reading too quickly and in a short while had devoured all the literature available regarding trips and expeditions from a female perspective. The next thing she did was try to develop an interest for other kinds of reading that would keep her busy.

On the other hand, for Devlin, getting used to his new status as a married man was not proving too easy a task. He dedicated all his attention to his work these days, while he tried to tackle the fact that, from now on, a woman would live in his house, take on his name and eat at his table. Although Harmony George did not turn out to be a demanding or exacting wife—in fact, she seemed to settle for very little and even tried to become invisible to him— her presence there disquieted him, and he wasn't sure why. Hence, most days he avoided her as best as he could and to have any intimate conversations with her. He refused to create a bond between them that he would have to break later on, probably forcibly. He held on, tooth-and-nail, to the well-measured distance that had opened up between them and to the pleasantries that could answer any question and fill any gaps.

Harmony had noticed his strange attitude and had no other option but to put it down to his character. After all, she didn't know him well. She hadn't tried to get too close to him either; her refuge was the library and the mountain of volumes waiting for her each day. It wasn't so bad, she would tell herself, trying to smile. At least, her aunt and uncle weren't there.

In only a few days, the duke and the duchess had received a stream of visiting cards that burst out of the silver tray at the entry hall. The London families—who were coming back home after the Christmas and New Year's holidays—were eager to have a look at the new duchess. If they could, they would have surely peeped through the keyhole to spy on the couple everybody was talking about.

Waldegrave declined all invitations and requests to visit, including those of Talbot and his wife, who even turned up one day without prior warning at the doors of the mansion. Limsey took charge of dealing with them with his glacial elegance, paying no attention to their protestations. Harmony experienced a joy out of this world when she found out. Of all the inhabitants of London, her aunt and uncle were the ones she least wished to see.

However, Harmony suspected that, in a short time, the pleasant routine that brought her such serenity would end. The ice would melt, the activity in the city and the parliament would restart, and perhaps Devlin would not spend much time at home any more. He would go back to his business trips, some likely to take him out of the country and overseas, and she... she wasn't sure what would happen to her then.

Would he decide to keep her secluded in Waldegrave Terrace, out of sight of his friends and acquaintances?

Although not fully aware of it, Harmony had started to fear that moment. What would happen to her once that parenthesis of time came to an end?

One afternoon, Devlin was required to leave the cold trench, as he usually thought of his work space. A leak on the ceiling of his study required they call the bricklayers. The price to pay was his forced removal from that room and the subsequent transfer to the library. When she saw him arrive, carrying his papers under his arm and an amusing expression of defeat, Harmony greeted him with a smile from the Winchester sofa she had made her own. The library was the second most appropriate place to work. There, Devlin had everything he needed close at hand, including a writing desk that was a copy of his, but it meant he had to cohabit with his wife. Although he didn't really want to do it, he ended up accepting it stoically.

Once settled there, he tried to focus on the letter he was writing to one of his New Jersey advisors. But despite his efforts, his gaze easily deviated from the page, blank still, to the image of Harmony, whose presence was as or even more evident than the damn leak. The young woman was motionless, silent and absent, like one of Madame Tussauds's smug dolls, her book resting on her lap, as if her whole world lived in those pages. He envied her concentration, her relaxed posture and the slight smile that increased and decreased on her face as she kept on reading. His pale and slender fingers turned the pages impatiently.

She was wearing her hair up in a high and large chignon. He had a mind to walk up to her and remove the hairpins which prevented him from enjoying the glory of her hair. She was reclined on the sofa, subtly revealing her ankles covered by silk stockings, which every so often she touched distractedly. Devlin strained his eyes to elucidate the colour of the delicate feminine garment. As soon as he realised he was engaged in such a dull task, he abandoned his intention and, scolding himself in silence, tried to concentrate again on the piece of paper before him.

How weird! In general, he didn't fall prey to distractions so easily. He didn't wish to know what colour were her stockings, what she was reading or what she was thinking right then. It wasn't any of his business.

'Do you think it will snow soon?'

The question pulled him out of his task again a few minutes later. Harmony was looking through the window at the white outline of the city that seemed as quiet and still as she had been a moment ago. It looked as if it had frozen over after the last storm.

Devlin replied, awkwardly, 'I hope so. We should have left for Winchcombe already.'

'What is in Winchcombe?'

'Sheep, turkeys, horses... so don't get too excited.' He ensured his voice evidenced his marked lack of interest.

'I bet it could be a good home for Iolanthe.'

He sighed, feeling weary. 'Harmony, don't start again. Iolanthe is where he should be. Isn't that what you wanted? 'A place where he would be appreciated', according to your own words?'

A couple of days earlier, Iolanthe had been acquired, at a price disgracefully low, by a horse breeder from Surrey. Mr Rusch, a successful businessman, had a reputation for being good and patient with his horses, and that must have been a comfort to Harmony, who must have thought that a man with a good eye, like him, was unlikely to do something as silly as putting a champion to work as a plough horse. Before he went to his new home, she had said goodbye to him and sent him off with her best wishes. Devlin, on his part, felt as if a heavy weight had lifted off his shoulders.

'I wanted you to give him a chance, not to get rid of him. In any case, I think Mr Rusch will do a better job,' she said with a shrug, sending him a sly look. 'He is the King Midas of horse-racing; they call him that in the circuit, hadn't you heard? They say he can turn a fat mule into a fireball.'

Devlin looked at her, a warning in his eyes, while trying very hard to hold back a smile. Was she mocking him, the sly girl? 'Well! I'll shut up.'

He put an end to the matter and returned his attention back to his letter, or at least that was his intention. She turned around, prancing along the bookshelves, once more absorbed by the books. Despite his efforts, his gaze followed her.

He looked at the letter again. Damn it, it might as well have been written in Chinese. To his embarrassment, he couldn't even remember why he had decided to get hold of paper and quill. His body was there, settled on his majestic chair, ready to fulfil the responsibilities pertaining to a man of his elevated status, but his mind was following each movement of that young girl, as if he were a pathetic hot-headed youth.

He put his quill to one side and let out a resigned sigh, but with that irritating feeling of defeat, came as well a rush of joy he had not counted on. He had intended to do that, even if it meant having to break the rules he had self-imposed.

He wandered slowly down the long corridors, his hands in his trouser pockets, peering over here and there, merely intent on finding her. It wasn't long before he discovered the little instigator high up on a ladder he used to locate the most inaccessible volumes. She was rummaging around the section over which she now reigned supreme, oblivious to the fact that he was looking at her. He could almost see himself eyeing her with burning interest, something she was totally unaware of, his expression that of a predator.

His view of her, from such a privileged perspective, was paradisiac. It wasn't only the roundness of her hips, her narrow waist, the provoking swell of her derrière... She seemed totally oblivious to her charms, and that was the most stimulating part of it.

'Is everything all right up there?' he asked, resting his hands on the bottom steps of the ladder.

Harmony got startled, but as soon as she saw him at the foot of the ladder, she offered him a smile that evidenced her satisfaction.

'I am not afraid of heights, if that's what you're asking,' she said, determinedly carrying on with her task, checking the spines of the tomes and discarding one after another until she found the volume that would be the lucky one to be rescued from oblivion. 'What are you doing here? Weren't you busy with your letter, Mr Important Physicist, and to top it all, Duke?'

'Is it a touch of sarcasm I detect?' he reacted, tilting his head.

'You've noticed, Your Grace. Aren't you truly brilliant!'

Devlin laughed in a genuinely relaxed manner.

'Insolent little girl! How dare you talk like that to somebody who is holding the ladder you're on? If I wanted to, I could—'

'Don't you dare!' she growled, guessing his intention of scaring her.

All of a sudden, he didn't know quite well where from, he felt a touch of uneasiness. He didn't like to see her up on that ladder.

'Best to come down now. It is dangerous for you to be up there.'

'No. I've just discovered this section and want to check it out.'

'You could slip and break your neck. Listen to me. I'll ask Peter to bring down all the books, and that way you can look over them later, but on firm footing.'

Harmony ended up obeying him, albeit not without a bit of resentment. 'All right, Granddad,' she mocked.

'Are you familiar with the term déjà senti?' he asked her as he helped her climb down. She shook her head, amused. 'It is when you experience the sensation that you have already lived something. It is very strange and it just happened to me… with you,' he added.

When her feet finally touched the floor, he did not remove his hands from her waist. They remained locked into each other's gaze for a long while. He was burning up with the attraction that was beginning to cloud his mind. As for her, she eyed him with a measure of mistrust.

'How interesting,' she ended up saying, with an elusive smile.

After that, she turned and began to walk away from him. Devlin wanted to follow her, to ask her what had happened, but decided to take that reaction as a reminder of his determination; that of keeping away from her.

'Listen! I need to ask you what that is,' he heard Harmony pipe up all of a sudden.

It was the next day of their forced coexistence. Devlin raised his eyes from his unfinished task to look at what his wife's index finger was pointing. It was the monstrosity that Thomas Edison had sent him two years earlier. He had only tried it once—the same day he got it—and now it lay forgotten in a corner of the room, behind the desk. Of all of Tom's inventions, that was the one he thought had the least future.

'It's an office machine. It's a prototype, nothing else.'

Harmony raised her eyebrows quizzically. 'Well, and what does it do?'

He sighed. He had to accept the fact that he would not get any work done that day, the same as the previous day, and the day before that. 'Come. I'll show you.'

He stood up from his seat and went straight for the object of her curiosity. She followed him, seemingly moved by an eagerness bordering on childishness. The artefact was composed of a grooved cylinder covered by a sheet of pewter and was attached to a simple mechanism. Devlin frowned as he tried to remember how to make it work: he pressed a couple of buttons here and there, and he winded a metallic handle on and on.

Harmony gave a start when the device produced a crackling noise; then, a wavering and throaty voice began to recite a poem over a blurry background. Devlin enjoyed her reaction, smiling as he watched her. She opened exorbitantly her onyx eyes, as still as when she devoured her books, as if the smallest movement could deprive her of a single word of Tom's brief test speech.

He had heard that, in New Jersey, the first reaction of the women of the Menlo Park Factory to the weird contraption had been to faint, but Harmony seemed to be having too much fun to imitate them.

'It is magic!' she said a minute later.

'No, it is inventiveness,' he retorted.

'But... how?'

'It is called a wax cylinder or phonograph,' he said with a smile. 'The tube captures the sound waves and transforms them into a vibration. The needle picks up that vibration and then transforms it into sound.' He didn't think it necessary to expand into complicated explanations about the way the invention worked. Anyway, Harmony would not pay attention to him. 'It is the first device known to man that can record sounds and repeat them at any point, as many times as one wants.'

She sighed while the convoluted voice of the inventor carried on rolling. Devlin realised Harmony was awed, like most people, by things that felt familiar to him.

He had to admit that he often used that advantage of his to seduce women, not because he needed a bit of help, but because he found it quite amusing.

Science, in and of itself was exciting, at least that was what he thought, and managing to surprise the females by unveiling some technological device greatly excited him.

The sound finally died out, and Harmony relaxed her shoulders that had been looking tense all that time. 'And is that all it can do?'

'For now. Edison is extremely busy with his study of electricity, and I think he has not managed to discover how to find a practical use for this invention yet.'

She looked at the machine, frowning, her arms folded. She evaluated it seriously and, after a moment, said something that would turn his world upside down.

'Well, he should use it for music.'

Devlin took his eyes off the phonograph and looked, incredulous, at his wife. 'What did you say?'

'A family could listen to thousands of pieces of music without having to hire an orchestra every time,' she said, pacing up and down the room, apparently moved by a peculiar stroke of inspiration. 'Doesn't it happen to you that you attend a recital and don't want it to end? It surely happens to me,' she said with a laugh.

Devlin thought it was an incredibly beautiful sound. He was suddenly unable to move, his eyes fixed on hers, caught under her spell.

She carried on, 'I would listen to Mendelssohn until the machine melted. I always ask Esther to play Mendelssohn, but she gets bored quickly or gets tired, and I am always left wishing for more. It is very disappointing. There should be... Devlin, what's the matter?'

Harmony looked at her husband's astonished expression, feeling quite surprised herself. Her mind was in a whirl. What had she just said to cause him to do this? She had no idea! And she was not in a position to find out with Waldegrave's mouth glued to hers, as he kissed her with the eagerness of a man dying of hunger.

His assault was feverish and somewhat aggressive, like Harmony would never have imagined a kiss could be; she felt as if she was a small child, defenceless, caught in the jaws of a skilled predator. And the worst thing about it was that she wanted to be mercilessly devoured.

His hands encircled her throat and held her, possessively, so that it would not occur to her to try to escape from his sensual restraint. As if she would. With each passing second, Waldegrave went further. He licked the inside of her mouth, used his teeth to gnaw her lower lip with an impetus midway between pleasure and pain, shattering each one of her thoughts. She realised she was sitting on the edge of the desk with her legs open; between them was her nimble and suddenly carefree husband.

Devlin's tongue tangled up and twisted in hers. His hands journeyed eagerly up and down the layers of her clothing. His left moved to cradle one of her breasts, caressing it over her dress, then climbed up to the place where bone combs held her hair. His right hand began rummaging under her skirt. He caught an ankle and went up her calf, encased by a stocking, regaling her with an intoxicating sensation. She could feel her pulse running out of control as he touched her throat and started to kiss her there.

Shortly after, she was feeling desperate and excited in the same measure, while Waldegrave did what he wanted with her. Desire sparked between them, and she would not have been surprised if their clothes had started falling off at any moment.

But then he stopped. He jumped away from her, as if he had suddenly burned himself. Harmony looked at him, astonished; his hair had come loose and untidy, his clothes were ruffled, mirroring her own appearance. Panting and with trembling hands, he looked back at her. His wild eyes looked like those of a man who, totally unintentionally, had committed a crime.

Frustrated and hurt, Harmony wondered why he had stopped; why he didn't carry on kissing her; why he hadn't tried anything similar since their wedding night. She tried to say something, ask anything, but then he, looking horrified, left the room, leaving her as eager and sorrowful as she had felt the first night of their intimacy. The only one they had shared.

It seemed to her as if Devlin had just woken up from a dream. One where he had been frolicking with a woman... and when he woke up he had discovered a completely different one he wasn't interested in.

Hours passed by in the quiet and empty library. She understood that he would not come back, that he regretted his ardent reaction and now he would start looking for another place to work while his study was being repaired. Sadness enveloped her like a merciless cloud, accompanied by the disappointment of not being attractive enough to keep him interested until the end.

She did not see him again that day. She dined alone and did not bump into him in the corridor. She went to bed without saying goodnight to him, with only her dreams for company, those dreams where he appeared and behaved as if he truly loved her.

Sometimes Harmony fantasised that he turned up at midnight, removed the blankets and lay next to her. The dream she had had a few days ago had come back at night, tormenting her, harassing her. She could never have believed that the sweet sensation of drowning and the need her body felt for him, which she didn't know how to relieve, could turn into such a torture. She convinced herself that she should have no expectations; that marriages worked like that and that the best thing to do, for her own good, was to remind herself that she had never been happy with the idea of getting married.

Why should she be eager for a proper marriage now? Why did she wish to enjoy the conjugal bliss she'd never expected or even wanted?

From the first day of their marriage, she had promised herself that she would remain secluded in the library, would go for long walks around Waldegrave Terrace or would engage in crafts and would never again be a bother to the duke, but then had arrived the 'flood', as he had referred to it, and they had discovered that that space, although huge and full of things to keep both of them busy, became small when they were both present.

During their time sharing the library, Harmony asked him to explain how the telephone worked, or how a generator of electricity transformed the water into energy to feed the devices and the lampposts. He, patient and generous to a fault, answered all her questions, putting to good use—without even realising it—that genius of his that proved so attractive, that made her feel halfway between admiring and devoted, and then all his indifference would disappear. She gave him the wings he never seemed to have allowed himself to explore, without any thought of the consequences.

She always listened to him in silence, wishing to be one of those complicated technical terms his tongue caressed when he pronounced them, or one of those scientific topics that woke such a passion in him. His intelligence, his wisdom, the evidence of his knowledge of the world left her speechless, much more than his physical beauty.

She thought of all the women who had enjoyed his company in the past, his attentions, his passion. The blood thickened in her veins as it if was tar. Jealousy, rage, sadness, an amalgam of vile and weakening emotions harassed her.

'Love is the thirst for beauty and goodness,' she mumbled to herself.

She'd just completed the equation. She had been taken with his beauty, which she had made the mistake of underestimating. Now, she had also discovered the goodness inherent to his being and felt that her heart was in extreme danger. His goodness was expressed in his work ethos which lacked in boastfulness or self-complacency. He was always working till late in the night, buried in papers, books, blueprints, and designs that someday would turn up into benefits for the houses of England and perhaps the world.

If he had wanted to, he could have evaded his duty. Some lords had accommodating styles of life; they lived off the rent of their lands and titles. They squandered their annual allowances and did not take up their seats in parliament to create laws and compensate with their work for the right to enjoy such privileges that were unthinkable for the rest of the citizens. Devlin wasn't like that. He dreamed of a world full of technological advancements. He had a big heart and was far-sighted.

How would she be able to live with such a revelation from now on?

How would she deal with her strong desire to be by his side, with her growing and unforeseen devotion for him linked to the desire that flooded her body each morning, night, and dawn?

That day, when he introduced her to the phonograph and kissed her again, Harmony knew she had reached rock bottom.

A few days had passed. That morning, Harmony sat up in bed and looked toward the window, her heart sinking. It was snowing heavily, to the point that the outside had become a thick grey blanket that stood out in the night. The cold managed to penetrate the walls, soaking through the bricks and bones, causing her to shiver in spite of the fireplace working full blast. Harmony could not remember a harshest winter and felt sorry for the people who did not benefit from a solid roof like theirs. However, it wasn't the cold or the worry for her fellow beings that had robbed her of her sleep. It was her own being that shivered due to her unsated need, which Devlin had fuelled with that kiss at the library. It was her desire to be next to him, to be caressed by him, to feel him, which kept hitting at her from inside her guts, dispelling her sleep.

She told herself she had to do something about it, even if it was madness. Then, she got out of bed and rushed like a whirlwind to the door that linked both rooms. When her hand touched the handle, cowardice, or perhaps clarity, stopped her on her tracks.

What the hell was happening to her? How could she expose herself to an imminent rejection that would totally bury her weak self-confidence? If he had abstained from seeking her out for the last few days it was because he no longer desired her. The interest in her he had shown on their wedding night had decreased, perhaps when he realised that their marriage had no future.

But, was it so bad to enjoy another night together? Whom would they hurt if they did? He could experience desire for her again; she could do something to revive his passion. Her hesitation was stubborn, but her curiosity for what would happen if she summoned the courage to cross that door was even more stubborn.

She got rid of her doubts with expedient urgency. She tried, unsuccessfully, to give her wild hair a civilised appearance. She decided that it was worth the risk of being rejected. If Waldegrave asked her to leave, she would understand and would leave without delay. She would be happy knowing she had tried it and had conquered one of her fears. Perhaps, after that, she could look him in the eyes with the certainty that nothing else would ever happen between them.

She breathed in deeply and turned the door handle with extreme care. The only light illuminating his bedroom came from the large fireplace, which projected a golden shine over the furniture, the walls, and his gigantic bed. Harmony felt terrified, her mouth dry; she seriously considered the option of turning around and going back to her room with her head hung low, but she had not made it so far only to chicken out.

She moved forward, her eyes fixed on the bedhead and the point where Devlin's head rested on the pillow. She knew he was awake as soon as she noticed the regular pattern of his breathing change. She felt observed, the thought giving her goose bumps. Her heart hammered against her ribs and something other than cold made her shake from head to toe.

She stopped in front of him, summoning all her courage. She could not see his eyes clearly or his facial expression in the twilight, but she registered his bold gaze as he looked her up and down admiringly.

Then, she had a revelation. She wanted to do something to tempt him, a thing she would have never considered if her common sense had not abandoned her a couple of minutes ago. Steeling herself, she unbuttoned the buttons of her nightshift one by one. Luckily, the one she was wearing was fastened up front and the buttons were not so close to each other as to take an eternity to get them undone. She did it with a measured slowness that did not correspond with the urgency pushing her on. While she opened her shift, she became conscious, like never before, of her femininity, of all the possibilities hiding in her body. She felt pretty, even.

Her nightdress dropped onto the carpet, which muffled any possible noise. Harmony was totally naked and prayed that Devlin, on seeing her, would remember the sensation that had possessed him during their wedding night.

He replied panting softly. He pulled the blanket to one side so she could join him. Harmony almost bobbed up and down in delight. That simple action gave her licence to continue. Immediately, she rushed towards him and climbed on the bed next to him. The warmth that welcomed her made the heat from the fireplace pale in comparison. It was his body and nothing else. It was all she had been looking for.

Harmony lay on her side, resting her elbow on the pillow and her head on the palm of her hand; Devlin's posture mirrored hers.

'I was wondering if you were feeling as cold as I,' she whispered.

'Probably, if I wandered around the house naked like you.'

She smiled at him. 'What other option did you give me?'

He sighed and kept quiet for a moment. 'So you have been waiting for me.'

'Yes,' she whispered. 'It's that, the first night, you... Why haven't you come back again?' She looked away, ashamed, although it was so dark that perhaps he would not have noticed it.

He took another long moment to reply. 'Harmony, I have been honest with you from day one, haven't I?'

She nodded. It was true. He had never lied to her; he had never given her a wrong impression of what that marriage would be like, apart from that first night. For some reason, his reminder unleashed an uncomfortable banging on the pit of her stomach.

'I never planned for us to have a wedding night,' he carried on, as if he had heard her thoughts. Not sure of how to reply, she kept quiet as he continued, 'And that is because I never had any intentions of entering into a conventional marriage relationship with you. We both know why we are here. We both know what I did to you.'

Right then, just as it had arrived, her self-confidence abandoned her like a carriage that had taken her to a faraway and unknown location, and had then taken off without warning, abandoning her to her luck. Harmony swallowed hard to try and get rid of the lump that had formed inside her throat.

'Are you talking about that kiss at Felton House?' she whispered feebly.

'It was more than a kiss.'

'And was it quite so bad for you?'

'For God's sake, Harmony! I am not the offended party in all this...' His words evidenced his frustration and a trace of bitterness.

'I don't know why you attach so much importance to it. I know you were drunk, and if you had known you would end up atop a woman as... as plain as me you would never have touched a bottle of liquor, but... it hasn't been so bad. At least for me.' She was grateful for the darkness as she realised she had blushed.

Devlin seemed to ponder over her words for a bit, then said, 'Are you being serious?'

'Totally.'

'But, it's just that... I...' He still hesitated.

His concern over honour—that she had considered ridiculous and extreme before—was starting to feel adorable to her. At that point, what aspect of his personality she did not find totally captivating? she wondered, downcast, then said, 'I do admit, I was a bit scared at first, but until that day I had never believed it possible that a man like you could kiss somebody like me.'

He sighed. 'Harmony, I am not an exceptional man. I have so many defects you would be horrified if you knew.'

'And who doesn't? I only see the good in you.'

'You are very sweet,' he replied, a few seconds later.

His reply was so brief that something inside her broke. I am an idiot, she kept repeating to herself inwardly. Had she thought that his rejection would not knock her down, would not totally crush her? How wrong had she been! How little did she know herself! She had arrived there looking for his body, his caresses, had disrobed herself like a whore and had almost ended up confessing her inconvenient feelings.

Why had she expected not to feel afraid? She had overestimated herself. She had ruined everything. 'Well, I think I'm no longer feeling as cold,' she said finally, her voice evidently transformed by her disappointment. She sat up, ready to escape as quickly as possible.

'Where are you going?'

'Good night.'

Devlin grabbed her waist when she was about to stand up. With a sudden movement, he pulled her back onto the mattress. Harmony bounced back with a gasp, and all of a sudden he was on top of her. Devlin was holding her by the wrists, as he had done that night at Felton House. His masculine face was a few inches from hers, and his long and heavy body was weighing her down, causing a bubbling inside her belly.

'What do you want, Harmony? Why don't you tell me once and for all?' he grunted in her ear.

Furious, she gritted her teeth. How did he dare ask her that? Did he intend to humiliate her on top of rejecting her? 'We shouldn't have got married!'

'Really? You undress yourself and get into my bed to complain about our marriage? Couldn't you wait until breakfast, my dear wife?'

'Why did you bring me to your home? You should have listened to me, Devlin. Now we are both unhappy because of that. I never intended to go running to tell everybody about that episode you so regret.'

'Perhaps not you, but what about your uncle? He would have done it!'

'I cannot be held responsible for his actions.'

'You came here seeking something!' He shook her impatiently, but not enough to hurt her. 'Tell me what it is you want, damn it!'

'Do you really need me to tell you?' she replied bitterly.

'Oh, yes. I need to hear it from your lips.'

'Why, Your Grace? To flatter your ego? In your eyes, I'm nothing more than the ordinary niece of the horse dealer who cheated on you, and I am far from being as pretty as those women you like. You don't desire me!'

'Would you like to bet on it?'

As he asked her that, Devlin grabbed her hand harshly and took it to his groin area. Harmony panted, between surprised and ashamed on groping the rigid protuberance that seemed about to burst through her husband's tight undergarments. Fascinated and intimidated in equal measure, she remained like that for a second, only for the time required to preserve her dignity. Afterwards, she removed her hand as if it had been burned.

Devlin no longer kept her immobilised, perhaps because she had recanted, but he did not move away as much as an inch either. 'Do you know why we had a wedding night?' he asked.

Harmony tried to read his eyes in the dark, but it was a useless attempt. Waldegrave's long hair created a sombre mask; only a few locks escaped the golden hue of the fireplace. His visage remained inscrutable. That was why she paid attention to his voice, that exuded... rage? Impotence? Anxiety?

'Against my best interests and all my plans, I desire you, Miss George. I do, and I wish I didn't, because this marriage will finish me off before it starts.'

'What do you mean?' she dared to ask, despite it being quite obvious.

'I refuse to keep talking while you are naked under me,' he grunted. 'Is it all right with you if we leave the discussion for later?' Devlin flopped onto her and kissed her with uncharacteristic ardour.

When their mouths melted into each other, any trace of her hesitation vanished. She tangled her fingers on his lank and silky hair while kissing him with desperation and exploring his mouth as he had done with hers in other occasions. Devlin seemed delighted by her effusiveness, to the point where he chased her tongue and held her to suck on it intensely.

He moved one hand down her body, fondling her side and moving waywardly, until it found a breast. He massaged it with the palm of his hand, and that made Harmony writhe excitedly. After that, it was his mouth that started dancing along her naked body, his wet and hot tongue caressing her nipples to later devour them. First one, then the other, then back to the first one.

While she twisted and turned, prey to a scandalous pleasure, Harmony desired Devlin's mouth in forbidden places, and contemplated some ideas that should have made her feel ashamed. She held on to her husband's strong shoulders, hair and his firm and muscular back, while he carried on pleasuring her.

His right hand climbed down to her crotch, the place where she most needed him, and provoked a weak moan as he deeply massaged her. He did it with scientific precision, stopping long enough for her to feel it fully and accelerating at other points, almost driving her crazy.

'Is this what you want?' he growled in a husky and voracious voice.

Harmony felt herself aflame, and for a moment felt like laughing. Her hips instinctively followed the voluptuous movement of Devlin's hand, like a puppet on a string. The relentless play of his fingers, which went in and out of her warm passage, had smashed to pieces her ability to reason, her capacity to blush, and any scrap of logic left in her head.

'No,' she panted, rummaging for the erect member with her hand. She found it and circled it hard, a gesture that spoke loud and clear. Devlin's moan after such daring made her smile proudly.

'Well. Then you'll have it,' he groaned, as if in agony.

She was waiting impatiently for him to jump on her again, like the first time, to cover her with his body and make love to her, but then he surprised her by lifting her up carefully, and guiding her until he made her face the bedhead.

To begin with, she felt disoriented. She was on her knees, naked and with her hands holding onto the sumptuous design of the wrought iron bars. She was not sure he had understood the message.

Devlin, his feet on the floor now, removed his simple undergarment and contemplated her full of excitement, his chest lifting and falling with his heavy breathing. He saw her turn her head and look at him, adoration alight in her eyes. She was trembling all over.

He climbed again onto the bed, hugged her waist, kneeling down as she was. His member stuck to the glorious swell of her derrière and his hip rocked wildly on top of her as soon as they touched. Her abundant hair brushed his chest, his throat, his face. He sighed in response to the marvellous pleasure that contact caused him. He had desired her like that since he had first seen her naked by accident.

Now he would give her what she desired… and he would also obtain what he yearned for.

His hands moved her hair to the side, uncovering her silky back and shoulders, which he kissed with extraordinary eagerness. Whilst he did, he began to follow with his hands the structure of her legs, her firm hips, her round and slender behind, turned golden in the light of the fireplace. His kisses all over her back caused her to writhe with desire. Devlin bit her from time to time and licked her when he so fancied, without leaving an inch of her body without pampering.

Then came the moment when the desire started to undermine his sanity. He would not resist much longer outside of her.

'Hold on tight,' he ordered her in a hoarse voice, pressing her hands against the bedhead bars.

Harmony obeyed while he opened up her legs with extreme delicacy. Afterwards, Devlin slowly penetrated in her wet cavity while he held hard onto her hips. The girl moaned in surprise and pleasure when she perceived the slow invasion of her core. She received the kisses he lavished upon her in the process and treasured each sensation, each sound, and each brush. She extended her head back, taken over by a strange spell, without missing a single detail of such exquisite incursion.

How she wished that moment would never end.

Once immersed inside her depths, Devlin began to move at a maddening rhythm. He was playing with her, torturing her with his slowness and captivating her with his sudden speed. He drew circles and long lines that ended up deep inside her body, harder and harder, deeper and deeper.

Harmony instinctively closed her eyes, enjoying that sweet plundering, with her hands holding tight onto the iron bars as if her life depended on it. She sighed when Devlin's hands began travelling compulsively up and down her whole body. Her breasts, her belly, and her perspiring thighs received her husband's expert attentions. And although she thought it absurd, she felt more beautiful than she had thought humanly possible.

Every time he moaned something in her ear, spurred by the passion, she melted like a liquid flame. She turned to steal a kiss each time, and he bit her shoulders or her throat, as he could not control himself. He had become obsessed with her hair, it seemed; he buried his face in it every time he had the chance, absorbed its perfume of rose water and rosemary, and ruffled or pulled at it softly.

It was a perfect dance, sensual and sensory; two bodies primordially connected, looking for each other for the second time, and in their search they had been blessed with the joy of encounter.

Devlin's hips were doing all the work while Harmony remained rigid, with her hands holding tight to the bedposts, to the point that her knuckles turned white.

After a few minutes, she had lost consciousness of her own voice, which was transformed into reckless screams of pleasure, her ears filling with the wild creaking of the bed and the animal growls of Devlin, who repeated her name in an insane litany.

They ended up exhausted, with their sweaty hands glued to the bars of the headboard, as if that was their only hold on sanity.

Waldegrave was the first one to move away, his heart thumping in his chest. He took Harmony's languorous body and rested it on the untidy bed. Her face looked relaxed by the dim light of the room, her messy hair a dark fan atop the pillow. She looked like a nymph rescued from the water, or a mermaid sleeping on a rock.

Harmony fell into a deep sleep, and Devlin strove to clean her between her thighs with exquisite care. He used a sponge soaked in hot water from the tap, and afterwards a towel that he also used to clean himself.

Strangely enough, he enjoyed that act that he had never performed for any of his previous lovers, but he did not stop to ask himself why.

When he finished, he snuggled up to her. What did it matter now? He had already gone too far.

Chapter 9

Harmony found out that Devlin's bed was more comfortable than hers, but she felt too lazy to ponder that thought. She simply felt a jab of capricious envy and sleepily tossed and turned between the blankets.

She stretched her arm to hold onto the bodily warmth her husband had left behind before getting up for his usual morning walk, and discovered that the sheets were cold, and that meant he had left hours ago. She pouted, disappointed. She didn't know what the clock said, but she was convinced it was later than she had ever woken up since her arrival at Waldegrave Terrace. Her belly growled and that persuaded her to jump out of the bed.

And then, she heard the rattling of a carriage approaching the main entrance to the mansion. Intrigued, she got up and peeked through the window, its panes slightly steamed-up due to the recent blizzard; she prayed it wasn't her aunt and uncle again, demanding crumbs of attention. A few days back, she had received an absurd letter written by her uncle where he asked about her new life as a married woman, her health and all kinds of nonsense, or that was what he was trying to make her believe. Harmony had chosen to ignore it, convinced that he was only faking it.

When she managed to glimpse a small cabriolet climbing energetically up the hill, Harmony ruled out the intrusion of her previous legal tutors. It was too ostentatious a vehicle, drawn by a pair of jet black horses, which for sure must have been part of the fleet of carriages of a distinguished nobleman. She noticed that on the side there was a majestic crest, a 'C' prominently displayed in its centre.

Before the cart had stopped completely, the door of the cabriolet opened with a loud bang, then a woman stormed out of it like a whirlwind, stumbled on the snow that had not been swept away yet, and rushed like a runaway horse to the door. Harmony followed her with her eyes wide in horror, until she disappeared from her visual field. What she heard next was a series of knocks on the door and an avalanche of incomprehensible shouting. Promptly, she wrapped herself on her négligée and prepared to go downstairs to find out the identity of that woman and what she was trying to achieve creating such a ruckus. She felt a sudden attack of worry; perhaps it was a neighbour or an acquaintance of the family who was in trouble. Whoever it was, Harmony hoped they would be able to do something to help her.

She leaped out and rushed down the two floors, but she paused before proceeding to the main floor, obeying a sudden fit of caution. From the top of the stairs she was able to survey, astonished, what was taking place in the front hall. Limsey had allowed the stranger in: a young blonde lady wearing a warm winter dress that covered her throat. The woman brought in with her a halo of insanity that gave Harmony goose bumps.

Her beautiful façade contrasted woefully with her dreadful manners, with her coarse speech, with the crazy and furious way in which she kept glancing around her, as if she were a dangerous wild beast just freed from her cage. Harmony realised that the woman was clenching her fists so hard that she wondered if the palms of her hands would end up all bloodied and pierced by her own fingernails.

The stranger was behaving like a tornado, sweeping everything in her wake, with an air of authority that made Harmony roll her eyes. She didn't need any more clues to understand that the woman had been there before and was familiar with every single object and every nook and cranny of the mansion. Perhaps she had lived in Waldegrave Terrace at some point, Harmony thought with unease.

'My Lady, His Grace, the duke, has gone for his usual constitutional...,' the butler was telling her in his usual reverential tone, although perhaps a bit softened.

'I couldn't care less if he is riding the very same Victoria Regina!' she was screaming like a banshee. 'Send for him, Limsey! Tell him I'm here. If he doesn't come here to face me, I swear to God that I'll set fire to his damn Waldegrave Terrace.'

The butler's expression was one of worry and astonishment, when it should have been one of horror in view of that threat.

'My Goodness, Lady Colvile, you don't need to use such a language, My Lady.'

'How dare you, you old buffoon? Shut your mouth and go fetch Waldegrave!'

Lady Colvile! Harmony thought in horror. She was the woman who had tried to kill herself over him. His ex-lover. And she was there, in Waldegrave Terrace, making a scene and demanding to see her husband.

'Forgive me, please.' Strangely enough, the butler's words didn't suggest servility but a great skill, as if he knew perfectly well how to deal with such a difficult lady. 'I'll send somebody to fetch the duke.'

As soon as Limsey turned around to do his duty, one of the doors of the main entrance opened. Devlin appeared on the lintel, looking ruffled as he normally did on his return from one of his walks, an inscrutable look on his face.

As soon as she saw him, Lady Colvile shifted from her aggressive stance. A triumphant smile bloomed on her beautiful face, causing Harmony's guts to knot.

'Devlin.'

'Laurel.'

'You look well,' she said, after kissing him, her lips lingeringly on each cheek.

'I saw your carriage from the hill. To what do we owe this noisy surprise?'

'What's the matter?' she said laughing bitterly. 'Aren't you happy to see me? Are you not going to wish me a Happy New Year?'

'No offense, but for a while now your presence has been causing me a certain unease.' Devlin's tone remained unperturbed.

'I can see that you are still mad at me. It doesn't matter. I know you will forgive me anyway. You always do, don't you?'

'Laurel, can I help you with anything?'

'In fact you can. You could clear out a matter that has made me feel ill since yesterday. I heard a terrible rumour as soon as I returned to the city, and I have come so you can refute it.'

'Seriously? And what's that terrible thing they are saying about me?'

'That you got married, and to a sad nobody!' She laughed again, this time evidencing a sinister sense of humour. Harmony swallowed. Was that truly what they were saying? She did not manage to quieten down the violent beating inside her heart. 'That she is the daughter of a horse dealer or something like that and that you are hiding her here, God knows why.'

Devlin's expression turned contrite. He gazed at her with evident patience, crossing his arms. Harmony held her breath, waiting for his reply.

'So now I am a monster that imprisons women in his castle,' he grumbled, but he didn't look upset or offended. 'The people from London must be bored to sickness.'

141

'Is it a lie, then?'

'No woman gets here against her will.'

'You know perfectly well what I am asking you, Devlin. Stop playing with me. Are you married? Have you brought one of your wenches to live here in Waldegrave Terrace?'

'Best if you keep your composure, Laurel,' he warned her, calmly. 'You know well how your tantrums end up like.'

'This one will end up worse if you don't tell me the truth.'

'Damn you! What do you want me to tell you? Why do you feel entitled to come here to ask me questions——?'

'Damn you, Devlin Sawyer! How dare you question me? How can you still harbour doubts? All these years I've done nothing but wait for you while I see you parade with a gang of whores. When I see that you are tired of one, not a day goes by before you fancy another one just as odious.'

Harmony wanted to glue her ears shut to stop listening to the woman's desperate words, and whatever Devlin had to tell her. Lady Colvile loved him; in her morbid way, but she did, and that truth was unbearable to hear. She thought it best to get away from there, making the most of not having been seen but, darned her luck, just then she gave herself away, unwittingly. When she stepped back to return to her bedroom, her foot got tangled up on her nightgown and made her stumble. She held tight onto the stairs' marble balustrade, and that at least prevented her from tumbling onto the floor, but her wail was heard by Devlin and Lady Colvile. Both looked up and found her standing there.

The woman stepped forward, no doubt to be able to mercilessly judge Harmony. Her half-closed blue eyes, full of wild surprise and scepticism, made Harmony shudder, and she straightened up as much as she could, despite her tremor, because right then she realised she was scared of the other woman. Something was clamouring inside of her suggesting that Lady Colvile, a woman capable of trying to take her own life, was dangerous to a worrying extent.

She glimpsed at Devlin, looking to him for help, but he did not seem happy with her sudden appearance. Quite the opposite. She noticed he was angry. Angry at her?

'It can't be,' the blonde woman looked at her from head to toe, her contempt mixed with amusement, but she never managed to look her in the eye. She then fixed her gaze on the gold ring Harmony was wearing on the middle finger of her right hand, which was clutching the balustrade.

Laurel burst out laughing in a macabre-sounding way, like a fairy tale witch that had created the perfect spell. Her reaction surprised Harmony, who was expecting anything but that. The woman laughed for a long time, to the point that her knees began to buckle.

'Laurel...' Devlin grabbed her by the elbows, without managing to quieten down the malefic laughter that was beginning to choke inside his ex-lover's throat. 'Laurel...'

'It isn't true,' she said, without pausing her laughter, her voice transfigured. 'It can't be true. She is not... She is not... It does not... No, this must be a joke!'

'Leave!' said Devlin with a wave, furious, this time addressing Harmony. His eyes transmitted a sense of urgency. 'Get out of here.'

She was too shocked to move, though, partly because of her husband's extreme indulgence towards the odious woman. Why didn't he kick her out once and for all? Didn't he realise that she was deriding his wife? Hadn't he noticed that she thought she was an inferior creature and was being disrespectful towards her with that mocking and outrageous laughter of hers?

For no evident reason, Lady Colvile's amusement transformed into ear-splitting crying. The woman began to shake her head and prance about furiously while Devlin held her by the arms from behind. Her screams were heart-breaking, enraged, and her eyes seemed as if they were trying to pierce into Harmony's body, like sharpened daggers.

Harmony watched Lady Colvile and could not help but feel horrified by this awful scene, but not as much as by Devlin's weird attitude. His forehead was now resting on the nape of Lady Colvile's neck as his arms encircled her waist.

She thought he was whispering calming words in her ear—or where they loving words?—while the woman raised her head directing a lethal and twisted look at her as her screams made her ears bleed.

Harmony returned to her bedroom after Limsey and one of the maids had helped Devlin control the volatile Lady Colvile. Now she was walking up and down her room, feeling empty of hunger, thirst, peace, and the scrap of happiness she had hardly had a chance to enjoy earlier.

She didn't know what had happened to her husband and the scandalous woman, but twenty minutes later she was dying to go back downstairs. What should a wife do at a time like this? she wondered, dejected. Should she go down there and claim him? Should she send Lady Colvile back home? She was sure that was the thing to do, although...

The door opened with a slight noise, but it sufficed to make her jump anyway. Mary entered, a laundry basket held against her hip and a distressed look in her eyes that suggested sympathy. Or was it pity?

'Mary, what is happening down there?' she asked but the maid averted her eyes. She tried to talk but nothing coherent came out of her mouth; perhaps they had ordered her to keep quiet. 'Where are my husband and Lady Colvile?' she insisted.

'They are sitting at the breakfast table, My Lady,' she said.

'What? And why didn't anybody come to tell me about it? Why is he having breakfast with her and not with me?'

The girl shrugged, piteously.

'The duke asked Mr Limsey not to be disturbed, My Lady.'

Harmony didn't want to hear any further warnings. She asked the maid to help her do her hair and dressed with the first thing she found in her closet. Then, she got ready to go downstairs immediately to settle things with her husband.

Why was Devlin doing that to her? Why was he excluding her from her own home and giving so much importance to that woman? What kind of hold did Lady Colvile have over him?

While she rushed downstairs, she was certain everything would end up badly, that her intrusion would turn the duke's stomach, but if she stayed in her room, pretending that the presence of that woman didn't hurt her, if she allowed him such affront, she would end up getting ill. After the previous night, for better or for worse, she felt more bound to him than ever. God help her, but she felt she had rights over him.

On the way, she bumped into the butler, who tried to talk to her and even chased after her down the gallery, but Harmony turned a deaf ear to his words and slipped nimbly away. She strode determinedly towards the place where she knew she'd meet her husband. She opened the double doors of the breakfast room noisily. The scene that welcomed her made her heart ache. Devlin was sitting at the table and Lady Colville occupied a seat very close to him, the same one that would correspond to the lady of the house, where Harmony had sat during their first conversations as husband and wife. The same place where she had looked at him enraptured; the same spot where she had begun to feel like the lady of the house. And now it was taken up by that woman who had mocked her, who had looked at her with disgust.

Waldegrave was holding a teapot and pouring water in the cup of his guest, while she observed the steaming liquid with an empty gaze, her eyes puffy from crying. Lady Colvile was in a curled position, her hands resting under the table. Her harmless appearance surprised Harmony, until the woman looked up and noticed her standing there shaking with jealousy and despair.

Then, Lady Colvile's face revealed her hatred.

On seeing Harmony, Devlin frowned, evidently irritated. He looked at his wife as if she were a trespasser that had slipped into his property. 'What are you doing here?' he mumbled as he dropped the teapot on the table with a loud clink of the porcelain. 'I ordered them to bring you breakfast to your room.'

'They didn't,' she replied with a forced smile, so much so that it felt like a wince.

She walked through the room, feeling as if she was moving through quicksand, and pulled back another chair to sit on, before the astonished Limsey had a chance to do it for her.

Waldegrave puffed angrily, but abstained himself from saying anything, or at least didn't find a valid reason to throw her out of his precious dining room. He looked at Lady Colvile, who had followed her rival's movements like a viper watching a mouse. Now that she looked at her up close, Harmony was more aware of her beauty, of her porcelain complexion reddened by the tears and her fury, of the purple bags under her blue bloodshot eyes, and of her blonde hair that remained beautiful even when messed up.

After a few agonising seconds, Harmony realised that Waldegrave had not introduced them and that only increased her uneasiness. Good grief! How small did he made her feel! A servant brought her something she could not identify. She had not come down to eat, but to make her presence felt, to ensure that woman knew Devlin was married and that, if she was looking for him to rekindle the romantic relationship with her, she would find a wife not ready to give him up.

'Right now, the people of the city imagine that, at least, although perhaps lacking in name or fortune, you must be a stunning beauty,' said Lady Colvile in a gravelly voice.

The words fell on Harmony like a bucket of frozen water, and her eyes travelled sharply from her untouched plate to the other woman.

'I can't wait for them to meet you and be totally disappointed,' added Lady Colvile bitterly.

'Laurel...' Devlin cut in weakly.

'Did you perhaps use a blindfold or simply jumped on him like a crow in the dark?' She carried on, regardless.

Harmony felt like dying when confronted by the furious accusation, because it evidenced that Devlin had talked to Lady Colvile about the garden at Felton House.

'A coarse and desperate method that was, but for your good luck it worked, didn't it? You knew that such an honourable man would accept the marriage as an appropriate solution,' Lady Colvile went on and curiously, without looking her in the eye. 'But, how long will you retain next to you a husband you have trapped with tricks, stupid girl? You are not pretty, and you already know that. You don't know him, and I doubt you are intelligent enough for that.' She tilted her head, pretending to feel pity. 'Poor girl. Let me tell you that you are condemned to be one of those disposable women we all hear about, destined for the role of breeding mares.'

'Laurel...'

The blonde leaned forward and, rather than paying heed to Devlin's weak warnings, carried on spitting venom at Harmony.

'That, of course, can only happen if he has the stomach to fuck you...' Lady Colvile was gesturing energetically now, and a vein seemed about to burst in her temple. 'A drunk or spurned man takes anything, the first thing he is offered, but a sober man is not so well disposed. Sometimes he might need the cover of darkness to perform such an act. And I bet that, with you, there will be no twilight allowed...'

A painful silence fell over the room, to the point that even Limsey, who remained standing near the table, lowered his head in a hint of pity. Harmony had not noticed she'd been crying until a tear tumbled down her chin and landed on her hand that was closed in a shaky fist, even though it would never hit anything. The rage she felt was extinguished by a wave of humiliation that engulfed her then, leaving her totally defenceless.

In the past, she had possessed a quick tongue that she had used to answer back to anybody who challenged her: her uncle John, Aunt Minnie, Miss Andersen, and even Waldegrave himself... but Lady Colvile's attack had left her speechless, had deprived her of all her strength, of any ability to defend herself, and that was why she had hit her where it hurt the most. She had discovered a new suffering, her Achilles heel. Harmony had never been bothered about not being pretty and refined, but now she understood that in the world of those kinds of people, beauty was an acceptable consolation if you did not own a title or an important fortune. She did not possess any of those three things, and therefore she was at the mercy of a society that disqualified those who did not fulfil their expectations. And the worst thing about it was that she had discovered that now she minded the fact that she was not beautiful. For heaven's sake! How she minded!

She turned to look at Devlin, but he was immersed in a strange mutism as if he was unable to find an argument to refute what Lady Colvile had said. My God, he was of the same opinion as she was! He had already told her. He had touched her that night in the garden of Felton House because he was drunk, and now that he wasn't, he had no reason to keep doing it. Unless she jumped on him in the dark.

Harmony could not find a reason to remain there a second longer. She stood up with a lethargy that kept gaining intensity as she left the dining hall and moved away as fast as her legs would carry her. Much worse than Lady Colvile's terrible insults, Harmony was hurt by Devlin's complicit silence; she was hurt by his indifference, and by the discovery that she mattered so little to him.

Why hadn't he defended her? Why hadn't he made that harpy shut up? Why did he appear to be defending that woman instead, when his wife was being morally battered in the cruelest possible way? Harmony wondered all that as she cried in her bedroom now, her face buried in the pillow.

All the admiration and respect that had been growing inside her for him had collapsed the instant he decided to keep quiet before his ex-lover's threats. Lady Colvile had caused her the biggest humiliation of her whole life, had reminded her that she was a thing of no importance and fell short of her husband, and he had not dared contradict her. Harmony was sure he had kept out of it because he thought the blonde woman was right. Waldegrave had stopped seeking her at night because he felt no desire for her, and if what Lady Colvile had said about men was true, the previous night he had given in to making love to her only because Harmony had offered herself to him in the darkness, like a whore, and he had simply taken what was being offered.

A colossal fury took hold of her. She punched her other pillow, wishing she could be less fragile, less stupid; wishing to be able to get rid of the feelings that began to develop within and to be again the same girl who had confronted her aunt and uncle in the past, the creepy Andrew Curson, and anybody else who'd ever wanted to take advantage of her. If only she had managed to gather the courage to scream in that woman's face, to tell her that she was a pusillanimous suicidal woman and that although Harmony might not have many qualities, she had something she lacked: dignity, self-respect, beautiful dreams, and a zest for life. She was not wondering around crying for another woman's husband, making a show of herself, and evoking people's pity.

She wished she could have told her all that to her face and smiled like a villainess.

She picked up the object closest to her, a brush with an ebony handle, and hurled it against a full-length mirror. It luckily hit the frame, which ended up with a dent. A mighty tension in her head began to grow with the threat of a migraine.

Later on, Mary brought her some smelling salts—as Harmony's migraine had only grown in the meantime—and a cup of tea as she had declined any food, but the drink wound up getting cold in the teapot. Harmony kept crying and crying, sometimes feeling rage, others self-pity. And sometimes she did it because she felt certain her marriage had collapsed even before it had taken shape.

'Don't cry any more, My Lady,' her faithful maid told her. 'That woman has the devil inside. Or that's what the cook says, and she's known her since that woman was a child.'

'Mary... does she and my husband—?'

The girl swallowed hard before replying, 'I don't know, My Lady.'

Harmony did not believe her. People said that Lady Colvile was his lover; that she had tried to cut her throat because of him. Her presence there and the intimate way they treated each other—full of familiarity—had confirmed it. She wouldn't be surprised if they resumed their relationship soon.

Why was she surprised? Why was she hurt? Powerful men did this. Even married men had women everywhere and nobody dared question them. The reason why they got married, in the first place, was to follow the dictates of good manners. Once they had complied with the required formalities, Waldegrave had no further moral commitment towards her. If she had thought he would behave lovingly towards her, she was very wrong. The best thing to do was to understand it once and for all.

At nightfall, there was a knock on her bedroom door. Harmony jumped up, believing it was her husband coming to offer her the explanation she deserved, but disillusionment slapped her on the face. Devlin didn't knock on the door, she chided herself. He simply walked in whenever he felt like it. It was the butler, that disagreeable and stuffy man, who had surely come to torture her even more.

Once Harmony had given him permission to come in, Limsey walked in quietly, no doubt maintaining a rigid posture. She refused to look at him. She didn't want him to see her face haggard and puffy from her persistent crying.

'I was wondering if Your Grace needed anything.'

Harmony forgot her decision and raised her eyes, surprised. It was the first time he had addressed her with the courtesy she deserved as the wife of a duke. She looked at him awkwardly and slightly suspicious. She noticed that the hatred she had assumed he felt towards her had disappeared from his blue eyes and now his face sported a genuinely kind expression.

'I... no,' she stammered. 'Is that woman still here?'

'Lady Colvile is in the mansion,' he replied with a hint of sorrow. 'The duke has sent a maid to look after her.'

'Incredible,' she shook her head, indignant and hurt, 'Limsey, you know that woman is evil. You have seen her; she has even insulted you. Why does everybody treat her with such regard?'

Limsey stiffened up before replying solemnly, 'I have served this family for over forty years, Your Grace, but it does not matter that I have been here longer than some of the family members or the furniture. I don't belong to it. My job here does not consist of feeling affection or misgivings towards any of them, or towards those who surround them and act in consequence. I am here to serve.'

Harmony was fully aware of that. That was why he had been so polite towards her, despite that hint of disapproval on his face that not even all of the world's training could conceal. It was clear that Limsey had felt sorry for her after Lady Colvile had showered her with such a tirade of insults, and that had made her deserving of the butler's empathy. After all, he had also suffered her abuse, even if he did it with stoicism, protected by his pompous professionalism.

'And what about my husband?'

'I cannot talk on behalf of the duke beyond offering my humble opinion. And I only would dare to say that his compassion often exceeds the worthiness of those who are in receipt of it.'

'Compassion?' Harmony stood up at once. 'Why should he feel compassion for her? She behaves as if she owns Waldegrave Terrace when she does not; she is rude and hysterical. She has insulted me, and I don't even know her.'

'It is not my place to comment on such subjects, My Lady.' He lowered his head.

'Oh, you are right, Limsey. I apologise. I should not have put you in a difficult position by asking you such questions. You are not the one who should answer them.'

'I beg you not to get desperate. There will be a time to settle all your doubts, Your Grace. Patience... and above all, keep strong.'

The man handed her a handkerchief he had retrieved from a drawer on the bedside table. Harmony accepted it, grateful. She offered him a sad smile as she dried an indiscrete tear she had not felt rolling down her cheek.

''Your Grace'... You had never addressed me that way before, Limsey. Perhaps I have finally earned it?' she asked sharply.

Limsey looked at her with a serious expression and, emphasising each word, told her: 'There is only a duchess here, and that is you.'

149

Harmony stared at him without blinking. He had given her a clear message. But, would she be courageous enough to adopt her role? Would she dare to start behaving like a duchess?

A loud scream, which came from not too far way, made her jump. She exchanged a horrified look with Limsey, and they both left the room to find out what was happening. Harmony saw Katty, one of the maids, leaving one of the rooms at the back. The girl, who could not have been over sixteen years old, was weeping and rubbing her face hard.

'What's happening, Katty?' she asked, alarmed.

'She hit me,' she whimpered, constantly rubbing her cheek with the palm of her hand. 'I was combing her hair, and I brushed that wound on her neck accidentally. She hit me and told me that if I did it again, she would stab me in the face with the scissors.'

Harmony felt her blood boil. Bloody woman. It seemed that Lady Colvile's fury made no distinctions. She spread it evenly with the most disturbing impunity. She examined Katty's bruised cheek. One of the mad woman's fingernails had caused a slight cut on the poor girl's cheekbone. This had to end.

She turned to look at Limsey, who appeared sad. His eyes shone with a sorrow that, of course, he could not voice out loud. He simply observed his lady expectantly. No. It was more of a challenging look. She swallowed hard and stuck out her chest. 'Go to get that injury looked at and go back to your room afterwards,' she told the girl, who looked at her with her eyes wide open. 'You don't have to look after that woman any longer.'

'But the duke—'

'It doesn't matter what the duke says, Katty. I order you to go back to your room and not to do anything for Lady Colvile, not even bring her a glass of water. Have I made myself clear?'

She nodded and scurried downstairs like a scared mouse.

'Where is that incompetent little whore hiding?'

Harmony squinted when she saw the detested Lady Colvile, dressed in a nightgown with her blond locks down, appear striding furiously down the corridor. She seemed surprised to see her and stopped at a prudential distance, glaring at her again, her eyes full of contempt.

'You don't deserve to be looked after by any of the members of staff in this house,' Harmony rebuked her. 'Are you not happy having spewed out insults left, right and centre and behaved like a crazy woman? Now you dare hit one of my maids too? You should be grateful we have offered you shelter here—'

'How dare you talk to me like that, little bug?'

'I am the Duchess of Waldegrave, like it or not.'

'Don't get too comfortable with that borrowed title.'

'Don't you get used to turning up here every time you fancy making a spectacle of yourself. Next time, Limsey will shut the door on your face!' She noticed the aforementioned, who stood next to her, lower his head to hide a smile and she added, 'And I'll be watching you from now on. It's time to stop with the poor-me act, Lady Colvile.'

'I see you've taken to your role. It will make it all the funnier when I see you leave this house with your head down, your ugly defeated mug and your broken dreams. I know you won't last long, whatever your name is. I've seen women come and go into Devlin's life, but I'm the only one who remains, do you hear me? It's always been like that and things won't change for you, who has all the attractiveness of a rotten egg.'

Harmony breathed in deeply, forcing herself to keep her composure. She shouldn't care if Lady Colvile was right or not, she only needed to put her in her place, to stop her from believing that she had the right to offend and assault everybody. 'I pray you go back to the chamber we have so kindly offered you to spend the night. Nobody will come to help you.'

The woman laughed out loud. 'I won't stay in any guest room. Waldegrave is waiting for me in his bedroom.'

Harmony swallowed hard to get rid of the lump that had formed in her throat. Her sudden courage began to crumble and the blonde woman took advantage of it.

'Don't be surprised. He's asked me to accompany him tonight. He feels quite lonely; his bed has not been properly warmed up.'

'Stop telling lies...'

Lady Colvile tutted. 'What? Don't you believe me? Little girl, for aristocrats it is perfectly normal, isn't it, Limsey?' She addressed the butler in a casual tone. 'How many women paraded by the bedroom door of the previous Duke of Waldegrave while the duchess, pregnant, snivelled? One hundred and two? They've even heard about it on the other side of the pond!' She laughed. 'They need somebody to warm their beds, either because the woman by their side is indisposed, or because she is too repugnant to contemplate upon. Didn't you know?'

Harmony had been knocked out and felt so disgusted that she thought she might be sick all over the floor.

'Oh, dear, you love him... It seems that your tiny little heart will suffer when he tramples all over it. You should have thought about that before hurling yourself at him at Felton House. He told me he was so drunk that he could have jumped a goat and not been any the wiser.'

'Enough!' she shouted, incapable of listening to her any longer.

'Don't blame me if you don't know how to treat a man. He needs release, and as you don't know how to satisfy him, he has asked me to help him with that, and if it's not me, it will be somebody else, have no doubt about that!'

'Get out of here! Leave this minute! I don't care if it's snowing!' she was screaming like a banshee while Limsey tried to hold her back.

Lady Colvile looked at her with a self-satisfied smile. She had managed to make her lose her cool and behave as her rival had done to begin with: like a mad woman.

Devlin appeared around the stairway bend right that moment. He was wearing his sleeves rolled up, no cravat or stiff collar, and his dark grey waistcoat was crumpled. His appearance, together with his loose and unkempt hair, gave him a strange look. Harmony also noticed that he had bags under his eyes and his boots were wet. Had he been out, perhaps?

The duke stood between the two women and pierced them with his eyes as he demanded an explanation.

'Your wife is throwing me out of here,' Lady Colvile stated, seemingly distressed. 'She has asked me to leave in this infernal weather. Limsey can confirm it!'

He turned to look at her angrily. 'I beg you to show some understanding,' he mumbled.

Understanding? What did he want her to understand? That he missed his lover and had decided to bring her to live in the house he shared with his wife? 'But...'

'We'll talk later. Go to your room,' that was all he told her. Then he addressed the butler. 'Limsey, I don't know what the hell you're doing here. I've been looking for you for a long while.'

'Yes... I beg your forgiveness, Your Grace. How can I be of service?'

'I no longer have need of you. Your work is done for today. You can retire.'

The man threw Harmony a sympathetic look. After wishing good night to all those present and bowing subserviently, although nobody paid him any heed, he stepped away, his gait refined and quiet as usual.

'Laurel, go back to your room, for God's sake,' Devlin told the blonde woman, whose gaze went from one to the other, as if she was deciding if she should do as he asked or stay and keep up the fight.

'Remember what I've told you,' she muttered, piercing Harmony with her stare. Then, she disappeared down the corridor, towards the bedroom she had been assigned.

Harmony kept looking at her, her fists clenched, while the woman walked ceremoniously, as if she were the Lady of Waldegrave Terrace.

'Can you tell me who the hell that woman is and why she believes she has the right to turn this house on its head?'

'Not now,' he said, in a tired tone, moving away.

'Not now? When then?' Harmony grabbed his sleeve to prevent him from leaving without answering her questions.

'Have you lost your mind?' He roared, pulling away from her rude hold. 'I am exhausted, Harmony. We'll talk tomorrow. Go to sleep.'

'No, I won't go to sleep until you tell me what's happening. When will that woman leave? Why did you bring her here?'

'I didn't bring her here!' he shouted, his eyes popping out with rage.

'She says you invited her to your bed, that you miss her and...'

'Damn it! Are you going to start like Laurel?' he howled and she looked back at him indignantly. 'Use your common sense!' he added.

'Your Grace...' One of the grooms, a young man, had approached without either of them noticing. His expression was one of extreme discomfort at having to witness an argument between the owners of the house, but it seemed that the matter that had brought him there was so important that it merited the interruption.

'What's the matter, Peter?'

'Your Grace, the man is ready to leave. He is waiting for the first instalment of his payment,' the boy whispered, looking meekly at the floor, perhaps to remedy his intromission.

Devlin nodded. 'It's all right. You can retire now. I'll take care of it.'

'What man...?' Harmony asked, but the duke was already on his way to the stairs. 'Devlin, what man——?'

'Stop being a nuisance!' he warned her, furious, pointing at her with his index finger. 'I won't repeat it again. Go back to your bedroom or I'll have to put you there under lock and chain. And perhaps tomorrow, when you've come back to your senses, we can talk.'

A tear had started to roll down her cheek, but she rushed to remove it with a sweep of her hand, so he would not see it. She did not recognise him, or perhaps she had forgotten he could be like that: a despot and a hostile man. 'That's what you're really like——'

'I haven't pretended to be what I am not. What you see is what you get.'

Having said that, he walked away, following the groom, while Harmony stayed alone in the corridor, going over his and Lady Colvile's words.

'You love him,' she had said, mocking her, after sowing the seeds of uncertainty in the mind and heart of her victim. She had read her hurt, had sniffed at her desperation and her fear of losing him, even though Harmony had not been aware that was what she was silently declaring. And she was horrified to have to admit the evil viper was right.

All that night she didn't manage to rest for longer than two undisrupted hours. All kind of horrifying scenes populated her dreams. Lady Colvile naked, slipping into Devlin's room, and moaning sensually as she walked through the door. Afterwards, she saw in her dream the same woman, sneaking into Harmony's room carrying a pair of scissors in her hand. That had caused her to wake up agitated and with a muddled head.

At that point she left the bed and went straight for the door communicating the two bedrooms. She wasn't sure what she was going to tell him. Perhaps the truth: that she was afraid, that she did not want to lose him, that she wished to trust in him, but only if he agreed to explain to her what was happening. She found the door locked, and she felt terribly disappointed. Then, she decided to go to the corridor and try her luck with the door that led to his bedroom from there.

Once in the dark and deserted corridor, she glimpsed a movement at the end, by the bedroom door of that harpy, Colvile. She ran to hide behind one of the columns, prepared to face her if the awful woman dared to try to enter her husband's bedroom, as she had threatened. But the surprise she experienced felt like a sharp dagger to her entrails. It was Devlin. Devlin, her husband, was leaving that woman's bedroom to return to his own.

Chapter 10

In the morning, she was feeling so bad that she thought she was ill. She doubted she could manage to survive another day like that, putting up with the presence and the insults of her husband's lover, who remained in Waldegrave Terrace according to what Mary and Prudence had told her.

She thought about leaving the mansion, going for good, but she did not have anywhere to go, and she'd rather jump into the freezing waters of the Thames than go back to Uncle John's place. Besides, Devlin would not take long to find her and return her to his castle, his golden cage, where he kept her away from the preying eyes of his peers and of society to make everybody believe their marriage was totally proper.

When her thoughts were starting to stray into those paths, the clatter from the wheels of a carriage echoed climbing up the hill towards the property. Harmony ran to the window to see the vehicle coming from a distance, and waited to see who it was. She hoped it wouldn't be another pretty and mad woman coming to brag about keeping her husband entertained.

The carriage, without a crest or a coat of arms on it to identify its origin, made slow progress along the road that was now cleared of snow. After a few minutes, a jet-black man dressed in a maroon tweed suit, climbed down from it. Harmony frowned; she had seen many people from the colonies, servants, workers at the market or the railway, but none dressed like that man. She was wondering who he might be, until a second visitor climbed out of the carriage behind him.

The gentleman removed his elegant hat, revealing his red-greying hair, and a well kempt moustache and beard. Harmony could not guess his age from her position, but he wasn't a young man, by any means. The visitor clutched the walking stick the other man had handed him—that she now realised was his footman—and looked thoughtful at Waldegrave Terrace.

Devlin came out to welcome him with a gentle handshake. After greeting each other with limited enthusiasm that was not lacking in tension, they exchanged a few words Harmony wished she could hear. She couldn't make out her husband's expression, as he had his back to her, but she could see the visitor's face who, despite the distance, expressed clear shame and dejection. She even saw him reach to his face with his right hand, saddened, while he listened to the duke's narrative. The latter, however, was patting him on the shoulder in a probable sign of leniency.

Then, both of them turned around and Harmony, afraid of being seen, crouched behind the curtain with a start. But they hadn't turned to look at her, as she realised later. Lady Colvile soon appeared in the scene, fighting against the dark skinned man, who had moved quickly to subdue her and deposit her inside the carriage. Soon, the woman's screams became audible. She started swearing, cursing the servants and then the duke, whose face Harmony could not make out.

She was accusing him of having called those men, of having handed her to them once again, and of having turned his back on her while she cried inconsolably. The red-haired gentleman was shaking his head. He was the vivid image of desperation and was offering her calming caresses that she rejected. Laurel shook her head and screamed, as if they had shown her a scorpion up close. 'I'll do it again, Devlin! I'll do it again, and I won't fail this time! And it will be all your fault!' she was shouting, her voice turned hoarse.

Harmony brought the palm of her hand to her mouth, and that made her realise she'd been crying too. She wasn't sure why. That woman was mad and had no qualms. Nobody in their right mind would behave that way. She hoped that man, whom she imagined must have been her father, could help her come to her senses.

In the end, they managed to have her sit in the carriage without any further struggle. Devlin said goodbye to the gentleman and offered him a few words that seemed to reassure him. The man rubbed his eyes with the back of his hand and patted the duke's back. Then, he and his footman entered the carriage as well, obviously ready to leave behind them that embarrassing episode.

Lady Colvile appeared behind the window, catching her unawares. She couldn't observe her expression in detail, but she felt the other woman's gaze fixed on her, and noticed the shine in her eyes due to the effect of the accumulation of tears in them. She did not make a celebratory gesture in respect of her pain, whatever it was, but to tell the truth, her warning had come true down to the last word:

They had closed the doors of Waldegrave Terrace on her face, and she had seen her being dragged out, but it did not cause her any pleasure.

When the carriage set off in the direction of the town centre with Laurel in it, Devlin experienced a huge relief. He finally exhaled the full stream of air he had been holding in for the last twenty-four hours. He had not had a bath, had not eaten properly, and he had slept even less with such a threatening presence at home.

The unexpected arrival of Lady Colvile and her violent ravings had affected him more than he would have imagined, and that was because he was afraid of what she could do in such a state, even more than on that fateful night after the New Year's ball when she had tried to take her own life.

Damn her! Why did she have to turn up now and in such a shameful state? The news of his marriage must have affected her badly enough to make her go back to her old ways. Devlin rubbed the nape of his neck with the palm of his hand, now aware of his physical aches and pains.

The erratic and tormented Laurel wasn't his problem. In truth, she had never been. The only thing he had tried to do, over the last few hours, was not to disturb her too much, to protect her from herself and to prevent her from doing something stupid again. That was why he had installed her so close to him and had gone to check on her every hour, worried that he might find her swimming in her own blood, with her neck broken, or hanging from the window with a blanket tied around her neck. The servants, visibly afraid, had refused to implement that task, and he had not had the courage to force anybody to do it, which was why he'd done it himself. Thank God it had all come to a satisfying end.

He went back to the mansion, where he bumped onto Limsey's worried face.

'Where is she?' he asked after a long sigh.

'In her chamber, Your Grace,' Limsey replied softly. 'The maid has told me she has not eaten anything since yesterday. There are corpses with a more lifelike appearance than hers, if I may add.'

Harmony. He wished he could have protected her from such a painful experience, but it hadn't been in his power. Damn Colvile, he had taken too long to come and pick up Laurel. The man he had paid had done a good job looking in every brothel and every gambling den in the city until he'd found him. If it hadn't been for Gresham, who had trustworthy connections in the underworld, Devlin would still be running around the city like an idiot trying to find him.

With the ugly matter now solved, he knew he had to go to find Harmony and offer her some explanation, although, deep down in his heart, he did not want to do it. He had never had to give explanations to anybody, but if that matter would end up becoming the trigger of future fights with her, he'd rather be honest about what had happened. Therefore, he strode with determination towards her room.

'Your Grace, excuse me, but I think you should see this, before you go upstairs,' Limsey said, holding out the tray with the letters. 'They arrived early today.'

'I'll check them out later.'

'I'm afraid I must insist, Your Grace.' With a grave expression, Limsey held the tray in front of his chest and bowed. He almost bumped his nose on it.

Devlin frowned but finally acquiesced. He started going through a thin bunch of letters, showing little interest. All of them were addressed to his wife. 'They are not for me,' he grumbled.

'Oh, yes! I forgot! This... I've been grossly negligent, Your Grace, and I apologise for it. I'm afraid I have accidentally spotted this...' he tapped with his index finger on a square piece of paper that was set apart from the envelopes, 'but they handed it like that... without an envelope. I suggest, My Lord, that you check it out immediately. I assure you that it is a matter of the utmost importance.'

Limsey didn't seem ashamed, but insisted that he have a look at the damned bit of paper. Devlin clicked his tongue and picked it up, without fully understanding the reason for such obstinacy, which only wasted more of his time. He didn't see any writing in the piece of paper and, impatient, turned it around to discover an image on the other side: a beautiful swan emerging from a blue lake. It had a blue ribbon on its neck and next to it one could glimpse a slightly hazy rosebush in bloom. The whole scene was contained within a frame of flowers, ivy, ribbons and all kinds of feminine kitsch. It was a card... A birthday card. Devlin felt his chest shake on reading the inscription below the drawing:

'Happy Birthday, Harmony.'

Was it her birthday? Damn it... he didn't know. She hadn't told him. He hadn't made any effort to check her file and keep track of it. It was her birthday, for pity's sake, and Devlin had missed it completely.

'Twelfth of January, a beautiful day to come into the world, don't you think, My Lord?' Limsey prodded him while he rocked on his heels, somewhat amused.

'My God,' he whispered. 'I had no idea. Did you know about it?'

'No, Your Grace. Of course not.'

He felt stupid for simply asking such a question. Of course nobody knew it, not even him, who was her husband. If he had bothered to make the effort to let her talk, to ask her questions... Oh, damn. It was her birthday and he'd done nothing but worry her. Right now she must be feeling devastated, when she should feel happy and be surrounded by love and affection.

He looked back at the card, signed by Esther Collins, one of her friends probably. He picked up the letters, imagining they must all have been sent with the same intention—to send her good tidings—and then put them away in the inside pocket of his jacket, before starting towards his wife's chamber.

'Eh, My Lord...'

Devlin, who had climbed two steps already, turned around, annoyed. 'What now, Limsey? Is it perhaps Victoria's Jubilee? What else have I missed?'

'Nothing else, My Lord, there is still plenty of time left for the Jubilee,' he said, his voice sarcastic and more than a little smug. 'If I may, I suggest you don't approach the duchess with empty hands. You don't want to disappoint her, do you?'

He then pointed at a bouquet of freshly cut white roses, surely straight from the mansion's greenhouse. Devlin realized the clever man had ordered to have them cut and delivered as soon as he had seen Harmony's birthday card. In moments such as those, Devlin truly appreciated having someone as good as Rupert Limsey at his service.

'Limsey, you old fox! You're a genius!' Devlin picked up the roses, and wearing a spontaneous smile, climbed the steps two at a time, determined to set things right.

Limsey smiled to himself as he patted his hair, his heart warming at the thought of his kind intervention. With his hands behind his back, and rocking again on his heels, he started humming a little ditty, convinced that very soon that hall would shake under the patter of a bunch of little kids' feet.

The door opened and closed slowly. Harmony didn't need to look in that direction to know Devlin was the one who had entered the chamber. She could feel his presence, which lit up any room, even more so than one of those incandescent carbon lights, or more than the sun itself when the windows were open wide. His scent of musk and the forcefulness of his gait on the carpet also betrayed him. She hated herself on experiencing a gust of pleasure.

In a few seconds she heard his brief greeting, but she refused to answer.

She remained seated on the window sill, on a long cushion. Her eyes rested on the London outline, on the sky that was blue and clear and slowly started to win its battle against the winter.

'Lady Colvile has gone,' he said, sidestepping her silence.

Then, her restless mind could no longer think of reasons to keep quiet. 'It will be a relief for the servants.' Her voice oozed sarcasm, pain and a trace of anger. 'There will be nobody to attack them. And I imagine I will be able to breathe easily too from now on.'

She heard him let out a long sigh, and she spied out of the corner of her eye how he shifted his weight from one foot to another, and then went back to his initial posture.

'Harmony, what happened has upset us all, but nobody could have prevented it.'

'Of course someone could have...' She turned around to tell him that he could have done it. He could have prevented Lady Colvile from breaking in a thousand pieces that incipient attempt at happiness that had bloomed between them, but she stopped on glancing at the scene she had in front of her eyes, which she would have never imagined possible. Devlin was holding a bouquet of white flowers and was offering them to her with a look that could well be described as remorseful.

Was she truly seeing that? Had he brought her roses?

'I'm sorry...' he stammered. 'Happy... happy birthday, Harmony.'

Her birthday. She had totally forgotten it. For the last few hours, she had not thought of anything else but the torture Lady Colvile's visit had been and the horrible vision of Devlin exiting her bedroom after a furtive tête-à-tête. It pained her to think that in other circumstances, she would have melted at his feet on seeing the beautiful present. But too much water had run under the bridge. The pain she was feeling could not be appeased by a bouquet of roses or a few words. Perhaps he hadn't even chosen them himself, she thought, with sorrow. He might not even regret what had happened.

She looked away from the gift, refusing to show any appreciation for it, as she had done with Worth's dress.

Evidently disappointed, Devlin left the flowers on the breakfast table. 'You asked me for an explanation. I've come to give it to you,' he said in a low voice.

She looked at him harshly. 'It is too late for that. You should have done it yesterday, not now, when that horrible woman has already achieved her goal.'

'What goal?'

Harmony stood up to confront him. If he was trying to act dumb, it was his problem. She had no qualms about listing the awful things she had caused, the trail of violence and destruction that harpy had left in her wake.

'Lady Colvile has turned this house upside down with her horrendous behaviour,' she spat out. 'She has offended Limsey, has wounded Katty on the face, and she has shouted at me that I am such a nobody that I don't deserve you as a husband, after accusing me of tricking you into making you marry me. And she's made it amply clear that you belong to her.'

'That is not true. She and I... Harmony—'

'You let her vilify me!'

Harmony didn't know what he had seen in her face, but his expression tensed up suddenly. He averted his gaze for a while, but then he turned to glue his eyes on hers. 'I thought you had realised—'

'The only thing I've realised is that you have not even a modicum of respect for your wife who, unfortunately, is I.' She gasped before carrying on. She tried to swallow her tears, but knew her efforts would be useless. 'Look, I don't aspire to your love, but at least you could respect the fact that I now hold your name and, if somebody offends me, they also offend your precious title. You allowed her to call me the most horrible things she could think of and your silence has served to remind me that you are of the same opinion.'

He raised his chin and said through clenched teeth, 'Is your self-confidence so fragile that you are disturbed by a few words? You must admit that you believe everything she has told you, Harmony. You must admit that you feel lowly, that you don't think you are worthy of the position you occupy by my side; it's the only thing that can explain why you are so discomfited by the delusions of a mad woman.'

'You promised me you would protect me, do you remember? It was the only thing I expected of you, but you can't even do that.'

'Damn it, Harmony. Laurel is crazy! Do you understand? Truly crazy! I am not being condescending with her. She is ill! Her mind does not work properly!'

'That is quite evident. But you are doing nothing but feeding her madness, giving her wings and humouring her to the detriment of everybody else, as if you could not allow yourself to contradict her, as if you feel remorseful on seeing her like that.'

His gaze darkened. 'Laurel has been under psychiatric care for years. In that time, she has hurt herself and those in her proximity. The only thing I did was to try to prevent her from doing something similar to what she did a year ago. Do you know what she did—?'

'Yes,' she interrupted him. 'She tried to kill herself before your eyes. The whole of London knows about it. And you must have done something terrible to provoke her to do it, mustn't you? What did you do to her, Devlin? Did you promise to marry her and didn't follow through? Were you unfaithful to her with that Anita? Is it your fault that she is so mad?'

'Shut up! You don't know what you're talking about!'

'I don't know anything about it because you never tell me anything. You have pushed me aside; you have excluded me from your life, while you have talked to her about us, about what happened at Felton House. You have more trust in a woman who should be locked up in a mental institution than you have in me, your wife.'

'Do I need to remind you of the circumstances of our marriage?' He almost spat out the words. 'We didn't get married to become confidants or make each other happy.'

'Of course, you married me to avoid your name being tarnished after what happened. You are always your first consideration, Waldegrave. You don't care if you have to trample all over other people. Your priority is to safeguard your interest and you don't care an iota about others. You don't care if you make me terribly unhappy.'

He couldn't find anything else to say from what she could tell. He clenched his fists and picked up the bunch of roses, the sad an inanimate witness to their argument. Furious, he hurled it at the door. The stems hit the wood and spread all around. The beautiful gift had ended up turned into a mess of leafs and petals.

He then proceeded to remove a bundle of papers from his jacket pocket and lay them down the table where the bouquet had been moments earlier. Harmony guessed they were birthday cards, and a tear streamed down her face. At least she would get the comfort of receiving the good wishes from the people who really loved her, the people who appreciated her for being who she was and would never hurt her like that man had done.

'We will leave tomorrow for Winchcombe,' he said through gritted teeth. 'Be ready to depart first thing tomorrow morning. We have waited long enough for the weather to improve. If we keep sitting here waiting for everything to be perfect we'll never make any progress.'

As soon as he'd said that, he left the room banging the door behind him.

Devlin walked down the corridor, away from Harmony's room, seething. She could never have guessed how difficult it had been for him to hand her that bunch of roses and wait on baited breath for her to accept it.

He couldn't remember the last time he had submitted to a woman's opinion. He hadn't even done it for Lady Lovelance, as their relationship had never gone that far, but with other women he had always been the one to assume the position of power. He was the one who chose his lovers, who made them wait, who decided when and where they would meet, how far they could go, and when the relationship was over. He was used to pull the strings around him, like a selfish and fickle god, and that was why what had just happened had thrown him off-kilter. Thinking that a nice gesture he had invested true affection in—something so uncommon and strange for Devlin Sawyer—had been rejected, tore him apart.

As he waited, like an idiot, for her to take the flowers, he had thought that a bouquet of roses was too little and felt sorry for not having visited the jewellery at Waldegrave Terrace; he could have brought her a pair of diamond earrings or a sapphire necklace.

Fear had followed his hesitation when she dared reject him. She had accused him of a load of nonsense, of being the cause of Laurel's madness even. Her allegations had hurt him and enraged him at the same time, and that made him feel angry at himself. Why had he allowed himself to be manipulated by a hysterical brat? Devlin didn't owe her any explanations, in the first place. She was supposed to abide by whatever he decided without complaint, but instead, she believed she had the right to question him, to openly accuse him. Harmony was turning into a problem incredibly quickly, and it was his fault.

He had to put a stop to the situation once and for all; he had to stop being weak with her. Perhaps he should find a lover to help him cancel any sexual attraction he might feel towards his wife, forget about her bed forever, stop watching her like an idiot while she read, and strengthen his plan of creating an unbridgeable chasm between the two.

If he had ever wavered on his determination to push her away from his side permanently, now he had even more reasons than before: He had to install her in Winchcombe and limit their communication to written correspondence only, as he once did with his mother, before things got worse for the two of them, especially for him.

Chapter 11

They started the journey under the pale light of the convalescent January sun. During the stretch by carriage, Harmony watched the icy and muddy streets of London go by until they reached the vicinity of Victoria Station. Throughout the ride, she behaved coldly, keeping further away from him than she had been from the beginning of that terrible mistake they called marriage. Devlin didn't do anything to break the silence that had settled between them either. He kept to himself his anxious and bitter thoughts. His unease remained buried deep in some remote compartment of his mind.

Harmony climbed onto the first class carriage of their train, worried that the long journey awaiting them in that narrow compartment would unleash a new argument but, to her surprise, Devlin didn't intend to travel in the same compartment with her. She spent the entire journey alone, unable to leaf through any of the books she had brought with her or even to sleep, while the train carried her to an uncertain destination.

Hours later, the trip ended. Her husband, looking particularly hostile, appeared at the door of the compartment and hurried her down.

Outside of the station, a coachman and a footman waited for them. They looked serious and bowed ceremoniously when the duke introduced her as his wife. The men looked after her luggage, and in a short time the horses were on their way to Sudeley Castle.

What Harmony saw through the window was a snowy valley, under a grey and opaque dome. The trees didn't have any attire other than a ton of frozen sawdust. In the distance appeared some honey-coloured stone cottages, almost totally buried under the snow, and a few cows on their way to the river. Farther away, she glimpsed the fences of some country houses, the silhouettes of stone buildings, the smoke from chimneys, a couple of factories, a church and a mill. To her eyes, Winchcombe looked like a typical English town, rural and industrial at once.

Sudeley Castle appeared a moment later, and it wasn't Devlin who pointed it out but her intuition. She held her breath on seeing the magnificent building dating from the times of Henry VIII. The stone mansion, Tudor style, took up a generous portion of Cotswolds land and was surrounded by white trees. From a distance, she appreciated the intricate structure of the castle, the long wings and the seemingly thousands of glass windows that shone under the pale rays of the sun at dusk.

The walls of Sudeley had been silent witnesses of the history of England. They had seen battles, plundering, exiles and torrid romances between members of the royalty. There was even a wing still in ruins after suffering the onslaught of the Civil War. It had also been the official and occasional residence of a large number of noblemen. The ancestors of Devlin, who held the title of Baron of Sudeley, had taken possession of the castle—which had belonged to countless owners through the centuries—to restore it, and had managed to improve on it over time. At least that was what Harmony had read in some of the books in the library.

In other circumstances, she would have felt happy and excited about living in such a place, but she could not help but see Sudeley as a huge prison.

The carriage entered the estate and followed a road bordered by trees until it came to a stop in front of the sumptuous main double door. An army of servants came out to greet their master in perfect formation. The women wore black dresses, white bonnets and aprons, and the men, black livery trimmed in green, and pristine white gloves. An older woman, wearing a sober grey dress with white collar and cuffs—the housekeeper, Harmony imagined—headed the retinue with an exemplary stance.

Harmony, who had not expected such a reception, hesitated before leaving the carriage. She stumbled slightly and if it had not been for the footman who helped her step down, she would have ended up on her knees on the snow. The young man caught her and helped her up. Her husband, on the other hand, only gave her a sinister look. That was, for sure, not the first impression a duchess should have given her servants.

Right then, a beautiful woman with a jubilant smile came out of the castle walking fast. Harmony only saw her profile, but she did not overlook her extraordinary beauty, her magnificent elegance, even though she was committing a serious breach of protocol, running as she held up her skirt with both hands. She wore her jet black hair up in a hairdo that was simple yet sophisticated, revealing a snow-white complexion, without spots or freckles.

Miss Andersen would have composed sonnets to celebrate the grace and beauty of this lady.

'Devlin!' she cried out as she ran down the entry steps.

Harmony was astonished. She had no inkling that anybody else, apart from the servants, lived at Sudeley. Her worry started gnawing at her when that same woman lunged at her husband, tightly embracing him.

'Son, it's good to have you finally here,' she muttered.

Son? That woman was his mother?

Had Waldegrave been such an idiot as not to mention the fact that his mother lived in Sudeley? Harmony took a step back; an uncontrollable thumping in her chest prevented her from hearing the low voice conversation that passed between them. She wondered what was going through his head; the woman was looking at him full of affection, while Devlin kept a circumspect and aloof posture, as if it was an inconvenience to be the recipient of such fuss.

Harmony swallowed hard, making an effort to keep her coolness despite such surprise. She had not expected to have a mother-in-law waiting for her at her new home, a woman she'd never heard about, a woman whose existence had been completely unknown to her until now. What type of woman would she be? Would she admit her into her family or would she reject her out of hand? What kind of mother-in-law awaited her?

It did not take the lady long to notice Harmony's presence. She turned to look at her, curious, tilting her head. Then, the girl noticed that her right eye was covered with an eye-patch, in the same blue-violet colour as her dress. 'Hello,' she greeted her with a smile that was both puzzled and amused.

'Hello,' Harmony replied in a stifled voice.

'Son, aren't you going to tell me who this young woman is?'

Devlin rolled his eyes, looking put upon and not even bothering to pretend otherwise. 'Mother, I introduce you to my wife, Harmony.'

A collective gasp was heard when the servants standing up in formation digested the news. The lady opened wide her only visible eye until it looked as if it was about to pop out of her face. Her astonishment disfigured her beautiful features.

As Harmony had started to suspect, the bastard had hidden from her his marriage. He had kept it a secret from his own mother, for crying out loud! For the first time, she wished to inflict physical pain upon him. She realised she was clenching tight her kid-gloved fists.

Devlin's mother held her breath. She looked at them in turn; first him, with incredulity and reproach, then her, with a serious inquisitorial look, but then she seemed to regain the composure demanded by her elevated social class. Harmony wondered if, in order to survive, she too would have to mutilate her capacity for surprise together with her will. The dowager duchess blinked repeatedly and smoothed her skirt, obviously trying to keep calm.

'You could have mentioned in your last letter that you had got married,' she admonished her son.

'I wasn't married at the time,' he whispered, not looking her in the eye. His expression reminded her of an icicle. 'Harmony, this is my mother, Corine.'

'My pleasure,' said his mother.

'The pleasure is all mine, Duchess.'

'No. You are the duchess now, I imagine,' she observed, with not a trace of resentment in her voice. She looked back at her son. 'How did this happen?'

'I'll satisfy your curiosity later on, if you don't mind. Right now, I'm exhausted.'

Devlin crossed the main door wearily, while the two women and the whole compliment of servants watched him go. Then, Harmony found herself face to face with Corine; she had to make an effort to keep looking her in the eye, not only because she was sure the woman would address her at any moment, but also because she felt a bit odd about watching somebody wearing an eye patch. It made her feel so uneasy that she would have rather follow her husband. However, her mother-in-law deserved a polite gesture after such rude behaviour, and as she would not get it from her son, it was her duty to behave courteously.

'If it is any consolation, I didn't know until today that Devlin had a mother,' she told her, as an apology.

Corine looked at her with interest. 'Don't worry; he isn't particularly talkative. I hope you like to talk more than he does, because we have a long chat ahead of us.' With that, Corine beckoned her in, then asked a maid to show Harmony to her bedroom.

Harmony was surprised on seeing the room she was given wasn't connected to her husband's like in Waldegrave Terrace. In fact, Devlin's chamber was at least eight doors away from hers, as the maid informed her, and although she tried to convince herself that she did not mind, the truth was that it broke her heart. It was as if the thickness of one wall wasn't enough, and he had decided to put seven more between them.

She thought about her mother-in-law, Corine, that beautiful woman of fragile appearance, and she felt certain empathy. She had come to believe that Devlin reserved his coldness just for her, but now it was clear that his mother seemed just as bitter about his attitude as she was. Why hadn't he told her he had got married? He had had enough time to send her a letter or a telegram. How could he be so discourteous?

Next morning, she met her at the breakfast lounge. She wasn't surprised on not seeing Devlin there. She was getting used to his absences, to his silences and to the fact that a chasm was opening between them. Harmony was sure that, as soon as he went back to the city, it would be the end of everything. She would remain there, buried next to the mother he didn't tolerate either, and perhaps that would be her home until he decided to replace her with another woman.

An old gentleman with grey hair and a neat beard sat with her mother-in-law, and he was sitting at the head of the table where she'd expected to see Devlin. She saw him as she walked in and was torn between curiosity and fear. Gradually, as she approached, she became more aware of his regal presence, of the patrician air surrounding him. He was an intimidating man at first sight, and not only due to his noble face and his refined tweed suit. He had his blue eyes half-opened in a wordless plea, and his lips, a bit cracked, formed a severe grin as he saw her approach with a hesitant gait. It was as if that gentleman was trying to decide if Harmony was worthy of his blessing or not, and judging by the harshness of his look, she could guess she had lost her battle.

'Good day,' she said.

The gentleman set down the cup of Minton porcelain on its dish and straightened up, but did not reply to the greeting.

'Good morning,' replied Corine, who was now wearing a white eye-patch, the same colour of her fine lace blouse. 'I hope you had a good rest.'

'Yes, yes. Thank you.'

The lady addressed the old man, speaking a few decibels more loudly. 'Dad, this is Harmony, Devlin's wife. Harmony, this is my father, Sir Malcolm Radley.'

It couldn't be true. So, Devlin's grandfather on his mother's side lived also in Sudeley.

'Oh, so that's her...' the man grumbled without taking his inexorable eyes off her. 'The clever girl who managed to catch my grandson. What an achievement...'

Harmony felt her legs would stop holding her in an upright position any moment now. The butler's disapproval was one thing, and the dislike of her husband's grandfather was a completely different one. She doubted that a man as intimidating as the one in front of her would change his opinion as Limsey had done.

'Dad...' Corine reprimanded him, her voice full of tension.

'What? She is clever!' Sir Malcolm insisted, in the tone of an adolescent becoming defensive on hearing his mother's warning. 'It's easier to catch an elephant with a slingshot than that slippery young man. In my time, I didn't put on such airs. I never had a title but was very handsome; at least that helped me cajole your mother, and a few others like her.'

'Dad!' Corine admonished him once more.

'But Devlin truly is a hard nut to crack. The princess's cousin was close to selling her soul to the devil to get the title of duchess... and Laurel Kirkeby,' he let loose a sickly laugh while slightly tapping the table, 'that poor deranged girl almost ended up in the other world in her attempt to grab the boy's attention, and she didn't manage it even then.'

'Dad, for God's sake, what happened to Laurel is not something to joke about.'

'But she didn't even know where the jugular is! That, strangely enough, was a good thing for her. Do you imagine what would have happened if that silly girl had the slightest notion of anatomy? She would be in the cemetery feeding the worms right now, although, if you ask me, it would be better for her to spend a year vacationing in Bedlam.'

'Don't be cruel! It isn't Laurel's fault to be the way she is!' Corine shook her head, exasperated. 'And don't mention death at this table, if you don't mind. It is in very poor taste.'

'Yes, yes. Because it will come looking for me.' He dismissed his daughter's comment with a sudden shake of the hands. 'I've called him before and look at me; I'm still in one piece, to the disappointment of many. I'll probably last longer than the two of you.'

'You are incorrigible. You will not behave even in the presence of your grandson's wife. She'll think we are all crazy in this family.'

Sir Malcolm returned his attention to Harmony, who wasn't sure if she should tiptoe out of the dining room or remain there and wait for her own share of dark humour. Sir Malcolm had mentioned Lady Colvile, had laughed out loud at her suicide attempt, and now, she was sure he was getting ready to open fire on her too.

'Ah, you're still there.' He looked at her, intrigued, and she had to swallow hard. 'I'm sure you played a better hand than those two softies, didn't you, love? What was it? What did you do, little witch? A pact with Beelzebub?'

Harmony's mouth shaped into an 'O' that probably did not manage to reflect the size of her indignation. Sir Malcom kept looking at her expectant, as did his daughter, who let off a nervous laugh as her only reply. Then, the gentleman started laughing with such enthusiasm that Harmony thought he would die of a respiratory arrest. He had a breathless and hoarse laughter that made her think of the neighing of a horse with lung problems.

In a few seconds he recovered; and even had time to dry a tear. How that damn trickster enjoyed embarrassing her... He had called her a witch and was now laughing at her!

'Go on! I'm only joking, girl. If looks could kill...' he said, still fighting the laughter. 'Come closer, let me look at you.' He beckoned to her to approach.

Harmony could not fathom where the intimidating attitude he had showed a moment ago had gone. Old trickster! All this time, he had been pulling her leg!

Harmony looked at Corine without quite managing to close her jaw completely, disturbed still by Sir Malcolm Radley's gall. The dowager duchess rolled her only visible eye, as if she was used to her father's jokes, and signalled for her to do as he had asked.

'Sit close to me,' he insisted.

Harmony obeyed. She occupied the chair next to the elderly man while she thought of a suitable reply. A servant poured her some tea.

'Are you not concerned that I might put a spell on you as well?'

'I'd feel flattered.'

'Not that kind of spell.'

Corine could not avoid another chuckle.

Sir Malcolm looked at her thoughtfully for a moment, then said, 'Young one, I survived opium in China, four surgeries, two of them without Chloroform, and a marriage to the most irritating woman in the whole of England.' As she listened, Harmony observed Corine with the corner of her eye. The woman looked ashamed in the extreme, hiding her face with the palm of her hand. 'You'll need to use better tricks to break this old man,' he added.

Harmony smiled genuinely for the first time in a long while and Sir Malcolm mirrored her expression before biting on a bread roll.

'In that case, I'll have to think of something.'

'You must forgive my father, Harmony,' said Corine. 'He doesn't have a filter when he talks, as you will have noticed.'

'No, it's fine,' she granted.

Sir Malcolm carried on eating his breakfast eagerly as if nothing had happened. 'Are there any other members of the family living at Sudeley?'

'No, dear. Only us.'

'Your husband seemed to be in a hurry this morning,' the elderly man observed matter-of-factly, without looking up from his meal. 'He hardly greeted me and went straight to the factory. I hope the lazy idiots there haven't caused another accident as they did last summer. I don't trust them since then. They almost set the whole building on fire. What a bunch of worthless individuals!'

'Factory? Which factory?'

'The factory of lightbulbs and generators,' her mother-in-law looked at her, surprised, 'It is based in Winchcombe.'

'I see.' Harmony blushed. She didn't know Devlin had a factory where they made lightbulbs. All this time she had been led to believe that his activity centred on politics and that, like most aristocrats, he lived on private income thanks to the proceeds from his properties. How many other things would she have to find out from the mouths of other people?

'Do you know if there were any problems?' Sir Malcolm insisted, rising an eyebrow.

'No. I don't know anything.' She was too ashamed to look at the other people at the table, and focused on eating and trying to hide at all costs the fact that she and her husband were a couple of strangers.

Corine placed the cutlery on the table, on each side of her plate, and looked at her intently. Harmony could almost hear the questions fleeting around in her mind, fighting to rush out of her mouth accompanied by a litany of reprimands. Perhaps she had already reached a conclusion.

For a few minutes, only the tinkling of the cutlery and the plates was heard, and she thought the matter had been closed... until Sir Malcolm piped up, 'Do you know? I was also caught in a compromising situation with my future wife when we were young.'

Harmony avoided looking at the elderly man and paused, the cup of tea halfway to her mouth. How on earth did he know?

'Gladys was a really sappy woman, beautiful as no woman I'd ever seen before, but even the freshest apples can spoil.'

'Dad. For goodness sake!'

Sir Malcolm carried on as if he had not heard his daughter. 'I had been trying to draw her attention for months, but she was an icicle, extremely pretentious. I wanted to prove that Gladys wasn't really like that, that there was blood running through her veins, like in any other girl's, and I was not going to stop until I had achieved that, so I looked for her at the ball that Lady Paynell, my great-aunt, gave.'

Harmony blinked profusely. At least there was a family anecdote she'd already heard about, she realised with amusement.

'She was sitting at the piano, playing I don't know what piece by Schubert. I greeted her and told her that her performance was extraordinary, that it moved my soul. She looked at me disdainfully and carried on playing as if I was only a column made of plaster. Then I told her that the instrument had belonged to Antonio Salieri in person, and that he had gifted it to a woman in my family, in exchange for a pretty special kind of favour. She stopped playing and looked up, curious. I knew I had finally managed to attract the attention of that snotty woman after so many months. She asked me what that favour had been, and then I came closer—'

'And then somebody arrived and found the two of you talking alone,' Harmony finished.

Sir Malcolm awarded her with a mischievous smile. His blue eyes sparkled with an unexpectedly youthful shine. 'No, gorgeous. The truth is that there was no further talk after that, because I had my tongue down her throat. And that was how they found us.'

She had to bite her lips to avoid bursting into laughter because that would have irritated Corine, but when she turned to check her mother-in-law's reaction, she realised she was doing the same: she pretended to be wiping her mouth with a napkin to hide her smile. She already knew that private version of the story, like Devlin, most likely.

'Well. I think Harmony has had enough of you and your escapades, Dad,' Corine reacted, finally. 'Wasn't Lord Gardiner going to come to play cards with you?'

'That old fool doesn't even know in which century we live in,' he grumbled. 'I bet he has forgotten again.'

Corine offered to show the castle to her daughter-in-law. Later, she took her for a walk around the splendid gardens of Sudeley and showed her the legendary ruins. It was all covered in snow.

'I am so sorry I didn't have a chance to warn you about my father,' Corine told her as they were leaving the walls of the castle behind. 'He was an incorrigible dandy when he was young, and as you'll have realised, he still behaves in the same way. I think that now that Mother is no longer with us, he misses those days.'

'He is adorable,' she said with a smile. 'As long as he doesn't start picking on the family.'

Corine started laughing. 'Believe me; he does it all the time. I'm afraid you must be ready for it.'

They reached a large rectangular pond right next to the ruined wing of the castle. Corine told her that area had been discarded by the restorers, because it had almost completely collapsed under a cannon assault during the Civil War. There was hardly anything left but a row of walls of different heights open to the elements, its floors invaded by tree roots. In the spring—her mother-in-law informed her—the weeds grew up to six ft. The honeysuckle grew through the windows with its hefty stems, and the gardening staff had to work hard to get rid of the poison ivy and all the parasitical plants. Apart from that—she assured her—there were flowers growing here that were unknown in other counties, and she expected she'd love them as soon as she saw them in bloom.

Harmony was truly impressed. It was an extraordinary place.

In the opposite direction, she glimpsed a luxuriant forest of frosty trees, large boxwood and bushes covered in snow that looked like sugary desserts. She felt a chilly wind freeze her cheeks, forcing her to wrap her fur coat tightly around her.

Corine pointed at a small chapel they would spend more time visiting at some other point. The building served as a mausoleum for Catherine Parr, Henry VIII's sixth wife, who spent the final days of her life at Sudeley. Harmony remembered having read something about it, but it was only a few brief paragraphs in one of the books. She promised herself she would read more about the life of the Protestant queen.

'Harmony, I've been trying all morning to find the right way to approach the matter of your marriage to my son,' Corine confessed as they started down the path next to the stone walls, 'but now I wonder if such a thing exists.'

She had been expecting an interrogation on the part of the dowager duchess, even more so after Sir Malcom's comments during breakfast. She shrugged. 'I thought it would have been obvious.'

'What would have been obvious, dear?'

'The fact that we have nothing in common and we don't even know each other,' she replied sadly. 'Devlin married me because it was the right thing to do.'

'And... exactly what compelled him to do it?'

'Your father already guessed it,' she said cringing. 'The need to protect his reputation, I think, or perhaps mine. I'm no longer sure.'

'Why don't you explain it to me?' The lady whispered, taking hold of her arm, in a gesture that obviously attempted to give her confidence. 'Don't think that I am a busybody who's always meddling on everybody's business.

It's just that I feel the responsibility to help with this. For heaven's sake, Devlin is my child. And so are you, being his wife.'

A variety of flowers dotted the edge of the road. They had broken through the thin carpet of snow, rebelling against the hostile environment, with tiny leaves and delicate stems.

In that moment, she knew she would tell her mother-in-law everything, even if she did not have to. She could have refused to do it and left that task to her husband, but Corine was kind, splendid, and had greeted her into her realm without the reluctance expected of a woman of such high breeding. But even so, Harmony decided she could not tell her the whole truth without sounding as a needy and pathetic little thing, dispossessed of her inheritance and condemned to be brought up by the meanest and most repugnant couple in the country, her only living relatives.

She started talking, telling her about her chance encounter with Devlin in the gardens of Felton House, explaining that she had got there after giving into a rebellious impulse and that she was only trying to leave the party through the mansion's back door, to prevent her governess and her aunt and uncle from finding her. She told her about her argument with the drunken duke, about the blow she threw at him to get him to set her loose and allow her to climb over the iron door. Then, her cheeks burning, and not only due to the cold wind of the Cotswolds, she mentioned the fall and the kiss on the gravel, followed by the scuffle that was witnessed, with horror, by the viscountess and Miss Andersen.

'Harmony, did my son hurt you?' Corine asked, halting along the path.

'No! Of course not!' Harmony shook her head profusely. 'He only kissed me and that's when Lady Fenton and my governess found us.'

'And they turned up because you were shouting, didn't they?'

'No,' she looked away, ashamed. 'The truth is that I didn't shout.'

'But you could have done.'

She looked down. 'Yes, I could have, but I didn't.'

The dowager duchess looked at her with her single eye in sight, which seemed quite capable of making her feel uneasy by itself. It was evident that she had discovered a detail in her account that she'd found to be of interest.

'Sorry.' Corine shook her head and resumed strolling by the ruins, causing Harmony to do the same. 'What happened afterwards?'

'We met at Lord Felton's library with my aunt and uncle. There, Devlin apologised to my family in front of the viscount and his wife. The whole matter was almost settled when my uncle raised his voice and urged Waldegrave to marry me.'

'A reasonable demand.'

'We got married early in the year. It was very hasty…'

'And the marriage has not been all that friendly?'

Harmony shook her head, holding back the tears. 'Devlin wanted to bring me here earlier, I imagine to drop me here and then go back to London as if nothing had happened, but the bad weather didn't make it possible.'

Remembering all that, made her realise how unhappy she was. She had been an idiot to believe that after that night in her husband's chamber things would change, that such an unusual union would become a true marriage. She bemoaned having abandoned her dreams to travel, to lead her life away from everybody—a dream she had nursed for years—exchanging it for the one of obtaining Waldegrave's love at some point.

The truth was that he had never as much as entertained the thought of loving her or considering her a wife, and he had never intended to have a wedding night. His intention had always been to have her under his power, to prevent her from going around calling his honour into question, saying that he had attacked her in that garden while being inebriated. If it had not been for her uncle's huge ambition, Harmony would have likely managed to convince him that she was not that kind of woman and would have made him forget about it. Perhaps she should had asked him for the ten thousand pounds and escaped from England. 'I wish I hadn't gone to that ball,' she whispered in the end, thoughtfully.

'But you did, and what's done is done,' Corine took hold of her arm again, 'I don't think everything is lost yet, Harmony. Tell me one thing; do you love him?'

'No!'

Corine pressed her lips. She didn't look like she had believed her, and Harmony cursed herself for not being convincing enough. Her companion paused for a long while, seemingly reflecting upon things, while they retraced their steps to return to the castle.

'Devlin is no villain. I don't intend to defend him, in fact, right now I want to throttle him, but I think it fair you should know: his life has not been easy. He was fourteen when his father died and had to take charge of the duchy. My father wanted to help him, but he declined his offer insisting he could do it himself. Heyworth, his father, was very hard on him when he was a child, and that's why he finds it so difficult to trust people. He is stubborn, somewhat capricious, and he is too early to judge because he thinks he'll be betrayed at a moment's notice. But that is a side of him that cannot undermine his best qualities. You need to win him over, to dig into him, to discover his best side.'

His good side. Harmony had suspected he had one, but she'd become convinced the opposite was true when she saw him leaving the bedroom of that dreadful Lady Colvile. A man who cheats on his wife in her own home with a woman with mental health problems could not be a good person. She didn't care for the conventions of the society he had grown in, or the rights conferred upon him for being a man and also a powerful aristocrat. If he wanted to cavort with another woman, why hadn't he gone elsewhere? Why hadn't he been more discreet? Why hadn't he waited until he had dropped her at Sudeley, to save her from such humiliation?

She refused to answer Corine's comment, too upset and hurt now that her wounds—still fresh—had been disturbed. Perhaps it would be better if she held tight to those feelings, if she sought refuge in them so Waldegrave would not be able to hurt her ever again. She should start to build up a wall to protect herself from him, to remind herself that the two of them were not destined to be a couple.

'Consider me your ally, Harmony.'

The girl smiled, but it was a smile devoid of joy.

Devlin leaned on the iron balustrade and eyed the fantastic Sawyer Light Factory, his brow creased. He wasn't sure if he should feel like the important businessman he intended to be or like a lonely child seeking refuge in his complex toys.

Far from feeling satisfied by the success of his factory that had been set up once he had acquired the patents to manufacture the Edison lightbulbs in mass in the United Kingdom, he had found multiple mistakes in the process. He had criticised the results provided by the managers, looked harshly at the workmen who wandered around doing nothing, and had finally come up with new ideas to double the production which had left many speechless. It was the first time he had complained so much.

He couldn't understand what was going on with him, and he didn't fancy finding out either. He wanted to be able to bury himself there, between those walls, as Charles Darwin had done in the laboratory of Dawn House, or Thomas Edison in the invention factory in Menlo Park. Tom worked ceaselessly, ate and turned the lives of his workers into hell with his mad genius demands. Sometimes he would spend weeks working without seeing the light of day, pushing his resistance to the limit until he collapsed, exhausted. Last year, when he had visited him in New Jersey, he had observed his work habits; he had felt they were irrational and unhealthy—although tremendously effective—but right now he only believed that method could work to keep him away from that scheming brat he had for a wife.

That day he had listened to reports, had spoken to the personnel and had exposed his ideas. He had spent more time there than he used to when he visited the factory, and it was the first time they saw him without a jacket, his sleeves rolled up to his elbows atop the waistcoat. He had stuck his nose everywhere, interfering even in the rational use of work materials and the time of arrival of the workers. As a consequence, people had felt intimidated and nervous. It seemed that Waldegrave had come to tighten everybody's screws with a new sense of stubbornness.

In the administrative part of the factory worked young women in diverse positions: receptionists, telephone operators, and typists. Some were widows of limited resources sent by Lady Lovelance's foundation that had been trained and had joined the workforce with the duke's blessing. There were also workers from other factories that had found better conditions and benefits at the Sawyer Light Factory. One of these women was Cherry Lucas, who was in charge of paying the salaries, a position that gave her certain pre-eminence.

Cherry was a rather shameless red-haired girl and had always tried to tempt Devlin with her formidable breasts and her prominent curves. Whenever he visited the place, the woman would find a way to stop him with some excuse or other to bend over and offer him a glimpse of her glorious neckline.

This time had been no exception. Cherry had approached him swinging her hips, greeting him with a long and exaggerated curtsey. As he always did, Devlin had observed the rounded hill of her bosom again for a few moments, and then looked back at her blue eyes. He had to admit it; the woman was quite pretty. Cherry had addressed him in whispers and batted her eyelids, clearly intent on attracting his attention while thanking him for the presents he had sent to the children of the workers. One of the beneficiaries was Ben, her seven-year-old son, whose father had ended up in prison.

While he listened to her talking, Devlin admired Cherry with more interest than he'd ever shown until then. He looked at her invitingly, thinking about all the enjoyment he had deprived himself of until then. He had been ignoring her for months, holding onto the notion that a man in his position should not get involved with working-class women, but now he felt more inclined to change his opinion. Perhaps a night spent with the ardent red-haired lass would help him forget his problems for a bit.

Then, taking advantage of the fact that they were alone and out of sight from the rest of workers, Devlin had asked Cherry where she lived and, after listening to her reply, he asked if she would be interested in him coming to pick her up to go for a drink. The woman agreed even before he had finished talking and offered him a smile brimming with naughty intentions.

As soon as he had moved away from Cherry, Devlin's eyes had bumped onto a phonograph standing in the corner of a far-away desk; it was another one of the prototypes Edison had sent him, and he had ordered for it to be taken apart to understand how it worked. He had forgotten he had it at the Sawyer Light Factory. Then, his heart gave a painful holt, his mind flying to Waldegrave Terrace Library, where he could almost feel again Harmony's fascination on listening to Tom's brief message. He didn't comprehend what intention drew him to the device, but his chest filled up with a debilitating feeling.

The memory of that moment made him sway as he stood at the edge of the production area now, watching his workers. He had just entered the building again, his mind still full of his musings. 'It should be used to record music,' he mumbled, remembering Harmony's exact words.

'What are you saying, Your Grace?' inquired Mr Monroe, the head of production of the factory, who had approached him quietly to ask him a question and had overheard him thinking out loud.

Devlin turned to look at his employee, but he was still absorbed in his thoughts. 'Music.'

'An excellent idea, My Lord,' Monroe praised. 'It will resuscitate that piece of junk that was about to end up in the scrap yard.'

'It wasn't my idea, but my wife's.'

Cherry Lucas heard those words, as did a dozen employees who were in the vicinity, and she dropped the pile of folders she was carrying, unintentionally. 'I was unaware you had got married, My Lord,' said Monroe. 'My congratulations. And congratulate your wife for such a magnificent idea.'

Devlin was no longer sure he wanted to bed Cherry. He didn't even bother to look at her as she bent over to pick up the folders, a posture that gave him, and the rest of men, the best seat in the house to fully appreciate her bosom.

At the day's close, when he was on his way to leave the factory, she approached him once more. With extreme discretion, the woman dared rest a hand on his chest, and then said her goodbye, gazing suggestively at him. She obviously wanted to make clear that she did not mind his being married, and that she was eagerly awaiting their promised rendezvous.

'I'll see you tonight, Your Grace,' she reminded him before she left.

Chapter 12

Once at his study in Sudeley, Devlin retrieved a bottle of brandy from a drawer. He intended to relax and remain there until it was time to go pick up Cherry Lucas. He had planned it all during his carriage journey; he would take her to a discreet inn, away from Winchcombe. Without wasting any time in useless conversations, he'd bed her and, depending on how he felt afterwards, he'd consider the possibility of taking her as a lover for his visits to the county. A rather promising idea.

But if it was all that easy, why couldn't he stop feeling as if he had a thorn stuck in his chest, as if he was about to step onto a bed of burning coals? An annoying little voice kept whispering the word 'danger' and, despite his determination, it made him feel fearful. What should he be afraid of? What could he lose if he sought the company of a woman who would satisfy his physical needs and would not make him feel as terribly confused as Harmony did?

He wanted to turn off that voice with a swig of liquor; he wanted to rebel and prove that he was not a weakling. He was lord and master of his emotions. No silly girl could turn his life upside down. He filled his glass with liquor and downed it in one go.

Corine opened the study door and poked half her body in. She'd knocked three times, which had seriously annoyed him, because he knew he could no longer dismiss her.

'Son, you have spent the whole day out,' she noted calmly as she entered the study without having been issued an invitation. 'A problem at the factory?'

'Why do you think there was a problem?'

'Because when you visit, you don't normally spend the whole day in town.' She smiled knowingly, and he had the feeling that either she was unaware of his bad mood or she simply did not care an iota. 'Didn't you say once that it was a very common place and that your ancestors had built their fortress in a pigsty?'

'Indeed,' he mumbled while he refilled his glass. 'Any other duke would be waiting for the farm animals, the sacks of grain, and the bales of wool which are the source of our income to come knocking at the door of the castle.'

Corine raised an eyebrow and tilted her head, staring at him. Then she folded her arms and spoke very slowly. 'You know perfectly well I don't mean that. You have people there who are more than capable of supervising the work. Why are you so worried?' She looked at him with a hint of worry. 'Oh, for God's sake. Don't tell me you have gone to pester those good people who break their backs every day for you, to triple their productivity. It would be very thoughtless of you.'

'Mother, if those people break their backs is because I pay them a lot of money to do it. And I'd pay them more if they gave me three times the profit.' He sighed because he knew she would not just leave. What the hell did she want? 'Seeing as you're already here, why don't you have a drink with me?'

'No!' Corine sat on a chair in front of him, then smiled at him, as if weighing him up and down. 'You'd perhaps like to hear that this morning I had a most revealing chat with my daughter-in-law.'

There was his answer. Devlin focused his eyes on the bottom of his glass of brandy, and the amber liquid suddenly darkened. A bout of anxiety took hold of him. 'I am always amazed at your ability to gain people's trust in such a short time.'

'I didn't do anything...' she replied in an innocent-sounding tone, but Devlin felt a cloud of suspiciousness materialise around him. '...other than be kind and ask the right questions. She is a sweet girl, I must admit. Granddad loves her,' she added.

'Granddad? Seriously?' He kept his gaze fixed on the liquor.

'You must see them together,' she chuckled, 'I think it was love at first sight. My father might be an eternal adolescent and a foul-mouthed and saucy old man, but you know that his assessments of the human soul are indisputable.'

Devlin gazed at Corine, squinting. 'What do you want from me?'

'A few simple answers.'

'I thought your conversation with Harmony had been revealing,' he stood up and paced the room, 'I am sure she told you everything. You should believe her.'

'I do. But I also want to know what you feel.'

182

'What does it matter what I feel? An innocent girl is approached in a dark garden by a drunken duke, and a few days later she marries him. Everything is right with the world, isn't it? I have behaved as expected of a gentleman. You should be proud of me, Mother.'

'Devlin, please. Be sparing with your sarcasm or it will lose its power. I am your mother. I know you, even if you hide under that armour of bitterness. I refuse to believe your father killed everything good in you.'

'You know I don't like you to mention him,' he demanded, gritting his teeth.

Corine retracted. She must have known she was treading muddy waters. 'Why are you like this? Is it due to that baroness who rejected you?'

He looked at her, frowning. He hadn't even thought about Victory for the last few days.

'My friend in London kept me well informed of what went on between you and her.'

'I see, but nothing is going on with the baroness.' As soon as he vocalised that thought, Devlin realised it was true. Victory was already out of his head, of his heart, or wherever she had invaded. A feeling of relief shot through him, but only briefly, because he was well aware that he had only jumped out of the pan to fall into the fire.

'My friend wrote to me that you seemed to be deeply in love with her.'

'I've told you that is behind me now, Mother.'

'There must be a reason for you to behave like such an idiot.'

He growled in reply.

'This... I mean, a marriage can only become hell if we allow it to. It's a decision you make. You know I speak from personal experience.'

'Of course,' his tone oozed the harshest sarcasm, 'I learned that from observing you half of my life.'

Corine swallowed hard. She forced herself to ignore his taunts. 'I only want to help you, Devlin. You are my son, and it hurts me to see that you keep away from the house to avoid your wife.'

'You don't understand, Mother.'

'Listen, I do understand,' she said in a sad tone. He quietened his thoughts and decided to listen attentively. 'You were drunk, spurned, and didn't know what you were doing. You kissed the first woman that crossed your path, and it was a girl you would never had looked at under normal circumstances. A girl who does not fit in the ideal of beauty we are used to, who comes from a humble family, without fortune or influences; I'd dare say she's even vulgar. It's evident that our friends will not approve of Harmony, and she will have difficulty fitting in. She might even become the laughing stock of our society as soon as she makes the slightest error,' she paused to check his reaction, 'Spending your life next to somebody who does not live up to your expectations, who is not your equal, must be torture, my son.'

He didn't say anything. He had paused by the window, his arms akimbo, but his attention remained trained on his mother. He went over her words while he asked himself at which point in that story everything had changed. When had that initial, logical and perfectly convincing version of things, turned into something else?

Corine smiled triumphantly to herself as she observed her son's face reflected on the window. A vehement confirmation of all her cruel conjectures would have been so simple; she was almost expecting it, but his silence spoke volumes, as did his face of sweet uneasiness. It was full of confusion and he was clearly confronted with a feeling that was perturbing and celestial at once. His, right then, was a vision she wished she could treasure forever.

She could bet anything that her son had fallen for the angelical charms of Harmony George, that troubled and abandoned girl that quietly begged for protection. What she had so coldly recited to her son had seemed the perfect script for a miserable life, but something had happened as she spoke. She had felt it; she had seen it on his face. Devlin had fallen in love with that girl and, evidently, he wasn't even aware of it. Was it possible to be deeply proud of somebody and at the same time desperately want to beat him up to make him react?

Corine wanted to cry out in happiness, wanted to hug her son and then run to Harmony's chamber, wake her up and thank her for having been born and for having allowed him to lay his hands on her.

'You don't have to answer me. I see I have been right,' she piped up then. Devlin didn't turn around to look at her, and she carried on,. 'But, darling, you decided to marry her. You must come to terms with your decision, accept that she will accompany you for the rest of your life and that at some point she will be the mother of your heir. I'm afraid that even if you open fifty factories, you'll never be able to get far away enough from Harmony.'

He finally turned around, his expression impatient. He looked tormented almost, as if every word Corine pronounced had caused him physical pain. His obvious refusal to accept the facts was beginning to worry her. 'Mother, I have to go out in a few minutes. I would be grateful if we could put a close to this conversation.'

'What? Are you going out at this time of day?' She looked incredulous at the clock on the mantelpiece. It was almost ten in the evening. 'Where are you going?'

'It's none of your business.'

Even though he was running late for his meeting with Cherry Lucas, Devlin made himself comfortable on the sofa, poured himself more brandy, and fell into a sorrowful state of thoughtfulness. He loved his mother; however, he had to admit that sometimes he enjoyed not having her near. She was an absorbing, scheming and meddlesome woman and that without mentioning the fact that her presence brought to mind certain events that, even after a lot of time, still disturbed him.

Guilty or not of his misfortunes, his mother was a reminder of them, of those days when he had wished to be the son of other people, to have a different life—even if it was the life of one of those dirty and wild ragamuffins begging in the streets of London—or simply to cease to exist. She had also suffered, more than he did at the time, but Devlin had focused on avoiding drama, and preferred that each one experienced their own sorrow separately, and that was how it had been all this time, despite the fierce resistance she kept exerting.

He was sure his mother had cornered the girl with her questions that were probably unwise, inquisitive, and lacking in all tact, with the only objective of interfering in his marriage and daring to decide what the best for them was. Harmony had obviously not told her that he had hit her in the midst of his passionate assault, otherwise his mother's attitude would have been very different. Perhaps his wife had forgotten it, perhaps she had forgiven him. That thought, instead of comforting him, made him feel worse.

Harmony... Harmony... He could not stop saying her name or feeling a maelstrom of emotions disturbing his insides. He did not deserve her forgiveness, he admitted while he sipped his drink again. The liquor was starting to clear his mind, to defeat his pride. And now, it brought back his mother's words. She had called Harmony vulgar and he no longer remembered what other horrible things.

He had also had a poor opinion of her at some point, had underestimated her; he had told her to her face that she wasn't good enough for him. And even after all that, she had submitted herself to him, she had looked at him with tenderness, as if her nobility would not allow for a trace of rancour. She had entered his bed, frozen, begging for his caresses.

He sighed, dropping his head back, as he remembered that night when she gave him as a present the most sensual and breath-taking experience of his

185

whole existence. The intensity of that memory made him tremble. What did she have that attracted him so much? He had not discovered it yet.

After that passionate parenthesis, Laurel had arrived and with her the confrontations, the fury, and the collapse of his marriage. What would have happened between him and Harmony if his disturbed childhood friend had not turned up that day at Waldegrave Terrace? How far would that honeymoon have gone? He was terrified thinking about it. Harmony loved him; he was sure that for some strange reason she had fallen in love with him, but Devlin did not deserve that affection or her forgiveness of his aggression. He wasn't even sure he wanted to accept the feelings she was offering him. Perhaps Laurel's intrusion had been a good thing, after all.

Perhaps he should have listened to Harmony when she implored him not to force a marriage. If Talbot had insisted on discrediting him or on asking him for money as compensation, he could have easily sorted it out. After all, how had that individual even dared threaten a duke? Who was he, after all?

He knew that he'd completely lost control of the situation. He had assumed that a marriage would appease the Talbot family, that Harmony would feel less abused if he married her and offered her a life full of privileges she could not have access to otherwise. If they had lead separate lives there would have been no problem. Instead, he had turned his life into a maelstrom of emotions that did not align: desire, fear, tenderness...

When he turned around to look at the clock it was almost eleven, and he felt more inebriated than he would have expected. He stood up, and felt the world spin around him. He acknowledged he was in no condition to go out and decided that he would enjoy the favours of the factory's red-haired lass on some other occasion. He imagined she would not get angry because he had stood her up.

His feet took him stumbling outside of the study, then he climbed a floor up the winding staircase. Suddenly he was in Sudeley's long bedroom corridor, lit by the lightbulbs he had got installed a few months ago. The artificial light of an amber hue, conferred a curious perspective to the landscape paintings hung along the corridor.

Devlin's steps echoed on the floor as he peered at the row of doors that reached as far as his sight allowed. He stopped in front of her door all of sudden. He had followed an impulse that took hold of him as he walked upstairs. He had to talk to her; he had to put an end to it all before the damage was irreparable. Harmony was a good girl, despite everything. If he was sure of anything was that no woman with a lively spirit deserved to end up as a wife in exile, confined to a ghostly castle.

He opened her bedroom door with extreme care. Gloom dominated the inside of the room. The fireplace flames were consuming the firewood, and the Cotswolds wind tapped the glass of the windows lightly with a peculiar whistling sound. He slowly approached the four posted bed where his wife lay asleep, face up. She kept a static but relaxed position, typical of a deep sleep.

He stopped there to watch her silently. The bluish reflection of the night filtering through the window gave an alabaster hue to her visage and to the skin of her slim arms that were crossed over her head. The thick mane of her hair spread around her, bathing the pillow in delicate ringlets, dark as the night itself. Her chest moved up and down following the rhythm of her serene breathing. He contemplated, at great length, her half-open mouth, which whistled lightly while she remained lost in her dreams, whatever they might be.

While he controlled the impulse to caress her face, to touch with his fingers those rose cheeks that looked pale, like snowballs, Devlin wondered what his wife was dreaming about. He knew so little about her that he felt ashamed. Although it was true that he had decreed not to establish any kind of attachment to her, that he had told himself that he did not want to become more involved with her than was strictly necessary, right now, his eagerness to learn more about her sprang out of him by itself, as if he had just opened the cage of a dangerous animal. He yearned to enter her head, to know her thoughts, to access her memories, her fears, her wishes…

He noticed an open book resting on her belly, the cover up. Devlin remembered she was a bookworm and felt happy to know one important thing about her, at least. He strained his eyes, leaning forward to read what was written on the cover. Even in partial darkness he managed to decipher the title: A Woman's Journey around the World by Ida Pfeiffer.

He looked back at the image of his wife, who had just moved slightly and mumbled something unintelligible in her dream. He had to admit that he wanted her to wake up, while hating the thought of disrupting her rest. He wanted to make love to her and stay all night watching her at the same time.

Damn it! He ruffled his hair feeling a frustration that bordered on desperation. Why was this happening to him? It made no sense to love her. She had no merits, no worthy virtue; she was everything his mother had said, and she was also a troublesome girl who was about to push him down an abyss… Despite all that, he was unable to contain his wish to kiss her. It was madness. He was going crazy. It had to be that. Alcohol had pickled his neurones.

He could no longer resist his powerful impulse. He was going to kiss her there and then; he had to wake her up and confess to her what was happening to him, if he was able to find the right words. His intentions went further, in fact. He was determined to ask for her forgiveness for all the occasions when he had hurt her, or for not having talked about Laurel when he should have, and for not knowing her birthday. And afterwards, he would make love to her like that night in his bedroom at Waldegrave Terrace. To hell with the idea of letting her go!

He bent forward slowly, to avoid giving her a fright, and rested both hands on the pillow by her head before seeking her mouth. But then, a sudden movement caused the book atop of her to stumble. Immediately, the volume slipped and fell to the floor with a dry thud.

Harmony woke up startled and curled up under the blanket automatically. Immediately, she turned on the electric lamp on the bedside table. On noticing her husband's presence, she directed a quarrelsome look at him. 'What are you doing?' she grunted.

Devlin was astounded. He felt put off by the rudeness of the question, the scorn he perceived in it, as if he had been a mouse who had sneaked in through a hole on the wall. He found it difficult to adjust to such a reaction, because, until recently, his presence in a woman's bedroom would have been received with joy. 'I came to see how you were,' he said, feeling like slapping himself for having said such a stupid thing. It was totally unlike him.

'I am well,' she mumbled without changing her expression. 'Thanks.'

The moon seemed to highlight her expression of revulsion. The way she looked at him, oozing rejection, astonished him. No, more than that... It hurt him. It hurt him as if she had hit him in the face with the book. His mind replayed the memories of the morning of her birthday, when he had offered her a bunch of roses, and she had looked at him as if he was a sack of manure.

Harmony George knew how to hurt him.

'You're still upset,' he groaned.

'Nothing has changed, as far as I know.'

'Would you like to talk?'

Devlin detected a slight hesitation in her eyes, even a spark of true surprise, until a bitter determination took hold of her expression.

'What for, Your Grace?' she whispered. 'You don't need to make friends with me. I am your wife, and if I don't follow your lead on everything I'll pay the consequences, won't I?'

He didn't recognise the cold and sarcastic woman he had before him. Or was Harmony truly like that? Where was the kind and perceptive girl who had talked about listening to Mendelssohn in a phonograph until she made him melt, the one who had whispered in his bed that she only saw good in him?

'Don't worry about me,' she carried on, oozing bitterness. 'I'll behave the best I can while you're away. I promise you I won't be a problem, and I'll keep so out of everything that you'll forget my very existence. Now, your room is eight doors farther down,' she pointed with her finger in the direction of his bedroom. 'Why don't you leave and let me sleep in peace?'

'And if I don't want to go there?' he grumbled, irked by her rejection. 'What if I wish to spend the night in bed with my wife?'

'You are inebriated.'

'As if this was the first time you saw me like this.'

'Go to sleep, Devlin.'

'I don't want to go to sleep, damn it! I don't want to go anywhere! I want you!'

The bedroom was invaded by a desolate silence. Harmony looked at him, puzzled, for a long minute. A glint like a diamond's appeared in her eyes, evidence of her tears trying to find an escape route.

He wished she had understood the nature of that desperate confession, that she would have grasped the truth behind those words, but damn his bad luck and everything he had sown from the day he had seen her for the first time until that night; it wasn't to be.

'Really?' she whispered. 'Do you want us to draw the curtains, to turn off the lights and the fire, or do you think it is dark enough?'

He couldn't believe it. A mixture of rage and sadness enveloped him; the rage won, however. He found it difficult to believe that the Harmony of his memories had vanished after Lady Colvile's appearance, that she had allowed herself to be so disturbed by her words. It seemed that the matter was more serious than he had thought.

'All that damn bitterness is due to what Laurel told you?' he muttered. He didn't find it easy to deal with her obvious notion that she was inferior because it was so alien to him. 'Why are you so worried about the allegations of a mad woman?'

'I'm not worried about her,' she said sitting up on the bed and hurling the blanket to one side. Suddenly, she burst into tears, and added, 'I'm worried about being in a marriage where I don't have access to the most essential thing: my husband's respect. And it isn't only that: I feel I am in front of a total stranger, Devlin… Somebody who has not told me he has a factory or, worse still, a mother and a grandfather.'

He was speechless. The last thing she had said was true, but it was all in response to a strict policy that right now he had decided to lift.

'And you don't want to know who I am either, do you?' she carried on. 'You have no interest in getting to know me, in knowing if I am worthy of being loved because, as you told me once, I don't have the qualities you like in a woman.' Devlin wanted to tell her that he had discovered in her qualities he didn't even know existed, that he didn't know he could be obsessed by, that he had never thought he would need with such desperation, as if it was water he needed to survive. But those were not things he could easily confess, even less when she was attacking him so viciously.

'Good! Carry on as you have until now. On the one hand, living with that sickly bond that ties you to Lady Colvile, and on the other, dying of love for a woman who loves someone else.'

He hadn't expected such a thorough whipping. She was talking about Victory now, who else? Had his mother talked to her? 'She is no longer a part of my life.'

'And your relationship with your mother is terrible,' she added, as if she had not heard what he had just said.

'Don't tell me what kind of a relationship I should have with my family,' he growled, fed up.

Harmony was getting dangerously close to crossing a forbidden line, and he wasn't prepared to allow her to keep going. 'Why don't you explain it to me?'

'It's none of your business!' That was a dark and murky subject, a dungeon he did not wish to re-enter, God and the devil knew why. He realised he was trembling and sweating despite the cold. She must have been fully aware of his reaction but did not cease in her attempt at provoking him.

'I thought it was exclusively with me, but now I see that you are cruel even towards her,' she claimed. 'You keep her apart from your life; you don't look at her in the eye. I think you dislike her presence. You think I have problems with my self-confidence? I don't know how yours is, Your Grace, but I suspect it's much worse.'

Devlin felt a flash of rage piercing his chest, but instead of exploding, he tore at his messy hair, strode towards her angrily, and ended up grabbing her shoulders in a menacing manner. 'Enough!' he urged her with a sinister grunt. 'Shut up, once and for all.'

'What wouldn't I give for my mother to be alive still,' she replied, holding back the tears, 'but I cannot bring her back. Consumption took her away when I was ten, and it also took my father. I didn't even get to meet my grandparents.'

Devlin had no idea of that. He hadn't invested any time in reading the report, which was likely full of important details such as these. He regretted not having done it, and being unable to drop his pride and hug her and tell her that he was sorry. Strangely enough, he felt the wish to confess that, despite having experienced that sad episode, he was sure that her childhood had been healthier and happier than his, as he had only a mother and a grandfather while growing up.

'I didn't know that,' he whispered gruffly.

'Of course you didn't know,' she broke loose from his hold, 'you don't know anything about me. You don't know that I have nobody but my aunt and uncle, and you have a family you don't appreciate.'

'Stop giving your opinion on matters you know nothing about!'

She looked at him with extreme curiosity, when she should have been afraid of his threats. Why did she insist on that, damn it? Why didn't she let it lie? He knew that the mere mention of his family irritated him, no matter who brought it up, but he did not wish to let that rage loose against her. Harmony had no idea she was walking through a minefield that could blow them both up at any moment.

He sighed, aware he had to leave before she started again. Then his gaze fell on the book he had dropped accidentally as he moved to kiss her earlier, before everything got ruined.

'I know something about you,' he mocked her, like the drunkard he was, while he squatted with difficulty to pick up the book. 'I know you like those silly adventure books.'

Inexplicably, Harmony's face twisted in total horror on seeing Ida Pfeiffer's book on his hands. 'Give me that!' she shouted, sounding both furious and needy. Hysterical, she jumped on him to recover the book, as if she were a crazy desperate mother whose baby had been stolen. For a moment, Devlin felt like being evil and prevented her from reaching it, forcing her to fight with him to get it back. In part, it was her punishment for having refused to bed him.

'Come on, get it from me! I bet you can't!'

The girl jumped out of the bed, enraged, her arms outstretched as she tried to grab the book, but Devlin was a fair bit taller and kept it out of her reach. While he moved around the room—with limited skill due to his drunkenness—and challenged her to grab it from him, Harmony tried extremely hard to get it. She even grabbed a pillow and hit him with it a few times. Far from enraging him, that made him laugh.

He felt jealous of that damn book. What did she find in it that made her so desperate to get it back?

'Stop! Devlin, give it back to me!'

He had not grasped her anguish; he was simply having fun and punishing her, laughing at her and distracting himself from the most painful subject in the world for him. He would have liked for her to laugh with him as well, to put an end to that discussion; to push him onto the bed so he could finally forget everything. But the only things he got in exchange for his thoughtless attempts at distraction were her nervous screams and sobs that made him worry. 'What's wrong with you? It's only a silly book!'

'It isn't only a book!' she cried out amidst her tears.

'Harmony, calm down, for God's sake!' Frustrated, Devlin was about to give her back the object of her adoration, but a sudden movement on her part made Ida Pfeiffer's work slip from both their hands. To his horror, it fell into the fireplace.

Harmony screamed in panic on seeing it land between the flames. She ran and fell on her knees in front of the fire, her anguish and the amber colour of the fire hurting his eyes to watch, but it was too late. The fire charred the paper at a mind-blowing speed. Her attempts at getting it out of it with the poker proved useless. A Woman's Journey around the World became food for the flames and soon afterwards a pile of ashes.

'It's ruined,' she stated, sobbing.

'I... I'm so sorry,' he whispered.

Full of regret for what had happened and for having caused her such pain, Devlin placed a hand on her shoulder and leaned towards her. He would never have imagined—not in a thousand years—that she had been so attached to that thing. Had a lover given it to her? he thought, irritated.

Harmony moved away from him. She stood up and stared at him, her eyes aflame. 'You destroy everything you touch! That's what you know how to do best!' she screamed, her eyes full of tears.

He looked at her, shocked, and hurt by her words, which had the amazing power to become sharp and cutting when exiting her mouth. Like shards of glass, they pierced his skin, causing him untold pain.

Yes. She knew how to inflict pain on him, he concluded. And, perhaps, he deserved it. 'I didn't mean to... I'm sorry.'

'Get out of here,' she carried on, and then looked daggers at him with the angriest expression he'd ever seen. 'I wish you would have allowed me to jump that bloody fence!'

Chapter 13

That morning, she felt too hurt and angry to go to the breakfast room and pretend that nothing had happened. The previous night had seen her dreams go up in flames in such a literal manner that it had almost felt like a supernatural warning; as if something wanted to remind her forcibly that her destiny had taken an unstoppable turn, and that the new life she was starting would not allow her even a single glimpse of freedom.

Mrs Pfeiffer's book was the possession she had treasured the most during her time living at her Uncle's house. It was her last stronghold, and Devlin had hurled it into the fire in the heat of the discussion... Well, perhaps he had not hurled it in. Harmony had gone crazy, she had to admit. She had pulled it from him with force and he had let it go at the same time. As a result, the book had gone flying and landed right in the middle of the flames in the fireplace, where it ended up completely ruined.

In any case, he should not have taken it in the first place, she thought, furious. He had turned up in her chamber, drunk, and had demanded her company, something she was not prepared to give him.

When she saw A Woman's Journey around the World in her husband's hands, Harmony had felt a shudder running down her spine. Miss Andersen had warned her that no husband would like such reading matter, and that was why she had kept it strictly private. She had only allowed Devlin to see her carrying books written by the respectable wives of diplomats. Now she had nothing, as she did not consider the books in Waldegrave Terrace's library to be hers, or those at Sudeley. Her only real possession had been destroyed by fire.

She could at least use the resources available to go out and try to get some fresh air, something that was impossible inside the castle. She asked Louis, the coachman of the black cabriolet with the duchy of Waldegrave crest, to take her out for a ride. At some point, she asked him to stop in one of the streets. The weather had notably improved in the last two days and she felt like walking.

Ahead of her, at the other end of the street, a small park welcomed the first visitors of the morning. The snow was starting to thaw and the trees were beginning to shoot new leaves with languid tenacity. The sky was crystalline blue and brought to mind the beautiful spring just around the corner.

That day she had chosen to wear a brocade blouse and a dark green skirt, a narrow wing hat atop her voluminous quiff and a coffee-coloured jacket, but she had not imagined her presence would attract such attention. Immediately, she felt a crowd of eyes falling on her. Some pedestrians stopped, distracted on seeing her climb down the cabriolet. She imagined they must have been wondering who that smart woman was, coming to the village in one of the duke's magnificent coaches. If they saw the wedding ring in her finger, they would guess she was the new duchess.

She told Louis to wait for her, something the servant reluctantly agreed to. She walked along a lane full of shops: a tailor's, an inn, a barber shop, and a photography studio. A fairly busy pawnbroker's—from what she could see through the shop window—called her attention. Some peddlers offered her spices, fruits, and greenhouse flowers that she declined with a polite nod.

She saw a woman wrapped in a threadbare cape, holding by the arm a tiny and wan old woman. She assumed they were mother and daughter. She felt sorry because the latter seemed ill; she walked incredibly slowly, her breathing laboured and hoarse, and the other woman had to help her stay in an upright position. They were poor people; she knew it because of their callous and deformed hands, evidence of an entire life of hard work. Only after her innocent inspection did Harmony notice that the two women were staring at her. The younger one did it discreetly, her face half-hidden behind her cape. The old woman gazed at her with something akin to loathing.

That look surprised her. She didn't know the old woman. In fact, she didn't know anybody in Winchcombe. Why should she hate her? Was she mad, perhaps? Had she got her confused with somebody else?

She was about to cross the street when she glimpsed a small bookshop a short distance away. It had white stucco walls and glass cases on both sides of the wooden door exhibiting, obviously, the most recent books. A sign hanging atop the door read 'The Bookend'. Harmony smiled thinking that she might be able to get a new copy of A Woman's Journey around the World there.

She ignored the pointed looks of the people of Winchcombe and decided to enter The Bookend, climbing the five steps to the door. Once inside, she took in the mountains of books, and the seductive aroma of ink and paper that always incited her to do a frenzied search for the most attractive titles. The bookshop was considerably smaller than Hatchards, the shop in Piccadilly where she had found the first copy of her beloved book, but it seemed well stocked; a place where each nook and cranny was efficiently used to display books.

Unfortunately, the bookshop owner shook his head when she asked for the title she was looking for. Harmony felt such a wave of disillusionment that she declined to stay to check the selection available, as the kind man had suggested. She wasn't interested in any other book, only Mrs Pfeiffer's.

She exited the bookshop and, after climbing down the steps, spotted the old woman who had just looked at her with hatred. She was planted there, a few steps from her, observing her with the same hostility she was unable to unravel. The younger woman wasn't beside her. Harmony looked to her left and spotted her just as she was entering a modest paint shop.

'Eh… Good morning,' she heard then.

Harmony turned around to discover, behind her, a blonde lady looking at her with deliberate interest. She seemed to be in her mid-thirties, stunning, distinguished and well-dressed; she was wearing a light embroidered white coat on top of a cream-coloured suit, and a little hat decorated with exotic feathers. Her huge blue eyes betrayed a suspicious nature and a possible proclivity for gossip. Her lips opened up in a hesitant smile. She didn't know exactly why, but that lady reminded her of somebody.

In her arms, the woman carried a French white-and-coffee-coloured pug puppy that she petted continuously. Behind her, a maid in uniform held some parcels and, as did her mistress, kept watching Harmony, but with the discretion appropriate to a domestic servant.

'Good morning,' Harmony replied.

'Your Grace, it is you, isn't it?' She glanced at the gold ring in Harmony's fourth finger.

'Yes,' agreed Harmony, caressing the jewel with the other hand. She had the weird sensation that half the people there had their eyes fixed on her wedding ring. Was it possible that nobody had expected Waldegrave to marry or perhaps they had never thought he would take a wife like her?

The lady smiled, without further hesitation, and curtseyed gracefully. 'Allow me to introduce myself, Duchess. I'm the Viscountess of Burghill. My husband and I live nearby, in Cheltenham, and my parents are neighbours of the duke. We heard the good news. Congratulations on your marriage!'

'Many thanks, Lady Burghill. It's a pleasure to make your acquaintance.'

'Oh, please, call me Becky,' she smiled again, showing a row of pearly white teeth, 'I hope you like Winchcombe; it's a humble town, unpretentious, but people are affectionate and hard-working.'

Harmony could not avoid looking away then, to glance at the old woman whose threatening eyes remained fixed on her. All this time, she'd almost felt them drilling a hole in the back of her skull.

'Am I wrong suggesting that this is your first visit to the county?' she heard Lady Burghill ask so she turned to her again.

'You are not wrong, Becky.' She smiled and added, 'I've seen very little until now, but I think Winchcombe is quite charming. And it looks like a developing town.'

'You are very generous. We owe that to your husband, who has ostensibly improved the quality of life of the inhabitants. In other words, the light bulb factory has employed hundreds of people, and I have heard that more and more workers are joining, especially women. And, I've also heard that the salaries are higher than anywhere else in the county, and perhaps even in the neighbouring ones.' She paused for a moment then, perhaps to evaluate Harmony's reaction, and added, 'You have married a truly exceptional man, who is admired and respected by all.'

Harmony smiled. She would have preferred not to have felt so proud of Devlin, but she had to be fair. If all that was true, then her husband was a wonderful master. 'I'm happy to hear you say that.'

'Well, I don't wish to take too many liberties, but I'd love to carry on talking to you at some other point. It would be an honour if you came to have tea at home some time.'

Harmony thought that was an invaluable opportunity to make new friends. Lady Burghill seemed to be an affable person. 'It will be a pleasure, Becky.'

The viscountess smiled eagerly. 'Please, pass on my best wishes to your lovely mother-in-law, whom I have not visited for a long time. And if you need anything, do not hesitate to let me know.' She removed a cream-coloured calling card with her name printed on it from her purse and handed it to her. 'The Sawyer and the Kirkeby families have been friends for generations.'

Kirkeby. Strangely enough, that surname also sounded very familiar, she thought while she examined the card. Where had she heard it before?

'Becky, how did you find out the duke had married?' she asked, frowning, her eyes still fixed on the delicate letters printed on the card. 'I had imagined that my mother-in-law had perhaps told you recently, but you have just said you have not seen her for a while…'

Becky's smile receded as Harmony spoke, until an expression of slight awkwardness invaded her features. 'Yes, you see… My sister has mentioned something about your marriage to the duke.'

'Your sister?'

'Laurel… I mean, Lady Colvile.'

Harmony felt the air turn heavy and experienced difficulty breathing. Becky was Lady Colvile's sister; that notwithstanding, she was charming and civilised. She found it almost incredible that these women could share the same blood.

'My Lady, I am aware of what happened at Waldegrave Terrace,' Becky lowered her head, looking saddened, 'but I did not want to bring it up here, in the street. On behalf of my family, I want to offer you our most sincere apologies. What happened is beyond the pale. My sister is mad; she is not aware of her acts. I beg you to forgive her, please.'

'I understand, Becky. Do not worry,' Harmony felt obliged to show some maturity, or at least to lie for the sake of politeness. The truth was that she still felt crushed by that woman's words and by her husband's betrayal. 'I hope she is in better health now. Thank God your father arrived to take her home safe and sound.'

Becky frowned. 'My father? No. He has not set foot outside of the county for years now. He has been in poor health and the doctor has forbidden him to go travelling.'

'Oh. I'm so sorry, Becky. But, then, who came to pick her up?'

'Colvile. Her husband. He went to Hampstead to collect her.'

For a moment, Harmony believed she would be unable to carry on with the conversation. Becky's revelation had swept all thoughts from her mind, and for a few tense seconds, it took all her concentration to send oxygen to her lungs. Luckily, Becky was extremely eloquent and carried on talking without pause, giving her a chance to process her thoughts.

Lady Colvile was married. Harmony had chosen to believe she was a widow or divorced, but the woman had a husband, and he evidently maintained a good relationship with Waldegrave, judging by the brief exchange she had seen through her bedroom window. Did he perhaps ignore that the two had an illicit relationship, or did he prefer to turn a blind eye to that fact?

'You are so generous,' Becky continued, now having totally abandoned her joyful tone. 'You can't imagine how hard living with her illness has been for us. We have abandoned any hope of her cure,' she sniffled loudly, 'I don't know how poor Aldous manages; I mean Lord Colvile, of course. I admire his dedication to my poor sister; his love, his tolerance, and his attentions, that in her condition must be extreme. He has to look after her even when she's asleep, did you know? In case she tries to kill herself again… Oh, God, forgive me. I don't know what I'm saying.' Becky raised her fingers to her lips in anguish.

Harmony, however, felt paralysed. A mountain of contradictory ideas crowded in her head. Regret, guilt, sadness, relief—that she wasn't sure she should allow to develop inside her heart—were running through her nerve endings at the same time. Her memory replayed the episode in the dark corridor of the mansion when she had seen Devlin coming out of that woman's chamber.

'I hope the shameful incident with my sister won't be an obstacle to our future friendship, Madam,' added the viscountess, looking worried.

She smiled, shaking her head. 'Harmony. That's my name, Becky.'

She returned to Sudeley as soon as she said goodbye to the chatty Lady Burghill. On the journey back, her mind did not stop spinning the information she had been offered by that kind woman, who had turned out to be Lady Colvile's sister.

What if she had made a mistake when she judged her husband? What if he wasn't as she believed? Just thinking that those bitter days could have been due to an unfortunate misunderstanding made her head spin. Hope had managed to penetrate her regrets like a ray of sun sneaking through a crack into a dark cave. If she could talk to him and straighten things up perhaps everything could be mended. Before the arrival of that horrible woman, there had started to grow a pleasantly harmonious atmosphere in their shared life. If she could re-establish it, she was sure they could manage to become a good married couple.

She rushed down the lane to the carriage and stepped onto it without waiting for the coachman's assistance. When they arrived at the mansion, she strode inside purposefully. All that jumble of doubts that tortured her could vanish if she spoke to Devlin as soon as possible, if she asked him that, for the first time, both of them lay their pride aside and said what they thought without hurting each other.

'Harmony, where have you been? I was starting to get worried,' Corine said, hurrying to her as soon as she saw her cross the front door. 'The servants told me you had gone out early this morning without breakfasting.'

'Eh… I went to town.'

'To town? I would have accompanied you if you had asked me to.'

'I know, but I wanted to be alone.'

'You fought again, didn't you?'

The young woman nodded.

Corine sighed, looking weary. Her expression tittered between affection and pity. Harmony didn't accept the latter. Things were about to change, and she would not need to get used to being looked at that way.

'Excuse me, Corine. I need to see my husband.'

'Haven't you heard?' she asked her, standing in her way.

'Heard what?'

'Dear girl, Devlin left this morning.'

Her heart beat so thunderously that it shook her insides, as if she had been hit by an invisible wooden bat. Harmony knew what that mean, but she had to ask, 'What do you mean? Where has he gone?'

'Back to London. He's taken his things with him.'

With that brief explanation, all the illusions that had been building up during her journey back in the carriage collapsed around her, the way she imagined Sudeley's walls must have tumbled down during the war.

'I'm sorry, I thought you knew.' Corine took her hand without her realising it, probably aware of the tremor in her limbs. 'He left before you did. He hardly said goodbye to me and his grandfather. He said he had things to sort out.'

'He has already sorted one of them... by leaving me behind.'

'Don't say that,' her mother-in-law whispered. 'Come with me, come on. I'll ask Agnes to bring us something to eat in the greenhouse.'

Later, they were seated in front of a breakfast that was growing cold because they hadn't touched it once. Harmony was unaware of it, in the same way as she was unaware of the exuberance of the greenhouse garden around her, which grew protected from the rigours of winter. Sudeley's greenhouse, with its high walls and glass ceiling that offered great views of the ruins of the castle, provided shelter for hundreds of plants and trees of a variety of species. The flowers exhibited their ostentatious colours without fearing the harsh weather outside, while their roots were being fed by an innovative watering system.

There were gravel paths, benches in wrought iron, and elaborate plaster-of-Paris sculptures. The greenhouse would be a perfect refuge to share a private conversation and a tasty picnic if she ever were in the right mood. Harmony thought that she would have more than enough time to admire the place. After all, she was going to be there for a long, long time, to her regret.

'I've seen one of your friends in town… Lady Burghill,' she mumbled dejectedly. Corine smiled discretely at her, and she continued, 'She sends her best wishes.'

'Becky is an exceptional woman. I have her in high esteem.'

'And what about her sister, Lady Colvile?'

Corine furrowed her brow. The way in which Harmony had asked about Laurel had caused suspicions to rise in her mind. Had Kirkeby's daughter had something to do, perhaps, with the disagreements between Devlin and his wife? Unfortunately, it would be no surprise to her if she had. 'Laurel is a special case,' she said, choosing her words with extreme care. 'She should not be judged like a normal person, Harmony. She has never been one. The doctors say she is mad.'

'She behaved accordingly when she turned up at Waldegrave Terrace a few days ago. She demanded an explanation from Devlin for having married me; she insulted me, and did what she pleased for the two days she stayed at the mansion. If she had not come, perhaps Devlin and I…'

Corine closed her eyes, sorrowful. There was her answer. 'Dear girl, you should not take her seriously. She is jealous; she's always loved Devlin, and now that he is no longer available, she had no other course of action at her disposal than to attack you.'

'Now I realise that.' Harmony stirred her cup of tea absentmindedly. 'Her husband came to pick her up. He seemed mortified.'

'Colvile is a saint. Not many men would be prepared to put up with such a duty; but, as you see, he's so in love with her that he can overlook her madness. Before Colvile became interested in her, Kirkeby, her father, had lost all hope of finding her a husband. He had accepted that she would have no family of her own and one of her sisters would have to look after her until the end of her days.'

Harmony looked at her thoughtfully. 'What's wrong with her, Corine?'

'Since she was very young we knew she would be different.' Corine's voice took on a compassionate tone. 'She seemed to live in a separate world, an unfathomable one nobody else could access and nobody could rescue her from. Her parents resorted to many specialists, but none of them were of any help. At first, when she was only small, they thought she was blind, then deaf. Later they said she must be slow. She didn't speak until she was eight years of age.' Corine noticed Harmony shudder to hear this, then continued, 'And when she did speak, it was only to utter lies and obscenities. Her character became more and more bitter with time; as a young girl she was irascible, aggressive, and fickle to the point that her own mother told me once, with tears in her eyes, that she would have preferred Laurel had been stillborn.'

'I'd never heard of anything like that,' Harmony replied, looking horrified.

'Me neither.'

Harmony stopped playing with her tea and rubbed her brow with her fingertips. She could not believe she was starting to feel pity for Lady Colvile. 'At first, I didn't understand why Devlin refused to put her in her place,' she confessed, 'and that made me furious. Now I know he was only trying to protect her. I would have liked to know his reasons at the time.'

'My son has been shouldering the morbid affection she has for him for a long time. Laurel has told everybody that they have been lovers since they were young, and that's not true. Some people have decided to believe it, even when they know she is a pathological liar,' she sipped some tea and added, 'Some time ago, Devlin turned up at a crowded ball accompanied by a lady, and Laurel, who was there, caused a very embarrassing incident. When Devlin took her back home, trying to calm her down, she tried to kill herself in front of him, with a letter opener. But you already knew that, didn't you?'

Harmony nodded. 'Everybody knows.'

'Anyway. I'm sure that underneath that hostile mask, Laurel experiences a pain that nobody can imagine,' Corine whispered, as if she was trying to put to rest the story of that girl for whom she seemed to feel true compassion. 'But that is not Devlin's business, or yours. You two are married and must make your marriage work.'

'Did you have a good marriage?' Harmony asked, noticing Corine's beautiful face grow tense. Harmony remembered some of the horrible things Lady Colvile had shouted in her face: that the previous Duke of Waldegrave had had dozens of lovers, and that it wasn't a secret at all. The evident dismay in her mother-in-law's face proved to her that, at least on that count, Laurel had not lied to her. The fact of having brought up such a subject made her feel ashamed. 'I am extremely sorry. It's nothing to do with me.'

'Don't apologise.' Corine shook her head and raised her chin, her expression oozing dignity. 'Let's say that married life wasn't as I had expected, and perhaps that gives me licence to talk to you about it.'

They heard some discreet steps approaching the door. Mrs Frank, Sudeley's housekeeper, brought with her a tray stuffed with dark phials, cotton wool balls and a steaming container.

'Apologies for the interruption, Your Grace,' she said. 'It's time for your wash.'

'Oh, of course, Agnes!'

The housekeeper strode eagerly, resting the tray on a chair. Solicitous, she put on a pair of gloves and proceeded to mix inside a porcelain container the content of two phials. Afterwards, she picked up a cotton wool ball and soaked it in the mixture, using a pair of forceps. Harmony, who was absently watching it all, felt like asking what it was about, but something inside made her keep her peace. That was even more the case when she looked up from Mrs Frank's work and noticed that Corine had removed her eye patch. She didn't quite manage to control a jolt of horror on discovering the condition of her mother-in-law's right eye: it was out of alignment and embedded on the inside corner of the eye socket. The eye patch was required to hide that fact.

Ashamed for having reacted as she had, Harmony looked away from Corine. While Mrs Frank looked after the duchess, the girl's gaze wandered anywhere else: the greenhouse's glass ceiling, the late winter landscape beyond the fecund trees, the shiny silhouette of Sudeley's ruins, and the breakfast getting cold on the table.

'Many thanks, Agnes,' the dowager duchess told the obsequious servant when she had completed her task.

Mrs Frank removed the tray with its contents and disappeared through the door.

'Harmony…'

'Yes?' The girl's gaze remained elusive, even after her mother-in-law had returned the eye patch to its place. Corine had gone back to being the incredibly beautiful and solemn woman she had met outside of Sudeley.

'All this just because of my strabismus?' she inquired with a mocking and dismissive smile. 'Don't tell me it scares you!'

'No! It's only that it took me by surprise. I'm so sorry…'

'Don't feel sad for me,' she dismissed her reaction with a wave of her hands and then sipped on her cup of tea, 'I was ill years ago. Food poisoning. But it could have been worse, you know? There are people who die of it, so think me lucky.'

Strangely, the duchess's words had sounded acrimonious to her ears. However, she wanted to move on; she felt overwhelmed thinking of her pain, of how hard it must have been to lose the use of one eye. In spite of the short time they had known each other; she already felt genuine affection for her.

'As I was telling you before, Harmony, I love my son and wish to see him happy. I don't want to see his life turned into a battleground, and his own spouse turned into the enemy. That's an experience I don't wish on anyone.'

'Your son's happiness is not something I can play any part in.'

'You're wrong.'

'Didn't I tell you already how we ended up getting engaged? Do you think such a story can have anything but a wretched ending?'

'What does it matter how everything started? Things can change. In fact, they have happily changed, as far as I can see,' she said, smiling. Harmony looked at the older woman as if she had suddenly lost her mind. 'Can't you see it? Devlin loves you.'

Yes, the poor duchess had gone mad, the same as Lady Colvile and the old woman on the street in Winchcombe, Harmony thought sombrely. Either that or she had to be laughing at her. 'Of course not!' she grumbled.

Corine looked back at her, evidently astonished. 'I can't believe how blind you are.'

'No, you are the blind one!' To her surprise, she was shouting at her refined mother-in-law and pointing at her with a furious finger. How had they moved so quickly from one situation to the next? Right then, she didn't care. 'I don't know what you've seen in him, but I'm not stupid. I know why things happened the way they did.'

'I see you haven't noticed.'

'He might be tolerating my presence; and perhaps there is something in me he likes, but... but that is not love!'

Corine looked unblinkingly at her. 'You don't know him then.'

'And how would I get to know him when he is a block of ice, incapable of telling me that he owns a lightbulb factory, or that he has a grandfather and a mother?' she blurted out, her emotions getting the best of her. 'He hardly speaks to me, Corine; he hardly replies to my questions and never asks me anything! I'll tell you why. Because he doesn't want to know anything about me; because he cares little for me. He married me because he felt it was his duty to do it—'

'I've already told you, Harmony,' the woman insisted forcefully. 'Your husband is brilliant when it comes to his science and his businesses, but in regards to his feelings, he is... he is like a monkey with a kaleidoscope!' And suddenly, her only visible eye rolled in such way that Harmony would have started laughing if the situation had been slightly more cheerful. 'And know I'm talking like my father!'

They shared a sad smile that, at least, reduced the tension.

'Devlin doesn't harbour those kinds of feelings for me, Corine,' she whispered a moment later. 'Would he have left me here if that was the case?'

'I apologise for asking you this but... are you sure you haven't hurt him?'

Harmony grabbed the arm of the chair while her mind dissected the last conversation they had engaged in. It was true that they had said horrible things to each other; she could not remember exactly what. She had experienced fear, rage, and resentment. She had not considered the possibility that she might have hurt him too.

'He grabbed my book...' she muttered, 'and I tried to get it back because Miss Andersen... he should not have seen it.' Treacherous tears threatened to appear in her eyes. 'I didn't want him to believe... I'm not uncouth, Corine.'

Devlin's mother contemplated her tenderly for a few moments, then rushed to her side to comfort her. She embraced her as if she were her own daughter, and Harmony clanged onto her shoulders, grateful.

'It's all right, little one,' she kept saying. 'It's all right. You're nothing of the kind.'

'I'd like to say I forgot myself Corine, but the truth is that I've never been a true lady!' she said, crying, her face buried in her mother-in-law's shoulder.

'How soon you've returned from your trip to the countryside, Your Grace! We haven't even had a chance to miss you.'

Limsey hid his disappointment on seeing the duke arrive in a rented carriage. He didn't come back accompanied by his wife, and his face reflected spite in its purest form. That could only mean one thing. Now he knew his prayers and those of the entire personnel at Waldegrave Terrace for the duke and the duchess to make peace had fallen on deaf ears.

'Any news?' The duke said, looking both haggard and unkempt, as he handed Limsey his mink coat, hat and gloves. Limsey would not have been surprised if he had learned that the duke had been drinking during his train journey from Gloucestershire.

'Your study is ready for use again, Your Grace. The workers have done an excellent job, truly,' he replied, hoping to cheer him up, although at heart he understood that such a trifle would hardly cheer a man who had shown a propensity for loneliness and moodiness since childhood.

Waldegrave turned away from his servant, his brow etched deeply. He felt as if he had poured salty water on his wound that was still fresh. The reference to the study's newly repaired roof brought back to his memory the occasions when he had surreptitiously looked at his wife while she lay on her sofa doing something as innocent as reading one of her books. He remembered the wild kiss he had stolen from her in the library, in front of the phonograph, when he had tried to seduce her, and he had been the one who had ended up falling at her feet.

Fate had pulled his threads to drag him towards her, to make him taste her sweetness, and then, damn it, had shaken them again to pull them asunder. He couldn't even figure out how he had gone from hardly being able to tolerate her presence at Waldegrave Terrace to needing her in such a pressing way.

Be that as it may, it was best to stick to his original plan and put some distance between them, before their constant fights caused him more serious wounds.

Devlin entered his study, followed by his loyal servant that informed him of what had happened during his brief period of absence.

'I intended to send you your correspondence this afternoon,' Limsey said, giving an innocent intonation to his voice. 'It was lucky I didn't. I imagine now I only have to give the postman the duchess's post.'

Devlin glanced at the correspondence piled up on his desk. Looking through them quickly, he saw that they were letters, work reports, and a bunch of unmissable social invitations. Suddenly, John Talbot's name made him stop paying attention to anything else.

'Has that scoundrel come back?' he asked, frowning.

'I'm afraid he has, Sir, and sporting a less-than-cordial attitude as well. He insisted on seeing you and did not believe me when I told him you were out of London.'

'What's wrong with that individual?' he mumbled, bad-tempered on remembering the bitter and prideful face of Harmony's uncle. Just thinking he was related to such a scoundrel turned his stomach. Then, a discomforting thought crossed his mind. 'Do you think Talbot wants to make sure I'm taking good care of his niece?'

'In fact, Mr Talbot didn't ask after the duchess.'

He turned to look at the butler, incredulous. 'Are you sure?'

'Absolutely, Your Grace.'

Devlin was even more surprised now. 'Then, what the hell did he want?'

Limsey cleared his throat. 'I thought I heard the words 'business matter' in the middle of a diatribe full of grumbling, Your Grace,' he said in his usual mordant and ceremonious tone. 'But of course, I could have misheard it in the middle of such nonsensical hubbub.'

Devlin tutted. Get into business with that trickster? It had to be a damn joke. After the total fiasco with Iolanthe, Talbot should have been grateful that Waldegrave had married his niece; otherwise, his name would have become nothing by now but a vague memory in the horse racing business. A single negative comment of his would have put Talbot out of the picture in less than a week.

How could that lazy individual have the gall to turn up at his house and demand a non-prearranged meeting? Did he perhaps think that the marriage of his niece with the duke conferred him some kind of privilege? If that was the case, he would have to bring him down a peg.

'What should I say if he comes back, Your Grace?' Limsey asked.

'That I cannot see him,' he mumbled as he started writing on a piece of paper. 'And don't you dare give him an appointment.'

'Understood, Sir,' The butler smiled, mockingly.

'Limsey, there's something else… I want you to send somebody to the bookshop this minute. I need this book,' he gave him a piece of paper with the title and the name of the book in question. 'It's crucial that I get it this afternoon.'

The butler took the piece of paper and put it inside the pocket of his uniform, after discreetly glancing at it. 'You can count on it, Your Grace,' he said before he bowed and left.

After Limsey's departure, Devlin remained alone in his small and lonely empire. He raised his eyes to look at the state of the ceiling after the refurbishment; it looked impeccable, he acknowledged somewhat disdainfully.

He started reading his letters eagerly, hoping that some work matter would keep him occupied for the next few days. He found recent issues of American scientific magazines he was subscribed to; messages from old acquaintances congratulating him on his nuptials; a letter from his partners of Calder & Barrett, and another one from his good friend, Thomas Edison, about his progress in establishing the power plant in Pearl Street, New York—the first one of its kind—that would suffice to power twenty blocks of houses in one of the most important financial districts of the city.

Devlin was determined to make sure that London also had a source of reliable electric power, therefore he had done everything in his hands and more to get the parliament involved and his wealthier friends as investors to achieve it, but he could not honestly say that his efforts of the last few months had been too fruitful. He couldn't help but feel a sting of envy on realising the Americans would beat him to it.

A letter, the last one, awaited patiently its turn to be read. Devlin picked it up without much enthusiasm, expecting an onrush of flattery from a nosy countess determined to get an invitation to Waldegrave Terrace. On opening it and recognising the female voice behind the energetic and elegant calligraphy, his heart paused for a second. His back straightened up suddenly, no longer leaning on the back of the chair, and his incredulous eyes devoured hurriedly the beautifully traced lines, the words that were full of affection; the same ones he had been waiting to read for months, like a castaway waiting for the arrival of a rescue ship.

It was from Victory. Lady Lovelace.

The baroness greeted him warmly, brought him up-to-date with the progress of her foundation, and asked him to meet her.

Chapter 14

Devlin had no idea what to tell Lady Lovelance. On one hand, he was intrigued by her request to meet with him, but on the other, he worried that on doing so, the feelings that he had miraculously managed to get rid of would return with a vengeance. Nothing could be more catastrophic than discovering that the growing affection he had been feeling for his wife, his sweet Harmony, had been nothing but a cloud of smoke behind which Victory's name remained indelible in his heart.

Because he wasn't an impulsive man, he decided he would not reply until he was sure of what he wanted to tell her, and also of what he would feel if he saw her in front of him again. He was faced with a fight that, at the moment, he wasn't ready to confront.

He took advantage of the next few days to join the parliamentary activity and keep his mind occupied with the matters of the government. At that point, they were discussing the pitiful defeat of the British Troops in Laing's Neck at the hands of the Boer rebels of Transvaal. Devlin and his party peers bemoaned the fact and defended the idea of officially recommending an honourable withdrawal, and the immediate signature of an armistice, because the Crown regiments had dwindled alarmingly at the hands of the rebels. Any new attack by the British troops, now diminished in number and led by inexperienced military commanders after the death of the most experiences generals, would be heading for a humiliating defeat.

After the heated discussion that took place in the House, Devlin went to have a drink with Lord Felton in the Britannia, an exclusive pub in Kensington. More than anything, he wanted to avoid being approached by his friends and dodge the usual questions about his wife and their rushed marriage.

London had thawed; the streets were again a dynamic boiling pot of rough and vague voices, of the newspaper vendors' cries, of the bustling street commerce and the stink of smoke, ash, and horse manure. In Kensington, the landscape had improved dramatically. The air was cleaner and the view of the gardens a calming one. However, Devlin felt strange, as if he wasn't truly there, as if he were absent from his brand-new study at Waldegrave Terrace, from his seat at the House of Lords, the London streets, and his empty and icy bed.

As Devlin enjoyed a drink in the pub with Felton, the latter, relying on the trust they had in each other, asked him about his marriage. Devlin replied that Harmony and he were better now than a month ago, although that wasn't saying much. However, he did not need to say much. Even a blind man would be able to notice that he was feeling dejected, just by listening to his voice that was distant and gloomy. His good friend, Lord Felton, whom he addressed simply as Harvey, surely hadn't seen him looking like that even when Lady Lovelance had abandoned him for Lord Radnor.

'You should come for dinner one of these days,' Harvey suggested, breaking his reverie. 'Clarissa will be very happy to see you.'

Devlin gladly agreed and, instead of days, only hours passed before he was again at Felton House, the place where everything had started.

He dined with Harvey and his wife, Clarissa, who greeted him with her usual warmth. In contrast with what he had been expecting, the viscountess was discreet and avoided making too many mentions to his marriage. He assumed that Felton had probably asked her not to do it, having informed her of his unwillingness to talk about Harmony. Strangely enough, neither of them mentioned Lady Lovelance either, although Devlin knew of the friendship between the Feltons and his previous lover. Perhaps both of them had decided not to bother him with matters that could irk him.

Devlin didn't know if he should feel grateful for their kindness or be seriously upset, and started to worry that his friends might be pitying him. That was the last damn thing he needed: becoming an object of pity. 'Clarissa, my wife sends her apologies for not having worn the wedding dress you chose for her,' he piped up suddenly.

The viscountess looked at Devlin surprised, with the hint of a smile that finally won the battle over the subdued expression she had maintained throughout the whole dinner.

'Oh, please,' she exclaimed joyfully. 'She does not need to apologise. It was her wedding, her choice. I only offered her an option. Did she... did she tell you why she didn't wear it?' she asked, in a soft tone of voice.

Devlin sighed. 'It wasn't necessary. I'd bet it was to make her opinion count before accepting me for her husband.'

'A spirited woman. I like her!' said Clarissa.

You should have seen her on her birthday, he thought sarcastically.

'I hope she gets on well with Corine,' she went on.

Devlin hesitated. He wasn't sure that was possible. Corine had made clear the little confidence she had in Harmony; however, he hoped the maternal and protective side of the duchess would discover, sooner or later, the girl's tenderness and would soon become her defender. Or was that something he should fear, somehow?

'I hope so,' he replied, finally.

'I'd like to invite her home one of these days, if you'll agree.'

'I'll tell her,' he briefly replied.

He left a few hours later, with his friends sad and worried for him, he imagined. But the Feltons knew him well enough to dare interfere with his problems. They knew he was too proud to listen to advice and to other people's opinions.

As these thoughts circled in his mind, Devlin bemoaned being cold and circumspect and wished he was the kind of man who could accept other people's support, the kind who was able to admit to his weaknesses, free of the fear of being judged. Unfortunately for him, he wasn't that kind of man.

Back in Hampstead, he went straight to his study, and then to the drawer buried deepest in his desk. He had already delayed the reading of that document long enough. He had no excuses left. He moved aside several papers until he found the folder he had been avoiding for so long. Harmony's file.

Once he had finished reading those few pages, he knew that his wife was the daughter of the foreman of a small property in Surrey and of a woman who had been brought up in the local orphanage. Harmony's parents had fallen ill with tuberculosis, as had many of the villagers. Mr George, without close family to rely on, had sent his ten-year-old daughter to stay with some acquaintances in London, to prevent her from catching the illness. Unfortunately, the couple did not win the fight and died, away from their young daughter. The house where they lived had been burned down by order of the property's owners, as had others that had housed the sick and dying. Little Harmony had been sent to live with her father's half-brother, John Talbot, and his wife, Minnie, who had no children.

Devlin felt sad just thinking about all the hardships his wife had probably had to put up with. For God's sake, she was only a little girl when she lost her parents, and she had been dragged out of her home to be dropped into the life of two strangers. There must have been a reason why Harmony's father had not sent her to stay with that brother from the beginning. Perhaps he was not in contact with him; perhaps he did not trust him. 'And how could he trust such a swindler?' he wondered, getting increasingly angry.

Then, he remembered Harmony had once confessed to him that her education had started late. He hadn't even been polite enough to ask her why. He had not paid attention to it at the time, and that made him feel miserable. It might have been that John Talbot did not have enough money to pay for a good school when the time came, or he might be a miser, on top of a crook. He remembered the simple dress she had worn to the Christmas ball—the same one he had torn—and the sad wedding dress. Those were pieces of clothing made for somebody truly poor.

How was it that the owner of the property where Mr George worked had never looked after Harmony, or at least granted her a small sum for her maintenance, considering that her father had been a loyal employee occupying a position of trust for over fifteen years?

He had to find out the name of the property and of the villain who had washed his hands of the well-being of one of his closest employees. He asked his staff to get hold of Mr Peter Ashcroft, private investigator and author of the file on Harmony. Ashcroft, who was located by phone, was contrite for not having included all the details in his file, but he answered all his questions. The property was called Portington Park and it belonged to Lord Eastbury. Devlin thanked him and hung up the phone.

Lord Eastbury. He had seen him once, a long time ago, and remembered him as a grumpy and lonely old man who had moved out of London when he become a widower. He also knew that he had died under a year ago, and the title had passed to his grandson, young Daniel Eastbury.

Devlin was disappointed to realise he'd lost his chance to demand an explanation from old Eastbury for his slights towards the daughter of Mr George, but felt satisfied to know that Daniel, the new viscount, was accessible. He would obtain anything he wanted from him, if he played his cards right. He decided to talk to him after the next session at the House.

Right now he had other aims, he decided, as he put pen to paper to write a letter.

A few days later, Miss Penelope Andersen, Harmony's old governess, arrived at Waldegrave Terrace and was prompted to sit down in front of

Devlin at his study, her expression expectant.

'I must confess I'm intrigued, Your Grace,' she said smiling. 'I can't guess the purpose of this meeting. I hope the duchess is in good health.'

'Many thanks for your concern, Miss Andersen, and for coming here as soon as I requested your presence,' Devlin looked at her, making an effort to soften his usually rigid expression. If there was anybody capable of removing his doubts was that moralist lady to whom he owed, at least in part, his marriage. 'My wife's health is excellent.'

'I'm pleased to hear that. On the wedding day, as was to be expected, she was apprehensive, poor girl. Thankfully it all went very well, don't you think?' Devlin nodded, holding her gaze. 'I miss her so,' she sighed.

'I am sure, but I imagine the marriage of your former student has been a relief to you. I mean, I understand that you have another student and now you'll be able to give her your full attention.'

'Yes. Miss Thorton is a lovely girl. I won't lie to you, Your Grace, but I'm too old to take on the instruction of two girls. Since Harmony… I mean, since the duchess has not had a need for my services any longer, I feel a bit more at ease.'

His expression turned somewhat mocking. 'Did my wife cause you many troubles?'

'No! No, what would make you believe that?' Miss Andersen, startled, drank a long sip of tea, while Devlin held back his laughter. He couldn't imagine the types of devilries Harmony would have done in her period as student of the Honourable Miss Penelope Andersen. 'The duchess was a true angel; proper, disciplined, hard-working, obedient… She caused me no trouble at all, Your Grace. None at all…'

'Why did you take her on, to begin with?' he asked her, standing up and walking around the desk at a measured pace. 'Didn't you realise that at your age you were not in the best position to look after two young girls at the same time?'

'You see… I didn't accept her as my pupil at first, but Mr Talbot was very insistent.'

'Really? What did he say, exactly?'

Penelope Andersen swallowed hard, then looked up to the powerful man who was contemplating her from above, like a bird of prey ready to rip out all her secrets in an interrogation she had not seen coming. She cleared her throat, feeling slightly uneasy.

'He told me the story of her parents and how traumatic it had been, for him and his wife, to receive a girl with such background. I thought mostly of her, of course. Poor girl, losing her family in such a terrible way... I got worried, even, because I thought she might need some kind of help I wasn't able to provide for her. Luckily, when I met her I realised that she was only a shy and lonely girl, but eager for knowledge and orientation.'

'How did Talbot convince you of taking her on? I imagine he must have offered you a sum of money much higher than what you are used to receiving for your services.'

Penelope couldn't stop a sarcastic burst of laughter exploding out of her mouth. Devlin raised an interrogating eyebrow, making her stop immediately. 'No, Your Grace,' she replied, downcast. 'Nothing like that.'

'Then he swindled you.'

She swallowed hard. 'Your Grace, I don't think—'

'Answer, Miss Andersen,' he insisted. 'Please.'

She stirred in her seat. The request had sounded more like an order, and she did not dare question it, coming from the Duke of Waldegrave. She did not understand what the purpose of so many questions was, but she could do nothing but reply.

'I was simply... moved by her situation,' she mumbled while she kept turning around the small handbag on her lap with her hands. 'Mr Talbot told me that he had tried to convince other governesses, but none had accepted the job. I imagined that a girl like her, left to her own devices, without the education required to find a good husband, and... well, I wasn't going to allow Minnie Talbot to look after her!'

'Why hadn't anybody accepted her?'

She sent him a pained look. She shook her head, worried she might be about to say something that she'd later regret. But, she realised, she'd rather be on the duke's good side than fighting the corner for the despicable and vile John Talbot. 'Not everybody, in these hard times, agrees to reduce their fees by a fifty per cent, as he requested, Your Grace. Even if it is to educate a young orphan girl...'

'Was that bastard looking for a discount?'

Devlin felt his blood boil. His shout, and the loud noise his fist made when it struck the luxurious wood of the desk made the woman jump. Devlin forced himself to regain his composure and to apologise immediately. Damned Talbot had used his sleek patter to take advantage of the governess, and one should not forget his abhorrent attitude during the negotiation of his niece's education.

'I'm truly sorry, Miss Andersen.'

'Your Grace, I don't know why you're asking me all those questions,' the woman whispered, breathless. 'You already know John Talbot is a compelling and miserly man. I heard that he sold you a horse of doubtful provenance. Don't be surprised if his dirty tricks extend to other matters.'

'I'm not surprised, only disgusted.' And that was the case. How many things had Harmony been deprived of as a young girl? Devlin forced himself to go back to his ceremonious tone. 'That is the reason why Harmony's studies started so late, isn't it? Talbot lost invaluable time trying to find a victim who would agree to his unfair requests.'

'Yes. She was already seventeen when she came to me. I always start when the girls are fourteen. The poor girl didn't know where China was or what fork should be used to eat a salad.'

'Thanks for accepting, by the way,' he grumbled. 'I agonise just imagining Minnie Talbot teaching my wife geography or the proper use of cutlery.'

'God help us! That woman is only qualified to teach her how to devour a steak in half a minute!'

Devlin sighed. 'I hope that rascal, Talbot, paid you, at the very least.' Andersen looked down, mortified, causing him to grunt. 'It can't be! After all this time?'

'He promised to get me a pony or tame horse by the end of last year, and told me that with that he'd cover all the arrears. He assured me that he was getting it ready to be a champion and afterwards it would be worth a fortune,' she said regretfully. 'God help me, and I believed him like a little child would have! I haven't seen even a horseshoe yet, Your Grace.'

Devlin mumbled a curse. So the governess had fallen for the same trick. 'Don't worry, Miss Andersen,' he muttered. 'That makes two of us.'

It was peculiar. He had detested the woman, but now he understood he owed her so much. She had looked after Harmony, had got her ready for him and had obviously coaxed her to marry him as well. To tell the truth, right then he felt the total opposite emotion: an infinite gratitude for her. And a certain empathy, of course.

He went straight for his desk drawer, produced a chequebook, and started writing one up while the woman looked away. 'Miss Andersen, I'm very grateful for your visit this afternoon. I want you to know that I'm in debt to you for educating my wife so well. And, to be honest, I cannot imagine a duchess worthier of the title than she is.'

The governess wriggled in her seat, looking proud and happy. 'Your Grace, it has been a true honour for me.' She looked as if she could hardly speak from her joy. 'Oh, my God, I don't think in twenty-seven years as a governess I've ever been thanked by a husband—'

'Shame on them. I hope this amount will cover your fees in full, for all the time you've invested and, of course, the trouble you've gone to.'

Andersen took the cheque hesitantly and squinted to read it, her heart racing with excitement. When she saw the amount written down, she thought she was mistaken and moved the piece of paper back down on her lap, trying to compensate for her poor eyesight. No, it hadn't been a mistake, she realised, her eyes opening like plates in an instant. Waldegrave had paid her a small fortune. 'Good God! This is... too much!'

'No, it isn't, Miss Andersen.' Devlin smiled. 'It's yours, you have earned it.'

'Thanks, Your Grace... I...' Her voice faltered, her eyes filling up with tears. God only knew how badly she needed the money. 'You are very generous.'

'No. You have been.'

Harmony thought of Miss Penelope Andersen and realised how much she missed her. She wished she had been a more conscientious and competent student for her. That way, she would have profited more from her superb lessons and would have been able to face the preparation for the spring ball with more flair.

To distract her from her torpor after Devlin's departure for London, Corine had got her involved in that task, which seemed more complicated than she had been led to believe at first. Every year, when the ice melted in Winchcombe and the surrounding woods reawakened, the duchess offered a ball to the inhabitants of the town and the nearby villages. It was more of a folk party than an aristocratic event: one could see the town carpenter rubbing shoulders with the richest bourgeois of the region and the girls from the modest families—wearing dresses they had saved for the whole year—hoping that an unmarried and good-looking lord would notice them and ask them to dance.

It was a custom, more than a decade long, that the peers of the realm from the neighbouring areas would attend that event before leaving for London, and it had become a tradition that the well-off girls of marrying age would be seen there before the season started. There were also some who came deliberately from other cities to take part in this amusing Sudeley tradition and also to have a look at the property, which was a shining jewel of British history.

The working-class people, on their part, were also eagerly awaiting the spring ball. At the lightbulb and generators factory there was talk of nothing else, and that was also the case at church, in the market, and the shops in the high street. Some small producers, in gratitude for having been invited, offered their homemade cheese and milk, others did the same with their vegetables, preserves, meat and drinks. Even popular musicians offered to play for no pay. Corine accepted all the offers gracefully. Her intention was, of course, to promote a friendly coexistence among the inhabitants of the area without any class distinctions.

Weather permitting, the ball would take place in the gardens of the castle, her mother-in-law told Harmony as the carriage drove them to town. Luckily, twenty men and women from the town had offered their services to the housekeeper to collaborate on the hardest tasks. The men carried on their backs tons of meat that the women would later marinate in the kitchen. Others helped to carry the barrels of beer, crates of wine or the impressive floral arrangements that would be placed around the lake.

Therefore, they were facing an event of huge proportions, and Harmony only hoped that the teachings of Miss Andersen would help her succeed in such a test. A few days before her wedding, she had studied to know how to organise informal meals, formal balls for two hundred guests, and how to seat at the same table a European prince and a general, but a popular ball for such a variety of people?… She had to open up her mind and pray to heaven not to put her foot in it.

Luckily, spring wouldn't arrive for at least three weeks; although the ice had slipped from the tree branches, right now the cold was biting. Harmony observed Corine's eagerness for the arrival of spring, and she kept running up and down as if the ball was going to take place the very next day. She liked to deal with the invitations herself, closing the envelopes, pouring the sealing wax and pressing the Waldegrave signet ring. She went over the wine list with the butler and checked the amount of flour, eggs and strawberries for the cakes with the cook. During her walks in town, she often saw her mother-in-law greet a few acquaintances on their carriages and keenly invite them to the ball, to which they would all reply with pleased and satisfied smiles.

She definitely was a generous and well-liked woman. Harmony had learned to love her and respect her as a mother. Corine made no excuses and taught her everything a member of the Sawyer family should know: she told her about the notable family history and the impeccable lineage they came from; she guided her through the property and told her about Catherine Parr, the Protestant queen, who had been the most famous inhabitant of the medieval fortress. At the same time, she had become a good friend, one that did not lose faith in her, even though it was clear that her son had.

Corine, who returned her affection, had tried to sell her the idea that the ball was an unmissable opportunity to introduce herself formally as the new Duchess of Waldegrave. Yet, the idea of the ball filled Harmony with trepidation, and she had to make an effort to keep smiling every time it was brought up. What would the good people of Winchcombe say if they saw her without her husband during her formal presentation? Would they start to gossip behind her back? Would they deny her the respect they showed Devlin's mother?

She'd rather push those thoughts to one side, because there was no other option.

In contrast with her, Corine refused to fall prey to the loneliness and surrounded herself with good friends; some of them had come to visit her during the last few weeks. Among them was charming Becky, Lady Burghill, who had brought her two little children with her: a six-year-old girl called Cressida, and a boy of four called Albert. Harmony remembered fondly that day; it was the first time she had smiled after Devlin's departure. She had had tea with the children and then had shown them the greenhouse, while Sir Malcolm played cards with Lord Gardiner, to allow the nanny to have a rest. She also sensed that Becky needed to talk urgently to the duchess, alone.

Harmony very soon realised that Corine wasn't only her shoulder to cry on but also poor Becky's, who was still suffering due to her sister's mad ravings and to something related to her husband, Lord Burghill.

Harmony was sure that other friends also benefitted from her mother-in-law's timely comfort. Some ladies came often to ask for her advice or would stop her in the street to ask for her opinion about such and such thing, as if Corine belonged to a wise species whose opinion could determine success in certain matters. The admiration Winchcombe women professed for her was irrefutable.

Then, Harmony started to wonder why she had not remarried. As she had hinted, her marriage hadn't been totally happy. Devlin's father had not left good memories, as she had come to suspect. If this weren't the case, there would be at least one of his portraits hung at Sudeley, or the servants would not get nervous when Harmony asked about him. Of course, the wretched man had made Corine suffer for years. It was true that he had cheated on her even when she was pregnant. God only knew what other hardships her late husband had put her through.

Perhaps the haughty position of the duchess prevented her numerous suitors from getting their hopes up; perhaps her intimidating son was a deterrent for anybody who was thinking of getting close to her. But Corine deserved to be happy, so Harmony hoped that she'd find happiness someday.

Harmony decided to accompany Corine on one of her visits to town. It was a lovely afternoon and her mother-in-law had an errand to run, one connected with the ball, of course. The coachman stopped in front of the park; the ladies had decided to walk the last stretch of their journey. At the other side of the woods, which would bloom in a matter of weeks, was the imposing church of Saint Peter, dating back to Saxon times. Harmony had gone to Mass with her mother-in-law a couple of times. Corine was determined to invite Reverend Fleet and his family to the spring ball in person. Fleet was a young man, despite his almost total baldness, and he was much easier to get on with than the previous head of the church, who had retired due to old age a few weeks earlier. The new reverend and his wife, the shy and helpful Rosamunde, had just arrived in Winchcombe with their seven-month-old son.

Delighted to welcome them, the Fleets accepted the invitation of the duchesses and invited them to have tea in their pretty parish house. Rosamunde, who wasn't precisely talkative, was the one who told them about the new doctor who had arrived in town. It was then that the duchess insisted on showing him the same courtesy as a sign of welcome.

After saying goodbye to the reverend and his wife, they visited the local millinery with the intention of indulging in a feminine pastime. Sometime later they came out carrying loads of parcels the footman would not have been able to carry on his own.

Then, Harmony looked under the shade of a birch, the only tree that was totally green in the park, and saw the old woman who had gazed at her angrily during her first visit to Winchcombe. The woman was wrapped in a dirty woollen blanket; it was as dirty as her cheeks and the hands that poked out through it in a pair of ragged gloves. Surprisingly, she had the same angry expression that so disconcerted her, only this time it was not addressed at her but at her mother-in-law.

Harmony felt her heart twinge with distress. She no longer listened to the lively chat of her mother-in-law, or to the street noise. She had her eyes fixed on the woman they were getting increasingly close to, and something told her she should be careful with her. She was about to ask Corine who that old tramp was when she left her hiding place behind the birch and strode towards them angrily.

'Criminals!' She was screaming like a banshee, making Corine, who had not seen her until she was almost by her side, stop dead in her tracks. 'Criminals! You are criminals!'

Startled, the duchess dropped her parcels. A stream of handkerchiefs and a pair of tiny hats were strewn on the gravel. Harmony was shocked by the poor crazy woman's reaction; she wondered where her daughter would be and looked around without finding her. The people observing the unpleasant spectacle were the passers-by and the shopkeepers who had looked out of their shop windows to find out the reason for the racket. Everybody seemed too shocked to know how to react.

The old woman carried on calling them 'criminals' without qualms, while Corine, frightened, took a few steps back and asked the woman to calm down. Harmony decided to intervene, as nobody else did: 'Lady, stop swearing!'

The woman spat close to her shoes and glared at Corine. 'Criminal woman!' she said, her eyes glazed over, her teeth the colour of coffee. 'All of you, you are a family of criminals and will end up in hell!'

'Shut up! Shut up, impudent woman!' Corine replied, breathing fast and with her only eye shining furiously. 'Stop insulting my family or you'll have to bear the consequences.'

Then, she set off running towards the carriage. Harmony had never before seen her lose control, and up to that point, she would have sworn that Corine, Dowager Duchess of Waldegrave, would have been unable to pronounce such nasty words. Hadn't she been the one who had advised her not to lose her nerves due to the delusions of a crazy woman?

Harmony followed her, unable to fully process what had just happened. The footman had been left behind, picking up the shopping from the floor, as he must have imagined would be expected of him.

Blinded by rage, Corine dashed through the streets. She only wanted to reach the carriage and go back home at full speed. On seeing the luxurious cabriolet with the family crest parked at the end of the street, she felt a rush of relief. She strode to it at a fast pace but, unfortunately, didn't have the presence of mind to look both sides before crossing the street. By the time she was able to react, she was already under the hoofs of a huge shire horse.

The animal neighed and reared up when the horseman, who obviously had not seen her running out of the park, tried to stop it. Overcome by fear, Corine screamed. Her only defence was to step back, shocked, and cover her head with both her arms, as if that would stop the charge of the two-ton beast. Then, she lost her balance and fell to the floor. She could only wait for the horse to trample her mercilessly.

But it did not happen.

After managing to stabilize his mount with incredible dexterity, the horseman dismounted and ran towards the terrified woman, who was lying in the middle of the street. With a professional attitude, he grabbed her wrist to check her pulse and then proceeded to tap her lightly on the face to make her come back to her senses. Only when the lady opened her eyes and the commotion had passed, did Martin realise how beautiful she was. He had heard about the beauty of local women, and he had had opportunity confirm it a couple of times, but until that day, his third one in Winchcombe, he had never seen anyone like her before.

'Miss... Lady...' He didn't know how to address her and felt suddenly stupid. 'Are you feeling well? Would you like to come to my surgery?'

The lady blinked repeatedly. It took her a few seconds to focus her eyes, and when she was able to, she looked straight at him. They looked at each other for a few seconds.

'Corine, good God!' A young and agitated woman kneeled next to the lady in trouble, whose name Martin now knew. She must have been her sister, he guessed. 'Are you all right? Did the horse knock you over? Talk to me!'

Corine rubbed her brow as she tried to find her voice. Slowly, she had started to see the world clearly around her again. 'I'm fine,' she said when she was able to stand up with the help of Harmony and that stranger who was looking at her with excessive worry.

She felt dizzy and ashamed in equal parts. That rushed behaviour was not typical of her, not even when Gretty bothered her with her antics, and now she had just made a fool of herself in front of that handsome gentleman.

Only when Corine was able to drag her eyes away from his, did she realise that a large circle of onlookers had formed around them. All were looking at her with certain distress and perhaps a bit of pity. When she looked back at them, they lowered their eyes.

Louis, the coachman, had reached them and looked paler than a sheet of paper. Harmony, always adorable and helpful, handed her something that she had not managed to fully make out. When she did, her breath caught. Good God! Her eye patch! It had fallen off in the middle of all the commotion.

Feeling suddenly naked, she moaned in anguish. She recovered the piece of leather with urgency. Her daughter-in-law helped her put it in place while Louis and the handsome stranger moved the crowd along.

'Please, move away. The lady needs a bit of air,' he demanded, probably still horrified after seeing her deformed eye.

Perhaps that was the reason why he had looked at her with such insistence. Dear God! She wished the earth would open and swallow her up whole right then.

'Are you feeling well?' Harmony asked. 'You look... flustered.'

Corine chuckled, in what she hoped was a casual way, intending to dissipate the terrible shame gnawing at her insides. 'Don't be silly, Harmony. It was only a fright, nothing else. I'm better than ever! And we have to leave right away, because that new doctor won't invite himself to the ball!' she said, as she straightened her skirt with all the dignity of a Radley. Her mother, the always composed Lady Gladys Radley, had taught her to put on a brave face when problems arise. Then, she ordered the coachman: 'Louis, the coach!'

'Lady... I have to apologise,' said the handsome stranger as he approached her without a change in his keen expression. She raised the palm of her hand to her eye instinctively, and he went on, 'I... didn't see you. Luckily, this horse I've just bought is quite obedient, and I managed to make him stop right on time.'

'It's all right. It wasn't your fault, sir,' she replied with a dismissive smile. 'It's fine! You and your horse can leave in peace.'

Corine tried to leave, but the insistence of the stranger kept her there.

'The truth is that I'd rather examine you, if you don't mind.'

On seeing her questioning look, the gentleman decided to offer her an explanation. 'Allow me to introduce myself: my name is Martin Bradshawe. I'm a doctor, and I've just moved into town. I arrived only three days ago. I was coming back from buying the horse, and I met you crossing the street...' He smiled at her and what a smile that was! 'You were in a hurry, weren't you?'

'It's not possible,' she mumbled, cursing her bad luck.

So, that was the new doctor. She had imagined a frail old man, pale and wearing thick glasses, for sure not a well-built gentleman, with sand-coloured hair with exquisite touches of grey, and lively blue eyes.

'He won't invite himself, after all,' Harmony said, looking amused, although Corine could not see the funny side of the incident. She had just had another nasty encounter with Gretty, and if that wasn't enough, now she'd been terribly embarrassed in front of the brand new doctor, who had already discovered her worst feature. Oh! She only wanted to go back home as soon as possible.

'Wouldn't you like to come by my surgery?' he insisted with that hoarse voice of his. 'It isn't much. As I told you, I've just settled here, but I think I have everything I need to look after you. It's on the corner, next to the barbershop,' he pointed at the place with his index finger, 'Please, come with me.'

'Yes, Corine, I think it's best,' Harmony, that little traitor, parroted the doctor's preposterous request.

She shook her head with determination. She'd had enough. 'It won't be necessary, Dr Bradshawe. Thank you.'

'Well,' he replied, disappointed. 'It's been a... pleasure, Mrs... '

'The pleasure has been mine. Have a good day.'

Martin stood alone and confused in the middle of the street. The lady had set off, followed by her coachman, her supposed sister, and a footman that was concentrating on carrying some parcels.

What a strange woman, he thought while he covered his head again with his hat. She hadn't even told him her name. Although he wasn't stupid; the crest of a noble family was engraved on the door of the carriage she had entered. He had seen it, weeks back, in a book about Gloucestershire when he had not yet decided to leave his native Lancashire.

That woman was the Duchess of Waldegrave, the duke's wife.

Chapter 15

According to the English members of parliament, Daniel Eastbury was a total idiot. In the few months since he had taken the place of the old viscount, he had not shown any evidence of honouring his legacy, and it wasn't for lack of ideas but rather for having too many of them. It was a shame that, in their opinion, none of them were sufficiently good, intelligent or at the very least, rational.

Some maintained that his interventions were so insubstantial that he might as well save himself the bother. 'How does he dare oppose the Irish Agricultural Law, or suggest that the British should leave India?' people would ask. The daily jokes centred on this or that comment of his, his desperate babblings or his fantastic idealism. The lords could not hide a mocking laugh or a censoring shaking of the head when Eastbury's name was mentioned in a private conversation. In a brief time, the young man had become the jester of a court full of boastful vultures that did not accept new blood or consent to freethinking.

If the youth had dedicated his time to listening to his detractors rather than insisting on his projects, Waldegrave would not have had him in such great esteem. Eastbury was convinced that politics were his forte, and although he was aware that his ideas were 'a step ahead of the old colonial British model', that did not discourage him. That was enough for Waldegrave to feel some respect for him. After all, he himself had been the object of ridicule due to his electrification project, and there was no shortage of lords involved in gas companies that attacked him head on.

Eastbury, of course, felt honoured when the Duke of Waldegrave greeted him in a friendly manner, and even more so when he invited him to have lunch with him that afternoon at the sumptuous Criterion Restaurant in Piccadilly

Circus. Eastbury was a confessed lover of fine dining as was evidenced by his rotund belly.

After making some enquiries as to general matters, Devlin addressed the point he was interested in. He made him aware of his marriage to the daughter of one of the old managers at Portington Park. Eastbury's reaction was to opening his blue eyes as big as plates. Although he made no offensive comments, it was clear that he could hardly believe that the duke could have been interested in a modest girl brought up in the countryside. That bothered Devlin, but he decided to focus on the matter that had brought him there.

'Wait!' blurted out the blonde youth, an amused smile playing on his lips. 'I know her! I mean, I saw her a few times when I went there during my school holidays. Of course! The boys and I used to call her 'cricket', because…' Eastbury stopped talking on seeing the duke's warning look, which made his intentions quite clear. 'It doesn't matter. Please, send the duchess my congratulations on your nuptials.'

'I will,' Devlin said with an impatient sigh. 'Eastbury, I'll get straight to the point: I need your help. I'm trying to find out if your late grandfather left some money for the upkeep of my wife after the death of her parents. As you'll imagine, Mr George was one of the viscount's most trusted men, and I refuse to believe that his daughter would not have had access to your grandfather's support on becoming orphaned.'

Eastbury blinked. 'I… I'm afraid I'm not familiarised with the way my grandfather dealt with his previous employees, Your Grace. Why don't you ask directly Harm… I mean, the duchess?'

Devlin's expression became one of displeasure. A waiter had arrived with a teapot and poured a cup of tea each. 'If it was my intention to ask her, I would have already done it.'

'It's true. My apologies,' he mumbled, looking down. 'My grandfather Eustace was a generous man, Your Grace, but he was never a rich man. I remember that time. When the workers of his property died of tuberculosis, it all collapsed. It took him years to get it working again; he was ill himself for a while. To be honest, I don't think he would have had much at his disposal to offer those families.'

'I understand.' Devlin nodded, but he was far from feeling satisfied. 'However, I'd like to make sure. I'm not asking for much, Eastbury. Only that some old files are dusted off, and that some questions are put to the people who used to look after your grandfather's books, if they're still alive. There must be something that can be checked!'

'I'll do as you ask, Your Grace, although I can't promise you anything.'

He shrugged after taking the last sip. 'As I told you, my grandfather didn't have much to give, although I'm sure his intentions were good.'

'It will suffice if you try, Eastbury.'

Devlin had a hunch. He didn't mistrust Eastbury; to be honest, the old man wasn't known as a miser, as his grandson had said. His ill thoughts pointed in another direction.

From the moment he'd read Harmony's file and learned her story, he had felt in debt with her; he wanted to go back to Sudeley but had decided to sort out a couple of things first. He needed to redress the hurt he had caused her with that marriage, physical harm included, and he could think of nothing better than his determination to get to truly know her, to the point where he revealed aspects of her life that not even she was aware of.

A week later, Eastbury informed him that neither his assistant nor he had managed to find anything other than insubstantial paperwork inside the old viscount's files. They had gone over Portington Park's office and the modest London manor from top to bottom, but they had not managed to find a single bit of evidence of a stipend post mortem left for Mr George or his family, or for any other of the inhabitants of Eastbury's village.

Devlin felt frustrated. Perhaps it was true that Mr George had died in the most abject poverty, and Harmony's aunt and uncle had looked after her with great personal effort. He had no intention of guessing and that only left him one option.

It was time to settle scores with a well-known swindler.

The life of the Talbots had taken a happy turn since Harmony married the duke. Even though they had no fortune or contacts, they had soon managed to make the head of the rigid London society turn and pay them attention. They had begun to get included in the guest lists for the most important events in the city: balls, premieres, concerts, exhibitions. Minnie was the one who most profited from her sudden lucky break and the money Waldegrave had given them. She did not decline any invitation, and did not spare in the purchase of fancy clothing to impress her new acquaintances. Her husband had given her a coquettish cabriolet she used to go riding around the city, raising her fatty chin, showing off her new dresses, her outlandish fur coats, and the jewels she had never dreamed of having.

Unfortunately, her social climb turned into a debacle when the implacable aristocrats noticed her lack of class. The doors of good society slammed on their faces as quickly as they had open. Truth be told, the only reason they had given a safe conduct to the Talbot family—allowing them to enter their exclusive society—had been the pressing need to know the family of the lucky new duchess and to be able to make jokes at her expense, for a change.

However, that did not disappoint Minnie in the slightest. She still had money, jewels, and rank! The snobbish woman spent time with the friends she had obtained thanks to her money, went shopping along Bond Street, and visited the fashionable fancy restaurants, as if she were a lady of the bourgeoisie.

On the other side, John had shut himself away in his little office in the Whitechapel house, refusing to waste his time on his wife's nonsense. He had realised a long time ago that flattering aristocrats in their stuck-up parties would not get him what he had set out to do. While Minnie savoured the sweet taste of her sudden social bliss, he was racking his brains with a new project, the same one that had kept him sleepless for the last few weeks. John wasn't stupid and knew that Waldegrave's money would run out soon, and then he would go back to being a humble horse dealer. That was why he was determined to earn more, much more money, and those blueprints he had before him would give him enough to live comfortably for the rest of his life... if he got them into the right hands.

His greedy mind took flight, until Minnie interrupted him to let him know that she would go to the city centre to order new furniture for the parlour. John composed a huge smile and said goodbye with a tender kiss on her cheek, but as soon as the door of the office closed, his expression turned into one of disgust.

For a long while now, he had felt fed up with that woman and her vulgarity, with her unnecessary and bothersome chat, with the voracious appetite that had given her the figure of a Pacific walrus. Even her bird-like croaking laughter bothered him.

He contemplated her through the window as she climbed into the cabriolet with gruelling difficulty. It was a child's game to keep Minnie Talbot occupied, he thought, oozing disgust. A couple of toys, a pantry stuffed with food, and a wardrobe full of feminine whims kept her fully content. Good for him, he thought as he waved goodbye at her. Now that his wife was fully devoted to wasting time on her nonsense, he could dedicate his to spoil the voluptuous dancer waiting for him every Friday in the refined cabaret of Madame Juliette and, of course, to put into practice the project that would turn him into a rich man.

A shadow crossed his face when he returned to his place in front of the bare desk. He thought of his niece, that silly girl who had not replied to any of his letters, and neither had Waldegrave. Harmony played a key part in his plans, and he could not afford to be in bad terms with her. He would write to her again; he would ask for a visit to her mansion. He would even behave like a father in order to avoid being thrown out of her place. The brat had turned up to be clever, he thought, a glint of admiration in his half-closed eyes. She had caught a duke; he didn't know what mysterious charms she had used, but she had done it as soon as she learned she was destitute, and with that marriage she had sorted out the rest of her life. But, she was mad if she believed he would be satisfied with what Waldegrave had paid out before the wedding. John Talbot would make sure he also got to share in the booty she now had access to, whatever it took.

He picked up a quill and drafted a new letter. This time he addressed it to the Castle of Sudeley, where that ungrateful girl would surely be, enjoying the assets of her extraordinarily wealthy husband. Harmony and Waldegrave had kept themselves removed from the public eye during the first weeks of their marriage. John imagined the duke must be feeling ashamed of the girl and would keep her in hiding for as long as he could. If that was the case, there would be no better hiding place than the majestic castle next to the Cotswolds, in the county of Gloucestershire.

Once he finished writing the letter, he went straight to the shed, mounted his bay horse and rode unhurriedly towards the rented stable where he kept his animals, his operation's headquarters. In a few weeks the races would get underway, and the season's main events—where John aspired to have his horses take part—would start.

Another one of his most immediate plans was to fix a couple of races in order to get one or two wins on the tracks. The minor scandal caused by Iolanthe and the constant defeats of his animals had muddied his already dilapidated reputation, and nothing would be better than a gust of glory to clean up his name and that of his business. For that reason, John had joined forces with a couple of important men in the world of horse racing. The men were no more than smartly dressed delinquents who made their opponents quake in their boots, but John was sure that he could handle them and bring them to his way of thinking. Apart from money and redemption, that connection seemed to hold the promise of profitable associations.

With this new and promising impetus, perhaps by spring he would not need to live off the pyrrhic prizes of his winning horses, or of the sale of his animals.

When he reached the stables, he surveyed his beasts that were settled in a well-protected box. He instructed the stable hands and scolded one of them, who had allowed the fire of the stove to die away.

229

Then, when he was about to pick up a riding whip to punish the guilty hand, he saw the duke entering the stable, and ended his reprimand abruptly with a satisfied smirk. The duke had read his letter. What would he be there for, otherwise?

'Your Grace, what a pleasure to see you in this humble stable!' He felt it was unnecessary to bow, as they were now related, but he decided to flatter as much as possible that unbearable and conceited man who looked at everything with an expression of disgust. 'If I had known you were coming I would have ordered them to clean up this hole, but as you know, the beasts are our business.'

'How kind of you, Talbot,' the duke replied with a smirk, as he glanced at the stable floor that was heaped with the accumulated manure. 'But you should know that this is not the kind of dirt that damages your business.'

John clamped his lips, feeling impotent. The brat had not got over his failure with Iolanthe, but he was not going to throw it in his face right now. He had to be more subtle. He pretended not to have grasped the malice of his comment.

'Please, accompany me to my office. You should not be made to breathe in this putrid air.' John guided him to the end of the corridor, where his office was located, a small but clean room he used to meet his clients and settled deals. 'Do you fancy a drink? I've just purchased a good brandy.'

Devlin shook his head. 'Don't go to such trouble, Talbot. I won't take up much of your time,' he said after sitting down.

'Not at all, Your Grace. After all, we are now family, aren't we?' He pretended not to notice the dismay in Devlin's face and went on, 'Tell me, please, how is my beloved little girl? Minnie and I miss her so; the house isn't the same without her laughter. We tried to visit her at Waldegrave Terrace, but that rough butler of yours prevented us from seeing her.'

'Mr Talbot, I'm afraid you have not taken into account the fact that it is totally uncivilised to turn up at somebody else's house without an invitation, more so if it is the residence of a duke and a duchess just married. But thanks for your concern, anyway. My wife is in excellent health.'

'I… I am very pleased to hear that,' he said, having to swallow the stream of insults the damn pompous man had uttered. 'I apologise for our interference. It wasn't our intention to disturb you… and please, send our best regards to the duchess. I am sure she misses us as well.'

Devlin gritted his teeth and wondered if that could be true, and the notion bothered him for a moment. In reality, what opinion did Harmony have of her aunt and uncle? He cursed himself again because he'd never been interested in finding out her opinion on anything.

'I always wanted to be like a father for her,' Talbot added. 'You see, God didn't bless my wife and me with a child, but when Harmony came into our lives, we felt so fortunate that we poured on her all the love we could never give our own child.'

John Talbot felt increasingly uneasy by this meeting. He swallowed hard when the duke's face turned into a hard mask of scepticism before he said, 'Really? If you loved her so much why didn't you allow her to study before she'd reached seventeen?'

John was left speechless by the bluntness of this comment, but he managed to keep his cool.

'I'm really indignant about that, Talbot. My wife spent seven years in total darkness. What can you tell me about that?'

John Talbot clenched how jaw, his mind racing. So, that idiot had shared family intimacies with Waldegrave. Why hadn't he considered that possibility? Did she mention Curson and her forced engagement? Did she tell the duke that he had helped himself to her inheritance? In spite of himself, he started sweating like a pig. He hadn't seen such a thing coming.

'Your Grace, my wife and I do not belong to the bourgeoisie. I make an honest living and, unfortunately, that is not enough to offer my family a life full of comforts. I always wanted… My Minnie and I always wanted the best for Harmony, a refined governess who would offer her a good education and teach her everything a decent woman needs to know, but that was beyond our means. When Harmony arrived in our lives, free state education was just in its beginnings in the country, and there weren't enough schools for all the children. Blessed be Miss Andersen,' he looked up, 'who appeared like a Godsend angel, although a bit later than we would have wished.'

Devlin furrowed his brow and willed himself to restrain his anger as he said, 'Yes, Miss Andersen! She's still waiting for her nag, as a matter of fact. I expect you to have it ready before next year.' Devlin hadn't fallen for Talbot's cheap speech. He wasn't precisely a poor man, or at the very least he hadn't always been one. Devlin had had him investigated. 'I understand that your businesses were quite profitable at certain times in the past. You even had your own stables in Newmarket and Ascot, full of purebloods, stables that were quite far from this pigsty you rent now. You bred true champions and sold them to American businessmen.'

John Talbot rubbed his temple, lips pressed together. He was cornered. Damned Waldegrave. He had seriously underestimated him. That man, with his power and contacts, had access to his full record. Even with that, he didn't allow himself to fall prey to fear, because the duke didn't seem to know the most important thing. If he had known about Harmony's inheritance and about Curson, he would have screamed it to his face. Perhaps the stupid girl had not told him out of shame. Better that way. That gave him an important advantage. For now, his only objective was to survive the interrogation unscathed and to finish smoothing things out with his future partner.

'Your sources are good, Your Grace,' he stood up to release the tension in his muscles and started pacing up and down the narrow room, 'but are they good enough to have made you aware that one day I lost everything?'

'Yes. I know that as well.'

'You can judge me as you like, Waldegrave, but you know I managed to get my niece an excellent governess, whom I intend to pay everything I owe, to the last penny.' John stopped in front of the only window in the room, whose opaque glass hardly allowed him to see the mucky streets of Whitechapel outside. 'My methods have never been the most appropriate, that is true, and that's why I've failed at business a couple of times, but that has never stopped me.'

'And what about your brother? Didn't he leave any assets?'

That question confirmed Talbot's suspicions. The duke wasn't aware of the existence of Harmony's inheritance, and for John's own good he had to remain ignorant of it, at whatever cost. He let out an ironic and melancholy laugh that he hoped would sound convincing to the duke's ears.

'My half-brother, God have him in his glory, never had much property, and his wife was just an orphan. Landon kept the books of Portington Park which, as I imagine, you must already know isn't as magnificent a property as Sudeley or Waldegrave Terrace. He did what he could for Harmony, but died ill and poor, and I carried on with the job.'

Devlin pondered the horse dealer's words. Was it possible that he was looking for something that did not exist? Perhaps that man, with his unorthodox manners, really loved Harmony and had managed to get her a quality education, even if it had meant he had to swindle the governess. He did not approve of his methods, but he valued his efforts to not have his niece suffer the miseries of state education, with all its defects.

'Tell me the truth, Waldegrave, are you disappointed in her? Has she brought shame to you? Do you regret having made her your wife?'

'I have nothing to reproach Harmony about.'

'That's what I thought,' he smiled. 'She's a magnificent young lady, isn't she?'

'The best.'

John Talbot laughed inwardly. It hadn't been that complicated, after all. It seemed that he had found the Duke of Waldegrave's Achilles' heel and, he had to admit, he was very surprised by it. 'I find your concern for my niece quite touching. One could say that you feel affection for her. That's very good. My wife and I thought it would be a disaster for you to take a girl like our Harmony for your wife, a simple girl with no refinements, but now I am delighted with your kind heart.'

Devlin nodded quietly and stood up, wishing to put an end to the whole matter. He felt embarrassed by Talbot's attention. There was a shade of falsehood in him that he found repugnant, but that meant nothing if the man was related to Harmony. If she approved of it, he'd have to invite him home often, he'd have to tolerate his sweet-tooth wife at the table, and then he might even have to chit-chat with them. Just thinking about it made him feel dizzy.

Furthermore, he didn't want to have to listen to him say that Devlin loved Harmony because he had a good heart. What he felt for his wife had nothing to do with pity, or goodness…

'I take care of what's mine, Talbot,' Devlin said, taking on his ducal and haughty attitude again. 'I regret that my wife, the Duchess of Waldegrave, has suffered some deprivations, and I will not forgive you for it, but I can swear to you that from now on I will provide her with all the luxuries she's ever dreamed of.'

'I don't doubt that.' John Talbot nodded with a greedy smile. Devlin made as if to leave, but the other man stopped him. 'Wait, Waldegrave. I presume you have read the letter I sent you a few weeks ago.'

John Talbot tried to smile earnestly as he waited for Waldegrave's response.

'I've read it,' the duke finally replied with evident disdain. 'I'm sorry to inform you, Mr Talbot, that I am not interested in becoming your partner in the building of a race course.'

John had been waiting for an answer like that, and he did not feel dejected. A good salesman, after all, knew that the real sale started with an objection, and he had new ideas bubbling in his head, new strategies to put into practice. He would find a way to make him change his mind. 'I advise you to think about it.'

Waldegrave waved ambiguously and left with a cold 'good afternoon'. John ignored his haughtiness and his excessive conceit, qualities typical of the aristocrats he so disliked.

He extracted from his pocket the letter addressed to Harmony, which he had thought of giving to one of the stable hands with the order of putting it in a post box. He examined it in detail, smiling naughtily, before tearing it up into little pieces that ended up inside the fire. He wouldn't need to behave in an excessively paternal manner towards her.

Dr Martin Bradshawe did not receive the invitation to the spring ball from Corine's hands; it was delivered by a messenger from Sudeley. Harmony made sure the doctor received it, aware that her mother-in-law had started behaving in a very strange way since the incident at Winchcombe.

'She's the town's madwoman, dear girl,' she had told her, nonchalantly, when she had asked her what had happened there. 'Mad people do and say mad things. Poor Gretty hurls stones at the baker if he does not give her a scone and a cup of milk, and she tells me horrible things when she sees me. That's life.'

Then, her mother-in-law had asked her to keep it a secret, to avoid worrying Sir Malcolm and Devlin over something she considered an absolute idiocy. Harmony shrugged and decided to forget the matter.

The winter was saying its goodbye to Winchcombe with an icy and prolonged rain. It had stopped snowing weeks ago and the cold had reduced considerably, but that afternoon, the temperature dropped to unexpected levels. Harmony watched the rain pour down the tarnished windows. Behind that thick blanket of rain she could just make out a ghostly mist.

She checked her correspondence with apathy. She hoped Limsey hadn't sent her any more sickly-sweet letters from her aunt and uncle addressed to Waldegrave Terrace. In the last two months, the pair had shown more affection to her than they had in the previous eleven years. Her aunt showed an interest in her affairs and asked her to have tea with her at the mansion 'to catch up'. As for her uncle, he had mentioned the project of building a race course that had him very 'excited'. Never before had he offered to discuss his business plans with her. When had that changed?

Luckily, inside the parcel Limsey had sent her were no letters from her suddenly affectionate relatives. Instead, she found enthusiastic replies from Fanny, Esther, and Sally. Her three friends had managed to obtain permission from their fathers to come to Winchcombe to attend the spring ball, accompanied by their governesses, of course. The good news made her smile with genuine joy. She could finally see them! She missed them so much. She was so eager to talk to them that she could hardly wait for them to come to visit her.

However, her joy ended when there were no more letters left, and she realised that there was none from Devlin. His hurtful silence continued. Of course, she had not dared write to him either, and that made her as guilty as him. Was that how the rest of their lives would be like? she wondered as she dropped on the sofa of the beige parlour where she spent her afternoons receiving her mother-in-law's visits or having tea. Was it truly her fate to languish in Sudeley like the duchess, whose existence everybody was aware of but very few had actually witnessed? It was true that her life there was easy and peaceful, all her needs were covered, and there was even room for extravagant luxuries... but Harmony had never dreamed of having an easy life, but a happy one.

Her old dream of travelling like Mrs Pfeiffer now seemed so far away that it felt like something from a different life; a childlike and crazy whim reserved for fearless and decided spirits, not like her, who was rather insecure and cowardly. Harmony was so unlucky that the members of the batak tribe would have surely eaten her alive even before she had crossed the border of their lands.

In all honesty, she could not say that she did not enjoy life in the castle a bit. Corine was a good friend, loyal and understanding. She had even become her confidant. Sir Malcolm, on his part, was charming, and his relaxed conversations, full of anecdotes from his youth, made her cry with laughter. She valued his wisdom, his extraordinary ability to see things from a very acute perspective, not exempt of humour, something increasingly rare, being—as he was—a nobleman of an advanced age. Unfortunately, for Harmony it wasn't enough to count on the company of Corine and her father. They were not her real family, no matter how hard she wished that to be the case.

How long would that morbid relationship, which made her and her husband so unhappy, last for? What was the future of that marriage that was forged on mistakes and guilt, of that act that had never made any sense? If she was sure of anything was that things would not carry on like that for long. Somebody would have to let go, somebody would have to take the first step. If they carried on like that, in a few years Harmony would fall ill or the desperation would drive her mad. And she'd rather be poor very far from there than end up in her old age the sad wife of a man for whom she meant so little.

Her life would be more bearable if she did not love him so much, if her only objective was to possess a title and to have at her disposal a catalogue of luxuries. But the truth was that she loved him, she had to admit with a huge pain in her chest. She loved him, and the thought of him preferring another woman made her shake with fear. She imagined he could be right now in the arms of one of his lovers... or of the Baroness of Lovelance, his true love.

What was Waldegrave waiting for then? Perhaps that Harmony would make things easy for him, being the one who'd decide to leave first. Then he would not have to pay any debts to her uncle, or to face his guilt or the social stigma of having abandoned his wife.

When Harmony decided to look at things from another angle, tears flooded her eyes again. Maybe he was waiting for her... He was playing with her, trying to tire her out, to make her think how she was thinking now... and she would not make him wait any longer.

'My little witch,' Sir Malcolm, always so quiet, materialized suddenly next to her looking worried. 'Why are you crying? What have they done to you?'

Harmony jumped, startled, but it was too late to hide her tears. She was soaked in sadness and did not feel up to denying that her heart was broken. Above all, she was tired of living a life that felt alien to her.

She sobbed and finally confessed, her voice hasty and dejected, 'I don't want to carry on with this, Granddad. I can't carry on with this marriage, or live in this house like a duchess when I don't feel like one. I'll leave!'

'You'll leave? But... where will you go?'

'I don't know... But I can stay here no longer. Devlin does not love me. He never will. He married me because... because he made a mistake, because he was drunk and he kissed me in that filthy garden. He didn't know who I was. He had never looked at me, he never had... because I'm not interesting or educated enough, because I don't come from an important and rich family... and because... because I'm ugly!'

She had difficulty articulating her final thought. She'd never allowed herself to be convinced by the belief that physical beauty was the source of great benefits, love included, but right now, she was feeling so bad that she'd started to believe it. Her sails were bereft of wind, her desolation had started to cloud her judgement and everything she'd believed until now had become uncertain.

Sir Malcolm observed her in silence, a silence long and unalterable, as if he was trying to assimilate the gravity of her words. Harmony looked up to evaluate the reaction that would follow. Although she was determined to reject compassion, a part of her, even if it was a minuscule part, was longingly hoping for it.

'Yes,' the old man agreed after a minute of undaunted pondering. 'The fact is that you look hideous when you cry.' She didn't know how, but Harmony felt paralysed, to her utter shame, before a caustic Sir Malcolm, whose gaze sparkled with intelligence. What had he said? 'Poor little

Harmony, Duchess of Disgrace, Lady of Self-Pity,' he went on, 'The worst kind of ugliness I can detect in your person is that of your poor self-esteem, dear girl. And I'm afraid that neither dresses nor make-up can hide something like that.'

Harmony blinked, baffled. With the last of her strength she wiped away the tears covering her face. 'You... you don't understand.'

'Go on, carry on crying about your bad luck, dear girl, as if you were Mary Magdalene,' he ridiculed, leaning forward. 'It's very likely that things will get sorted that way, and the pot of gold at the other end of the rainbow will come to you faster as well.'

'Sir Malcolm...'

'I know my grandson well enough to guess that he would not tolerate the company of a pusillanimous woman, even if she was a ravishing beauty, an anointed queen or... or even if they'd put a rifle to his head to force him to say 'yes' in front of the presbytery,' he grumbled, leaving her as astonished as she had felt when she had first met him, his diaphanous blue gaze steady, like a fountain of pure wisdom acquired from resolutely striding down the paths of life. 'So, either I'm getting too old, or you're too silly to understand that you're the only woman capable of taming that pig-headed man.'

Harmony opened her mouth to reply, but Devlin's grandfather was already making his way to the door, leaning on his walking stick, his gait slow and measured. She shook her head to try to clear her head after such an unexpected shock.

Before crossing the threshold, Sir Malcolm turned around to look at her and say, 'One more thing: I'll send the housemaid to clean the mirrors in your chamber. Somebody has been living in darkness for too long.'

The Mary Alice Bird Foundation had its headquarters at 53 Warren Street, an ancient building that had just started to present a much kinder face to the world thanks to the careful refurbishment work. Devlin had visited it a couple of times when it was only a dive with cracked and leaky walls that was often used as a hideout for criminals. Victory had taken him to see it before it was officially acquired, and he had given her a less than hopeful opinion. Now, looking at its façade from the street, the place looked closer to what she had planned to do with it. He had to admit that, once again, he had been excessively prejudiced.

At least, he hoped not to have made a mistake by turning up there. He had stopped postponing his decision to visit Victory, convinced that it was silly to believe that he would suddenly succumb to his friend's charms. It had been a long while since Devlin had last thought about her in a romantic manner, but he was aware that perhaps the pain and the frustration he had once felt due to her rejection could resurface with that new meeting. Even with that, he talked himself into getting out of the carriage and striding onward with determination.

In the narrow street, he saw a group of weak-looking women waiting in front of a fence newly painted in black. Their humble clothes and sun-tanned skins made him think they were country women, or perhaps local factory workers. Some were seated on the pavement holding small kids on their arms; others, dressed in black crêpe, conversed with the doorman.

Devlin felt sorry for them because he knew they were poor widows and were there because they had nowhere else to go. The Foundation had been created to help people with that profile, women who, after losing their husbands, were deprived of home and sustenance for their families. Without support or training to get a gainful employment that would cover their needs, many of them ended up becoming prostitutes or beggars, and their children would-be delinquents. Lady Lovelance—a kind-hearted and unorthodox widow—had insisted on changing that dreadful reality by creating a help centre for helpless widows which offered them refuge, food, and trained them to get a proper job. Her vision had conquered the heart of England, and she had managed to get any lord or member of the gentry who prided himself on being prosperous and a Good Samaritan to donate thousands of pounds to the cause; him included.

The doorman greeted him with a bow. As soon as Devlin set foot inside of the building, he noticed that it had been refurbished to perfection. A lady in black greeted him in the impeccable lobby with a respectful bow. Devlin recognised her. She was one of Victory's assistants, also a widow. The woman guided him to the first floor, where her boss was, while she talked to him about the water features they were about to install, and thanked him for having gifted them the electrical energy plant that powered the whole building.

Devlin looked at everything with satisfaction. Where before there had been rubble and dirt, now they had built a spacious patio with walkways where the 'guests', as the residents were called, could go for a stroll. Where he had seen ruined walls and flimsy ceilings, now he found faultlessly built solid rooms.

He couldn't feel anything other than satisfaction and pride for his dear friend, even if that meant admitting that he had been wrong, underestimating the building. Victory had transformed a miserable hovel into a place full of spirit, a building oozing hope.

Then, when he reached the first floor, he finally saw her. It was her, more beautiful and stubborn than ever. She was holding a paintbrush while giving directions to three painters, who seemed reluctant to contradict such a tenacious woman. She had her raven black hair braided, and wore a simple grey woollen dress, evidently chosen so she could move with ease among the building works... or perhaps to avoid intimidating the group of women who came from the most abject poverty.

Victory. The same woman that had inserted in his brain the word matrimony, had obtained his sympathy, and had earned his respect. The woman that had turned her own misery into an opportunity for the less fortunate women. Devlin realised then that the fire that woman had lit in him had nothing to do with love, or even passion. The turmoil of his feelings had more to do with the admiration he felt on thinking that somebody had built a house for others with her own efforts.

Their eyes met, and they both smiled. She rushed to finish her conversation with the painter and then left the room to allow them to carry on working. Devlin observed that the dark grey dress had a white paint stain on the side; she also sported another one on her cheek, and her skirts were caked in plaster, but she did not seemed bothered by her appearance.

'Look what a kind heart with a handful of the right friendships can achieve,' Devlin joked on seeing her approach.

Victory laughed. 'Well said, Your Grace. A kind heart cannot achieve anything without a purpose... and let's not forget those right friendships.'

'This is... incredible,' he said, looking around at the facilities again. 'I can see you are fulfilling your dream of helping the widows. I've seen dozens here, and outside there must be fifty or sixty more.'

'We don't have enough space for all of them,' she said in a sad tone, 'at least not until they give us the other building. We only accept old women and those who have young children. The rest of them will be distributed to nearby refuges and will be able to come here to have their meals and to attend the classes.'

'Then they are not alone. I'm sure you'll know how to protect them.'

'This is also your achievement,' she mumbled in a mock-accusing tone. 'Don't pretend as if it had nothing to do with you... I'm so happy to see you, Devlin.'

'I'm also happy to see you, Victory.'

They wandered around the new and shiny facilities of the foundation, which included spacious classrooms, two floors full of well-appointed bedrooms, workshops, a chapel, and an infirmary. Victory told him about the building she had just bought thanks to the extra funds from the charity event organised at Waldegrave Terrace. The building was planned to house the guests' bedrooms, and a huge community canteen that would feed even the homeless children of the London slums.

While he listened to the enthusiastic speech of Lady Lovelance, Devlin admitted that it felt strange to walk with her on his arm again. The sensation that had consumed him in the past, however, wasn't at all the same. With each new discovery his mood improved, his calculating mind relaxed and gave him more time to focus on the upbeat conversation.

'Devlin, the reason I asked you to come is…' she suddenly said, 'is because I want to return to you the necklace you gave me last winter.'

His memory brought back to him the ostentatious gift he had given her a few months ago, which he hardly remembered: a ruby and white diamonds necklace that the jeweller had praised to extremes. Victory had worn it during the ball, and then he had noticed she seemed uncomfortable and nervous. He had even thought that she disliked it.

'Why do you want to give it back to me? It's yours.'

'It isn't right for me to have it. You know you gave it to me under different circumstances,' she shook her head energetically, 'I can't keep it.'

'That's fine. Then sell it and use the money for the foundation.'

Victory looked at him with her huge blue eyes open wide. 'Are you… sure?'

'I wouldn't do anything with it in my safe, and if I know something for certain is that I can't give it to another woman.'

'Well, that's true. I could find an art teacher, a music teacher, and buy some instruments…'

'You will be able to do much more than that,' he mumbled, remembering the enormous sum he had paid for the jewel. 'Tell me one thing, did Radnor ask you to give it back to me?'

'No. He told me he didn't mind what I did with the necklace, and if I tried to return it to you, he was sure you would tell me exactly what you have just said,' she bit her lip, 'I had also thought about selling it, but I knew that I should inform you of it anyway. Many thanks, Devlin.'

'How are things with him?'

Her face lit up. 'He is all I want,' she confessed, without a doubt of hesitation or cynicism, as they started walking again. 'Isn't it strange when something we had never thought of having, and we hadn't even wanted, arrives in our lives and suddenly it becomes the centre of everything? It's as if fate or God knows better what we need than we do and puts it on our path, like an unexpected blessing, waiting for us to get wise enough to realise it.'

Devlin thought of Harmony and his chest collapsed with the feeling he had not managed to fully accept yet. Victory had described his own situation and, with that, she had read him with admirable precision. She possessed the words he needed to hear and the courage required to pronounce them.

'The prize for that act of faith could be no other than total happiness,' she carried on. Now, seeming aware of how her words had impressed him, she said: 'I heard you... got married.'

Devlin thought of the likely source of the to-be-expected update: Lady Felton. He was fully aware of the friendship that united the two women and, judging by the natural affinity of the female sex for sharing all possible information with their closest friends, he wouldn't be surprised if, by now, Victory knew even the smallest details of his marriage to Harmony.

'In fact, yes. We got married at the beginning of the year.'

Victory seemed to be waiting for a follow-up to that brief sentence but on seeing it did not arrive, she decided to interrogate him. 'And? How is she?'

He took a moment to remember his wife; her delicious fondness for travel books, her fresh wit, her implacable tenderness, the way her exquisite body fitted perfectly into his side when they were in bed...

'Devlin!' Victory called out, impatient.

'She is... sweet, witty...' he babbled, 'but if you provoke her she can be very churlish.'

The despondent look of the baroness showed how disappointed she was in him. His sad attempt at trying to look impassive and indifferent, at making her believe he wasn't irremediably in love with his wife, must have seemed pathetic to her.

'Don't be afraid to give yourself to somebody, Devlin,' she murmured, looking him in the eye with a trace of pity. 'If you don't do it you will regret it someday and perhaps it will be too late by then.'

Devlin sighed, tormented. His eyes wandered around the desolate landscape outside the window in front of him; those defenceless ladies in the street had lost everything, as had Harmony when she was only a child. He would have given anything to spare her such an experience, to have been able to protect her in some way. He would have lived a hundred times through his childhood pains, his father's beatings, to save her from her suffering.

God, he truly loved her, he acknowledged, terrified. And he felt relieved when he finally did. Perhaps she wasn't the most beautiful, or the most intelligent, or the most exemplary woman, but she was all those things in a measure simply perfect; she possessed an irresistible bouquet of virtues and singularities that suggested to him that she was precisely what he needed.

He loved her, but perhaps it was too late to do something about it. It was likely that he had avoided giving himself fully to her for too long, and the last train was leaving as he arrived at the station.

'I have underestimated her all this time,' he said with a heavy heart. 'I've made her think that she is not good enough for me, when I am the one who doesn't deserve her. I think she'd be better off without me, Victory.'

'Why don't you let her decide that?'

'Do you think she will be able to forgive me? You have no idea what we've been through!'

'It's true, I don't know. But I know one thing. It's not easy to resist a truly repentant man,' she smiled, raising one of her perfect black eyebrows. 'But if she makes it difficult for you, you can always crawl and beg a bit, can't you? For God's sake, Waldegrave, what are you doing wasting your time here with me?'

Chapter 16

The spring dance at Sudeley opened with a brazing welcome march. The ladies and gentlemen paraded in their elegant attires around the dance floor, as desirous of exhibiting themselves as of having fun with the music of the band. From their position as lookouts, the mothers and the escorts observed the movements of the elegant dance, ensuring the good behaviour of the dancers and praising once more the extraordinary taste of the dowager duchess.

A large number of families of the entire region had gathered there, in the terrific main hall of the castle, to celebrate the arrival of the—so eagerly expected—station of the flowers, the start of the crop season in Gloucestershire and the start of the London season, as the most frivolous would say. The music was chosen to suit all tastes, and the same was the case for the food and the entertainment. The local society was diverse and it was easy to discover the most recent news of the town with such a heterogeneous offer of individuals with whom to converse. The parents of the local debutantes had a golden opportunity to show their daughters off to the eligible bachelors, and they tried their best to stand out in a sea of fierce competitors. For the last few years, that event had become an unavoidable engagement for the people of the county, which nobody wanted to be left out of.

Harmony was sorry that it was too icy to use the outdoor space of the castle. She would have liked to make use of the newly budding gardens, the magnificent lake, and the views of the ruins but, like her mother-in-law, she was happy with the result of weeks of planning. Her mind had been busy and that was something she'd felt grateful for. She imagined that after that night she would have to find a new project to keep her active.

It all was going very well, except that when people were introduced to her they frowned and enquired after her husband. Then she had to explain that, unfortunately, Waldegrave's businesses in London had kept him there against his will. The more she repeated her speech, the more stupid she felt, but that was not the case for Corine, who seemed used to telling lies on behalf of her son. She was a great actress. Luckily, the guests believed everything they were told easily enough, or at least they pretended to.

Harmony was happy to see Fanny, Esther, and Sally again. They could not believe she had truly become a duchess. Her friends had arrived there a couple of days ago, and they'd had ample time to catch up. Esther was being courted by an excellent gentleman the rest approved of, to her outmost joy, and it was eagerly anticipated that soon the aforementioned man would talk to Mr. Collins to ask for her hand in marriage.

Sally, in turn, was in no hurry to walk down the aisle, because it was only her second season. Her father had promised her a Grand Tour for her next holiday.

'Can you imagine, Harmony?' she had told her with the theatricals she was well known for. 'I'll be travelling the world like Mrs Ida Pfeiffer. I could visit the tribe of the anthropophagus and of those that collect human heads in Borneo... What are they called?'

'Bataks! But I doubt it very much that Mrs Bonifonte will allow you to socialise with the anthropophagi,' she warned her, mockingly.

'It doesn't matter!' Esther joked. 'They wouldn't eat Sally for fear of getting poisoned and Mrs Bonifonte, poor thing, with her meagre flesh; the batak wouldn't even have enough to stuff a pie.'

They burst out laughing and Harmony, happily, felt as she had in the good old times.

'Now, I understand why Miss Andersen forbade you to bring that book to class,' Fanny said, still trying to control her laughter. 'Those ideas are bound to corrupt innocent minds such as ours.'

The answer to that joke was a new stream of guffaws. It was lucky that the girls' governesses were having a nap at that point.

Fanny, her closest friend, who carried on her lessons with Miss Andersen, stunned her and made her feel proud in equal measure when she confessed to her that very soon she would start a period of preparation to begin her university studies. Her goal was to become a doctor, a big challenge for a woman at the time.

Harmony had heard that some universities had women among their body of students, but enrolling formally was hard, even in those who allowed for it, and more in careers as elitist as Medicine. Fanny knew she would have to fight all the way: to get admitted, to be granted a degree, and to be allowed to work as a doctor, but Harmony knew her friend's determination and was sure that she would not give up.

'I'd rather fight that fight than get married, Harmony,' Fanny had told her looking serious when they were alone. 'I'm not the delicate damsel Miss Andersen and my parents think... I... will wear trousers and will enter the morgue to rummage inside of the bodies. And one day I'll heal others, as well as a man can.'

'Better than a man!' Harmony corrected her, among tears of pride. 'You'll do it, Fanny,' she encouraged her as she gave her a tight embrace. 'You'll make Andersen cry in distress but, damn it! I'll have a doctor friend!'

Now that she had met again her three kindred spirits, her heart oozed happiness, even with Devlin's absence still paining her.

Thank God the march had finally come to an end. Harmony felt suddenly exhausted when the music paused, but then she realised that she had been working extremely hard during the last few weeks, and her body was just starting to show the exhaustion she had not allowed it to feel. The only thing she wanted to do right now was to go up to her bedroom, drop on her soft bed, and perhaps eat something on the way, but she was not ready to ruin her debut as a hostess, and she would never dare to disappoint Corine. As she walked down the corridor, she promised herself that she would only briefly visit her chamber, lay down for a couple of minutes and then she would pour some water on her face before going down again.

'Are you all right, My Lady?'

Harmony's eyes met the kind and professional gaze of Dr Martin Bradshawe, who was entering the vestibule through the front door. He looked impeccable in a black tuxedo, closely shaved and with his greying brown hair combed back. He was a truly attractive man, and maturity suited him really well. She greeted him with a smile, happy that he had accepted the invitation, but then dismissed his comment. 'Oh, don't worry about me, Dr Bradshawe. I'm just exhausted!'

'You seem to have a different colouring today,' he insisted before shaking his head. 'Or is it, perhaps, that electric lighting I can't get used to?'

Harmony laughed. 'You take your job seriously, but you aren't here in your professional capacity but to have fun. I'm happy you've come!'

He scratched his jaw shyly. 'Thank you for the invitation. I thought that after that terrible incident in front of the park I'd be exiled from Winchcombe forever.'

'Don't say that. We were lucky to have crossed paths with an experienced jockey and not with a car driven by some madman.'

'Is the duchess well?'

'Very well. I'm sure she'll be happy to see you again.'

'Are you sure?' The doctor raised his eyebrows sceptically. 'I suspect I haven't made too good a first impression.'

'Nonsense!' She glanced behind him, but she didn't see any companion. 'Didn't you bring your wife?'

'I'm a widower.'

'Oh. I'm so sorry. Reverend Fleet didn't mention it.'

'Don't worry. I didn't tell him either. I imagine I'm still a stranger in town. People are reluctant to visit a new doctor, don't you think?'

'Then you've come to the right place to be seen and known,' she smiled, 'Why don't you come with me to the hall? I'd like to introduce you to the other guests.'

Martin felt his heart bloom with enthusiasm about attending the ball as he offered his arm to the nice lady, and then realised they had not been introduced. He didn't even know her name, for God's sake, and she was, surely, a member of the aristocratic Sawyer family. Was there a worse and more deliberate way to make a fool of himself?

As he guided her towards the big hall, he confessed regretfully, 'My Lady, until a few seconds ago I thought it was humanly impossible to be more ashamed, but now I realised that I've managed to do it. I'm afraid I have to admit that I don't know your name.'

'Oh, of course! After that rushed meeting, I don't blame you,' she replied, unconcerned. 'I'm the Duchess of Waldegrave, Harmony, and your hostess this afternoon.'

'The Duchess of...?' He blinked several times, trying to clear his head. If that young woman was the duke's wife, then, who was the lady he'd almost trampled over with his horse outside the park? 'Oh, I'm confused, Your Grace. I thought the duchess was the other lady...'

'No... I mean, yes...' The young woman shook her head. She seemed amused by his confusion. 'You see, Dr Bradshawe, Corine is—'

But then, the lady who was the object of their conversation made her entry into the vestibule. She was an exquisite apparition that left Martin breathless.

He had to admit that his memory hadn't done justice to her extraordinary beauty, to her presence that was charged with certain mysticism, and to that terse and somewhat nervous look that discomfited him. She wore her hair, shiny and black like onyx, up, her hairdo highlighting her alabaster face and her delicate neck. Her velvet dress, which stylised her figure, was wine-coloured with tiny embroidered golden petals. That detail led Martin to mentally compare that woman to a rose, and like an authentic rose, she was probably not devoid of thorns.

'Doctor Bradshawe,' she greeted him in a strangled voice. Her fingers creeped up, subconsciously, he imagined, to the place where her eye patch that matched the colour of her dress, was affixed, before moving away again.

'Your Grace…'

'Welcome to Sudeley,' she told him as she offered him the back of her hand, which he kissed.

Martin thanked her, still overcome by the proximity of the woman.

'This is the appropriate way to meet somebody,' the young woman who had welcomed him said, somewhat mockingly. 'I was telling the doctor that we are both duchesses.'

'It isn't so,' the other woman contradicted her. 'The only duchess is this young lady. She is married to my son, the duke, and I… well, have been consigned to history, I believe.' She started to play with the lace in her gloves. 'The title has become a sort of a nickname that people will forget slowly, or that's what I hope.'

Martin felt compelled to tell her that a creature such as she could never be forgotten, but in the end he managed to keep his mouth shut. After all, she was a duchess, and he had to keep some distance. God help him, but that was going to be the most difficult thing he had tried to do in his whole life.

'All right, as you like!' mumbled the duke's wife as she disentangled herself from Martin's arm. 'I was about to guide Dr Bradshawe to the main hall to introduce him to the rest of the guests, but I imagine you'll be better at it than I am, don't you think, Corine? Would you do him the honour?'

'Of course,' she muttered. 'Will you come with me, doctor?'

'It will be my pleasure.'

Harmony smiled to herself, pleased, watching them as they walked away arm in arm. They could not stop looking at each other, and they were lucky that there were two footmen whose job was to open the doors of the grand hall with great ceremony. Nobody in their right mind could have denied the wave of sparks that flooded the room, once the two got together. Could they…?

He was a widower, had just arrived into town and knew very few people; Corine had been alone for a really long time, as far as she knew, and if she was sure of one thing was that she deserved to fall in love again, this time, with a good man.

All of a sudden, Harmony felt full of joy on imagining the possibilities of a future union between Bradshawe and her mother-in-law. Nothing could make her happier.

On her way to her chamber she hummed a song that she interrupted every so often in order to let out a yawn. She was truly exhausted, especially considering the evening had just started. When she entered her room, she planned to lie down on her comfortable bed to rest for a few minutes. The presence of an unusual object on her pillow, however, made her forget her intentions.

Harmony couldn't believe her eyes. Her hands picked up the beautiful book bound in deep crimson leather with golden filigrees, and her heart started beating faster. No, she wasn't imagining it, she thought as she caressed the silky surface, as a frivolous woman would caress Dacca muslin. A Woman's Journey around the World, she read; it was engraved in golden letters on the spine, a collection of words that tasted delicious to her. It was a much more elegant and larger version than her old edition, the one that had ended up as improvised firewood in the fireplace. She turned the pages slowly, spellbound and elated, while wondering where the book had come from. Soon she discovered that it was an 1850 edition. A first edition!

Who had left such a precious gift for her? One of the girls? No! Harmony hadn't told them she had lost her beloved book; only Corine knew that it had turned into ashes after her last fight with Devlin. It must have been her, then, she thought, hugging the refined book to her chest. What a beautiful present, she thought, smiling.

The delightful surprise had removed all trace of sleep from her being, and she did not find any reason to remain in her room. She decided to climb down and continue playing hostess of the party. She could not afford the luxury of neglecting her guests now that Corine was going to be so busy getting to know the attractive and friendly doctor Bradshawe.

While she walked across the hall, full of people, some guests approached her and kept her busy with their conversation. Harmony smiled at them and again felt she had to justify her husband's absence. It was becoming very tedious.

When she had reached the drawing room reserved for the matrons and governesses, her look crossed with Miss Andersen's. Harmony had not had a chance to sit down to talk to her; the bustle of the preparations of the party and the activities of the last two days with her friends had absorbed her completely. The woman looked happy and relaxed, holding a glass of champagne while she kept her eyes on her fine student, the future doctor

Fanny Thorton. She wondered if her friend had already informed her of her plans, and she immediately decided that she hadn't, otherwise Andersen would be looking heartbroken, drying floods of tears from her face.

'Oh, look at yourself. You make a splendid duchess,' she said with a melancholy smile when Harmony sat next to her. 'I'm so proud of you, Harmony. I must confess that I had my highest hopes placed on Fanny, and not so much on you,' she whispered, so nobody else could hear her.

'I know, Miss Andersen. I know.'

'I worried that you might become one of those tomboys who protest in front of Parliament, demanding the vote for women. But you haven't failed me. You have become a refined lady, and an exemplary wife. Her Grace, the dowager duchess, only has complimentary things to say about you, and I know she isn't wrong. She even congratulated me on my work, can you believe it?' she commented, ecstatic.

Harmony smiled, amused. Miss Andersen seemed to have drunk more glasses of champagne than usual, and that was extremely odd; her role as chaperone at dances and public events for the last few years had been beyond reproach. In any case, she thought it charming that she had started to enjoy herself. Fanny gave her no reasons to worry; with her, it had been the opposite.

'You are the best governess, Miss Andersen. I thank you for what you've done for me these last few years. You are a real angel.'

'Oh, I'm only an old stubborn woman who wants what's best for her girls,' she sipped her glass and added, 'I wanted the best for Fanny, but...' She started sobbing.

Oh dear. So she did know about Fanny. 'Miss Andersen, I know. Fanny wants to be a doctor...' She consoled her. 'You should be proud of her.'

'I know, I know, and I am happy for her, I assure you,' she said trying to swallow her tears. 'But God knows what pitfalls await her at that university. The men will harass her, will try to dissuade her with pranks and who knows what else. Do you think I don't know how this works, Harmony? My dear girl won't have an easy time in that place ruled by men.'

'She does not want to pursue easy things; that's the issue,' she muttered. 'She'll manage, Miss Andersen. Fanny is stronger than you think.'

'That's what I hope, dear.'

'You will be able to start with another student,' she went on, trying to cheer her up. 'Perhaps the next one will be less conflictive than us.'

'Not for now. I'll have a holiday,' she said, as she dried the corner of her eyes with a handkerchief. 'You two have been a true challenge, and I need some time to recover before taking on another pupil. I am infinitely grateful for the money the duke gifted me, otherwise—'

'Money? What money?'

'Oh, my God!' The governess covered her mouth with the palm of her hand. 'I wasn't planning on telling you! Look what this champagne made me do!'

'What money are you talking about, Miss Andersen?'

'Your husband summoned me to Waldegrave Terrace a few days ago. He asked me some pretty strange questions about your education, and why you had started so late. He seemed eager to learn everything. I think he was worried about you.'

'Why would he do such a thing?' she whispered.

'I don't know but, as you see, I had no other option but to tell him the truth. I told him about the empty offers I received from your uncle, who tried to convince me to take your mentoring on. The duke was very persistent, dear. In the end, when I confessed that your uncle owed me a lot of money, he wrote me a very generous cheque. I didn't have the heart to refuse it!'

'Don't worry, Miss Andersen.' Harmony was astonished. She fixed her eyes on the dancing couples, but not her mind, which was working at full speed. 'Whatever he has paid you, I'm sure you deserve, and more.'

'Your husband is a generous man. And he loves you; I have no doubt about that.' Harmony smiled at her with little conviction, and Miss Andersen added, 'It's a shame that he couldn't be here today.'

'His businesses keep him busy in London,' she explained mechanically.

'I know that,' Andersen said in reply while she picked up another glass.

Harmony stood up to carry on with her role as hostess, which basically consisted of walking around the hall to talk a little to the guests, show an interest in their businesses and ensure everything was in order. Several times, servants approached her to ask her something and she gave firm replies, although deep down she had no idea what was best. She looked around trying to find Corine, the only one who could support her in her role. Then, she saw her dancing with Doctor Bradshawe. Farther away was Sir Malcolm, who was doing the same with a lady of his age.

When she caught sight of the refreshments' table, her stomach grumbled. She hadn't realized she was hungry until then so she went there and piled up a dish of sautéed sirloin with truffles, crab, and some cheese and toast. Luckily, the other guests hovering around the table seemed to be as famished as she was and did not pay attention to the amount of food she had served herself or the huge effort she was making not to gulp it down all in one bite.

While she enjoyed her food, Harmony carried on paying attention to the ball, as would do a good hostess. The music had morphed into an energetic waltz, and the couples were spinning around the dance floor with extraordinary precision.

Her gaze stopped then on Lady Burghill who was pacing up and down a faraway corner of the hall. Her face betrayed anxiety and worry. Her husband was trying to calm her, but the viscountess seemed on the verge of collapsing. Harmony wondered if it would be appropriate to go there and ask her what the matter was. Perhaps it was something she could take care of.

After finishing the meal, she went to the powder room to tidy herself up before going back to the party. She had decided to approach Becky and ask her what was happening. She hoped not to sound like a busybody.

On her way to the powder room, she found two young women somewhat worse for drink in the corridor whispering to each other, and they waved at her when she walked by. Harmony replied in kind. Inside the powder room she washed her hands and removed any trace of food from her mouth. She wet her face and then dried it with a towel. Once she had finished, she was ready to go back to the ballroom.

Returning to the corridor, she bumped into the person she would have least expected to see at that ball.

At first, she doubted it was her. She looked totally different; her face free from the injected eyes and the demented bags under them. Now her gaze was a diaphanous blue under the amber shine of the lamps. Her visage had also transformed from manic to totally calm. Her blonde hair, although tangled, looked more civilised, giving her the semblance of a fairy... or of an avenging sorceress. She wore a dark suit under a woollen cape, the hood draped over her back, as were her long tresses. Laurel Kirkeby displayed an irrefutable, but not beatific, beauty.

She shouldn't have been admitted inside. That woman is dangerous, she thought with fear. She had dared to come to her home—the dreadful woman—to ruin her party, to carry on ruining her existence.

Where were the young girls she had seen lazing about in the corridor? Was somebody else nearby? She looked at her coldly, and Laurel did not speak. Then Harmony decided to leave, even if it meant looking like a coward. She had to warn Becky that her sister was here and make her remove her as soon as possible.

'Wait, Harmony,' Laurel called after her, causing her to stop and pierce her with her eyes. 'What are you doing here?' she growled. 'Who let you in?'

Laurel, who was intentionally avoiding her eyes, hesitated. 'Nobody,' she finally whispered.

'Devlin isn't at Sudeley, so you're wasting your time! You won't find him here. You managed to render us apart, so you should feel satisfied.'

'I didn't come because of him,' she said shaking her head as if she was desperately trying to focus on the conversation. 'I understand why you don't want to see me.'

Harmony snorted, exasperated. Then she started talking, moved by the rage burning inside her chest. 'You do? Really? Do you understand that you came to my house, offended and abused my servants, insulted me in the cruellest and most inhuman manner possible, said horrible things about romping around with my husband and demanded an explanation from him for having married me? Do you understand that you might have destroyed my marriage forever, Lady Colvile?'

Laurel was attentively listening to her speech, but her gestures revealed neither satisfaction nor sadness.

'Of course you understand! That's why you've come here, to mock me, to rub your triumph in my face.'

'No... no, I'm mad, Harmony...'

She looked at her, indignant. 'I believe you, but I suspect you're not as crazy as not to realise that your attitude destroys others, and destroys you in the process as well. Your sister, Lady Burghill, suffers for you, as does your husband.' Laurel's look darkened for the first time when Harmony mentioned Colvile. 'Think of them, for the love of God. You should think about it or at least—'

'The doctor told my mother that the sermons are useless,' Laurel told her with a nerve that Harmony could hardly believe possible.

Harmony threw her hands up and looked skyward, as if begging for a bit of patience. Then she let them fall to her sides. She'd never had such a pointless conversation before. It seemed that her entreaties didn't have the slightest effect on the woman. 'Is that all, then? We have to put up with your bad moods and your delusions just like that, only because you don't care for sermons?'

Laurel thought for a minute, but Harmony was no longer expecting a coherent answer. Yes, the girl was crazy. Mad as a hatter! But right now she didn't look like the type of madwoman who might assault her, as she did the first time she met her at Waldegrave Terrace, but rather an extremely confused and amusing one.

'I believe so,' Laurel said with a shrug, as if that released her from any responsibility for her evil conduct. 'I only came here to apologise. I don't want you to hate me. Sometimes I tell lies, and one of them is that I'm Waldegrave's lover. Don't believe me. He's never given me as much as a kiss.'

Harmony, inexplicably, was moved by her sincerity and the enigmatic touch of innocence her words revealed. Was the young girl that looked like a just-awaken fay the same woman who a few months back had shouted obscenities at her with her eyes popping out of their sockets? She couldn't believe it. Her rage diminished until it turned into a quiet serenity. Surprisingly enough, she no longer wanted to scream at her.

'Ah, and he's never said anything about attacking a goat!' she carried on, as if nothing had happened. 'He's too elegant for that,' she said with a chuckle.

Laurel's words left Harmony confused, her feelings tittering between rage and the most absurd sympathy she had ever felt for anybody in her life. She wanted to laugh and cry over Lady Colvile's lost sanity. Without a doubt, it felt more like a strange dream than the type of conversation one could have in the solemn corridors of Sudeley. She was expecting the woman to vanish momentarily, leaving her to think she'd imagined everything and feeling intent to retire immediately and get some rest.

'Laurel!' a desperate voice echoed behind Harmony. Becky was running towards them followed by a footman.

'Oh, damn!' Laurel mumbled on realising her sister had spotted her. 'I have to leave. It was a pleasure to talk to you again, Your Grace. See you soon!'

She curtsied in the most polite manner, picked up her skirts and stormed off running in the opposite direction to her older sister. Her mouth agape, Harmony saw her leave towards the gardens, like a hare running from the hunting dogs, and then melt into the darkness.

That evening was turning into the longest, most astonishing and eventful of her whole life. After the Christmas ball at Felton House, of course. And, to her utter disbelief, she still had to wait a few hours longer until it would be over.

Becky would not stop apologising for her sister's crazy intrusion. She had confessed to her that since she was a child, Laurel would escape from home and return a few days later without showing any remorse. She had not lost that habit once she grew older and got married. Nobody ever knew where she had been or what she had done, and she'd never been caught in the prank. This time it wasn't an exception; Laurel had disappeared a few days ago and her family, used to her mischief, could do nothing but hope and wait for her return in one piece.

A few hours earlier, Becky had been informed that they had seen her sister outside of Sudeley. Her biggest fear was that she would come to the spring ball with the intention of assaulting the hostess and turning the event into a real tragedy. To calm her down, Harmony disclosed to her the brief conversation they had, but her words didn't achieve the expected effect. Viscountess Burghill was desolate.

After that unusual encounter, Harmony ordered a discreet raid outside of the castle to locate Lady Colvile and send her back to her family. Nobody, apart from Lord and Lady Burghill, Harmony herself and the servants, knew what had happened. Poor Becky had begged her not to tell others, and she had given her word that nobody else would know about it. Not even Devlin or Corine.

With the raid outside still ongoing, Harmony returned to the hall, exhausted and overwhelmed. She felt it was her duty to wander around the grand hall with a smile that in no way reflected her shock.

'Are you feeling well, dear girl?' her mother-in-law, who had sneaked up on her, wanted to know.

It was evident that she had spent the last few hours in an enchanted cloud. Harmony nodded enthusiastically although, deep down, she was exhausted in body and soul. She could not wait for the moment when the ball would end and she could go to bed, although she doubted that she would manage to get to sleep even then.

'Yes, yes. And what about you? It seems that Bradshawe and you are having a good time. I'm happy for both of you.'

The duchess blushed slightly and a smile spread over her precious face, giving it an exquisitely youthful charm.

'Doctor Bradshawe is a gentleman. Did you know he is a widower? His children have just got into Eaton. I have invited him for tea tomorrow!'

Harmony tried to show her delight, but the only thing she seemed capable of was offering her a sad smile.

Corine eyed Harmony with concern. The girl seemed exhausted, making her feel remorseful on realizing what she'd done: she had lumbered her with all the responsibility for the ball while she allowed herself to be dazzled by the charming new doctor. The poor girl seemed to be on the verge of collapse. 'Oh, darling,' she mumbled. 'I've been thoughtless! I've abandoned you with that horrible load on your shoulders! You should go to bed this instant!'

'And offend our guests with my absence? No way! Miss Andersen says that to be a good hostess one has to make sure that her guests are comfortable and well looked after.'

Corine thought that show of strength was adorable; it was clear that Harmony was destined to be an extraordinary duchess. If only Devlin were capable of putting to one side that stupid pride of his, as she had asked him to do in her last few letters...

She took her by the hand. 'You have worked extremely hard.'

'Somebody has to do it.' Harmony sighed, and her dark eyes shone, filled with dejection.

Harmony tried to smile but only she knew the kind of upset she felt. Devlin's absence still weighed heavily on her like a yoke. Corine studied her, anguished, in that way that so upset Harmony, because it made her feel as if she deserved her pity. She had to change that, she had to stop looking helpless and decadent. Otherwise, nobody would take her seriously. Wherever she went she would always be the shy and unattractive orphan, the devastated divorced woman. And if she was going to start again elsewhere, she would have to build up her own strength, to bury deep her most pathetic feelings.

She was determined. Tomorrow she would write to Devlin the letter that had been going around in her head for several days. The letter in which she would ask him for the divorce. After that, she didn't know what her life would bring, but if she was sure of something it was that she would not stay where she was not needed... or where she was not loved.

'Give him a bit more time.' Corine seemed to have read her mind. 'I beg you.'

She smiled ironically. She didn't want to torture her. Corine had been good and patient with her, and she hoped to keep her as a friend once everything was over. She remembered that lovely gesture that had obviously been Corine's, and it made her feel warm inside again. 'Many thanks for the book. You shouldn't have done it.'

Corine looked at her, tilting her head with obvious surprise. 'What are you talking about?'

'About the book you left in my chamber. I saw it a few hours ago.'

'I haven't left any book in your room, dear.' She looked at her humorously. 'It seems that somebody is more tired than she'd like to admit.'

Right when Harmony was about to contradict her, the enthusiastic murmurs of a group of guests that were looking out through the picture windows interrupted their conversation. Corine, bitten by evident curiosity, approached them and did the same.

'Harmony, look!' she exclaimed a second later. Harmony approached her and, intrigued, looked to the top of the main tower. Two huge torches had been placed there to highlight the superb silhouette of the castle. Against the light of those two balls of fire, she caught sight of a flag waving at its pinnacle, depicting the erect figure of a lion and four swords. And then she knew the reason for the commotion. 'Do you know what it means?'

She exchanged a look of astonishment and absurd hope with her mother-in-law, a hope that threatened to topple down the thoughts she had been harbouring inside her head. Of course she knew. The flag of Waldegrave's duchy was only raised when Devlin was at home. Her heart summersaulted.

Then they heard an ovation spreading through the room. The guests had stopped paying attention to the dance in order to bow at the master of the house, who was entering the big hall with the pomp of a general returning triumphant from battle. Devlin Sawyer, Duke of Waldegrave, looked ravishing in attire made-to-measure by the best, including a black tailcoat, silk waistcoat, and white gloves. His lank and long hair, as was the fashion, was neatly combed back, tied up with a ribbon at the nape of the neck, uncovering the beauty of his virile features, the perfect lines of his archangelic face, the green eyes frenziedly scrutinising the crowds under the cascade of lights from the glass chandelier.

Those eyes shone enigmatically on meeting another pair, dark and bright, at the farthest end of the room, and he moved towards them with a reckless sense of urgency.

Harmony observed her husband, fighting between love and astonishment, swimming in a river of desperate questions, as he strode towards her. It was the same Devlin, imposing, intimidating and absolutely beautiful, who had prevented her from climbing up the fence at Felton House, who had reluctantly put a wedding ring on her finger in that gloomy ceremony, and who had made love to her in his warm bed at Waldegrave Terrace. He had come back home, and she was unable to guess why, no matter how hard she tried. Hope surged through her again, in the same instant as fear reared its ugly face, like a cold and threatening snake slithering up her spine, ready to bite.

When Devlin reached her, her heart experienced an unexpected ecstasy and accelerated to beat at a dizzying speed. She managed to see inside his eyes more clearly. In that stubborn look, in his determined expression and energetic posture, she could sense a determination that made her tremble.

Her mind wandered through her memories. It took her back to a nook of her past, right back to the moment when he, engrossed, was looking at Lady Lovelance at Ascot's Racecourse. His eyes oozed an impetuous love that would make any woman dream. Harmony had not been an exception. She had also secretly wished to be looked at with the same impetus, to be the object of such feelings.

She found it difficult to believe that the same man, who shortly afterwards had only looked at Harmony with indifference, was there now, in front of her, and was looking at her, not with the same ardour as he had the widowed baroness, but with something even more overwhelming and so real that she could almost touch it with her fingers.

'Hello, wife.'

Chapter 17

Harmony couldn't understand how she'd ended up in Devlin's arms, twirling to the sound of a slow waltz in the middle of a crowded ballroom, being watched by hundreds of eyes.

Despite her efforts, she had difficulty keeping her composure. Her face must have betrayed her deep excitement; the shaking of her hands must have been evident even to the most absentminded of guests, without mentioning that her heart had not yet recovered from the surprise of seeing her husband again after weeks of absence, of an endless silence, and after a chain of pitiful thoughts that threatened to crush her sanity. Right then, she must have looked awfully out of sorts.

She could almost hear Miss Andersen telling her off, insisting that that kind of behaviour was not what was expected of a duchess.

When she felt strong enough to face Waldegrave, she found he had a relaxed and calm expression, the total opposite to hers. His lips were trying to control an amused smile. Was the rake mocking her? She clenched her jaw, itching to stomp on his foot without looking like a clumsy or—worse still, uncivilised—creature.

'My first... my first official ball and you get here late,' she reproached him, sulking, making sure she didn't raise her voice and trying to be on her best behaviour.

He looked at her with a hint of tenderness and some mischievousness.

'My valet was very surprised on seeing me this evening. My clothes were not ready and... Well, he had to do his best... Oh well.'

'Really? Is that your best excuse?'

'In fact, no. I seem to remember that you did not invite me.'

'Don't be ridiculous,' she mumbled, looking nervously around. 'Does a duke need an invitation to a ball in his own castle?'

'Yes, when the duchess has made amply clear that she does not wish to see him.' That truly threw her. As she clearly remembered, that night she had thrown him out of her chamber, in hysterics, after the incident with the book. 'You didn't even write to me,' he complained in an offended and somewhat theatrical tone.

Was that a joke? she wondered as her jaw dropped, seemingly about to touch the floor. 'You didn't either!'

'But you were the one who threw me out—'

'Devlin, for the love of God, this isn't a competition!' She looked around nervously. The guests were observing them as if they were a pair of exotic fishes in a huge fishbowl moving gracefully their delicate and colourful fins in some extravagant dance. They both felt compelled to smile. 'Let's carry on dancing.'

'Good.'

'Good!'

'You look beautiful tonight,' he said.

Harmony got tangled up in her own skirts on hearing that and took hold of his arm to avoid ending up sprawled on the floor. Luckily, nobody seemed to notice her awkward stumble. After that confusing statement, she looked at him from behind her eyelashes, with her head low and her cheeks flushed.

'Don't you believe me? Well, your loss,' he mocked her.

She had a right to be sceptical. She'd never been a beauty and she'd never minded that, therefore she didn't know what to do with compliments.

'Did you miss me?' he asked, then. It was as if the scoundrel had decided to corner her right there, in front of that crowd that seemed to be making an effort to read their lips. Harmony started to sweat. She wasn't prepared to answer that question. Not when she wasn't sure yet what he intended to achieve with such a surprising appearance. 'That's what I thought,' he said, reading into her silence.

He trapped her again in his gaze, which now shone with calm certainty. Then, the couples started to move around the hall, ready to restart the dancing.

'Thanks for replacing my book.' It was the only thing she managed to say after a moment, when she was released from being the centre of attention.

'It was no bother,' he mumbled. They were quiet for a bit, until he added: 'That woman is crazy, by the way.'

'Which woman?'

'That author, Ida.'

Harmony jumped. It was lucky that Miss Andersen wasn't listening to their conversation; otherwise, she would have already collapsed on the floor, suffering a stroke.

'Did you read it?' she asked him, horrified.

'On the train,' he nodded, 'I didn't have anything else at hand, unfortunately.'

'And what did you think?' She hoped that her husband would at least highlight the anthropological interest of the book.

'What did I think of it? Well, I found it disturbingly offensive!'

She clenched her teeth. Why was she surprised? He was a renowned physicist, a brilliant man who was respected by the entire scientific community. Above all, he was a man, and the same as the rest of his sex, so he questioned the aptitude of a woman to do certain things. She only managed to feel disappointed.

'And what offended you so badly, My Lord? That a woman goes travelling alone and has no qualms about leaving her husband at home? That she has the guts to do something so daring?'

He took his time observing her. He seemed somewhat hurt. 'No,' he mumbled, 'that my wife seems to be more interested in learning about cannibals and hunters than in making love to me.'

Harmony looked at him with tears in her eyes. 'What makes you think...?' Then she understood what he was talking about. She had rejected him that night, and she wasn't sure where she'd got the strength from. Too many things had happened; Lady Colvile's appearance, his unpleasantness during the journey to Sudeley, the disdainful way in which he had talked about his marriage to his family and, finally, the incident with the book.

'You worship that thing,' he accused her.

Was that jealousy permeating his voice? 'That 'thing' has made me forget many sorrowful moments. It kept me company when I was alone, when I wanted to forget who I was and, for an instant, imagine that my life was... another. A happier one.' Her voice faded slowly.

'Are you talking about when you went to live with the Talbot family?'

She was so surprised he had guessed that she could only reply with a nod.

Devlin didn't say anything else. Looking kindly at her, he hugged her against him while the waltz kept on playing at its sedate rhythm. He kept quiet for a minute, for which Harmony felt grateful. That gave her time to process what was happening. When had she passed from total sadness to that state of sweet serenity? She was in Devlin's arms; he was holding her firmly and possessively, making her feel safe. The closeness of his body also awakened sensations that had been asleep inside her until that instant, but she didn't understand yet what that was all about. His sudden return, the look in his eyes, had filled her heart with hope when she believed it had even lost its capacity to keep beating.

She imagined she would get answers to the questions haunting her brain later on.

'Even with that, I think I enjoyed it,' he added suddenly.

'What did you enjoy?'

'The book.'

Harmony opened her eyes wide. 'Seriously?'

Devlin smiled in that way that made her go weak at the knees, as if her legs were made of cheese melting on the fire. It was an intimate smile he had rarely shown her, but she had treasured it in her memory.

'I must acknowledge certain... beauty in the rebellion of a woman,' he said mockingly. 'It's good to test one's limits. And a journey around the world can't harm anybody. On the contrary, whoever does not travel will always be full of prejudice.'

'That isn't what the rest of men think. They believe that a gentleman travelling is the Cid or Sir Lancelot, but a lady... she's an odd fish.'

'Odd, for sure... but odd things are often the most fascinating,' he whispered in her ear, making all her heart race. His voice oozed sensuality and she even thought it was a double entendre. 'However, I wouldn't like to be in the shoes of that lady's husband, for sure,' he carried on, 'Although, if you're thinking of imitating the adventures of Mrs Pfeiffer, I ask you to at least consider taking me with you.'

She looked at him, incredulous. 'You——?'

He nodded, smiling. 'I can be an exceptional travel companion.'

Harmony chuckled. 'You, Your Grace, riding among Bedouins, eating roasted termites for breakfast, sleeping out in the open with only the sky and the stars for a roof?' she said mockingly.

'Only if you sleep with me,' he whispered.

She stared at him, electrified and lax. Was he talking seriously? 'We are not talking about a simple pleasure trip, like the ones you're used to, but of an expedition with a limited budget.' Harmony hardly recognised her own voice; now it sounded too high and breathless. A drop of sweat ran down her back. 'No expensive hotels or ocean liners with private cabins and champagne.'

'Don't underestimate me. I can adapt to anything. I'm a planner, well-prepared; I am a good map reader and understand many languages well. And, being a scientist will come handy. I can teach you how to sterilise water with a chunk of copper.'

'That would be very useful,' she smiled, flustered. She didn't know how much longer she would manage to control herself and not jump on him and kiss him. 'Devlin, thanks for what you did for Miss Andersen.'

'I did it for you.'

They looked at each other for a long time, without realising that their dance steps had turned repetitive and no longer followed the music.

'Do you know what we should do?' he whispered enticingly.

'What?'

'Get rid of all these people and go to bed.'

The rest of the dancers had already forgotten about them. The effects of alcohol were starting to become evident in their mood. The laughter, the tipsy conversations, and the change in the type of music, from solemn to jovial, let the two know that it was the right moment to retire.

'We don't need to kick them out for that. Just get me out of here,' she said.

Devlin took her hand gently and guided her through the happy crowd, avoiding with impeccable tact the attempts of their guests to keep them there a bit longer. He greeted them all but spent no longer than a minute of conversation with each one before moving on. That tedious ritual soon ended when they reached the vestibule. From there, they rushed to the wing that contained the bedrooms.

When they got to the first private nook, Devlin did not hold back any longer. He pushed his wife against a column and kissed her passionately. The desire had pulsated through him since he had seen her at the other end of the big hall, enveloped in that exquisite green emerald dress that complimented her shape, the curves of her figure, her perfect bosom, and the delicate outline of her clavicles. The vision of her expression of innocent surprise, her black eyes shining like agate and her half-open lips, had driven him crazy. He had discovered in her a beauty that he had missed at first, and a perfection that did not cease to scare him. That woman was made for him. He had prayed to heaven for the necessary restraint not to sling her over his shoulder and take her upstairs without a word as soon as he saw her.

Now that they were far away from the interfering looks of the people of Winchcombe, he could savour her at his own pace; he could squeeze her in his arms, as he was doing right now, and seek inside of her mouth what he had been yearning for, to the point of experiencing the same physical pain he had felt during the long weeks they'd spent apart.

Devlin let loose a groan of desire when his mouth moved away from hers and started to travel hungrily down her perfumed throat. Harmony threw her head back, as far back as the column behind her allowed, and caressed his shoulders through his clothing. She was panting hard, and her breasts went up and down as if trying to keep up. Devlin leaned forward and kissed both peaks with daring insolence. He introduced his tongue through the edges of her corset, and down the shortcut the generous neckline of her dress offered, while his covetous hands massaged them over the fine materials of the corset.

His mouth assaulted her lips again with violent and burning kisses. He penetrated her mouth with his tongue and caressed hers with precise lashes. She sucked it, first shyly, then eagerly, until Devlin felt he was about to lose the little sanity he had left in the face of her passion. A guttural moan escaped his chest. Then, he saw himself holding her by the hips and pressing her against his turgid groin that was extraordinarily rigid and soon began to pulsate with a movement that mirrored wild mating. The two were riding in the wings of the most febrile desire they'd ever experienced.

Harmony, who stirred like a pampered cat, received the sweet thrushes of her husband. She found that game captivating and scandalous at once: their hips fused, rubbing, and their mouths tangled up, as if they could not get close enough. It was all just a sample of what awaited them once they reached their chamber. She hugged his shoulders shakily, untied the bow holding his silky hair back and submerged her fingers into the fine threads. It was so glorious to feel his kisses again, his burning caresses, his body promising a devastating pleasure.

When he was about to lift her skirt to remove any barrier made of clothing left between them, her heart wavered, pushed and pulled by a blend of emotions.

'Devlin… not here,' she whispered, breathless. 'I fear somebody might come—'

'We are at home,' he said, offering her a pirate smile. His voice had taken on a seductive harshness. 'If I want to have my wife right here and somebody is rude enough to turn up, he'll have no other option but to turn around and leave.'

She squinted and looked at him, her pitch rising in mock horror.

'Not so fast, Your Grace. You and I must behave in a civilised manner. At least when we are not behind closed doors.'

'Mm?' He pierced her with his shiny eyes; they looked like those of a predator about to jump on its prey. 'How uncivilised can you possibly be, dear wife?'

Harmony raised an eyebrow.

'You won't find out if you stay here, you silly,' she teased, then set off running upstairs.

Devlin felt dizzy with desire as he began to follow her with nimble strides, giving her a small advantage in the exciting game that was driving him mad. Naughty chuckles flooded the corridors of the castle, alternating with fast steps and wild panting. Very soon they reached the doors of Harmony's chamber and entered it like two runaway horses. Two maids stared at them and, horrified, left the room with their eyes glued to the floor. The couple burst out laughing when they disappeared.

The interruption, however, gave them a chance to recover their breath and the opportunity for their excitement to grow further. Harmony slithered towards the huge bed, eagerly watched by her husband. She picked up the book, which she had left on top of the blankets, and put it on the bedside table next to a lit lamp. Trembling with desire, Devlin got rid of the frock coat, hurling it at the first place he could. He did the same with the shoes and the gloves. She imitated him at a slow cadence, holding his warm and craving look.

When he realised she was about to let her hair loose, he rushed to help her. With exquisite care, he released her from the constraints of the hairpins shaping the hairdo, then slowly undid the locks of her voluminous hair, the ringlets he had dreamt of burying his face in. He devoured her with his eyes as he worked through her hair, enjoying the beauty of her dark leonine mane as it bounced over the slim and snow-white shoulders. Once he had finished, he held her from the back and eagerly breathed in the aroma of her hair. Rose water with a trace of rosemary. Delicious.

Harmony felt herself tremble all over as he began to trace the shoulder of her neck with warm kisses. With each one, he sent small waves of pleasure to every bit of her body. She closed her eyes and surrendered to his sweet attentions. Even her toes writhed due to his mouth's invasion.

Devlin's heart was racing as his agile hands began to toil at the row of buttons of her dress. Parsimoniously, he undid them one by one, although he wished to tore the dress and shorten his agony. The heavy piece of clothing fell to the floor in a harsh swish. He caressed his wife atop the almost see-through chemise and savoured the curves of her body. He released her from the prison of her corset with notable dexterity, loosening the ribbons until it dropped onto the floor. He carried on untying the ribbons of her drawers which, on leaving her, offered him an incredible view of her hips that were slightly rounded, and her bottom that was pale and well-formed. Bending over, he rolled down her tights and kissed every inch of her legs as they were revealed. Very soon, Harmony was naked under the favourable transparency of the chemise.

Grabbing her by the hips, he made her turn around to see her better. She was perfect, damn perfect. Had she put on some weight? Her breasts looked fuller, her curves more rounded. And it wasn't only what his eyes could see but also what his spirit recognised when he was next to her; her tenderness, her wit, her idealistic and determined leanings, her hunger for liberty, her simple and at the same time clever way of looking at the world. Why hadn't he noticed it before that night at Felton House? Why had he spent so much time without her? Why had he tried to convince himself that he did not love her and that it would be better to push her aside?

Still standing by the bed with her, he extended his hand to her to help her step out of the mountain of clothes lying on the floor around her. When she did it, his thirsty mouth got glued onto hers. His senses jolted with the excitement on savouring her taste again. But then she moved away, and he puzzled at her expression.

Could he see doubt fluttering in her eyes?

'Tell me what this is,' she demanded, her voice indicating distress.

'Harmony—'

'Will you spend a few hours with me and then leave again tomorrow? Do you think I'm stupid and my only role is to sate you every time you feel like it?'

'No.'

She looked like she was holding back tears, and Devlin felt his chest tighten. She obviously did not believe that his care and attention were motivated by true feelings. And how could she? He had treated her as if she were another piece of furniture. He had told her many times and in different ways that she meant nothing to him. He had even offended her by putting up with Laurel's presence in Waldegrave Terrace without giving her an explanation.

'Why did you leave in the first place?' she insisted.

'I had to or we would have hurt each other even more. We were not at our best.'

'And what changed since then, Devlin?' She confronted him, raising her chin. 'Did you suddenly start seeing me as pretty and elegant? Do you think that now I deserve to be introduced as your wife?'

Devlin could not say a word. With each sentence Harmony pronounced, he hated himself a bit more. He had made her believe all that, that she did not deserve his affection or the approval of those around her.

'You cannot come back and expect me to be waiting with my arms and my legs open,' she carried on after getting rid brusquely of the tears that were threatening to brim over. 'If you think that I'll play that part for you, you're mistaken!'

'I'm sorry, damn it!' he growled, impotent and desperate. 'It hasn't been easy for me either to assimilate all that has happened to us in the last few months. I'm here because I want to start again, Harmony,' his voice softened, 'We didn't start up well but, don't you want to find out what will happen to us if we give each other another chance?'

She was immobile, with her arms folded, in front of the lone flame burning on the fireplace. Her eyes contemplated, with a melancholy glow, the sad mutation of the firewood into ambers.

'I know what will happen,' she mumbled sadly, without removing her eyes from the fire. 'I will fall in love with you even more; I will love you to the point where the little I have left of me won't be mine any longer, until my whole being is crushed. And even then I'll carry on loving you.'

Devlin's hands were shaking, impatient to touch her. He moved to do it, but she moved away to avoid his touch.

'That's why it's best to end it all here,' she said, causing a wave of horror to run through him.

'No! No, of course it won't finish here!'

Her look was as incredulous as it was exhausted. 'You are an egotistical and foolish man! Why do you insist on remaining married to me? I don't understand it, Devlin! Haven't you had enough of this marriage? You're a man, a duke, for the love of God! Nobody would say a word against you if you chose to divorce me. Not even I would oppose if you wanted to do it!' She covered her lips with her fingers and closed her eyes tight, as if she could not believe what she'd just said. 'Don't you want to live with somebody you truly love?'

'It's what I intend to do.'

Harmony blinked, baffled. Silence enveloped them for an instant.

'You aren't like any woman I've ever met,' he whispered and his eyes shone, full of love and surrender. 'I thought that would be good for me, but it's ended up being my downfall! There's no aspect of you that I discover that I don't end up loving like a madman. It is terrifying. It's scary to know that a person can have so much power over another one as you have over me; that my peace depends so much on you, as if I had lost control over my own life. It is scary, but it's also the best thing that has ever happened to me. That's why I kept away from you at Waldegrave Terrace, because I knew that with each minute I spent in your company, I was feeding that monster that's gnawing at my sanity. But I don't even care any longer. I choose you, and I choose this monster that's devouring me.'

Harmony listened, frozen and incredulous, fearing that her legs were about to stop holding her up. Devlin's words had dragged her into a world of dreams that she had caressed with her thoughts, but in which she'd never wish to stay for fear of heartbreak.

That's when he took hold of her hands, which felt icy cold. He kissed them repeatedly, and she raised them to caress his face, delighting in tracing its lines with her fingertips, feeling him with a new awareness.

'Devlin... Devlin...' She could only repeat his name over and over. The swelling in her chest didn't allow her to do anything else.

'I had to leave to discover that I can't live without you and that, even if I could, I don't want to,' he said then, putting his arms around her and caressing her through her thin chemise. 'Harmony, I'm not playing games. I'm throwing myself at your feet. I want us to carry on being married; I want you to forgive me for all the pain I've caused you from the very first moment we met... because I've been blind, or rather, because I've refused to see your light.'

'I forgive you,' she whispered, brimming with love.

'I'm very sorry about Laurel...'

'I know! I don't want to talk about her,' she muttered.

'That's all right.' He smiled tenderly. 'I love you, wife. I don't think I've ever needed anything as much as I need to be with you right now.'

'I love you, husband... and if you carry on talking, I'll die right here.'

Her wild kiss quieted him down completely as she pulled him towards her with the desperate need that was hollowing her inside. She took his face and his shoulders in her hands, caressing them urgently, as if her soul depended on it. She pulled at his cravat and hurled it away carelessly while he deepened the kiss. Her fingers began to look desperately for the openings in his clothes.

Tenderness gave way to lust.

'You are beautiful... more than you will ever realise,' Devlin whispered when he had her naked in front of him.

Harmony smiled. She took it more as a loving compliment than as an unquestionable truth. If he loved her, he would see her as beautiful, because his heart would recognise the ties that had been woven between them in the moments they had shared, happy and even unhappy. This was what love was, wasn't it? The ability to look at the other person with the heart and not with the eyes.

Next, they were lying on the bed in an entanglement of arms, legs, and naked torsos. The kisses and the caresses came and went, melting into both bodies.

Devlin thought he was about to lose his mind from the joy he felt as he held her in his arms. 'I'm not joking. You're truly beautiful,' he said breathlessly while his lips traced a path of kisses over her pale abdomen that was a little more swollen than he remembered. 'You are Harmony, aren't you? Your name suggests that everything in you is exactly as it should be.'

Harmony laughed, feeling drunk with elation. She was amused by her husband's newfound eagerness. She was about to reply to him with a sarcastic joke, but then an unexpected tingle of pleasure ran through her, from head to toe. Devlin, the rogue, was kissing her in her most private place, and these were not tender kisses, but rather shameless, hungry.

Every coherent thought left her mind. Her left hand reached for support on the wrought iron headboard and her right on her husband's lank mane, whose tongue was beginning to twist voraciously around her sex. It wasn't long until a powerful wave of ecstasy, like the one she had experimented in his bedroom at Waldegrave Terrace, swept her feelings like a raging hurricane.

When she opened her eyes again, Devlin had positioned himself on top of her. His hair was tangled, and his eyes that were burning with fire let her know that his need was pressing. Then he penetrated her hard, alight with passion and love. A moan of relief left her lips on being reunited with the warmth of his body, the incredible hardness that filled her up completely. She felt as if she were coming alive again now that he was fully inside of her. How desperately she had longed for him, night after night, without ever admitting it.

Then, Devlin started to move atop of her, with long and powerful charges, without leaving a single inch of her body immune to the devastating pleasure. She let him carry on, surrendering without any scruples, delighting in the pleasure his splendid body offered her. If Devlin loved her as she did him, then there would be no more pain or misery. From now on, she would not deny him anything.

She felt the sudden need to bring him closer to her. She circled his hips with her legs and kissed him hard. His masculine back was soaked in sweat despite the cold slipping into the room, his muscles tense and stone-like to the touch of her hands. He was so wonderful like that, his face tensed up by lust, his body loving her as if his life depended on it. Harmony was

269

overflowing with love for him.

Devlin's thrusts increased in power, his moans got louder and, at the same time, the pleasure increased for both. A few minutes passed until an explosion of lust, hot and primitive, enveloped them.

They ended up wet and sweaty on top of a tangle of blankets, both of them making superhuman efforts to recover their breaths. When it finally happened, Harmony nestled by his side, hugged his chest and whispered that she loved him.

Devlin listened to her words of love, his heart rejoicing. He drank up those words, savoured her with his soul, his heart now open and peaceful after the assurance of her surrender. He also wanted to talk to her about love, he wished to release the words no woman had ever inspired before. They were crowding in his throat, eager to be finally freed. But then he heard his wife let out a sigh of total happiness and, immediately, a soft snore warned him that his romantic discourse would have to wait until the following day.

Even in the throes of the most miserable unhappiness, Harmony had admitted on occasion that the spring mornings at Winchcombe were captivating. That specific morning, however, seemed to her especially beautiful. She wasn't sure if it was her new mood that allowed her to see everything through rose-tinted glasses, but the truth was that the air she was breathing felt purer, and it was filled with the aroma of pastures green anew. The sunrays, filtering through the wide open windows, seemed to carry with them certain sweeping energy; the birds were waking up from their dream to sing joyful tunes.

She hoped all mornings would be like this one, she thought, and turned her head on the pillow with a sleepy smile.

Had she thought it was morning? It was noon already, she realised on looking at the wall clock. She sat up quickly, feeling achy and disoriented for an instant. The previous night had been full of contrasting emotions, and her mind had been so busy processing them all that she had forgotten the fact that her body was also exhausted.

Then she realised that her husband, half dressed, was observing her, unconcerned, from one of the sofas. His naked feet rested on the foot of the bed, and his right hand held a steamy cup.

'Good morning, wife.'

'Good morning, reckless man,' she grumbled, holding back a smile. 'Why have you allowed me to sleep until now?'

'Why should I wake you up?' He stood up and walked towards her, his

270

steps lazy and sensuous. Harmony looked up and down his fit body, his strong and bulging muscles in full display as he was wearing only pyjama bottoms. A jolt of desire ran through her. She accepted his morning kiss with her senses open and the memory of the previous night still on her skin. 'You fell unconscious. It seems that you enjoyed yourself a lot last night.'

'I was exhausted.' She smiled after drinking the cup of coffee he had offered her and added, 'Being a duchess and throwing a party are not easy things. My jaw hurts from smiling so much and my feet… oh, I think they are swollen.'

'Welcome to the frivolous and empty world of aristocracy, Madame,' he joked as he massaged her feet with expert strokes. 'I think I'll have to compensate you for all this trouble.'

The relief and the pleasure from his massage fell on her like a warm cascade. She moaned, then dropped on the bed to enjoy the generous ministrations of her husband.

'Your Grace, your skill as a masseur dazzles me,' she purred. 'You should abandon science and politics and turn this into your profession.'

'I can do it all,' he replied with gall and nerve, while his hands started to climb up her thighs. 'I'm very accomplished, in general, and I have a bunch of talents you don't know anything about yet.'

'You're so vain!'

Devlin carried on massaging her with both hands. They travelled up her legs causing a pleasant heat to rise there. Harmony was over the moon. They had confessed their love for each other and now they were playing around in bed. How had all that happened?

'Wasn't my mother with you?'

'She was my mentor,' she purred with her eyes closed. 'She manages fantastically well in society, as if she had been born for the role. I don't know how she does it.'

Harmony remembered that Corine had spent a big part of the ball in the company of the handsome Dr Bradshawe and quietly smiled. Instinctively, she knew that she should hide that information from her husband.

'You're right. She never gets a hair out of place during one of her social events,' he agreed. 'It's her greatest talent. In truth, it's her only talent.'

The cloud of charm that surrounded them vanished suddenly. Her heart broke on hearing Devlin refer to his mother like that. She couldn't understand the reason for such hostility yet. 'If that's what you believe, then you don't know your own mother,' she grumbled, annoyed at him. She got out of bed and dressed behind the folding screen. 'I'm dying of hunger. Aren't you?'

Devlin looked at her, evidently confused, still sitting on the bed. 'Is anything the matter?'

'I've been asking myself that since I arrived here,' she shrugged as she put her chemise on, 'Corine Radley is the woman I owe your being to, no less. A tender and kind woman that worries about you, even if you find it difficult to believe. She does not deserve you behaving towards her like a cynical bastard, Devlin.'

A shade of rage, mixed with vulnerability, crossed his green eyes. Harmony had never seen him display such an expression. She wanted to console him, to hug him, but she would not do it until he was totally honest with her. She couldn't just let the matter go, as if it wasn't her problem, and pretend everything was fine. Any matters that affected that man had become her problem too.

'A cynical bastard,' he repeated. 'Is that what you see when you look at me?'

'What did she do to you, Devlin? What is Corine's sin? Why don't you love her?' Her husband's only reaction was to glue his eyes to the carpet, where the clothes that had gone flying the previous night were piled up still. Impotent in the face of his silence, she walked to him. 'I'm your wife. You know that sooner or later I'll find out, perhaps by accident, perhaps because she'll tell me. But I don't want to hear it from someone else. I want you to tell me. I want you to share it with me.'

She had expected an angry reaction, like the one of that fateful night before he had left Sudeley, but she was surprised by his meek reply:

'Not today,' he whispered, and the irritation that had started to show in his face vanished. Then he gave her a weak smile that contained a promise.

An hour later they went downstairs, arm in arm.

The servants had finished clearing and cleaning the whole place, and it looked as shiny and tidy as usual. Harmony thought of her friends, the governesses and other guests who had stayed the night at the castle. She hoped they hadn't felt offended because she had not come down earlier to greet them. Luckily, Miss Frank, who was supervising the cleaning tasks, informed them that the guests had not got up yet.

As soon as they reached the early blooming gardens of Sudeley, they heard complicit laughs nearby. Devlin stopped, intrigued, and exchanged a questioning look with her. Harmony followed him to the castle's country dining room, which had remained forgotten during the winter. It was an idyllic place, located near the boxwood maze and the splendid marble fountain decorating the centre of the garden. In that wing, fragrant branches of honeysuckle—with its bell-like leaves—had already climbed up to the second floor. A few primroses, violets, and wild roses splashed with colour the romantic landscape.

Then they spotted Corine, sitting at the table under the huge umbrella, next to Dr Martin Bradshawe. They were chatting in a relaxed and affable tone, as if they were long-term friends that had happily met again. Before them there was a tea service and a tray of sandwiches that lay forgotten in the heat of the intimate conversation.

Harmony couldn't avoid noticing an air of close comradery, perhaps a bit too close, and wondered if Devlin had noticed it as well. She observed her husband sideways and realised that he was eyeing the scene with certain ill will. It was evident that he did not like what he was seeing.

As soon as Dr Bradshawe became aware of the presence of the newcomers, he stood up, his expression serious. Corine, on the other hand, smiled, unconcerned.

'My darlings,' she greeted them with a huge smile, ignoring her son's clear upset. 'I hope you have enjoyed a good rest. Especially you, Harmony. You were a wonderful hostess, don't you think, Dr Bradshawe?'

Harmony noticed Devlin's uncomfortable reaction to Corine's familiarity with the stranger.

'Good afternoon, Mother,' Devlin's voice grew cold, 'I see the ball has brought you new friends. Aren't you going to introduce us?'

He looked at the doctor with a rigid questioning expression, but Bradshawe seemed undaunted. His posture remained erect and respectful, although Harmony could have sworn that he had also noticed the duke's unexpected hostility.

'Of course, how silly of me!' Corine said, 'My Lord, meet Dr Martin Bardshawe, Winchcombe's new doctor. Doctor Bradshawe, this is my son, His Grace, the Duke of Waldegrave.'

'It's a pleasure to finally meet you, Your Grace.' The doctor greeted him with a bow he then extended to Harmony. 'Good afternoon, Your Grace.'

'So... you're the new doctor. Where do you work?' Devlin asked, frowning.

'At the surgery Dr Dillard used to look after, in the High Street. It's a small place but conveniently located and where I feel very comfortable, Your Grace.'

'And what happened to the good doctor Dillard? Don't tell me he has retired.'

'I'm sorry to have to inform you that the arthrosis he was suffering from has gotten worse. He has gone to the house of one of his daughters, in Devon, to rest. I've been lucky enough to come to Gloucestershire at the request of the bailiff to take his place at the surgery, from where I'm happy to offer you my services.'

'It's very kind of you, but we already have a doctor. Dr Shapiro.'

'Dr Shapiro has left the county for a while, Devlin,' Corine pointed out. 'I've asked Dr Bradshawe to take his place.'

That didn't please Devlin, who tensed up like a piano chord. He looked suspiciously at his mother, who replied in kind, her eyes like burning arrows. The conversation was turning sinister.

'Then, will you stay in Winchcombe permanently?' Devlin insisted, piercing the doctor with his stare.

Bradshawe hesitated for a moment, but then he stated, 'Yes. At least that's my intention.'

'Be careful with your intentions.' The sentence was said in a whisper, but all those present felt the threatening intent behind it.

'Devlin, you are inconveniencing my guest,' Corine said with a fake smile. 'This interrogation is in awful taste.'

'Don't worry, Mother. I am not feeling uncomfortable at all,' said Devlin, his expression impassive. He was being a perfect gentleman—Harmony thought—and she was bearing her husband's terrible character with admirable serenity.

'Your Grace, I find Winchcombe happily suited to the exercise of my profession,' said the doctor, 'and if circumstances prevent me from staying here, then… there's no place where a doctor is not needed. However, I hope this could become my new home.'

Waldegrave snorted. 'Of course. I imagine my mother invited you to the ball and to have tea this afternoon as a welcome gesture to our county. It's very typical of her to rally to newcomers,' Devlin said, then addressing Corine, 'although I don't remember seeing you laugh this way with Reverend Fleet or the retired colonel who moved here recently.'

'And how would you possibly know that, my son, if you're never at home?' she objected.

'Please, Mother—!'

'Devlin, enough…' Harmony whispered, pressing his arm.

What on Earth was that? Why was Devlin behaving like a stupid pompous man with the kind and gentle Doctor Bradshawe? It wasn't as if he'd found him kissing his mother. It was absurd from every angle.

'Your Grace, I understand your surprise when faced with the presence of a stranger in your property,' the doctor said in a calm tone. 'I can assure you that my intention is not to offend you or your family at all. I apologise for having caused this embarrassing episode. I am also sorry for having earned your mistrust with such little effort. I'll leave Sudeley if so you wish.'

Devlin's look was challenging, and Corine's full of apprehensive expectation. Indignant, Harmony stared at her husband, who seemed to be weighing up the idea. He wouldn't dare throw him out of Sudeley, would he?

'Good, if you insist.'

'What's wrong with you, Devlin?' Corine muttered.

Dr Bradshawe nodded resignedly, and walked towards Corine—who was still open-mouthed due to her son's abusive behaviour—with a defeated expression. In the meantime, Harmony turned to face Devlin to demand an explanation.

'Why did you do that?' she whispered, furious. 'Apologise! Ask him to stay!'

'Harmony, you don't understand.'

'What don't I understand? Your mother has made a friend—'

'Bradshawe, are you leaving already? I've just asked for the cards,' Devlin's grandfather, as showy and well-dressed as usual, appeared around a bend of the garden, escorted by his personal valet.

'Sir Malcolm,' the doctor smiled at him with affection, 'I'm afraid we'll have to leave our card game for another day. I have to leave right away.'

Sir Malcolm clearly sensed the accumulated tension by glancing at the faces of those present. 'Really? With so many sick people here?'

'I'm sorry, My Lord. I'll be waiting for you at my surgery whenever you wish to come,' the doctor said to Devlin, 'I shall leave, Your Grace, but not before I tell you that you cannot destroy my friendship with your mother. Only the duchess has the power to deprive me of it. Good afternoon.'

Harmony couldn't believe what was happening. Devlin had thrown Dr Bradshawe out of Sudeley, had annoyed his mother and now was evidently giving her a huge migraine. Corine seemed heartbroken with her arms folded, like a young girl whom they'd forbidden to get in touch with her intended. Harmony felt like hitting her husband. She wasn't aware of that stubborn vein in his character, and she was awfully horrified by it.

Dr Bradshawe picked up his hat from a nearby chair and put it on with determination, in a gesture of diehard pride, before setting off back to the castle.

All the while, Devlin oozed arrogance as he looked at him stiffly, like a warrior who had been declared the winner before even entering the battle field.

Harmony, who had started to breathe very fast in angst, saw how the gardens darkened and the trees danced above her, spinning vertiginously. Then, the world became a confused and fast black mass that switched off all her senses.

When she regained consciousness, she was lying on a chaise longue, inside a room with stained glass windows she had never seen before. The furniture was covered with white blankets, and so were the paintings, and some shapes she assumed must have been sculptures made her think that nobody had entered there for years. It must have been one of those forgotten spaces on the main floor of the castle.

The first face that appeared hovering above her was Dr Bradshawe's.

'Hello again,' he greeted her calmly.

'What happened?' she asked, her voice frail.

'You fainted. Luckily, your husband is fast. He caught you as you fell. Otherwise you would have crashed onto the floor.'

'My husband is a cretin,' she muttered, remembering the scene that had upset her so much.

Devlin had behaved like an idiot. How dared he treat his mother and the honourable Dr Bradshawe as if they were a couple of obscene lovers?

'Perhaps, but he's worried about you,' he acknowledged, somewhat amused. 'And your mother-in-law, as far as I can see, falls also under his strict protective dome.'

Harmony heard Devlin arguing with Corine on the other side of the closed door. Although she could not hear his accusations clearly, she suspected he blamed Corine for everything that had happened. But then Harmony started processing the good doctor's words, and what her mind had not managed to decipher yet began to take shape inside her head. Devlin wasn't chastising his mother; he was protecting her... from a suitor.

Dr Bradshawe, kind and solicitous, comforted her. He asked her about her alimentation, her exercise habits, and if she had experimented a series of symptoms that he carefully listed. She replied openly to all his questions, happy to know that there were professionals as thorough as he was. In the past, she had sometimes fallen into the hands of uncouth doctors, and other times of indolent ones, like Dr Mortimer.

Dr Bradshawe processed all the information calmly and professionally.

'Harmony, as your new doctor, I'll ask you a final question, and it is very personal. I need you to reply to me in all honesty. All right?' She nodded, intrigued, and he continued, 'When was the last time you had your period?'

Thousands of thoughts crossed her mind, but none sufficiently coherent to become fully conscious. A surge of emotions flooded her; an infinite tenderness, a sensation of abundance and absolute happiness. She felt like crying and laughing at the same time... She also experienced hunger, and wished to go back to bed.

She was a puppet of her own feelings.

She had noticed her missing period a week ago and then she had completely forgotten about it, as if the omission would protect her from what she would have to face if her suspicions were true.

But now... now everything was different.

Dr Bradshawe smiled. He'd had his answer.

Meanwhile, the discussion outside the room got louder. Screams came and went, and it wasn't only Devlin's voice that made the foundations of the castle shake; Corine also knew how to raise her own. Harmony exchanged an apologetic look with the doctor, but he did not appear particularly shocked. Like the proper gentleman he was, he pretended as if nothing was happening, and was taking notes in a little note book he had produced from his jacket pocket.

Then, Devlin opened the door and rushed into the room like a whirlwind. His eyes, feverish and full of anxiety, calmed down when he saw that Harmony had regained her consciousness. He ran towards her, squatting in front of the chaise longue, and grabbed her arms.

'Thank God...'

She received his caresses, a silent evidence of the concern that was about to swallow him up, and kissed his hands lovingly, eager to comfort him.

'Dear girl, are you all right?' Corine asked. She had followed her son inside quietly.

Harmony only nodded in reply. She had not fully recovered from her surprise yet to offer a coherent explanation.

'Bradshawe, what's happened to my wife?' Devlin spoke in a forceful tone. 'One doesn't just faint like that for no reason! Talk now, man!'

'It will be better if she explains it to you, Your Grace.'

After addressing a meaningful look at Corine, the doctor invited her to leave the room with him. She was observing him with demanding curiosity, but in the end she obeyed. The door closed, leaving Harmony alone with her husband.

'I cannot believe that guy is truly a doctor,' Devlin growled. 'Did you hear what he said, the——?'

'Shh.... Forget about him—'

'Are you feeling well?' he asked, and Harmony nodded with a smile, but his expression grew serious. 'Don't do that to me again. Do you understand?' His tone was furious and at the same time apprehensive, to the point that she got frightened.

'Do what to you?'

'Faint... get ill... make me think that I could lose you...'

She held his face with exquisite tenderness. She kissed him long, her only intention that of calming him and reassuring him that she was in one piece. More than that. She was overjoyed. Devlin started to calm down thanks to Harmony's soft caress, and the contact with her tender lips.

'I'm here with you. Nothing has happened.'

'She left you in charge of that stupid ball, didn't she? She left you alone while she looked after her conquest... That's why you're so sickly, and why—'

'Devlin, enough,' she whispered, exhausted. 'Enough, for the love of God. I'm not ill. And stop blaming your mother for everything that happens around you. You look like a resentful child, and I hate not knowing the reason why.'

He sighed. His head dropped dejectedly over his wife's lap. Harmony rocked him with infinite reverence, as if he was the one in need of being looked after.

'I love you,' he muttered. 'Now I know since when. From the same day you told me the phonograph could be used for music... and I only realised the day I accidentally burned your book. You are so ingenious, so bold, and you don't even realise. You are the most beautiful and strong woman I have ever met, the most complete. You are all I need and I go mad just thinking something bad might happen to you.'

'I love you too, Devlin,' the tears had filled up her eyes, 'and I can't live knowing that you are full of resentment. It isn't good for you or for me. I want to clean up every trace of ill feeling from your heart. Let me do it.'

He shook his head, which remained cradled in her lap. 'I don't want to drag you into this quagmire.' His voice sounded muffled by her clothes.

'I don't mind! We'll go wherever you are, suffering, and we'll rescue you. Together.'

He seemed to digest her words with a light stupor. 'We, you said?' he raised his head and looked at her, stunned.

Then, Harmony smiled at him, her tears already streaming down her cheeks. She took his hand and placed it on her belly.

Devlin wavered, surprised, between looking at her and her belly that was pregnant with a beautiful promise.

'Yes. Our son and I.'

Chapter 18

The week had ended and Harmony had to say goodbye to her dear friends. Before leaving Sudeley to go back to their usual activities in London, Ester, Sally and Fanny covered her in kisses, hugs and good wishes for her pregnancy. As for Miss Andersen, she had been beside herself on hearing the happy news. She had cried her eyes out, as had done her beloved mother-in-law, Corine, who had commissioned from the seamstress maternity dresses and a ton of materials for knitting. Sir Malcolm, however, had not shown any surprise, to everyone's amazement.

'One has to be an idiot not to realise that. She only eats and screams, like Gladys did when she was pregnant with you, and like you did when you conceived Devlin,' he had told Corine, who had been too happy to complain to her rude father.

'Women! You all drive me crazy!' he had concluded.

Devlin was the one who had taken the good news in the most dramatic way, an unusual mixture of caution and frenzy. He'd go around paying an obsessive attention to his wife: what she ate, what she did when she got up and during the day, up until the time she went to bed. And even then he wouldn't leave her side. For Harmony it was all adorably disturbing.

He insisted on accompanying her every time she had to use the stairs, and he had even had the mad idea of carrying her in his arms every time she had to go up or down the castle. He even mentioned something about getting a lift installed—which would use a crane system—so that Harmony could move around safely. She hadn't taken it seriously until an engineer turned up to inspect the castle the next day. Harmony had rolled her eyes, but her complaints had not managed to dissuade Devlin from creating a 'secure environment', as he constantly repeated, for his pregnant wife and his son.

As if all that wasn't excessive enough, he had ordered that all stepladders, stools, and any other object that could be dangerous in the library be put under lock and key.

'Why don't you just cover the walls in my room with mats and put iron bars on the door so I don't escape?' Harmony had muttered, her arms folded, when she found him inspecting the outside of Sudeley trying to find the perfect place to install the lift.

'Don't give me ideas,' he had mumbled, concentrating on the task.

Devlin had come to accept Dr Bradshawe reluctantly as his wife's doctor, but not before requesting all kinds of accreditations, which the latter had supplied more amused than offended. In the end, it had turned out that Bradshawe was overqualified for the post, according to Waldegrave's consternation.

When the hustle and bustle of the spring ball had become just a nice, distant memory, Harmony felt that she could finally relax and start enjoying that new phase in her life.

Devlin hugged her when the two carriages carrying her friends and their governess disappeared in the horizon. That feeling of security, of total belonging, of growing hope was so nice.

So that was what happiness felt like... that ethereal sensation that for the first time in a long while she was savouring.

'Are you tired?' he asked her, holding her still.

'What could have tired me seeing that you don't let me do anything?'

'I don't know. I, perhaps.'

'That will never happen,' she smiled, madly in love, 'even if you tried your best.'

Devlin caressed her belly and kissed her tenderly; perhaps with excessive tenderness, although she enjoyed the protective side of her husband's character. It made her feel that nothing and nobody in the world had the power necessary to penetrate the sacred armour he had built around them.

'I know I've been a pain these days,' he said as they strolled back to the castle holding hands, 'but you know that nothing in the world would make me risk your life or the life of our little boy... or girl.'

'It's the only reason why I put up with your crazy notions,' she smiled.

When they were inside again, he muttered, 'I have to go to Surrey tomorrow.'

Harmony did not manage to hold back an expression of uneasiness, but at least she made the effort to correct it. The truth was that she was not ready to be apart from him again. 'Tomorrow?'

'The company that has to install the power lines at Godalming is due to start work soon. I must supervise everything and send a report to the minister and the rest of the members of parliament. If everything goes according to plan, next autumn we could become the first fully electrified town.'

'And you wouldn't miss it for anything, either,' she stated resignedly on seeing the shine in his eyes. 'It sounds captivating, but you're not planning on taking me with you.'

'When I heard about it, the day before I came back to Winchcombe, I thought about asking you to come with me, but now, in your state... I don't think it's a good idea.'

'It's all right.'

'I'll be back in five or six days,' he promised. 'I have no intention of being apart from you a minute longer than necessary. You'll be in good hands.'

She raised an eyebrow, suspicious.

'You mother's or Bradshawe's?'

He sighed, annoyed.

'He hasn't passed all the tests yet,' he whispered, narrowing his eyes, irritated. 'I could change my mind any minute and send for the best specialist in London.'

'You don't fool me; I know you like him now,' she smiled, smugly.

Devlin remained silent to hear these words, and his mind began whirling as he thought about the doctor again. Earlier on, while he assessed his suitability to become Harmony's official doctor, Devlin had had a few chats with him accompanied by a good brandy. He was extremely surprised by his professional references, his studies with well-known German doctors, his theories about the dosed use of Chloroform during the delivery and his wide knowledge on the newly implemented rules for asepsis and antisepsis as applied to surgical procedures. Soon, their conversations had become refreshing scientific debates. Devlin discovered that Bradshawe, in his youth, had been the assistant of Dr William Budd, the author of a brilliant publication about the contagious nature of typhoid fever, its transmission and prevention.

In spite of that, the doctor had to jump through some hoops yet to gain his confidence.

'Not enough,' he finally said.

Harmony puffed, aware that her husband's reticence had to do with Corine. Then she remembered the outstanding topic, that family mystery she had no access to, which she would have left alone if it did not compromise the peace of her family as it was doing.

'Will we be able to talk when you come back from Surrey?' she asked, her tone soft.

The news of her pregnancy had taken precedence over any other matter, had replaced the worry and tensions with a refreshing gust of happiness. Even then, Harmony knew she had to pre-empt the mater from escalating. Otherwise, the arguments between him and Corine would continue until they became untenable.

He looked at her, oozing uncertainty. 'I'll try.'

It was his only reply, but it was enough for her, for now.

The next day she had the difficult task of saying goodbye to her husband. She had difficulty letting go, even if it was only for five or six days. When would she be able to enjoy a calm marriage, without shocks, endless conflicts and unexpected separations?

What would she do without him all that time? Perhaps go back to her routine prior to their reconciliation. Although, she had to be honest and admit that she felt too tired for walks. She hoped that the pregnancy would not tire her for the rest of the months she had left, because she knew that even such an imposing library as Sudeley's would not keep her sufficiently entertained.

At least this time she knew Devlin would come back.

'Will there be women there?' she asked while they walked together down the platform at Gloucester train station.

Devlin gave her a devastatingly sensuous smile. He looked very handsome in a grey tweed suit and with a bowler hat crowning his masculine beauty. Harmony felt uncomfortable having to let him go. She had to admit that she was feeling jealous.

'Good God, I hope so, otherwise the species will be in danger of extinction in Godalming.'

'Don't be silly—'

'I won't have a chance to notice if there's a woman around because I'll be thinking of you all the time.' Playfully, he encircled her waist with his hands.

He kissed her long, embracing her with his sensual and warm mouth; he lingered in, caressing her tongue and biting her lower lip, as if he was trying to leave a mark behind, to leave a reminder that would make her think of him in his absence. As if that was necessary.

She thought she could hear some tutting, and she glimpsed some people giving them funny looks, no doubt alarmed by their open displays of affection, but she was too happy to pay them much notice.

'You'd better be back in five or six days, Waldegrave,' she whispered as soon as they moved apart. She was trying to look threatening, although it wasn't easy with the pleasant bubbling feeling rising up from her belly. 'And try not to get electrocuted.'

'I'll keep myself safe if you do the same, my love… When I come back I want to find you healthy and strong,' he told her, right when he was about to board the train. Then, before taking the step that would get him inside the huge steam contraption, he whispered in her ear, 'That will be the only way you'll be able to bear everything I am going to do to you.'

'Good morning, Mrs Frank,' Harmony greeted the housekeeper, who knocked on her door the following morning.

'Good morning, My Lady. I apologise for disturbing you, but there is a gentleman here asking to see you.'

Harmony looked at her, intrigued, pausing her brush in the middle of its journey across her long and curly hair. The maid who was helping her also looked at Mrs Frank, waiting to hear more.

'A gentleman? Dr Bradshawe?'

'No, My Lady. I don't know his name. He's in the parlour, with your mother-in-law. She asked me to come herself.'

Harmony frowned. Who would have come to see her?

She rolled her eyes, speculating that it might be the engineer who had come to install the lift, or perhaps a new doctor sent by her stubborn husband. The truth was that she was not prepared to put herself in the hands of anybody else but Martin Bradshawe, and she was not in the mood to offer her opinion about the contraption Devlin wanted her to use.

As soon as the maid had finished her voluminous hairdo, she exited her room and walked languidly down the corridor. Once she reached the stairs, Miss Frank, who had diligently escorted her, reached her hand out to her.

'Are you joking?' Harmony burst out, startled, on realising the woman wanted to guide her by the hand, as if she was sick or a little Princess Victoria whose neck had to be preserved in one piece to rule an empire.

'No, My Lady. One can't joke with your husband!' the housekeeper replied seriously.

This was Devlin's handiwork, of course. Because the woman didn't give her any option, she obeyed and took her hand, holding her laughter back. She felt ridiculous, but it didn't hurt to humour her husband and his obsessions. She climbed down carefully, holding on to the firm and competent Mrs Frank, wondering if that woman could do anything else other than lose her composure and start screaming if Harmony fell rolling downstairs. She chuckled to herself.

Once safe and sound on solid ground, she walked fast to the dowager duchess's lounge. She was on tenterhooks, eager to learn who had come to visit her.

Her expectation turned into disappointment when she entered the lounge. A pang of fury shot through her when she saw the tableau in front of her. John Talbot, dressed like a cocky youngster, had settled down comfortably on a Louis XV chair and was smiling with his hyena teeth at her mother-in-law, while holding a cup of tea at the height of his lying chin.

Even from a distance she could perceive the stink of his cologne, the stench of his intentions, and the falsehood of his polite manners, deliberately designed to flatter the person he was talking to and enmesh him or her as a perverse spider would a delicate butterfly.

John Talbot, her only blood relative; the man for whom love and kindness were unknown words, the man who had brought her up only giving her his disdain and then had robbed her of the little she had.

How dared he turn up at Sudeley without invitation? How dared he invade her sacred space, her family's home?

'Harmony, my dear girl.' Corine smiled on seeing her entering the lounge. 'I had no idea you had an uncle. You should have mentioned it before. Mr Talbot is a fascinating man. He was telling me about his business selling purebloods, and his project of building a race course!'

That's when her uncle John stood up and approached Harmony with an expression that made her feel sick. It was a smile so full of lies and of fake affection; only she could not be deceived. He kissed her brow and she had to summon all her self-control to not move away, sickened, and strike him down with her eyes.

'My little one, it's such a pleasure to see you after such a long time,' he crooned. 'Your aunt Minnie and I have missed you so much. Ah, how happy I am to see that you have become the mistress of this splendid home! Your father would have been so proud of you, my darling.'

She wondered if anybody else would be able to guess the malevolence behind his pretend poise or if only she, who knew him well, could. She scanned the room, looking for her aunt, but luckily she did not find her. She noticed the presence of Sir Malcolm, who seemed intensely focused, observing the scene from the solemnity of his chair.

'Uncle John, what are you doing in Sudeley?' She made an effort not to sound irritated. She even lifted a corner of her mouth to compose a faint smile.

'Well, I was on my way to Worcestershire to an exhibition, and I thought, 'why not surprise my beloved niece?' I haven't seen her since the wedding and, well…' He couldn't come up with another strategy than faking being embarrassed. He laughed bashfully, and even managed to give the impression that he was blushing. He was a damned good actor. 'Oh, good God. I hope I'm not causing any inconvenience. If that's the case, I'll leave straight away—'

'I wouldn't hear of it, Mr Talbot,' Corine, naively, stood up to defend the old fox. 'You and your wife are welcome at Sudeley. If the duke made you believe you would not be welcome, I offer my apologies. Now that we're family, we should not apply those absurd rules of etiquette.'

'I don't want to importune you, Madame,' he replied.

'Not another word,' Corine insisted. 'I invite you to stay at the castle as long as you like, in view of your engagement at Worcestershire. And Mrs Talbot and you can come to visit us any time you like. Harmony must be surrounded by love and care… now more than ever.'

No, Corine, I beg you… don't tell that scoundrel about my child… thought Harmony.

'Madame, you're a true angel,' he said, pretending to be moved, and bowed, lowering his bolding head. 'My wife will be ecstatic when she learns that she will be able to come to look after her most precious treasure.'

Harmony was speechless, her jaw clenching due to her unstoppable fury. Her uncle still had that damn black magic of his. Now she knew what he had come for: the beneficial connection to the Sawyer family, the shade of the thickest tree, the advantage that can only be provided by being related to a powerful family. It was his way to make money thanks to his new and valuable contacts! What else? Money, or the search for it, had always been his greatest goal in life.

Without fully knowing how, she sat next to her mother-in-law and took part in the conversation as much as she could. Time passed like a vague storm of words and fake smiles that made her feel dizzy. She felt her stomach doing summersaults every time he talked about her childhood, the immeasurable love Aunt Minnie and he had received her with when she lost her parents, and how her presence had filled the sad void in their lives caused by the impossibility to conceive their own children…

Dirty lies!

The worst thing about it was that Harmony could not expose him. What would her new family think of her if she repudiated the people who, for better or worse, had brought her up? They would question her loyalty, her gratitude, her humanity. They would condemn her for it!

Corine was listening to Uncle John's pathetic speech with evident emotion, while Devlin's grandfather maintained a serious demeanour that, she suspected, did little to reveal what he was truly thinking.

Then Corine said, 'Dad, let's give Harmony and her uncle a bit of privacy. We have monopolized them long enough.'

Sir Malcolm—who had a made one or two laconic comments during the tedious conversation—stood up with his usual promptness. He said goodbye to Harmony and her uncle with a curt nod. Then he disappeared with his daughter without uttering another word. Usually, the old man never missed an opportunity to make a joke or blurt out one of his caustic remarks. Harmony wasn't sure what to make of his cold demeanour.

When the doors of the lounge clicked closed, Harmony pierced the despicable intruder with her eyes.

'An exhibition in Worcestershire... I see you are as good at lying as you've always been.'

Uncle John grinned his hyena smile.

'Harmony, or should I say, Your Grace,' he bowed with a mocking smile. 'Is that the regard you show for your uncle, the man you owe all this to?'

'I don't owe you anything,' she growled through clenched teeth. 'You are the one who owes me. I hope you haven't forgotten it.'

'Well, I hope you don't intend to demand money from me now that you're wealthier than Cleopatra, or do you?' He laughed, derisively. 'Avarice is contemptible, niece. You should know that.' He wandered around the room examining each painting, each sculpture, and each decorative piece with his vulturine eyes. 'And thanks for answering my letters,' he said sarcastically, 'If I'm not wrong, I sent you four with no reply. It isn't very flattering for your family to know that you want to cut off all contact with them.'

'I had nothing to reply,' she said, her voice trailing off.

'Really? But I wrote to you about my project. Don't you remember?' He picked up a valuable clockwork device from the mantelpiece and examined it in detail. 'You could have offered me your opinion.'

'Some time ago you told me that a brat like me could not understand anything about horse races. I haven't matured much since then.'

'You remember that, do you?' He laughed again, distracted by his covetous reflection. 'I hope you didn't take it badly. The truth is that I'm very interested in your opinion, dear niece. It is a project I strongly believe in. And unfortunately, I'm running out of time. The work should have started already but certain problems...' he paused ominously, 'and the lack of a business partner have put a stop to it.'

''You should never sell a bad horse close to your own home,'' she challenged him. 'Have you ever heard that saying? Your lack of support is due to the bad reputation that precedes you. Nobody will do business with you with such a bad track record and with Devlin thinking of you less than anybody else does.'

'I know that I don't have the approval of the duke,' he said quietly. 'I hoped you would help me with that.'

'I?'

'Of course! You could put in a good word for me.'

Harmony's eyes opened up wide with outrage and surprise. She jumped up and suddenly felt slightly dizzy.

'How dare you ask me that?'

'In the name of the blood ties that join us,' he said very softly, making her sound like a hysterical woman. 'I know that I haven't been the best father to you all these years, Harmony... but you must admit, it could have been worse. I could have refused to accept you as a child. I was under no obligation to take charge of you. You would have ended up in an orphanage. If it hadn't been for my compassion, now you'd be a servant in a castle like this, or a factory worker... or you would be selling your body in the streets to get something to eat. Growing up at my place wasn't quite so terrible if you consider what I've saved you from. I hope you can at least admit that.'

Although she hated having to admit it, he was right. One of those grim scenarios would be her reality now if he and his wife hadn't opened the door of their home to her. Annoyed, she sighed.

'I know,' she growled. 'I know it could have been worse. But you could have let me go that night at Felton House. You would have got rid of me. I wouldn't even have complained about my inheritance. After all, I haven't told anybody about it. But instead of that you forced me to marry Curson. And when he hit me, you didn't defend me, Uncle John!'

He looked at her, evidently upset. He lay down the object he had been handling and approached her gingerly.

'Forgive me, dear girl,' he blurted out, and his voice cracked in a way that shook her. 'Forgive me! I could die of shame only thinking about it. I curse the hour I considered that bastard to become your husband. I only wanted to do my duty and leave you in the hands of a decent man that would look after you properly, but had no idea what a rascal that Curson truly was.' He took her hand and knelt down in front of her. Harmony could not believe what she was seeing: Her uncle was humiliating himself. 'I beg you, by all that's sacred, Harmony. Forgive this old fool who has failed you so many times. Forgive me!'

She hesitated for an instant, but then she remembered that her uncle was a master manipulator. He was a cunning snake-oil salesman, a relentless individual, and that scene wouldn't be happening if she hadn't become a rich woman. He needed to anchor himself in that wealth. He must be in dire straits to stoop down to the floor, she thought.

'You've never managed to trick me, Uncle John,' she slowly pronounced, shaking his hand off. 'Reserve your playacting for people who don't know you.'

On hearing that, he gave up on his failed attempt, stood up and looked at her for a long while, without showing any emotion.

'Keep your distance from my family,' she carried on, 'I won't allow you to settle here with your good-father-substitute mask to swindle my mother-in-law and try to do business with my husband. You're not welcome in my life! I'll tell Devlin you've been a horrible guardian. I'll tell him you robbed me of my inheritance, and he'll make sure you end up in prison.'

Uncle John's ruthless eyes squinted, sending her an evil look.

'Look at yourself, Harmony George! You've gone from pathetic wallflower to duchess. It seems that it hasn't taken you long to get used to your new status. Now you also insult and threaten, like all damned rich people do.' Now his look was oozing poison. 'I must be honest with you. I'm truly impressed. I thought you could become Curson's wife; I thought the little pigmy would break you in like a mare and if you revealed your true character, he'd know how to hit you where it hurts. After three or four black eyes, all women understand what their true place is.

'It was the future I had envisaged for you from the beginning. But you've shocked me with the enormity of your ability to get your own way. I don't know what kind of guiles you used, but you've managed to get into the bed of the Duke of Waldegrave, no less. You have acquired his title, and according to the servants' tales, you're also about to give him an heir!' He laughed out loud on seeing Harmony's flustered reaction, whose first impulse was to place a protective hand over her belly.

That miserable man had no right to know she was pregnant. It made her feel vulnerable.

'Bravo, little one. I realise you're not the fool I took you for. But you would be an ungrateful woman if you did not give some credit for such an achievement to your beloved uncle. After all, I was the one who gave you a hand to secure this profitable marriage, wasn't I?'

'You want some money. What a surprise!' She felt sickened.

'Yes. To tell you the truth, I need it desperately. My list of financial problems keeps growing.' Harmony was surprised that he'd admitted his disadvantage so easily. Normally he was proud when it came to money. 'Some very rude men want the money they won via an illegal betting scheme I organised. It's a lot of money, Harmony. I cannot get rid of them without selling everything I own, even the house and the horse breeding business. If I don't pay them back, they'll kill me.'

'You should have thought about the dangers of such a business.'

'It is too late for regrets. I need your help, Harmony.'

'Don't count on it! I'm not going to help you!'

'Of course you will.'

'And how are you going to force me to do it?'

He looked at her slyly.

'If you don't agree, I'll tell the whole truth to Waldegrave.'

Harmony clenched her fists, enraged.

'What are you talking about? What truth?'

'Well, the only plausible truth in all this; the only logical explanation for the fact that a coveted duke, such as Devlin Sawyer, has ended up marrying a little sewer rat, a nobody like you. Have you perhaps forgotten, my dear girl, how we planned the memorable ambush in the garden of Felton House?'

Harmony looked at him, uncomprehending.

He sat down, crossing his legs, showing off the control that little by little he was regaining. 'We spent all night doing nothing but follow Waldegrave's steps. We knew he was there, in the garden, getting drunk, clearly depressed and vulnerable. That was the perfect occasion to act, the moment for which Miss Andersen and I had been preparing you for months. We agreed that you would go there, distract him, taking advantage of his sorry state and the darkness to hide your lack of beauty. You would seduce him, and after a reasonable amount of time, Miss Andersen, worried for your safety, would turn up searching for you, accompanied by a respectable witness who would vouch for the loss of honour. And who would have been better than Viscountess Felton to see how Waldegrave had jumped on you and lifted your skirts?'

Harmony felt the world swirl and spin violently and endlessly around her, but her body had turned into stone. She could not hear her own breathing or the beating of her heart. Her insides had frozen, as had her will. Fear started gnawing at her to the point of clouding her mind and blocking her movements.

'And then we'd have the drama, the accusations, the guilt, the fear of scandal... the compromise,' He carried on explaining glibly what sounded, in fact, like a master plan created by a conspiratorial mind. 'In a world like this, things could not end in any other way. You've trapped a husband by using trickery, and the idiot didn't realise because he was as drunk as a bishop. Tell me that it does not sound like a very reasonable version of events. Tell me if anybody would dare refute it.'

'Devlin won't believe you.' Her voice had sounded more tremulous than she'd have wished. 'Those are only the lies invented by a disgustingly greedy man...'

'We won't know that until I tell him... Well, you've turned green,' he said laughing, evidently pleased. 'Perhaps you now understand why it is in your best interest to be on my side in this matter. If you don't do as I tell you, I'll tell Waldegrave that we set a trap so he'd feel morally obliged to marry you.'

'You won't lie to him! I'll talk to him first... I'll tell him...' she shouted, but then, a piercing pain in her abdomen, like an accurate lash, made her bend over.

'Oh, please! You're the one who's made me resort to this, Harmony,' he said, in his defence. 'I never thought it would be necessary to get to such extremes, but I find myself in such a complicated situation that I have no other option. I have nothing to lose. You, on the other hand...'

'I won't give you money... You can't...' Another sharp stab silenced her.

'Look at yourself, little one. You don't need to go through this.' He took her by the arm, guiding her to the sofa, where he helped her sit down. Then he started talking to her with fake kindness. 'You know everything is against you. When Waldegrave hears about it, perhaps he'll abhor you even more than when he felt obliged to take you for his wife. He won't give you a chance to explain. He'll find a way to make you pay. He'll take your child away from you; you can be certain of that. Then he'll divorce you, and he'll send you to a discreet exile or, in the worst-case scenario, he'll find a way to send you to prison. He's a powerful man, and I'm sure he'll have the means to do it if he knows he has been tricked.'

'He'll believe me,' she sobbed, overcome by pain.

'Would you swear it on your child's life?'

Harmony didn't say anything this time; her head was spinning wildly. She didn't want to take any oaths. She didn't dare.

'Ah, that's as I imagined... You only have to give me money, silly girl, something you have plenty of! In exchange, you'll be able to preserve everything you value in life. I don't ask for anything else! I don't ask you for anything that—'

Uncle John's words faded as Harmony's sight clouded.

She woke up with a strange buzzing in her ears; she didn't know exactly when. Corine's worried face was the first thing she saw when she finally opened her eyes.

'Harmony, are you feeling all right?' Harmony nodded, drowsy, and Corine carried on, 'My goodness, how badly your pregnancy is affecting you... I don't remember having gone through anything similar. I can see now that Devlin's precautions aren't at all excessive. I've already sent for Dr Bradshawe. He'll be here any minute now,' she told her as she compulsively fanned her.

'Did I faint again?'

'Yes, love. You uncle warned us you were unwell.'

Then, the memory of a sinister conversation invaded her mind. A threat, a lie that was painfully similar to the truth. The life she so loved and had hardly started enjoying was swaying dangerously. Her baby... Devlin... the family that now was the whole reason of her existence. She clenched her fists over the material of her skirt to conceal the trembling of her hands.

'My darling,' her uncle'a voice reached her ears like a horrific howl, 'The duchess has just given me the happy news. I had no idea, Harmony, otherwise, I wouldn't have bothered you with my problems. Agh! I'm an old fool. Forgive me, my daughter. What a blessing, you being with child. Your aunt Minnie will jump up and down when I tell her.' His voice, like that of an experienced actor, cracked in the last word.

Miserable liar!

She felt like crying due to her impotence, to the feverish fear that made her feel dangerously close to losing her mind. She swallowed the tears that were crowding her eyes, resorting to a self-control she didn't know she had.

That bastard had won; he had settled in her house, tricked her family and had her at his mercy. She closed her eyes and allowed Corine to caress her hair, as if that could comfort her. She focused on the maternal attentions she was receiving and desperately forced herself to believe in the words her mother-in-law was repeating.

'Everything will be all right, sweetheart. I promise you. Everything will pass.'

Her uncle left Sudeley two days later, taking with him the first cheque from the chequebook Devlin had given Harmony on getting married. The number written there was the whole amount contained in the last statement of her personal account, the one her husband had opened in her name and where he deposited her allowance. It was so much money that she was convinced she wouldn't hear from her uncle in a long time.

It wasn't a final solution to her problems, but at least a resolution that gave her some peace. She didn't want to ponder about why she had done it when she was innocent.

In any case, she gave him the money and tried to forget about it.

Corine did not pass up the opportunity to interrogate her. She had done it gently but, even with that, Harmony felt cornered.

'Ah, Harmony. I would have expected something like that from Devlin, but not from you,' she had told her that very same day, as soon as they were alone. 'Why didn't you talk to me about your aunt and uncle? I would have invited them to the spring ball. Are you ashamed of them, perhaps? I hope our ball has shown you that we don't judge people based on what they have.'

She ended up by admitting that she felt ashamed of the Talbots and doubted that they would be able to fit into the affluent lifestyle of the Sawyers. Although that was true, she still felt guilty. In the name of her happiness, she had started to spin a web of lies. She apologised to Corine. She, bless her, decided to comfort her instead of scolding her.

Once the matter that had caused her such turmoil was closed, Harmony tried to focus her attention on knitting and embroidering, the new tasks her mother-in-law had suggested she do until tea time. Unfortunately, she wasn't particularly skilled at either of them, as was the case with most crafts. Corine taught her with her renowned maternal patience. She talked to her about different types of knitting, styles and techniques with complicated names, and she ordered magazines with drawings of complicated designs, which Harmony was sure she would never learn to do until after the baby had already learned to walk. Corine showed her, proudly, the pieces she had created herself for fun: blankets, scarfs, gloves, pillows, handkerchiefs, and even a picture of a beautiful bird's nest.

Miss Andersen had tried to introduce Harmony to the feminine and proper world of embroidery, a task very suitable for a woman, but she had not turned out to be a skilled student. Her stitches, which refused to follow any pattern, never did what they should. And, she got easily bored, because her mind was always busy thinking of something else, like the books she wanted to have or the places she wanted to visit. Another failure to add to her long list.

Corine's extraordinary ability to do any type of housework made Harmony feel as rough as a mule at a horse fair by comparison. It wasn't easy to try to be a good duchess and to live up to a predecessor that embodied perfection.

Sometimes, only sometimes, she felt irritated by such perfection. She felt as if her mother-in-law enjoyed showing off her grace, her total suitability for any challenge that came her way.

She sighed to scare off her annoyed thoughts and straightened up on the sofa, ready to keep on working on the needlework she had in front of her, even if she had to fight the slight tremor in her hands and the bitter memory of her uncle's visit. It couldn't be that difficult to shape a silly sunflower, she thought, as she started stabbing at the piece of cloth, tracing the lines of its design as if her life depended on it.

She pondered using her allowance again if her uncle came back a few months later demanding more money. She would have to find an excuse to justify spending the whole of her monthly allocations... The needle went in and out of the cloth, leaving an acceptable yellow trace... Perhaps nobody would notice that the money went out as soon as it came in; perhaps she shouldn't worry that much. But if she had to give a reason for her expenses, she would say that she contributed to some charitable foundation, or that she'd indulged herself, but, what kind of thing could she have indulged in when she never left the house?... The threads were shaping into the petal of a sunflower... She had to come up with something else. She couldn't let Devlin find out that she was financing John Talbot, a man he abhorred. If he found out, he'd ask her the reason and she would have to...

'Damn!' Accidentally, she had pricked her thumb with the needle.

She lifted it to her mouth to suck the drop of blood spurting from it. When she realised she'd cursed in front of the exquisitely polite duchess, she raised her worried eyes towards her. Corine was looking at her, her eyes shining, evidently horrified. Harmony felt her blood heating up her neck and face. She had, now for sure, left her in no doubt of her daughter-in-law's vulgarity.

What an embarrassment!

Then, out of nowhere, she started to cry.

Quickly, Corine picked up her needlework, put it back in the sewing box and came to sit next to her.

'Oh, dear girl,' she comforted her. 'There's no need for that. Believe me; I say the same every time I find a good reason for it.'

'I'm so sorry.' Harmony hid her face behind her hands.

'You don't need to apologise.'

Corine stayed with her while her crying quieted down.

'This is not because of the pregnancy, is it?' she said shortly.

'Yes... I don't know.' Harmony avoided looking at her again. She silently prayed she wouldn't give herself away.

'I'd like to make sure you know that you can tell me anything,' her mother-in-law told her, placing a hand on top of hers.

'Thank you. I... think you're right...' she muttered. 'The pregnancy is not suiting me.'

Corine furrowed her brow deeply. She was aware of the way in which John Talbot's visit had affected Harmony's mood and couldn't help wondering why. She felt somewhat hurt by the girl's recent mutism, her determination to shoulder alone that load, because she had thought the level of trust they shared would allow for any kind of confidences.

'Let me help you with that,' she said, lifting her chin delicately. 'After all, I've gone through the same a couple of times... a long time ago, but I don't think things have changed too much since.'

Harmony heard the words and froze. 'Did you say a couple of times?' she whispered, contrite, on understanding that Corine was talking about pregnancies. 'Devlin has... or had... a brother...?' she mumbled.

'Yes,' Corine's look seemed lost in a fog of memories; some happy, but most of them horrible. 'There were three months left before the birth... it was a girl. But I lost her... Oh, but you don't want to hear that...!'

'No, no. I do, it's all right.'

'Harmony, in your condition, it's a terrible topic of conversation.'

'I don't see it that way. You must tell me. Do it, please.' She squeezed Corine's hand in hers and turned her body in her direction, expectant.

Corine straightened up on the sofa, relaxed her shoulders and looked at her with her only visible eye. Harmony swallowed on seeing the melancholy shining in that eye. She knew that what she was about to hear would be tough.

'I got married for love... I was very young then,' she started, but in contrast with the nature of the content of her speech, she sounded devastated. 'Heyworth Sawyer, Devlin's father, was the loveliest, handsomest, most educated, and intelligent man I had ever met. The first time I saw him was at a dinner, at the mansion of one of my father's friends who was celebrating his birthday. When we were introduced, it was as if the whole world had stopped for me; as if I'd been waiting for that moment, for that person, my whole life without knowing it,' she scowled, 'or that's what one thinks at seventeen.

'He courted me for a few months, with all the chaperone propriety required. He was always so proper and affable in front of my parents, and when we went for walks in the park. But we never talked alone other than twice, one of them when my father agreed to the engagement... so we could say that when we got married we were a couple of strangers.'

Corine paused for a while, and Harmony mulled over her words in that time. Shortly, Corine, went on, 'I wish I had known him better before the wedding; I wish I hadn't allowed myself to get dazzled by him. I would have realised that he drank until he lost control... and that was only one of his many vices.'

Harmony looked into her eyes, moved, but remained silent.

'When I got pregnant with Devlin,' she carried on, 'shortly after the wedding, I got to truly know him. When he was at home, he drank all day, at all times, with his friends or alone. And then he would sleep the whole day. He only managed to recover whenever Limsey prepared him some concoction that cured his hangover, or he would never have been fit enough to attend Parliament. Then he'd go travelling, and I wouldn't hear from him for weeks or even months. I always wondered where he was, what he was doing and if he also drank when he was away from home. I couldn't help worrying for his health.'

'It's terrible,' muttered Harmony sorrowfully.

'Not as terrible as what followed,' she whispered. 'I loved him. I wasn't going to let our lives go on with his drunkenness and hangovers. I told him he should look for a doctor, somebody who could help him, and he didn't take it too well. That night he hit me.'

Harmony flinched. She found it difficult to believe that somebody could lift a finger against gentle Corine, and more so Devlin's father. 'Did he beat you when you were pregnant?'

Corine nodded. 'He arrived one night with his depraved friends and a group of vulgar women, all of them inebriated. One could tell at once that the women were prostitutes. Of course, I went mad. I asked for an explanation; I demanded that all of them leave my house, but Heyworth shut me up and ordered me to go back to bed. One of the women, who could hardly remain upright, mocked my swollen belly and all of them laughed with her. Even he did. I refused to accept such disrespect; I complained, and then, furious, he grabbed me by the neck. I thought he would strangle me there and then. He told me that no woman could speak to him that way... and even less so a stupid brat who didn't even know how to satisfy him in bed.'

'Such a horrible man... What did you do, Corine?' Harmony asked, hardly aware that she was clenching her fists.

'That time I tried to defend myself, but even with all that had happened between us, I had yet to see Heyworth's true nature,' her mother-in-law whispered in monotone, her eyes glued to the carpet. 'He let go of me. He called one of those horrible women, one with her makeup smudged and her corset so low that one could see her nipples. He told me that I owed her more than I could imagine; that Ginger, as she was called, was the one who had kept his bed warm while I looked like a sickening sow, and that thanks to her skills, he had not got rid of me yet. He assured me that she could teach me how to satisfy a man, because, according to him, I had plenty to learn from a real woman. Then, the aforementioned Ginger approached, looking smug. She asked me to look closely at her... and started grabbing my husband right there. That was enough for me to leave the place, indignant, while his vile friends laughed at me...'

Harmony could hardly believe such villainy; she felt like bringing back to life the bastard to send him back to his grave.

'After that, I decided to create a wall between him and me. That humiliation made me realise that I had made a mistake marrying him. I tried to leave him, but my mother dissuaded me. She told me that it was my lot as a woman; that I had to put up with everything for my son, because if I enraged a duke, he'd make sure I was sorry for it. My father was always away travelling, so I doubt he ever found out what was happening in my marriage.

'When Devlin was born, I understood what my mother had meant. I couldn't just leave, because if I did, I would lose any rights over my son. If I escaped with him, he would find me, one way or another, to get his heir back, and then it would be worse for me.'

Harmony shuddered to hear all that. It wasn't that she saw her own situation mirrored in that macabre story, but she had shared the fear of losing a child and that made her think that perhaps she wasn't wrong trying to keep her uncle quiet.

'That's why I stayed and bore much more than you can imagine,' Corine added then.

'Is there even more?'

Corine nodded.

'The love I felt for Heyworth ended up becoming a repulsion. The visits of those women and many others to Waldegrave Terrace and to Sudeley didn't stop. I could often hear his scandals, his parties, and gave thanks because, at least, he was kept entertained, and he did not demand my company at night. For that, he had his prostitutes. I dedicated myself to looking after my little one and to ignore the beast that was my husband. But one night, after spending months away from London, he arrived home, alone, and looked for me.' She paused, then opened her mouth to speak anew, but the words would not come out.

Harmony imagined what she was trying to relay was most likely a dark and painful episode.

'And that was how I got pregnant again, four years after Devlin's birth,' Corine finally said, obviously sparing Harmony from the disturbing details.

'Why did you lose your daughter?' Harmony asked, saddened.

'It was during an argument with Heyworth. I no longer remember the reason for it. The truth is that I was furious; I wanted to go downstairs, to the garden... then I tripped on the stairs and rolled down to the main floor.' Corine evidently held back because she did not want to upset Harmony with excessively vivid descriptions. 'Devlin witnessed everything.'

'Oh, good grief. I'm not surprised he's so obsessive with me...' Harmony hid her face behind her hands, telling herself that she'd never again criticise her husband's efforts to look after her, even when she thought they were excessive. 'I'm sorry, Corine. You did not deserve to have to live with such a cruel husband. That man... I can't believe Devlin bears any relation to him. He was a monster!'

'I no longer think about him that way. I only remember him as a disturbed man.'

'Did Devlin know he treated you badly?'

'He found out soon enough. Devlin never reciprocated his father's affections; he was evasive and cold with him. I imagine he had a grudge against him. He preferred the company of his friends and their parents, or the servants. Heyworth blamed me for that; he used to say I had turned him against him, and he even denied that he was his flesh and blood. That was a subject we fought about often... He tried to gain Devlin's love and trust for years, but he never relented. Then, Heyworth realised it would never happen... and started to turn violent towards him as well.'

'Did he beat him too?'

'Yes, but, in contrast with me, Devlin hit him back. By the age of thirteen he had caused his father several bruises. I couldn't bear it.' Corine's eyes misted up, but she seemed intent on holding back the tears. After a pause, she went on, 'I couldn't bear my son throwing punches like my husband did. I worried he'd turn up the same... but when I tried to intervene he rejected me... Both of them did.'

'No, Devlin isn't like that!' Harmony stood up suddenly and started to pace up and down the room. 'He's never behaved in a violent manner towards anyone, at least not in my presence. He's not a beast like his father!'

'I know, sweetheart, and I thank God for that. I don't know what you'll think about this, Harmony, but both he and I felt very relieved when Heyworth left this world for good. I think all of our defences dropped.'

'Perhaps not all, Corine. Perhaps there is a defence still up.'

'That's a matter only Devlin can tell you about.'

'How did the old duke die?'

Corine took a moment to compose her reply. 'It was here, at Sudeley,' her voice sounded eerily mechanical, 'Devlin was about to celebrate his fifteenth birthday. Heyworth was drunk, of course. He had gone to visit the ruins.' She shrugged. 'I imagine he lost his balance in his drunken stupor because of the many holes there and must have tripped and fallen over the edge… We found his body flat out on the ground, his neck broken.'

Harmony didn't feel sorry in the slightest for that bastard. Although he was Devlin's father, she hated him. She couldn't even comprehend how her husband could possibly be descended from such a vile individual. She turned to look at her mother-in-law.

'You didn't deserve what that swine did to you,' she muttered. 'May the Lord forgive me, but I'm happy the devil took him away.'

Corine pressed her lips as she nodded her head. For a long time she had been of the belief that she deserved the bad treatment she received at the hands of Heyworth. The constant abuse and insults had blurred her perception of her duty, her marriage, and love itself but, thank God, all that had finished the day he died. That day, she had been born again.

Harmony was right. The devil had taken him away.

'I wasn't thinking of anything like this when I said I'd help you with your pregnancy,' she laughed, but her laughter didn't transmit good humour. 'This is the family you now belong to, Harmony. We're all full of scars… and perhaps the odd festering wound as well. I've told you all this, because I think it is fair you should know… and because I trust you. Perhaps you'll understand Devlin better now. I know my son will make an extraordinary father, because his nature is noble, loving… but not for what he's learned from his own father.'

Harmony was moved to hear these words, her heart giving a flutter. 'I have no doubt about it,' she said, feeling both moved and saddened for not being able to be as honest with her.

Then, she hugged her.

Chapter 19

Harmony's health improved significantly in the following days. The fatigue, the sickness, and the fainting had been left behind once she started the diet prescribed by Dr Bradshawe and a daily routine of walks around the flowery and exuberant gardens at Sudeley. Breathing the clean country smells, walking on the thick grass, and feeling the breeze of the Cotswolds stirring her hair made her feel incredibly well. To a great extent, she felt the atmosphere of her new home had contributed to her recovery.

During those days, she tried to forget about her uncle and his threats. She started to question the truth of the story he had told her—about some unsavoury characters demanding the money for some illegal bets—and ended up believing he had made it up to try to move her. That vile extortionist was surely spending the money of her allowance. Of course they had bought liquor and food in excess to throw a huge party at their Whitechapel house, as they used to do every time they had a shilling in their pockets. If he came looking for more money, she'd give him another cheque and everybody would be happy.

That afternoon, Harmony was feeling so well that she decided to take a tour of the town. Corine didn't oppose because it was clear that her exhaustion of a few days earlier was a thing of the past. She only imposed one condition, that she allowed Jane, her maid, to accompany her, and she ordered Louis to follow her very closely.

Harmony appreciated the care of her mother-in-law, whom she loved and respected, now even more so than before. The conversation about her husband threw some light on the unfathomable distance between Devlin and his mother. She had trembled in impotence whenever she reflected on it. It was so deplorable... whereas they should be closer due to their shared pain, they were utterly isolated.

She felt guilty for having criticised earlier on the 'tiresome perfectionism' of her mother-in-law and her 'perfect and pretentious' manners. Now that she could imagine the hell she had gone through, she realised that Corine Radley was a much stronger woman than she had anticipated. The finesse she evidenced concealed an incommensurable female strength.

Although she desperately tried to get rid of that thought, something told her that her mother-in-law had omitted a large part of the story of her marriage to the previous Duke of Waldegrave.

Once she reached the sunny and cool High Street of Winchcombe on foot, she bumped onto the keen greetings of a few passers-by who, grateful for having been invited to the spring ball, showed her their respects. That included the manager of the Telegraph Office, Mr Phelan, and his wife, who walked by her with their little three-year-old boy. The little one, shy and red-faced, brought a tender smile to her face. She smiled on thinking about her dear child, whom she'd soon be able to spoil and hug.

After a brief chat with the Phelan family, Harmony continued her walk.

She took the chance to wander around the local park, now blooming and full of walkers. She had a look at the shops, greeted the kind shop girls and picked up a few gifts. Afterwards, she entered The Bookend and passed the time choosing some new titles from a promising mountain of newly published books. But then she remembered she didn't have a shilling to pay for them. Her allowance for the last two months had gone straight to line the pockets of that conniving scoundrel, who, even from a distance, managed to turn her life into misery. A rush of bitterness destroyed the good humour she had felt all day. She left empty-handed, to the disappointment of the bookshop owner and her own.

As soon as she came out of The Bookend, a pair of bleary eyes, which mistrustfully inspected her from the pavement, caused her to halt.

She had already been the object of that fiery gaze that was full of an incomprehensible hatred, and she had decided to ignore it then. This time, however, she refused to do the same. It wasn't fair, and she had to do something about it.

It was an impulse more than anything else. Harmony stared at Gretty, her chin up to show her she was not afraid of her, and walked towards her, her steps slow and determined. Jane, her maid, looked flabbergasted on seeing her mistress approach the town's madwoman. Despite that, she followed her hesitantly.

The old woman, standing by one of the columns of a small building, tensed like a cat about to pounce on observing Harmony approach.

'Good morning, Gretty,' Harmony greeted her with an open smile. 'Nice day, don't you think? It isn't quite as cold. I hope your chest complaint is better now.'

The only reply she got was a morose look and something that sounded like a weak grunt.

'Your Grace, she's mad as a hatter,' Jane whispered. 'You're wasting your time.'

Harmony paid no heed to the warning. She retrieved from the bag Jane was carrying a box of sugary buns, a gift from the baker. She then offered her one, to the astonishment of the other two women. 'Do you fancy one of these? I've heard you love them.'

Gretty looked at the delicious treat. One could almost hear her saliva dripping as she seemed to fight against the temptation, like a squirrel that's been offered a handful of nuts. But, as any other wild creature would have done, Gretty ended up succumbing to the pull of the delicious morsel.

Without further hesitation, she grabbed the sugary bun and gobbled it down in one go. She chewed it with delight, more than Harmony could have imagined, without stopping to savour it.

'They taste good, don't they? Have another one.' Harmony offered her a second bun. She was surprised on seeing that she put that away inside the pocket of her worn out coat. Perhaps she wanted to eat it later... or was she thinking of giving it to somebody else? 'Now tell me, Gretty, do you still dislike me?'

The old woman adopted a less hostile expression, but it was far from kind. Her reservations remained in place. She cleaned the corners of her mouth with the lapel of her coat, while seemingly mulling over her answer. 'A family of criminals,' she muttered.

Harmony squinted. 'For God's sake, good woman, stop saying that.'

'Not you, they!' She gestured dismissively with her hand. 'You don't know anything, girl. You weren't even there.'

'What don't I know?' She rolled her eyes on remembering that she was trying to reason with somebody whose head wasn't properly screwed on. 'Please, Gretty, you can't go around saying horrible things about my family. Enough is enough.'

'A family of criminals!' she insisted, to Harmony's frustration.

'The Sawyer family has done nothing to you, or has it?' she said, clenching her teeth. 'You have no right to go spreading such horrible lies around town. The other day you almost got my mother-in-law trampled by a horse. Do you know what that means?'

Gretty looked at her, her eyes bulging and her lips closed tight, pulling a face that only a woman off-her-head could compose without any justification.

Jane moaned in fear and went back to find Louis, the coachman, who had taken advantage of the stop to give water to the horses.

'It isn't a lie, young girl,' the madwoman hissed. 'The woman pushed him.'

Harmony tutted.

'Which... which woman? Who are you talking—?'

'She did... I saw her!' She compulsively tapped her cheek with her index finger. 'She pushed her husband. I saw her. I saw her!'

Harmonly looked at her, mouth agape, feeling a strange numbness. It can't be true, was all she kept screaming inside her head. It can't be.

'I saw her,' the old woman insisted, flitting between dead-seriousness and uncontrollable laughter, typical of a disturbed woman. But even Harmony knew that mad people and children didn't have the slyness required to lie. 'I saw her... I—' Gretty continued.

Corine. She meant her, she realised, her mouth dry. Had Gretty seen the duchess push Heyworth Sawyer over the unprotected edge of the ruins at Sudeley? Would she truly have done it or was it only crazy talk? Was her mother-in-law a criminal, as the old woman had so often suggested as she shouted at her?

Good God... Corine...

She didn't blame her exactly. She herself had thanked God on hearing how that man had left this world, but to think that the sweet and prim Corine Radley, the splendorous Duchess of Waldegrave, had had no other option than to commit such a horrendous act, stung her heart.

Gretty took advantage of Harmony's confusion to grab hold of the box of sugary buns, and begin to run towards a crouching female figure that was calling her over from the street corner.

Even in the middle of that chaos, Harmony followed her with her eyes. She realised that the woman peering from behind the wall was the same one she had seen with Gretty the first time. Like she did on that icy day, she was wearing a heavy and frayed cape which half-covered her face and reached down to the edge of her skirt. Her hands were stained with something resembling paint. Harmony had deduced it was Gretty's daughter. When the old woman reached her and was greeted with what seemed to be an anxious sermon, Harmony was able to glimpse an inch of her face.

Impossible, she thought, shaking her head.

A blonde curl escaped the hood and reflected a sunray. And then she had no doubt about who was hiding behind the worn out clothes. As if it had not been bad enough to have to listen to Gretty's horrific revelations, now she had also become a witness to the forays of Laurel, Lady Colvile, who wandered around the streets of Winchcombe without a care in the world while nobody recognised her.

Louis and Jane arrived right when the two madwomen began to walk together down the street. Harmony now knew who Gretty would be sharing the sugary buns with.

Devlin returned to Sudeley on a sunny Saturday morning, after spending four days supervising and actively participating in the work of Calder & Barrett, the company holding the license for the installation of the public electricity service in Godalming.

The owners of the company, two tenacious electricians from Westminster Bridge Road that had obtained—and it wasn't easy—a contract with the town hall to supply electricity to the town, had offered him a grand reception. It wasn't a matter of generosity. Sawyer Light Factory had invested a large sum of money in the London firm to facilitate the installation that, otherwise, would have been only a dream.

A few months back, Calder & Barret had fought hard to get the approval of the authorities to bring electricity to the homes of Godalming, once the contract with the gas company Godalming Gas & Coke had expired. For a while, the advisability, or not, of installing such a 'complex' system had been a frequent topic of conversation in the markets, taverns and when the inhabitants got talking. The matter split the town into several competing sectors, ones pro and ones against that scandalous novelty. Some said that the calm of the town would be altered by those ghostly lights, and that installing them would take forever and be incredibly expensive, not to mention bothersome for the citizens.

To overcome the misgivings of the population, Calder & Barrett made a proposal that their gas rivals could not undercut; one that only an ingenious electrician with many ideas about how to exploit the available resources and a rich patron would be able to bring to fruition. The company suggested using and adapting the pylons and the gas lampposts already in existence to save themselves the bother of having to build a new power line. Waldegrave would supply the lightbulbs and the generators.

Those involved promised to accelerate the works to ensure that the basic structure would be ready in a month's time. As a result, the word of a respected aristocrat and of two renowned businessmen sufficed for the town hall to grant them a twelve-month permit to work.

Obtaining the license wasn't the most difficult thing; afterwards, other challenges arrived: once in possession of all the permits, the company built a factory, which worked thanks to the hydraulic power of two enormous waterwheels on the river Wey. The alternator would carry the energy up to the cables installed in Godalming High Street, and from there to the shops and nearby buildings. There was widespread reluctance to the innovation and Mr Calder and Mr Barrett, with the duke and his partners, had to spend much of their time selling the idea of the practical applications of electricity and dispelling the fears townspeople could have about it. A few pints at the pub or glasses of whisky went a long way to convince shop owners of the merits of the new system of lighting.

After installing the power lines and the incandescent light bulbs, they had the first public show, greeted with plenty of admiring gasps. Afterwards, there were public celebrations, fireworks, and street music performances; there was a crowd on the high street to share the pride of being the first British town with a public electricity supply.

The trip had been worth it, Devlin thought as he left Godalming in the morning train, but after all that bustle he wished for nothing else than to get home and be with his wife. He had lusted after her every day and every night in that lonely hotel room. He had thought about her, had enjoyed in silence the joy of knowing that she carried his child inside her. Now, nothing would prevent him from going back and looking after them both. He laughed when he thought that if he had not been happily married, he would have accepted the offer an attractive woman had made him in the hotel bar; after all, that was what his life had been like before he met the elusive and fascinating Miss George.

He felt overjoyed when he told that woman that he was not interested, because it was true; the weirdest and most tremendous truth of his life. There was only one woman for him, and she occupied all aspects of his life in an irreversible manner.

He arrived at Sudeley several hours later. He smiled when he saw her glowing excitedly, atop the steps. She was beautiful with her cream blouse and a blue taffeta skirt, her brown curls tumbling down her narrow shoulders and a hairdo partly up which highlighted the magnificence of her hair. In contrast with the last time he had seen her, her cheeks showed a wonderful blush, and he could bet she'd put some weight on.

She looked healthier and prettier, he concluded, happily.

Harmony felt a surge of joy in her heart as she smiled at Devlin sweetly. It was a happy coincidence that she had been alone in the house when he'd arrived. She was about to climb downstairs, but suddenly stopped. Perhaps it was something she saw in his eyes that forced her to think better of it and remain at the top step.

Devlin felt relieved to see her staying up there. Unexpectedly then, the horrific memory of a woman falling among much screaming and complaining, briefly flashed in his mind. That woman had rolled spectacularly downstairs and ended up flat at the bottom of the steps, with the lower part of her dress and her hands covered in blood.

Devlin shook his head to dispel that horrendous memory, a fragment of a childhood he did not want to remember. He ran upstairs, two steps at a time, to avoid delaying any further the meeting with his wife. He was up in an instant, holding her safely in his arms now. He finally hugged her and inhaled eagerly the celestial sandalwood aroma of her curls. He kissed her shoulders, her hair, her brow, and all the bits of her skin he had access to. He'd done the same on the night he had returned from London and had seen her playing the role of duchess valiantly. He had felt he loved her more than words could say… therefore he'd chosen a universal language and he did the same now.

'How did it go——?'

He placed his finger on his wife's lips to quiet her down.

'Later…' he whispered.

He gathered her in his arms without saying another word and took her to their chamber.

In the intimacy of their room, he undressed her and loved her without waiting any longer. He did it with such passion that he made her see stars. He was slow and delicate at first. Later, overtaken by the passion he had held back for endless days, he accelerated the rhythm until their ecstasy rose to the level of a gale. At the end, he turned into a fiery and vigorous lover, awaken by the willingness and the surrender of his magnificent and pregnant wife.

Harmony felt ecstasy surge through her like a freight train as she allowed Devlin's dexterous hands to dissolve the fears and worries on her mind. She permitted him to do as he wished, devoted to the desires of his body and the unquenchable urge that seemed to control him. How on Earth did he know better than her what she needed and desired? How did he forestall all her whims? What sibylline intuition allowed him to know her body better than she did, as if he possessed a map or a secret compass of her humanity?

Devlin couldn't believe his ears when, shy and excited in the same measure, Harmony asked him to teach her how to please him, as he so competently did for her. He knew that the mechanisms of pleasure were unfathomable, and that a woman with such limited experience—a wife first and foremost—would need more time to learn to perfection the nooks and crannies of the male body... unless she revealed her interest in learning how to do it. Devlin, fascinated by that rare and sublime request, born from true feminine innocence, decided to teach her.

Harmony tried her best, focusing her mind as Devlin showed her what to do. As a student, she had never been particularly gifted, but in that aspect she felt proud of herself: she had proven that she could be an exceptional student. Her husband was a patient and gentle teacher that instilled her with confidence and celebrated her progress with joy. Forgetting her own inhibitions, she followed the instructions as he whispered and moaned, his voice hoarse and the movements she was shown to do agonizingly demanding... In the process, by giving him pleasure, she found her own.

Devlin shivered with rapture while Harmony did as he asked, as he experienced the touch of her exquisite mouth and the effective movements of her hands. He tingled with the emotion of some of the creative ideas she introduced as well. She was so ingenious, so ready to break the rules, so authentic... like no other woman who'd shared his bed before. She would be a magnificent inventor, he thought while enjoying her generous ministrations, and taking care of her in turn.

The ecstasy invaded them as they delighted in the splendid art of pleasuring each other.

Harmony erupted in soft sobs then, and it caught her by surprise as her heart still raced. A mix of pleasure, pain, fear and an overwhelming joy had flooded her.

Devlin went crazy with worry, his brow creasing deeply. Thinking that he might have hurt her, he took her in his arms and rocked her, then dried with his cheeks the sweat from her brow and her tears. He apologised repeatedly and, after what felt like eternity to him, she smiled, reassuring him that everything was well.

Devlin sighed with relish, his heart blooming with love. He and Harmony had just made love for the third time that night. They were too exhausted to carry on, but while they recovered their strength they hugged in the dark.

'Why didn't you stay with me in our wedding night?' she asked playfully, as she nestled her head on his shoulder. 'Why did you leave without a word, without as much as a goodnight? I can't stop wondering about that.'

Devlin hesitated for a few moments; he had not expected that question. 'Darling, I'm sorry... I was ashamed.'

'What of?'

'Well... You made me lose control very quickly.'

'Me?' She started laughing now that she understood what he was talking about.

'Yes, you,' he purred, as he caressed her naked back, that vast and soft desert. 'It should not have happened so quickly, do you understand? But I imagine that, from the very beginning, you had that kind of power over me.'

'The power of making you lose control?' she teased him. 'Is it so bad?'

'Perhaps.'

Harmony eyed her husband with curiosity. He was being a little mysterious and she felt compelled to press on. 'Why do you say that?'

'I often think of that night at the Feltons' garden...' He was quiet for a minute, pondering, while she tried to keep up her good humour. 'I don't remember much about that night, but I'd like to know. Sometimes I wonder what happened exactly, but I'm ashamed to ask you. Now, however, a feel a bit more courageous. I'd like you to be sincere with me, Harmony.'

Harmony tensed up. If she'd known that subject would come up, she would have kept her mouth shut. 'Why? It doesn't matter.'

'It does to me. Tell me what happened.'

Harmony couldn't bear the very thought. If she spoke about it, it would be like walking the tightrope. She would have to be honest, tell him that she was trying to run away from her aunt and uncle and from the horrible marriage that awaited her with Andrew Curson. If Harmony told her husband that her uncle John had embezzled her inheritance, he'd go to demand compensation and her uncle, enraged and with nothing left to lose, would take the chance to blurt out that dirty lie of his that Harmony feared more than death itself, because it sounded like the absolute truth.

That damned man was right. Every detail was perfect to make Devlin believe that their meeting had been part of a plan to take advantage of him and put him in a morally compromising position. It was a rather logical explanation, which would displace any other certainty. And she had no way of disproving it, even less when her adversary was the most skilled liar of the entire England, a consummate actor. She didn't want to find out if the love Devlin felt for her could stand such a test.

'You... kissed me,' she finally muttered.

'I know, but I'm sure there's more.'

She had no option. She told him the same version she had offered Corine shortly after her arrival at Sudeley, the one that did not mention her stolen inheritance, her engagement to Curson, and her intention of running away for good from her unhappy life next to the Talbot family.

'I fought with my relatives and wanted to leave the party to go back home,' she said, matter-of-factly. 'The main door was full of people, and that's why I decided the best thing to do would be to leave through the garden door, but it was closed. I tried to climb it, but then you turned up. You stopped me because you thought I was going to kill myself,' she giggled nervously, 'You tried to bring me down, but I made it difficult for you. I even hit you to make you let me go once and for all... but then we slipped and fell down... and that is when you kissed me.'

Devlin had grown uncomfortable to hear the account of that horrific incident from her lips. 'Did I... try to rape you?' He almost died of shame when he asked that question, but he was not going to let another day go by without knowing.

'No!' Harmony stood up, looking horrified. She turned on the nearest lamp and looked at him, tense. 'I mean... I think you got a bit carried away. That's all. I... I wanted you to kiss me... to touch me. I let you do it, Devlin. I'm guilty of what happened! We both wanted it.'

'And what about the torn up dress... and the bruise on your chin?' he insisted, drawing himself up as well, hungry for replies.

Harmony held her breath, her mind whirling. How could she explain that? She'd forgotten the damned dress.

'Don't be afraid to tell me the truth. Please...'

They sat back on the bed, then kneeled on the soft mattress, staring at each other unblinkingly. He seemed stubborn and bold, and she managed, hardly knowing how, to resist the attack of a creeping wave of panic. Her thoughts were spinning at a vertiginous speed, entangling and creating a hateful jumble of urgency and desperation. Say something, for the love of God, she ordered herself inwardly. Say something or you'll lose him. You'll lose everything. You'll lose your child...

'Devlin, I...' she finally said with a sob. She closed her eyes to avoid having to look at him when she added, 'It must have been... the passion, I imagine.' First lie. She hated herself unmeasurably for being capable of committing such an act of cowardice... But not as much as she hated herself when she caught a glimpse of her husband's horrified face. 'But... I didn't notice... I swear.'

'Enough!' He jumped off the bed, looking like a nervous wreck.

'Devlin——!'

'How can you make excuses for me after I've done something like that?' he muttered, enraged, while he put on his nightshirt.

'You were drunk... you didn't know what you were doing.'

Devlin gritted his teeth, shame washing over him like a jet of dark water. To be honest, he did not need his wife's confirmation. He had already accepted the fact that he had assaulted her that night, although he did not remember anything. The fact that she excused his behaviour made him feel even more wretched.

He rested his hands on the wall and, shaking, let his head drop. A wave of shame confined him to that stance, as if he were a miserable convict.

'Yes,' he acknowledged in a low voice. 'I was drunk... like he used to be.'

'Who are you talking about?'

'My father.' He'd spat the words, his tone an amalgam of fury and resentment. Now he could no longer find a difference between his own behaviour and that of Heyworth Sawyer, the swine he'd learned to hate. 'He was a bastard who loved to drink all the time. And when he did, he assaulted my mother...'

Harmony couldn't believe her ears. 'You're nothing like that man!' she burst out crying, feeling impotent. He was the antithesis of such a monster. 'You're very wrong if you think you are even a little like him. Devlin, listen to me——!'

'I see that my mother has talked to you about the previous duke.'

'Yes, she has, but Devlin... Let me——'

In a sudden movement, he yanked himself off the wall, turned towards her and fell on his knees. He took her hands, as a sinner would do in front of a divine presence, and kissed them compulsively, begging for redemption. Harmony felt worse than a pile of dirt; she was the one who should be crawling on the floor, begging for his forgiveness... but she could not bring herself to pronounce the words that would soothe his pain. They would not come out of her mouth. Her panic about the possibility of losing the only man she'd ever loved and her little child had paralysed her capacity to do the right thing.

I'm a liar... a coward. Selfish. Heartless, she told herself while her husband begged for her forgiveness in a flaying litany.

'My God, Devlin! I have nothing to forgive you for.' Rivers of tears flowed down Harmony's cheeks. She grabbed his face and looked at him in a fit of determination. 'I love you. I love you more than I've ever loved anyone... The only thing I want is for us to be together, to bring up our child.' Her voice cracked as she pronounced the next words. 'Everything I do is for us, do you understand? I don't want anybody to ever hurt us. I don't want anybody to separate us. I can't...'

'You are too generous with me. I don't deserve it. I should give you a weapon and ask you to use it against me if I ever lay a finger on you like that again.'

She was the one who did not deserve him; now she understood that. 'Don't say that! Never say that again!'

She grabbed his hand and guided him back to bed, right when a fine spring rain started to fall on the gloomy prairies of Winchcombe. She remained next to him in silence for an undetermined period of time, comforting him with kisses and caresses in the warm refuge of her arms while a storm of guilt shook her insides. She repeated over and over again that she loved him, that for him she could do the most unthinkable and scariest of deeds and that, if necessary, she'd also die for him.

Finally, a truth came to light in that sea of lies when Devlin started to speak a few hours later. They'd remained together in bed all this time.

'He didn't only take his anger out on my mother.' His voice took on a cold and impersonal tone when he started telling his story. 'He took it out on me as well, sometimes only to discipline me, or at least that was what he used to say. He assured me that it was for my own good; that I had to toughen up and polish my character if I wanted to become the man my future social standing required. 'A man born to rule could be anything but a softie',' he mumbled bitterly.

'One night, in the middle of one of his outrageous parties, he entered my room. He woke me up and told me that he was going to introduce me to a friend of his, one of those women who always came home with him. He told me he was going to leave me alone with her, and that I could do whatever I wanted. He said: 'If you want to become a man, you have to learn how to treat a woman, and the sooner you do that the better.' I didn't know what he was talking about. I was nine.'

Harmony flinched in horror to hear that, but remained silent as he continued, 'He asked the woman to be patient with me and then he left us alone. I won't horrify you telling you the things that whore did to tempt a child,' he shook his head, 'Instead of exciting me, it made me feel disgusted and nervous. When she started touching me, I asked her to stop. She didn't listen to me. I couldn't put up with it any longer. I left. When my father learned that I had not consummated any acts with that woman, he beat me to a pulp... He started to doubt my virility and blamed my mother. He said that she'd spoiled me, turning me into an effeminate. Then he beat her as well.'

'For the love of God, you were only a child!' Harmony burst out as she sobbed and caressed his arm.

'I didn't mind my own pain. However, hers crushed me,' he carried on, 'She was going to have another child, do you realise? But she lost it after a fall downstairs. She was arguing with him... They were shouting at each other and... I thought I saw him pushing her.'

Harmony stopped her caresses, surprised. She had felt more and more horrified with each new revelation. Corine hadn't dared tell her the truth... Before she could say anything, Devlin added, 'When I became more aware of what he was doing I started to confront him, but I always ended up as bruised as she did, or even more.'

'Wasn't there anybody she could turn to?' she whispered.

'Whenever Waldegrave got up to one of his old tricks, the servants looked another way. Nobody dared challenge him; they feared him as if he was the devil, even the Winchcombe's bailiff and the police did. He was the most powerful man in the county,' he grumbled. 'I couldn't bear it when the holidays were over, because when I went back to school I had to leave her at his mercy. I asked her many times to run away, to hide in some hamlet, but she always said that it didn't matter where we went, because he'd find us. Sometimes I hated her for that, because deep down I believed she loved him... or loved his title, and that she'd allow him to maim her before abandoning him.'

'I hope you don't believe it still,' she told him while she caressed his hair. 'Nobody could love such a vile being... Not even a woman as generous as your mother.'

'What he did to her that summer, when I was fourteen... that was excessive,' he growled in a low voice. 'I was coming back from Eton. I was happy because the classes had finished and, finally, I'd see my mother after many months. When I entered her lounge, I saw her laid out on a sofa, the family doctor looking after her. She was wearing an eye-patch.'

Harmony looked at him, appalled as he continued, 'I didn't understand it, at first. I asked her what had happened and she told me she had been ill. I didn't believe her. I caught her by surprise and removed her eye-patch. Her eye was shattered and the orbit around it was swollen and bloodied.' Harmony noticed Devlin was clenching his fists and she tried to massage them to loosen them up.

'I knew then that it hadn't been long since that bastard beat her up again. So I went to the ruins, to the part where his cellar was, where I knew he'd be.

There, I confronted him as I had never done before, but he only laughed at me, telling me that I was only a pathetic child and that he was ashamed I shared his name. He even doubted I was really his son, because I hadn't inherited the supposed 'gift of the Sawyers',' he muttered, evidently disgusted. 'I screamed at him that I'd love to find out that I wasn't the son of a pathetic drunkard, an attacker of defenceless women, and I managed to provoke him, because he jumped on me, furious. We fought until we were exhausted. My mother appeared later, begging us to stop beating each other up, but then, Waldegrave picked up his bottle, smashed it up against the wall and brought it close to my face when I was at my weakest. He told my mother that he'd leave me one-eyed, like her, that perhaps that way we'd learn to respect him.'

Harmony couldn't breathe; she was shaking, wrapped up in the blanket that she was squeezing against her chest, unawares. She was listening to the story, transfixed and horrified by the baseness of that man against his own family.

'What happened next, Devlin?' She wondered if he'd be able to confess to her that his mother had intervened and pushed the old duke down the hole.

'My mother carried on crying, begging him to stop, and promised him that she'd do anything he asked if he let me be.' He kept quiet for a long while, then added, 'I would have liked to be the one who finished him off. But it didn't happen. Somebody turned up right at the moment when he was about to stab me in the face with a piece of broken glass.'

'Who?' Harmony exclaimed, her eyes about to pop out of their sockets.

'Limsey...'

Harmony gasped, surprised. She found it difficult to imagine the refined and sharp butler—that even then must have been advanced in years—taking part in a hand-to-hand fight with a man younger than him.

'He went for Waldegrave and managed to get him off me.'

Then, a terrifying idea sliced through Harmony's thoughts. 'Wait. Was he the one who...?'

Devlin looked back at her, his gaze hard and enigmatic. His green eyes shone, but not with rage or fear but with a serene acceptance. He didn't need to carry on telling the story. She had reached her own conclusion.

'It is our family secret, Harmony.'

She was petrified. Corine had not pushed Heyworth Sawyer; Limsey, the butler of Waldegrave Terrace, had done it, in a brave attempt at defending the son and the wife of his master. Bless you, Limsey.

'And it's safe with me, my love,' she said, caressing him.

'After that, my mother assigned Limsey to Waldegrave Terrace; she

314

thought it would be the best for him.'

She hurled herself into her husband's arms, eager to show him that she did not blame him for the death of such a horrible man, and even less for the action of the butler, who had courageously protected him like the good father Devlin never had. But then she remembered Gretty's angry accusation in town.

'Wait, Devlin… Gretty…' she piped up, moving away from him. 'The town's madwoman goes around telling everybody that your mother pushed the duke.'

'I know.' He held her face in his hands and left a trail of tiny kisses on her brow. 'She was the only witness. They brought her to Sudeley to clean the weeds and the undergrowth of the garden. I imagine she must have heard the noise, and when my mother peered over the void to look at the body lying in the garden, Gretty saw her… and assumed she was guilty. Don't worry… She's repeated it for many years and nobody believes her, and if somebody does, I'm sure he or she won't come to report her after all these years. As far as the law is concerned, the previous Duke of Waldegrave, a terrible drunkard who treated all the people of Winchcombe with scorn, plunged to his death without anybody's help.'

'Devlin…' She couldn't wait any longer to ask the question burning in her throat. 'Corine has always loved you; she tried to defend you, although she wasn't always successful. Why do you keep her apart from your life? Perhaps you blame her—?'

He tutted, evidently irritated.

'There were moments when I felt she was as guilty as he was for what happened to me. She could have run away with me, but she stayed here and let him carry on hurting us. When he went away travelling, she did nothing but lose herself in her balls and an endless catalogue of trifles.'

'It was her refuge, don't you understand it?'

'We could have taken advantage of Waldegrave's long absences to disappear,' he mumbled, resentful, 'but she never allowed it and I could never leave without her because—'

'Because you loved her too much to leave her at the mercy of that monster,' she said and he nodded. 'Perhaps you are right, Devlin, but nobody knows for certain what would have happened. Don't judge her so harshly. She is your mother. Perhaps Corine didn't want to deprive you of the opportunities you could only have access to as the son of a duke: your education, your—'

'I didn't care for any of that.'

She hugged his waist because she sensed then that he needed her contact. His muscles felt tense.

'Every time I look at her wearing that eye-patch...' he growled through clenched teeth, his eyes misting over.

She had never seen him as vulnerable and remained quiet with surprise as he went on, 'She seems so dignified wearing that, but I don't see her when I see it; I see that bastard who destroyed her life. She had been so stoical, without the slightest intention of leaving him... and I see myself at Eton too, doing anything but protecting her... I don't see her, Harmony. I see what that man did to us, what we allowed him to do to us.'

'Then, don't allow that wretched man that turned your lives into a tragedy to rob you of any more of the time you could spend next to your mother. Don't allow Heyworth Sawyer to keep making her suffer even after his death... because that is what he is doing. He is keeping you away from her; he makes you unhappy and he does the same to me, because I love you, Devlin.'

Devlin sat on the edge of the bed. He remained there, still and quiet. Harmony followed his movements with a pained gaze. She knew she would not manage to prick his conscience much more that night. Her husband was stubborn and had lived with that resentment and the bad memories for too long. But, at least she had managed to plant a seed in him; she had helped him unburden himself and had made him think. She hoped with all her heart that the seed would germinate. For now, it was the best she could do.

After a while he lay back down on the bed and she did the same, lying so close to him that the contact of their bodies created a pleasant touch. She kept looking at him for a long time; he had his gaze fixed on the half-open window that offered a partial view of the lowlands covered in shadows. Harmony caressed him without getting a response, and her mind filled up with fears. She decided then that she would tell him the truth about her uncle and his plan of asking her for money in exchange of keeping that 'truth' quiet. A truth that was only the macabre machination of a contemptible and greedy man.

But she couldn't do it yet. She had to prepare herself, to gather some courage, something she didn't have a lot of at the present time. She would wait until the matter of Devlin and his mother showed some evidence of improvement. Perhaps then she'd have to confront a more affable and perhaps even reconciled husband. And may God help her.

'Good night, my love,' she whispered and, half-asleep, felt Devlin's warm kiss on her brow.

For the first time in a long time, the entire family had breakfast together in the castle's country dining room, located a few inches away from the fragrant garden. The Cotswolds' climate, now cool and mild, offered them a gentle gift, hinting at the positive changes that were around the corner for the Sawyer family.

Harmony seemed pleased when she noticed that, little by little, Devlin was starting to leave to one side his resentment towards Corine. During their meals, he'd smiled at her several times, laughed at her jokes and showed an interest in her affairs, the same ones he had thought superfluous before.

The dowager duchess, overwhelmed and thankful for the gradual reconciliation between her and her son, looked for Harmony after breakfast. She had to know better than anybody else what was happening in the head of that unpredictable man. Then, her daughter-in-law told her about the little chat they had had a few nights earlier and the way he had opened up to her.

'I think the idea of being a father is softening him up.'

'That... and you, dear girl,' Corine replied, winking a Harmony. 'The influence you have over him is refreshing. I must give you thanks for the difference you have made on him, my girl. I don't recognise my own son, but luckily that is good.'

Harmony felt pleased to see the evident relief on Corine's face as she told her about the revelations Devlin had made her and the ones she had heard from Gretty in town. Corine didn't appear at all worried about the latter. She told her Gretty used to be Laurel Kirkeby's nursemaid and after the death of her family in a fire had progressively lost her mind. Laurel's mother had then decided that Gretty wasn't in a position to look after her daughter and threw her out. Limsey, who was Sudeley's butler at the time, had offered her a job as the assistant of the castle's gardener. Shortly after the death of the previous Duke of Waldegrave, Gretty stopped coming to Sudeley and took refuge in the forest, in the same charred shack where the members of her family had lost their lives. Since then, she had lived off the charity of the passersby and of the shopkeepers of Winchcombe's High Street, where she spent the whole day.

When she isn't running around with Lady Colvile, that is, Harmony thought on remembering the surly elderly woman running away down the street with the woman she used to think was a threat to her. Lunatics are likely to understand each other better than sane people are, she thought, smiling widely. That surprised her a bit. To tell the truth, she no longer held a grudge against the blonde who'd ruined her honeymoon.

'I hope you don't mind that Devlin told me about your eye,' she asked her mother-in-law, deciding to put an end to their talk about Gretty.

Corine waved her hand in a dismissive gesture.

'I'm happy he did. Nobody believes the story of the poisoning, anyway. A few days ago, Martin...' she blushed slightly, 'I mean, Dr Bradshawe, examined me and it didn't take him a second to identify the aftermath of a blow. In fact, he confessed to me that he knew the same day we met in front of the park. It was so shameful... I didn't have to explain anything to him. It seems he has a clear idea of how my life was like when my husband lived.'

'And why should you give him any explanation?'

Devlin's mother giggled naughtily and Harmony caught it as well. She had not missed the fact that between Corine and Dr Bradshawe a slight change had taken place, as if both of them had taken a step towards each other. Simply paying attention at the way they looked and smiled at each other was enough to realise that. The doctor visited Sudeley increasingly often, and Harmony was sure it wasn't only to supervise the progress of her pregnancy.

'I'm so happy for you, Corine,' she put a hand on top of hers, 'It's time somebody loves you as you deserve.'

'We'll see, dear girl,' she said, thoughtful. 'I think it's too early for that. But at my age, I'm afraid hope hasn't abandoned me yet.'

'And I'd rather it didn't!'

Corine smiled. She glanced, uncertain, to where Devlin was playing blackjack with Sir Malcolm.

'I'm worried about his reaction when he learns about it.'

'Don't let that stop you, Corine,' she sighed, 'It seems you have a long conversation with your son ahead of you.'

She turned to look at her husband, who had just lost for the third time in a row playing against his crafty grandfather. She was amused by his confused expression as he checked the hand of cards the old man had beaten him with.

She also had a conversation pending with Devlin, and each time she thought about it, she experienced an erratic heartbeat. The image of him heartbroken because he thought he had assaulted her haunted her dreams, making her feel miserable. She kept calling herself a coward; she hated herself for causing him such pain to protect her own skin. Despite that, her will was sealed with an unbreakable lock.

The previous afternoon, Devlin had asked her questions about her uncle's visit to Sudeley. Harmony had tried to avoid the subject, but he'd seemed determined to know what they had talked about and how she felt about it. It was as if suddenly he wanted to understand the nature of her relationship with her former guardian.

She had felt suffocated in the middle of that exhausting conversation. Then, the subject of the race course had come up. Devlin had openly asked her what she thought about going into partnership with her uncle to bring the project into fruition, and she had looked at him nervously and imploringly in equal measure. Do not ask me that, please, she'd kept shouting inside her head. If she said what she really thought, she'd spoil the aspirations of the vile opportunistic man... but if she gave her approval, perhaps her uncle would leave her in peace forever. In the end, her panic had decided for her. Pretending to fix an earring, she had turned her back on him, to avoid lying directly in her beloved husband's face, and said, 'I'm sure that, even if it came to nothing, you'd enjoy taking part in it.'

Damn it. She'd had no option. She wasn't ready to be sincere, to confront his perplexed expression and the shadow of a doubt that would darken his beautiful features as a consequence. And what if he does not believe me when I tell him the truth? she wondered now, terrified. She thought of her child. If Devlin wanted to, he'd take it away from her at birth.

'I was thinking about inviting your aunt and uncle next month...' Corine suggested out of the blue, dragging her violently away from her thoughts.

'No!' Her refusal escaped agonizing from her lips, before her brain had time to process it. Harmony knew then that she had exposed her true thoughts, because Corine looked at her, at first confused and then saddened, and it was as if her head had taken a heavy blow and it made her react.

'But Harmony, why—?'

'Corine, no. I beg you. Don't do it,' she pleaded. 'They aren't what you think.' An enraged voice shouted inside Harmony's mind then. What the hell was she waiting for? Hadn't she yet realised the harm her silence had caused?

If she carried on hesitating, her aunt and uncle would end up settling in her home, and by the time she had lost her fear of confessing everything to her husband, it would already be too late. Her uncle would demand more and more money, more privileges, and he'd take advantage of her total helplessness to handle his threats.

She had to speak as soon as possible. She had to confront her husband, even if that meant putting up with the heavy blow of his suspicions. Devlin loved her; he had told her that, and that love should be enough to make him believe her. Or shouldn't it?

She stood up, ready to go to Devlin and blurt out the truth without any further useless doubts. Corine called her, but she was no longer listening. Her mind was working hard trying to come up with a coherent explanation as her steps took her increasingly close to the stone table where Devlin was playing cards with Sir Malcolm.

When she was about to reach him, she saw Mrs Frank get there first. The housekeeper reached Devlin and told him something that made him frown. Harmony didn't manage to hear what it was.

Devlin stood up and walked towards the house. She kept looking at him as he walked away, and as she lost her chance to relieve herself from the confession that was now burning on her tongue. Well... she hoped to be able to retrieve that impetus later on.

'Somebody has arrived,' Corine said, glancing inside, and she felt as if somebody had pricked her side with a needle. What would she do if it was her uncle John?

She managed to calm herself down in a moment.

The old man pushed the two women to play a hand with him. Although she wasn't feeling up to it and had no idea of how to play cards, Harmony agreed, as she'd rather be doing anything else rather than having to undergo an interrogation by her mother-in-law, who kept looking at her with an increasingly suspicious expression. She'd rather not imagine the kind of thoughts that were crossing Corine's mind.

Later, Devlin reappeared. Harmony's heart somersaulted when she saw him approach hastily with a solemn expression. What had happened? Who had come? Why was Devlin looking at her that way?

'Love, come here, make yourself comfortable.' He helped her stand up from the chair and insisted that she sit on one of the comfortable settees in the shade before she had a chance to ask. Her hands began to sweat. Why was he trying to make her feel more comfortable? 'Harmony, listen to me. What I'm going to tell you is very serious.'

'Devlin, what has happened?' she asked with bated breath.

He looked at her, delaying his reply, or perhaps struggling to find the right words.

'Devlin?' Corine, who seemed as tense as Harmony was due to the intrigue her son's behaviour had built up, hurried him on. Sir Malcolm approached them, oozing curiosity and a modicum of worry. 'Talk at once, in the name of God! Who has come? What is happening?'

The duke looked at his wife.

'My love, your uncle has been murdered.'

Chapter 20

Before sharing the horrible news with his wife, Devlin had met inspector Peter Fitzgeoffrey, from Scotland Yard, in his study.

Fitzgeoffrey, a young man, sturdy and with a thick brown beard, observed everything gingerly. Devlin perceived a lively intellect in his gaze and in his meticulous voice that was finely tuned on addressing a powerful aristocrat to filter out any suggestion of a threat. He was, Devlin assumed, an astute country policeman newly promoted, determined to prove that he truly deserved his post.

When the inspector informed him of Talbot's death, Devlin looked at him flabbergasted. It had taken him totally by surprise. He thought of Harmony and how that would affect her. Although he had not managed to figure out the nature of the relationship between his wife and her previous guardian, he was sure that the death of the man who had looked after her since she was a child would break her heart.

Fitzgeoffrey told him that a couple of days earlier some vagrants had found Talbot's body floating in a channel of the Thames, near the district of Wapping, in the East End. Before being thrown into the river, the victim had been shot on the chest twice.

The widow had recognised the body and, according to the inspector, was inconsolable.

'It is public knowledge that your wife, the duchess, is related to the deceased, Your Grace,' Fitzgeoffrey said, his hands behind his back. 'That's why I've come personally to inform you of his death. You are an Honourable Member of the House of Lords, and I didn't think it in good taste to send you a telegram.'

'I am very grateful, Inspector,' Waldegrave said, still shocked by the news.

'Do you know who did it?'

'We suspect a group of crooks we've been trailing for a long time. A rabble engaged in fixing-up bets, frauds, and a long list of offences to do with horseracing. Mr Talbot was mixed-up in the group's businesses, as we were able to confirm when we checked his correspondence, which we intercepted in his Whitechapel office. He owed them money but had not been able to keep up with the payments.' He composed an expression of regret and added, 'I'm afraid that one cannot negotiate with such individuals, Your Grace. It is like making a pact with the devil. They always win.'

Devlin wasn't surprised that a man like John Talbot, whose dealings were full of cheating and deceit, ended up as he had. The man had been ambitious, even a visionary, he had to admit that, but the way he conducted his business, using all kinds of tricks and always looking for the shortest way to reach his goals, undermined that prodigious quality that most men lacked. It was a true shame.

And to think that he had been toying with the idea of providing his support to Talbot's project of building a race course. He would have done it for Harmony, of course; his intention had been to make her happy, as always. He had imagined that if her 'stepfather', or whatever Talbot had been for her, could have set up a legitimate and prosperous business, Harmony would have felt satisfied because, that way, she would have paid him back by far for everything he had done for her. For that reason he had asked her opinion on the matter and, in the end, he had received her shy but definite agreement.

Devlin had to admit that he had avoided discussing that thorny subject with her; he feared making her feel uncomfortable dragging up the bad dealings her uncle had been involved in, which were described in detail in the report he had commissioned. He didn't want to make her feel ashamed for Talbot's faults nor blame her unwittingly for things she had no responsibility for, like that time at Hampstead when, resentful of that swindler, he had ended up giving her a terribly hard time in front of her friends.

'But we will find the guilty party,' continued the inspector sternly, caressing his beard. 'For now, we must carry on investigating.'

'I'll be the one to inform my wife of her uncle's death, Inspector.'

Fitzgeoffrey nodded. Then he completed the other part of his job, asking questions and gathering information about Talbot and his activities. As an old client of the horse dealer, Devlin shared what he knew about him, without mentioning what he had uncovered through his personal investigation. Talbot was his relative, and now that he was dead there was no point in bringing to light his faults, which would only end up tainting his wife's reputation.

'I am sorry for having to be the bearer of such sad tidings, Your Grace.'

'Don't worry, Inspector. Thanks for going to the trouble of coming all the way here.'

The man nodded and turned to leave the study, but suddenly something made him stop.

'Ah, how forgetful of me!' He started rummaging around his sand-coloured fur-lined jacket. 'I almost forgot, Your Grace. As I told you, unfortunately we had to search Mr Talbot's papers as soon as we got the case, as you can imagine, for investigation purposes. Luckily, in Scotland Yard we have the legal power to intercept private correspondence.' He retrieved an envelope and handed it to him, grimacing. Confused, Devlin's eyes kept travelling from the policeman to the mysterious envelope and back. 'I hope you will excuse us.'

In her bedroom, Harmony was pacing up and down, still unable to assimilate the fact that her uncle John had left this Earth in such a violent manner. She hadn't managed to sob, to shed a tear or to say a word out loud; she was too shocked to react.

Devlin had told her what had happened after his meeting with the policeman. Now she realised that her uncle had not lied, after all; indeed, a band of crooks trying to collect on the money for illegal betting had been after him. She suspected they must have been his murderers. And he must have been aware of how dangerous they were, otherwise he would not have come to ask for the money so desperately, wouldn't have threatened her with such eagerness.

And now he is dead, she thought, dropping onto the upholstered chair.

It hurt her, of course. The death of the only blood relative she had left caused her a deep sorrow. Nobody deserved to die as he had, in such a cruel and dishonourable manner. She lamented that he'd always found it so difficult to do things appropriately... that he chose the path of corruption.

Then, she thought of her Aunt Minnie and her heart sunk even more. These two had been inseparable; they had shared something beyond her capacity for understanding. She imagined the poor woman must be crushed.

Was it guilt she was experiencing?

She refused to contemplate that feeling. After all, she had given her uncle all her money, despite not fully believing his explanations. She had accepted his terms. There was nothing else she could have done to save him from the reprisals of the criminals he had partnered with to rob the bookmakers.

His terms...

A Machiavellian thought penetrated the barriers of her conscience. Harmony stood up slowly and looked beyond the window of her chamber, where three workmen were hurrying to install the lift, the contraption her husband had ordered to be put in place to look after her and her baby. Now that Uncle John was dead, Devlin would never learn of his threats. She had been spared from the torture of having to explain what his uncle had devised to extort money from him, the infamy that had shaken her world and could have made him hate her before giving her a chance to defend herself.

He didn't need to learn about it.

She quickly dismissed that wicked thought. Before she learned of her uncle's death, Harmony had already decided to tell her husband the truth; it was the proper thing to do. She didn't want to keep secrets from him, and she didn't want him to carry on believing he had attacked her at Felton House, when it had been the despicable Andrew Curson who had done so.

However, she pondered that she could be sincere regarding Curson and could still hide Uncle John's threats, his horrible lies, and the money she had given him to keep him quiet. Devlin could learn of her failed engagement and nothing else.

No... she couldn't do that! If he found out Uncle John's plans from another source... he would never forgive her. And what if Aunt Minnie carried on threatening her?

She shook her head to get rid of such horrendous eventualities. She had no choice; she didn't want to lie to Devlin, her beloved husband. She hated the thought of wounding him; she hated looking him in the face and remembering that she had not been totally truthful.

It was decided. She would tell him everything... right now.

Feeling determined, she left the room where Corine had left her, a nervous wreck, in order to go to organise a whirlwind trip to London for everyone to attend the funeral. Harmony checked the corridors, her heart beating fast, her only goal to find Devlin and confess once and for all the truth burning inside her chest, which would not let her breathe easy until it had exploded out of her mouth.

She made her way downstairs carefully, holding onto the bannister with both hands, as he would have wanted, until she reached the main floor, hardly able to contain her impatience. She looked for him in his study, in the library, in the garden, in the stables... She asked the servants she met on the way, but nobody knew where to find him. Miss Frank told her that she had seen him coming out of the study, but she didn't know where he'd gone. Harmony knew for certain he had not left Sudeley, because Louis, the coachman, and the head groom who sometimes took on the role in his absence were in the stables.

A bad feeling had taken hold in her abdomen. She worried as she returned to the garden, on her way back from the stables, that something wasn't right.

Then, when she was about to lose hope, she spotted Sir Malcolm, who was walking back from the ruins at a slow pace with the help of a walking stick.

In the distance, Harmony exchanged a questioning look with him. The shine in his blue eyes that seemed nervous and sad threw her out. She didn't know what to make of it and that made her anxious. She approached him gingerly, instinctively cautious.

'Sir Malcolm...?'

The old man held onto the handle of his walking stick with both hands and pursed his lips, looking serious.

'You must talk to him.'

She understood it straight away; Devlin knew, somehow. Her head crowded with frenzied thoughts like fluttering birds that prevented her from thinking clearly. Her body shook in a sudden rush of panic; her hands, trembling and ice-cold, held tight onto her skirt. Her breathing became heavy and difficult due to the fast beating of her heart.

For the love of God. He knew it. She raised her hand to her brow.

How had he learned about it?

She looked at Sir Malcolm, ashamed, but without feeling up to making any excuses. She was only interested in what Devlin thought. He and he alone could forgive her... or condemn her.

She had to ask the old man where she could find her husband. Luckily, she didn't have to say anything. He pointed the end of his walking stick in the direction of the path to the ruins. Harmony wetted her lips and made an effort to take the first step to get there.

Even if she died of fear, even if her happiness—her whole life—was hanging from a thread right then, she had to find courage where there wasn't any and fight in the name of the truth. In the name of love...

She stepped onto the gravel path that crossed the stone arch opening onto the legendary ruins of Sudeley. The walls, built of honey-coloured stone and destroyed in the past by enemy attacks, were now covered with a thick layer of ivy and a multitude of cascading bougainvillaeas in bloom. The aroma of jasmine and the climbing roses assaulted her nostrils; she breathed the heady fragrances, trying to summon some of the courage she needed but, to her regret, she didn't manage it. Unsteadily, she stepped into the exuberant and colourful garden. The pheasants wandered freely around on the grass that had grown everywhere. The birds set each other off with their warbling, creating a scale of out of tune songs.

Harmony looked everywhere when she reached the most dilapidated part of the ruins. There, the hedges grew wild, and the brushwood grew side by side with the bellflowers and the geraniums. The elm trees, tall and lush, created a shadowed area that sometimes had offered her a refuge to read, but right now she could only see darkness, the setting of a horror story.

Then, she saw her husband, his back to her, standing still in front of the godforsaken pond. His rigid and immobile posture competed with the plaster of Paris statutes; a stillness that made her tremble. Harmony noticed that he was not wearing a jacket or a waistcoat, and his dark hair, not held back in a ponytail, flowed in the light wind of the Cotswolds. He had rolled up the sleeves of his untidy shirt. He was clutching a crumpled sheet of paper in his right hand. A letter, she imagined, which had perhaps been read and manipulated a thousand and one times in an attempt at understanding its inextricable content.

Harmony swallowed hard when she saw the scene. She advanced towards him, as if she was walking the tightrope, with shaky legs and an unbridled heart.

'Devlin…'

Her voice sounded croakier than she had expected, but that did not distract her. She carried on walking until she reached him. His beautiful profile was outlined by the light of dusk and the shadow the elms projected over that corner of the pond. The expression on the face of her husband, who refused to look at her, was stiff and unfathomable; severe enough to break her heart, because that confirmed he knew the dirty lie… and believed it.

'Devlin…'

He didn't reply nor abandon his reverie.

'Devlin, for the love of God,' she said with a sob after a short pause. She laid a shaky hand on his shoulder, expecting him to slap her off, but surprisingly, he didn't. He seemed stuck in his silence. 'Talk to me.'

Desperate, she shook his arm, but he didn't even blink.

She had to make him react, damn it! He could shout; insult her; demand explanations, anything but punish her with that condemnatory silence that gnawed at her soul. She ended up slapping him and punching him compulsively to force him to look at her.

'Talk to me!' she moaned, lost in her lonely fight. 'Say something, Devlin! What are you waiting for? Tell me that you hate me if that is what you feel right now!'

'What the hell do you want from me, Harmony George?' He yelled at the top of his lungs, causing all the birds to fly off scared, and the ducks to get into the water at full speed. He had ended her assault with his outbreak and right now was looking at her, troubled and irate. His green eyes were two powerful flames. 'Haven't you had enough? You have a title, money, all that's mine... What do I have left for you to plunder?'

She couldn't believe what she was hearing. She covered her mouth with a hand to suffocate a painful moan.

'Have you said plunder? Is that what you think I've done?'

'You and your... family,' he pronounced the last word with repulsion, 'I imagine there was nobody more stupid to trick, or I was so drunk that I became an easy prey.'

She kept shaking her head, the tears burning in her eyes as he went on, 'Tell me, did you choose me or did they? Did you meet every evening for dinner to plan how to make the stupid duke fall for your tricks so you could get all his money?'

'You are wrong.'

'I was... about you! I thought you were much better than this, but how wrong I was.'

'No, Devlin. Listen! I—'

'You wanted to ensure your future. Well done!' he insisted bitterly. 'You weren't the first débutante and probably won't be the last to use these kinds of ruses to catch a rich husband. Your resolution is almost admirable,' he growled sarcastically. 'I have always praised the skills of some poor devils to rise above the misery in which they were born, by any means necessary, but I won't be so complimentary towards you.' He lifted the piece of paper he was clutching so wildly. 'It seems that you don't know loyalty, not even towards your own accomplices.'

'What is that?'

'It's the letter your uncle, or your pimp... or whatever Talbot was to you, left behind. The police found it among his things. It seems he was thinking about betraying you, because he wrote it shortly before he was killed. It's a full-blown confession; I'm not sure if it was born from his remorse, or his wish to get even with you for not having complied with the agreement to share the booty. The latter would make you even worse than him...'

Harmony could hardly look at the piece of paper. Her eyes were flooded with tears. Everything around her had become blurry, and the whole world, it seemed, had lost its colour.

She didn't even have the strength to curse her uncle, who even dead had the power of destroying her. And the worst part of it all was that Devlin had believed him.

Disgusted, he explained to her the content of the letter, which said everything Uncle John had intended to say and much more. She felt sick but forced herself to control her nausea. It was her word against a dead man's, a very vicious and a lying individual.

'Did they force you, Harmony? Have you gone along with all this filth... or has it been your idea from the beginning and you merely got others to follow?'

She pierced him with her eyes. 'What does it matter, Waldegrave? It seems that my uncle's explanation has satisfied you. And you've become my judge and my executioner. It couldn't have been any other way, could it? You would never have turned your head to look at me unless I had used a trick of that kind. Now everything makes sense to you! It isn't love, not even attraction! It is a deception to make you fall into the trap. Well! I'll let you believe that because you seem desperate to do it.'

'Is that all you're going to tell me?' he shouted, his rage increasing further.

Harmony, which had started her retreat, stopped. It took her a few moments to decide but, despite her pain, she knew she had to release him from the horrible responsibility that she so cowardly had burdened him with. In the name of her love for him, she had to do it.

She dried her tears with the back of her hand and made an effort to look at him. 'No,' she murmured. 'No, Devlin, I owe you something still. Forgive me for not having told you before. I was a coward, and you didn't deserve it. You never tried to rape me; you never hit me.' He looked at her astonished then, and his fierce resistance shook slightly. 'You are unable to hurt anybody, even when you're drunk,' she said sobbing. 'I'm sorry for having made you believe that. I'm truly sorry.'

She tried to leave, but this time he held her arm and forced her to look at him.

'No, you won't leave! Not now!' he growled. 'Who did it? Was it you? Did you hurt yourself to confuse me and make your performance more realistic?'

Good God! Did he believe she was so abject? She could hardly believe he had said such a thing.

Harmony thought she was about to collapse, but her weakness obstinately turned into strength and rebellion. Perhaps it was her indomitable spirit that refused to be beaten down, that defended itself tooth and nail against such injustice.

'I'm not like your dear friend, Lady Colvile, Your Grace! Andrew Curson did this to me!' she blurted out bitterly. 'My fiancé.'

Devlin's jaw almost hit the ground. His shock, all his ire and his doubts, passed fleetingly over his face in the blink of an eye. His breathing visibly accelerated, his fists clenched in a fighting stance, his teeth cracked as he tightened his jaw, until his whole appearance was the embodiment of extreme rage.

'What...? What does that mean? Andrew Curson, the jockey? He hit you?'

Harmony nodded.

Devlin seethed with fury, his heart racing. That bastard had dared lay a finger on his wife. He started pacing by the edge of the lake, frightening Sudeley's fauna. He muttered curses, rubbed the nape of his neck and pulled at his hair repeatedly. He could almost feel that familiar red and engorged vein split his tense brow right down the middle.

'I don't understand. Explain it to me! Why do you say that he was your fiancé?'

'Because he was! My uncle chose him for me against my will. Five minutes before I bumped into you in the garden, he had tried to take liberties with me. He thought he had the right because my uncle had given him my hand... and because I slapped him, he got his own back on me,' she lowered her head, 'I'm sorry you took the blame for that. And I'm sorry for not having told you the truth when you finally asked me.'

Harmony and Curson? He had difficulty imagining her with another man. He felt his blood boil anew. Cursed be John Talbot if he had arranged a marriage of his niece to that son of a bitch and women beater. He wanted desperately to hit something... or somebody.

The rage, the sensation of utmost vulnerability he had felt from the moment he had read that damned letter had clouded his mind. Only his grandfather had managed to calm him slightly with his encouraging words. But now, his rage had another target. They had touched what was holiest to him... and he wanted revenge.

It wasn't me, after all... it was that... bastard... I'm going to finish him off! he thought to himself. Then he stared at her, looking for the flimsiest sign that she was lying while he grabbed her forearms, desperate. 'Tell me more,' he ordered her, hissing furiously.

Harmony bent her head, shook it with regret, then began to speak, 'I went to my aunt and uncle to tell them what Curson had done to me, and they didn't do anything. As if that weren't enough, Uncle John had earlier told me that I was broke, and that I had no other option but to marry, whether I like it or not. The inheritance my father had left me, and on which I had been planning to leave my uncle's damned house on my twenty first birthday had been used to pay his old debts.'

Devlin's mind kept boiling. So, an inheritance had indeed existed. And that petty thief had taken it. Or perhaps that was another lie...

Confused, he shook his head. Damn it... What should he believe? What if she was lying to him? What if this was only a new ruse she'd come up with, in the spur of the moment?

Furious and desperate, he looked at her again. He took her tearful face in his hands. He did not glimpse any evidence of falsehood in those dark and tired eyes, which were bravely defending themselves. But God only knew what they were hiding...

'Then you improvised,' he suggested. 'You thought I'd be a less disgusting husband than Curson. That's why you came to me...'

'I never wanted a husband!' she shouted, breaking the physical contact. 'That was why I was climbing that fence. I wanted to run away from the Talbots and from Curson, but you stopped me. How I wish you could remember something of what happened...' she furiously shook her head, 'But it doesn't matter! I have already begged for your forgiveness for not telling you the truth.'

'Yes, but you haven't told me why you didn't.'

Harmony straightened up. He was right; she would not deny that either. 'The day after you left for Godalming, Uncle John came to Sudeley. He told me that some men were after him because he owed them money and asked me for my help. Of course, I refused, because I knew if I agreed, he'd never stop. And I didn't believe him; I grew up with him and I know he is capable of making up the most blatant lies in order to get his own way.' She dried up a new stream of tears that were flowing down her cheeks and went on, 'He threatened to tell you that our meeting at the Christmas ball had been all a plan to 'catch you', if I didn't cooperate with him. You know it's a story anybody would believe,' she spat out bitterly.

Devlin felt the urge to contradict her but stopped himself, allowing her to continue, 'I dreaded you would believe him, as you have. Then, I gave him a cheque for the whole amount of my allowance money, hoping it would be enough for him to leave me alone for a while. Although I had the chance, I never got the nerve to confess it to you. I wasn't prepared to risk losing you, and you kicking me from your side. And I wasn't about to let you take our child away from me!'

'That's absurd! I wouldn't...'

He grabbed at his hair again and, overcome by a feeling of impotence, punched the air.

Was Harmony right? Would he have believed that story if he had heard it under different circumstances? He preferred to leave that thought to one side and also the fact that he had spent too many years mistrusting everything and everybody.

'Are you telling me the truth?'

'The whole truth!' she said firmly.

'I don't know what to think, damn it! I've been thinking about this letter over and over—'

'And even so, you've settled on the first thought that came into your head! You haven't even given me the benefit of the doubt. You have accepted it all without question.'

'Look at me,' he growled. She obeyed, despite her evident outrage.

Devlin looked at her for a long time. His brain was torn between doubt and the agonising hope of certainty. Neither seemed happy to set him free.

He loved her. He couldn't deny it... and she had proved that she loved him too.

Hadn't she been a good wife during all those months? An extremely sweet, compliant, and loving wife? Hadn't she managed to bring him closer to his mother and to touch his most sensitive chord without hurting him? Hadn't she scared off his most feared monsters? Hadn't she given him the extraordinary blessing of a child?

All that without asking for anything in return, he admitted with a sigh. He could not recall that she had ever demanded a particularly expensive dress, a piece of jewellery... not even a journey, something he was sure was more valuable to her than all the rest.

He approached gingerly, like a curious child would approach a tiny hare. He held her face, caressed her neck, her cheeks, the tufts of hair on her nape, then he brushed her brow with his nose. He'd realised that he desperately wanted to believe her, to tame his pride and allow her to do with him as she wished. He wanted to put an end to his hesitation and cover her with kisses, make love to her under the elm tree... and then go to find Andrew Curson to break his neck.

Anything but losing her!

For the love of God, he'd settle for anything if he did not have to let her go.

Harmony's heart leapt with relief. She accepted Devlin's caresses as she looked intently at him, without totally surrendering herself but without resisting herself either, because she needed desperately to feed on his touch. Harmony wanted him to believe her. She quietly prayed to God that he would.

'Against my nature, Harmony George,' he said first, his voice cracking, looking quite different to the cold and boastful man he had been earlier on. He went on, 'I surrender my pride, what I've most closely protected since I can remember… And I acknowledge my defeat. I can accept that you caught me by using a trick. I can live with that, because we have been happy nonetheless.' Their foreheads touched, but Harmony shut her eyes really tight, because she knew she could not accept what he was going to ask her. She could tell what he was about to say.

'I… will forget everything, I give you my word. Tell me the truth, in no uncertain terms and without softening the blow. Tell me that you thought about becoming my duchess and seeking my protection, because you could not tolerate that Talbot was forcing you to marry Curson, that abusive son of…' His voice faded away.

She couldn't have expected a man to make a bigger sacrifice, least of all one so powerful and arrogant, who was used to doing as he wished since he was fifteen. What Devlin was doing was crushing his pride. He had gone down on his knees in front of her, like the most devoted of lovers.

'Don't ask me that, Devlin,' she mumbled. 'I don't know if this is too much for you, but you'll have to believe me.'

He stood again, then stepped back a bit to better look at her.

'I didn't need anybody's protection,' she carried on. 'I didn't even care about not having any money; I was going to leave, regardless. I climbed on that fence ready to accept anything but a marriage, irrespective of who the groom might have been.'

Devlin looked at her, his mind churning with questions. Then, he remembered something from that night at the Fentons' garden. Or at least he thought he did.

He saw himself below her heavy skirts. She was perched on a ladder or something similar, with her body dangling at a reckless height. He was asking her to come down, warning her of the risks and got frustrated when she would not obey his orders.

Yes, that was what he had experienced in the library, when Harmony climbed up the ladder, insistent on reaching the most inaccessible books. That sensation of dread and fear, curiously familiar, had overtaken him then.

'Déjà senti.'

Harmony looked at him, frowning.

'What?'

He didn't reply. He dropped the letter which, caught in the wind, ended up in the pond, and kissed passionately the small and warm mouth of his wife. He pushed in, bit her lips, and drank from it to quench his extreme need.

A minute later, she pushed him away, with determination. 'Devlin, don't do this,' she muttered. 'I need you to believe me.'

'My love, I do believe you.'

'No! It's not true! You don't believe me and intend to leave it all as it is to avoid conflicts. When we argue again, in the future, you'll throw it in my face the first chance you have, and we'll both be hurt.' He looked at her, impotent, and she went on, 'I'll prove to you that I'm telling you the truth. I didn't conspire with the Talbots and even less so with Miss Andersen to 'catch you', and I didn't think either that marrying you would save me from Curson. I don't know how, but I'll prove my innocence to you.'

'Harmony...' he called after her as she left.

'Please, Devlin. Grant me this,' she moaned. 'Grant me this.'

Two days later, Devlin and his mother visited the cemetery of Nunhead in London to pay their respects to John Elliot Royce Talbot. Harmony had remained at Waldegrave Terrace, under the care of her loyal maids Mary and Prudence, who spared no cuddles and caresses for her. Harmony was saddened by having to remain in the house while the rest went to the funeral, but her pregnancy—as Corine had made her realise—did not fit in with the black crêpe or with the desolate setting of a cemetery.

The ceremony was conducted by an octogenarian priest, who was tedious and simple. Minnie Talbot cried all the time underneath a long black veil. The number of attendees didn't reach a dozen, between friends and acquaintances, people in the business of race horses and the inconvenient creditors of the deceased. Minnie Talbot's sisters took it upon themselves to get rid of the impertinent creditors with loud curses.

At the end, Devlin and Corine approached the widow to offer her their condolences, and told her they were at her disposal to help with any formalities. The woman thanked them with a croaky voice and then burst out crying again.

It was public knowledge that the few possessions of the Talbot family would be seized to settle the financial agreements that John Talbot had entered into before his death. After exchanging a few words with the family accountant, Devlin discovered that the money he had given the Talbots after his engagement to Harmony had been squandered in a long list of trifles and whims. He had difficulty comprehending how a man could spend a small fortune in such a short time, but that had been John Talbot. He thought that perhaps the man had expected the money to keep raining from the sky once his niece had married him.

At some point during the funeral, Devlin returned to his thoughts about his wife and the conversation they'd had a few days earlier. Since then, he had noticed she kept her distance, but at least she wasn't angry at him. He guessed she was still determined to prove her innocence, although he had asked her to forget the matter.

When he had read Talbot's letter, Devlin had felt mad with anger and disappointment; he had taken it as a given that she had tricked him, and now he felt ashamed. Harmony had bravely defended herself, had opened his eyes; she had told him things he had never wanted to hear. And everything had fallen into place. He believed her, and that was it.

'That woman needs help,' Corine, who stood beside him, said suddenly, interrupting his musings.

Devlin looked sideways at Minnie Talbot, whose sisters were trying to convince her to move away from her husband's grave. 'I know,' he mumbled, 'but perhaps she doesn't deserve it, at least not from us.'

Corine let out a sigh. 'I know that family behaved awfully towards Harmony, but... Good God, if nobody helps her, the poor woman will end up in the streets,' she frowned and added, 'Perhaps your friend, Lady Lovelance, could house her in her institution.'

'All right,' he sighed and added, 'I'll ask Harmony.'

'She won't refuse to do it, I know her.'

He looked at her with a smile full of tenderness and admiration. 'You're a saint, Mother.'

She dismissed his comment with a wave of her hand and he added, 'I never got to see your suffering; I never appreciated the enormity of your sacrifice.'

Corine froze when she heard these words, her mind going numb for a few moments. She was surprised by that sudden confession. She stopped and looked at him with her good eye open wide and her heart galloping in her chest, full to the brim with love.

'My dear son, that's what sacrifices are for.'

'Forgive me, Mother. I—'

'I don't have anything to forgive you for, Devlin,' she said with a sweet smile, putting an end to the subject.

His heart soaring with love and gratitude, Devlin took his mother's hand and kissed her knuckles over her black gloves, then guided her out of the place. The ceremony had finished, and the attendees were dispersing.

Then, he looked into the distance and stopped short when a fleeting movement behind a mouldy headstone caught his eye. What he saw make him feel pleased and enraged at once; he hadn't expected that meeting but now understood that the journey to London would be more fruitful than he had anticipated. Finally, he would enjoy getting satisfaction from meeting somebody whom he'd recently started to detest fiercely.

He asked Corine to wait for him inside the carriage and quickly walked towards the place where he'd glimpsed the suspicious movement earlier. He strode through the unattended grassy ground, towards a row of weathered plaster of Paris crosses. Further away, he saw the greenish and tarnished gravestone that had attracted his attention earlier. He kept reminding himself that he had to maintain his composure, but given the rage he was feeling—the same that had been tormenting him for days—he couldn't promise himself anything.

Behind the cracked stone he discovered a trembling pigmy, red-haired and with a cloudy gaze in his eyes. He was squatting next to a tomb, and not with the intention of paying his respects to the deceased, but to hide from something… or more accurately, somebody.

Devlin eyed him with scorn and disgust, and the vile man cringed visibly when he saw Devlin's shadow fall over him. Devlin looked down at him like a giant would look at a repugnant garden worm. Andrew Curson swallowed hard and looked back at him fearfully with his murine little eyes.

Curson felt himself tremble to the core with fear. He tried to stand up and pretend that he had not recognised him. He had come to attend John Talbot's funeral with the only intention of reminding the widow that he was still owed the profits for the fixed races.

'Good morning, Mr Curson,' Devlin greeted him with a kindness that did not reach his eyes, 'I haven't seen you at Mr Talbot's funeral. Are you not going to offer your condolences to the widow?'

'Yes, yes, Your Grace…' mumbled Curson in reply. 'Mm… Good morning. I was just on my way to say hello to Mrs Talbot and to offer her my services. It's… it's a shame what happened to poor John, don't you think?'

'A real shame,' Devlin stepped towards the jockey, who instinctively stepped back as if he was expecting an attack. 'I understand you held him in great esteem. Am I wrong?'

'Well… I don't think so, Your Grace,' he said as he adjusted his black fur-lined jacket nervously. 'We had some business deals. He was a good man… a good friend, I guess.'

'As close a friend as to offer you the hand of his niece in marriage?'

Curson, who had not seen that one coming, paled. 'Yes... well... no,' he muttered and he started sweating like a pig. 'Your Grace... You see... that's all in the past. I've heard that Harmony married you.'

A wave of rage engulfed him on hearing the name of his wife coming out of the lips of that despicable individual. Devlin buried his right fist inside of his overcoat to avoid being overcome by the impulse of smashing it against the nose of that miserable man.

'What did you say, Curson? Are you perhaps talking about the duchess?' he growled.

'Of course! I apologise, Your Grace!' he cringed. 'I mean the duchess. A truly exemplary young woman. Magnificent, if I might say so.'

Fed up with the useless exchange, Devlin decided to get straight to the point. The mere presence of somebody who had hurt his beloved Harmony turned his stomach. He couldn't guarantee his self-control if he had to spend another minute next to him.

'If you have such a high opinion of her, why did you dare assault her during the Christmas ball, you wretched worm?' he growled, clenching his jaw.

The face of the jockey, who ended up trapped against a stone, ran through the gamut of all possible colours. Obviously fearful, he was desperately scanning both exits of the cemetery, perhaps in an attempt to catch sight of somebody, in case he needed to ask for help.

'Your Grace, don't...' he whimpered pathetically. 'I don't know exactly what she told you but... Look, I'm very sorry. It was a misunderstanding. Is she all right? I didn't want to hurt her. I thought... I thought...'

'Did you think you could beat up a woman and get off scotch-free?'

'No, My Lord, please... forgive me. She was out of control. I'm very sorry! I hope I didn't hurt her. Oh, damn... I beg for your forgiveness.'

'You, damned coward...'

Furious, Devlin raised his fist, but he left it hanging there as he listened to the voice coming from his heart. It wasn't worth it; he would not manage to erase Harmony's old pain, or his mother's, by punishing that man. He eased off from his threatening posture, but looked defiant at the poor excuse for a man he had before him begging and crouching like the worm he truly was.

'The only reason why I won't break all your bones is because you are at a clear physical disadvantage, but be aware that I'll keep my eye on you, you pathetic piece of dirt. If I hear that you've laid a finger on another woman, I'll ruin you. Do you understand me? I'll send you to prison and when you come out, if you do, you won't find work again, not even to sweep up the muck from a stable's floor.'

'I understand, I understand, Your Grace,' panted Andrew Curson as he pressed his back against the stone, turned into a true weakling.

Devlin felt better after doing that, after putting in his place that woman beater having frightened him enough to seriously contemplate not doing it again. He was in earnest when he had told him he'd keep watch over him. Perhaps his fright would save another woman from being assaulted in the future.

Shortly later, when he entered the carriage and the horses got moving, Corine told him, indignantly, 'Son, for the love of God, we've come to a funeral, won't you erase that smile from your face?'

'No!' he said smiling even more widely.

Later on, he returned to the House of Lords where he was approached and congratulated by the other members for the recent and well publicised success of the installation of the hydro-electrical power station at Godalming. He was surprised on finding so many sympathisers when, not long ago, only few had supported his ideas. At some point they had been judged to be extravagant and daring.

He thanked them for the professional compliments and accepted, in a relaxed manner, the sudden and doubtful solidarity of his fiercest critics. He was in a good mood, despite just having attended a funeral, and he intended to keep feeling the same.

With an unusual hug, he greeted Lord Felton, who acknowledged his new mood with a mixture of surprise and incredulity. Devlin invited him and Clarissa to Waldegrave Terrace to dine with Harmony. Harvey accepted, delighted, and shared his good news: his beloved viscountess was expecting a child. Waldegrave also told him about Harmony's pregnancy and both fathers-to-be, overjoyed, congratulated each other.

Returning home, when he was about to reach his street on foot, a shout behind him made him turn around. Devlin saw Daniel Eastbury running towards him, his face reddened with the exertion.

'Goodness, you walk fast, Your Grace!' panted the rotund viscount when he finally reached him. 'You haven't given me any respite!'

'Eastbury, you need to exercise more,' he replied with a relaxed smile.

'You can say that again.' Eastbury dried the thin layer of sweat from his brow with his sleeve. 'My Lord, I didn't want you to leave without hearing the good news. My administrator has been making enquiries, talking to all of Mr George's friends and acquaintances and to reputed bankers.'

Then, Devlin remembered the favour he had asked of the viscount so long ago that he had forgotten about it. He looked at him, serious and anxious.

'And...?'

Eastbury smiled. 'My Lord, we have succeeded!'

Chapter 21

Harmony hoped that Miss Andersen could confirm her version of the story, but she seemed to be enjoying her holidays in France so much that it was unlikely she would remember to keep up with her correspondence. Even so, Harmony thought she would write to ask her for help. She had no idea who else she could appeal to.

She picked up paper and quill, wondering what she would write, but she forgot what she intended to do when the door connecting the two bedrooms opened. Her husband's gaze, warm and loving, melted her heart. She offered him a shy half-smile, the only one she had manage to bring to her face after their quarrel at the ruins, which she had miraculously managed to recover from, but not totally.

'How was the funeral?'

Devlin walked around the cream-coloured desk where she sat and, bending over, kissed her neck.

'The widow was in pieces. They say she'll lose the house, the stable, and the rest of her belongings. Talbot owed too much money. It seems that he had never honoured an agreement with anybody in his whole life, because that's the only possible explanation for the fact that he owes money to half the people in London.'

'That was what I feared,' Harmony said after pondering for a few moments. She wasn't tough enough to abandon her aunt Minnie... She was surprised to realize that, but it was true; she did not want to see her suffer. 'Devlin... Would it be too much to ask if—?'

'Do whatever you think you have to, my love,' he pre-empted her. 'My mother will be on your side; she has already hinted at it. I don't feel quite as generous after learning that those people treated you so meanly, but we'll do whatever you decide.'

'Thank you,' she smiled shyly at him and he replied in kind.

Devlin felt his heart twinge with dismay. He was hurt by the obvious distance she chose to keep from him, but he decided to respect it. Downcast, he leaned against the wall, crossing his arms.

'I bumped into Curson at the cemetery,' he piped up. She looked up at him teary-eyed and he went on, 'He tried to avoid me, like the coward he is. I approached him 'to say hello', and it wasn't hard to make him confess that he had assaulted you.'

'What did you do? Did you—?'

'No, no,' he said, his teeth clenched, when the memory of that despicable jockey crawling on the grass in front of him popped into his mind. 'I threatened him with sending him to prison if I heard about an assault on any other woman, although I might have been too soft on him. Dishonourable individuals such as him should be in prison.'

'Of course you weren't soft. Curson would have collapsed after your first punch, and you'd have been the one to end up in prison. I think you did the right thing. He started shouting when I slapped him that night, so you can imagine the kind of fuss he would have raised if you had punched him.'

He looked at her mockingly. 'Yes, My Lady, I know that you can neutralise a man if you want to.' He touched his forehead faking a pained expression jokingly. 'You don't need to boast about it.'

Harmony sulked, but then a naughty smile flashed on her face.

'Will you hold it against me for our entire lives?'

'Our entire lives...' he repeated, moving closer until he was squatting in front of her, 'I love that sentence, as long as it refers to you and me. Harmony, you have no idea how relieved I am, knowing that I wasn't the one who caused you that bruise, not even when I was out of control.'

'Me too, because if you had, I would have pulled your eyes out and fed them to you,' she said with a smirk.

'I know, my love. Now I know.'

He laid a kiss on her lips, the first one in several days, and it was as if the thin layers of ice slowly began to melt. He tasted her mouth where the fruity taste of tea hovered still. But he wouldn't carry on until he'd said everything he'd come to say.

'There's something else, Harmony.'

She moved back a bit and examined his serious expression.

'Oh, God, no. Now what?' she muttered, looking scared as she stood up. 'Don't tell me that despicable Curson accuses me of something else! Devlin, you cannot—'

'No, no, it's nothing to do with him. Calm down.'

'What's it about then?' She looked at him tensely, her hands clutching her hips that were now slightly more rounded due to the pregnancy.

'It's about Talbot and your inheritance.'

Harmony frowned and looked at him as if he was talking in a foreign language. Her inheritance had vanished in her uncle's hands. There was no point.

Then, he told her of the enquiries he had pursued with the help of Daniel Eastbury, the new master at Portington Park.

'Devlin, I'm very grateful, but I already told you that my uncle took all of the money my father had left me. He used it to pay his debts. It wasn't much, anyway.'

His brow etched deeply. 'My love, haven't you learned anything? Your uncle was incapable of paying a single debt. He owed money to half the city, and I have no idea how he managed to stay out of prison all these years.'

Devlin sighed and continued, 'With his glib tongue, his empty promises... I assure you that he had a big variety of abilities...'

As she listened, Harmony began to wonder. If her uncle had not paid his debts, then what had he done with her money? 'What exactly are you trying to tell me, Devlin?'

Devlin grabbed her hand and led her hastily to sit next to him in the purple chaise-longue. She hated it when he did that, as if he expected her to faint.

Devlin heaved a long sigh, then said, 'After much searching and talking to lots of people, Mr Coleman, Lord Eastbury's administrator, managed to find some of your father's papers, among them a copy of his will, where he left you a considerable amount of money, but there was no trace of it. He looked for the money for many days, without any result, until he asked for the help of a very influential banker, and he helped him find it. It seems that it has been sitting in a very well-hidden account. The bank staff confirmed to Coleman and the banker that the money had been there for quite a few years, untouched, because its owner had not appeared to claim it.'

Harmony was paralysed. Her temples were throbbing. 'My money...?' she murmured, stunned, and Devlin nodded. 'But... no. It must be a mistake. My uncle told me he had taken the money, that because he was my legal guardian he had the right to access it in an emergency. I hoped that emergency would never happen but... then, at Felton House, he told me about his debts. And—'

'He lied to you, Harmony. The money is still there. You are the only one authorised to access your inheritance. Not even Talbot had the right to touch a single penny. Your father made sure to include an explicit inheritance clause: you will be able to access your money once you come of age… or once you get married. Whatever happens first.'

'I…I had no idea.'

'Of course you had no idea. It wasn't in Talbot's interest that you be forewarned. It was all a ruse devised by that idiot.'

'He lied to me all these years.' Harmony stood up, as if in a trance. That miserable man! He kept her in total ignorance, perhaps while he tried to find a way to get his dirty hands on her money. Why was she surprised by the extremes that swine had gone to? 'And I believed him, like a silly—'

'Now I understand why he forced you to marry Curson. Once married, the money of your inheritance would come under your husband's control, according to the law.'

Harmony looked at him and gasped. 'But of course!' She moaned, indignant. 'Another one of his dirty dealings! My uncle, the idiot, could have gained access to my father's inheritance in exchange for a percentage. That's why my uncle didn't allow me to leave, and why he insisted so much that Andrew Curson had to be my husband.' She started pacing the bedroom as she went on, 'I imagine that when he had the bright idea of marrying me to you, he forgot about the few pennies the orphan had coming because you would bring him a much bigger reward.' Despite herself, she had begun to shout at full volume, hysterically.

Devlin cleared his throat. 'We're not talking about pennies exactly. You can see for yourself.'

He retrieved from his pocket a card, the one where Coleman had written the total amount in the account. Harmony froze on seeing so many numbers together; at first she thought it was a joke, but her husband's expression suggested he was serious. Good grief, how could it be so much money? she thought.

'The accumulation of ten years of interests,' he said, seemingly reading her thoughts. 'Talbot had left your inheritance to fatten up all this time. The bastard was pretty clever.'

Banks don't pay interest these days, she thought as she remembered that miserable thief's words. He had lied to her on that respect as well, and she, in her absolute ignorance, had believed him.

'Well? What are you going to do with all that money?' Devlin asked her while he pulled her towards him to sit on his lap.

Harmony let him hug her while she clasped the small card. With that amount of money she could not only have lived without concerns for a good while… She could also have travelled much more comfortably than Mrs Pfeiffer; she would have bought a house and started a new life alone. She would have been able to do so many things. It was strange to think that, until a few months back, such an idea had excited her. But now those dreams were a thing of the past. Now she had other desires, more tangible, more fascinating, and more important ones. Now she had Devlin, her husband, her great love, and her little child. She had a whole new family, completed by Corine and Malcolm, her grandfather.

She didn't need anything else; she was already wealthy in all that mattered.

She looked down at the card again. She was thankful to her father for having provided for her, but he, as well as her mother, would be ecstatic knowing that Harmony had found her place in the world next to Devlin, an upright and kind man. That could not be measured in money and was worth far more than any fortune.

She looked at Devlin with a wicked smile. 'I hear that Lady Lovelance has an institution that helps poor widows.'

He nodded with a big smile. 'I am sure she would do worthy things with that money.'

Devlin felt his heart swell with feeling as he planted little kisses on Harmony's temples, on her cheeks and her brow. All the while, his hands caressed her hair, then travelled down her sides, to the little bump in her belly and to her back.

'Harmony, listen to me…' He looked at her, overcome by love and longing. 'You have been very distant these last few days. I feel you are punishing me for having accused you so thoughtlessly.'

'It isn't like that—'

'And I know I deserve it,' he carried on as if he had not heard her, 'because the truth is that I caused that unfortunate quarrel. I didn't want to learn anything about you. When we got married, I was determined to keep you at a distance. I had no interest in getting to know you to find out if we were a good match.'

Harmony's heart twinged with sadness at the very thought of that impenetrable distance between them those first days of their relationship. Remaining silent, she let him carry on, 'At first, I wanted to avoid you falling in love with me so I could avoid an unnecessary drama if we got separated, but afterwards, I understood that the heart that was at greater risk was mine.'

'Devlin—'

'If I had accepted that truth early on, we wouldn't have needed to hide so many things from each other.' He sighed and added, 'I am sorry. I am very sorry, my love.'

Harmony took his face in her hands with urgency. 'I didn't intend to punish you,' she muttered, 'I only wanted to repair things between us and prove to you that I had not lied at the ruins. We deserve to start a new life together without half-truths, Devlin, without doubts, without guesses, without having to keep things quiet for fear of what the other might think.'

'But... we wouldn't be a British married couple then.' He raised an eyebrow jokingly.

She laughed and tousled his hair. The silly man had ruined her perfect speech.

'Well... Then let's be something better than a boring and standard British married couple, Devlin.'

Devlin felt his heart bloom with adoration for her. 'Let's be whatever you like; just don't ever kick me away from your side,' he said with humour as he caressed his own face with her warm hands; they were his perfect refuge of safety and comfort. 'I won't bear you thinking that you owe me anything, or that I could reproach you again for things I don't even remember. The only thing I know is that I believe you. I believe in you, my love... So, for goodness sake, don't force Miss Andersen to return from France only to sermon me. Spare me the hard time...'

Harmony frowned as she scratched her chin. The busybody that was her husband had obviously seen the heading of the letter she was writing to her old governess and had guessed her intentions.

'All right,' she sighed, 'No airing our private matters to Miss Andersen.'

'Thank God...' he whispered into her hair as he fumbled with her dress buttons. 'And, talking about private matters...'

Epilogue

Ascot Racecourse, Berkshire.
Spring 1882

Jacob Alexander Sawyer, Baron of Sudeley, had inherited his father's fondness for horses; at least for soft toy horses, as he seemed fascinated by the one Lady Esther Allington, one of his godmothers, had knitted for him as a present to celebrate his first six months on Earth.

Harmony settled him on the pram and gave him his beloved toy before the races started. In general, young aristocratic couples left their children at home to be looked after by one or several well-qualified nannies while they went out to have fun, but the Duke and Duchess of Waldegrave did not seem interested in following that tradition. For the racecourse public it was a novelty to see their Graces arrive with the child. Lords and ladies had sighed tenderly and forgotten their betting for a while to approach the proud parents, congratulate them and have a look at the little baron.

That morning, the little boy had visited the arms of over a dozen of fussy ladies to receive a stream of hungry kisses. Harmony was impressed he had not cried or fallen asleep, exhausted by such shaking and after seeing so many new faces. She couldn't help but feel proud of her little son's impeccable behaviour in society.

When Jake had turned six months' old, Harmony and Devlin decided to go back to Waldegrave Terrace, their residence in London, and leave behind their confinement at Sudeley. Corine had grown so accustomed to the presence of her son, Harmony and Jake, that she had felt despondent on having to see them go. However, she had ended up agreeing, because as Harmony had reminded her, she would have plenty to keep her occupied from now on. To be the hostess at Sudeley Castle was one thing, but to be the wife of a prestigious doctor was quite another; that was a task much more significant and demanding. Her life had changed forever. The newlywed grandmother in love had agreed with all that Harmony had suggested.

Grandfather Malcolm had said goodbye to them with big hugs. He was perhaps the happiest one about his daughter's new status, because now Corine did not spend too much time lecturing him, and more important still: he had found in Martin Bradshawe a permanent partner to play blackjack and pinnacle with, now that his old friend Lord Gardiner had passed away.

Once at Waldegrave Terrace, little Jake had plenty of arms to cuddle and pamper him, to the point that the new nanny wondered what on Earth they had hired her for. All the staff members adored the pretty baby and nobody spared on hugs and caresses to make him happy. Jake soon met Claire, the daughter of Lord and Lady Felton, who was born a few weeks after him, and they immediately made friends. In her, he found the perfect companion for his playpen fun, while their parents had a cup of tea in the garden.

And now, they had taken him to the racecourse so he could encounter the horses and the atmosphere that his father loved so much. He had not appeared too impressed so far, but Devlin did not lose hope that, very soon, he would begin to love the races, and that one day he'd also become passionate about science and inventions too. Often, Harmony scolded Devlin, insisting that he must keep his feet on the ground. She reminded him that Jake had to follow his own dreams, and if he wanted to do other things, like, travel the world or become a writer, it would be his decision and nobody else's. That discussion always ended up in a draw, for a change.

'What did you say was the name of the horse you bet on?' Harmony whispered to her husband as she leafed through the gazette.

'Royal Commander,' he replied as he looked after his son, who had started to bite eagerly at the head of his soft toy.

'Hmmm... It sounds rather pretentious.'

'I have a good tip,' he argued. 'And it has won six races in a row. Don't judge a horse by its name, my love.'

Harmony's eyes were fixed on the page, unblinking. Something had captured her attention to the point of making her gasp like a pretty little fish.

'It can't be.'

'What?'

She looked at him with a smirk.

'Iolanthe is racing.'

Devlin tutted, incredulous.

'Allow me.' He grabbed the gazette and confirmed with his own eyes that the horse he had sold a little over a year ago was listed among the competitors at the race. Mr Rusch, his owner, had given him a chance, it seemed. 'Well, so Iolanthe is back in business,' he muttered, but his voice was full of scepticism.

Harmony looked at him mischievously. She looked beautiful in her marine-green dress and her straw hat that was decorated with flowers and grosgrain ribbons. There was no doubt that being a mother suited her.

Devlin was crazier for her than ever.

'No, no way!' he complained, as he anticipated his wife's intentions. 'I seem to remember that I told you once that it was a crime to back a different horse to the one your husband has bet on.'

'And I remember that we agreed we would not be the typical boring English married couple,' she said craftily. 'We should put our good will to the test, don't you think? This is a good moment to do it.'

We've already brought our son to the racecourse and have exhibited him as if he was an exotic puppy. It would be two tests in one day, he thought, sarcastically, but he saved himself the effort.

'Do you want to embarrass me in front of all these people?' it sufficed him to ask.

'Don't be such a drama queen...' She looked at the baby, who was pouting as he clasped the snout of the soft toy animal with his plump hand. 'What do you say, Jake? Shall we back Iolanthe? After all, if we're in Dad's life, it is thanks to him, my love.'

The baby squealed, a natural reaction to the loving voice of his mother.

'Oh, perfect,' Devlin moaned, defeated, and dropped on his seat after signalling a footman to place a bet on her behalf.

Harmony laughed, patted her husband's cheek, and looked for the binoculars to check what was happening at the starting gate. The race was about to start and she was sure she knew who would win.

The End

About the author

Alexandra Risley, a journalist by training, decided to abandon the buzzing world of the news to devote herself to her true passion: literature.

Nine of her novels, in the subgenres of historical romance and young adult romance, have been published in Spanish by several Latin-American and Spanish publishing companies. *Harmony's Desire* was her first novel published on Amazon; it immediately became a bestseller, and its success has prompted its translation into English.

Apart from reading and writing, Alexandra loves keeping fit, travelling, and learning about new cultures. At present, she lives in Miami, USA, with her husband.